THIS
PRESENT
MADNESS

THIS
PRESENT
MADNESS

William Cory

Niche Publishing Co., Llc
Colorado Springs, Colorado

Niche Publishing Co, LLC
P. O. Box 62114
Colorado Springs, CO 80962

Printed in USA
Print Edition ISBN: 978-0-97295-671-0
Electronic Edition ISBN: 978-0-9729567-2-7

For Mrs. Martha Zabel,
my 11th grade English teacher
at Anaheim High School,
whose encouragement of my
writing still helps me
get started every day

Think about that, if you are
a teacher.

CONTENTS

7

EPIGRAPH

It is this present madness
    from which we must refrain
Though it may be relentless
    we must more than just abstain
Then find why it takes hold
    of our people's fragile minds
And makes them, young and old,
    Leave reason far behind

— anon

ONE

JUNE 24, 2016. FRIDAY.

The banner above the speaker's platform read "Texas State High School All-Star Band Welcome Picnic." Hot late-June winds gusting through Klyde Warren Park kept it flapping, competing in volume with the sounds of young people having fun.

Cassie Stevens smiled and spoke to the Dallas PD officer standing beside her table as he mopped his brow with a handkerchief. "Too bad it's not a Thanksgiving event, huh?"

The cop's polite chuckling at Cassie's comment was interrupted by a call on his shoulder mic, but it was covered up by the loud flapping banner. His intense reply grabbed her attention.

"Say again! *Repeat last?*"

It came through again. Cassie heard it this time. "*Code 6G! 6G! Gunfire north of platform!*"

The cop said something in reply as he squeezed between picnic tables and sprinted toward the other end of the park, where some of the young musicians were playing games. She could hear screams and yelling but couldn't tell if they were fearful or just more of what she'd been hearing all day. She ran out into the nearby open area, searching for her son. *Where was Mark?*

The adults began to panic as most of them heard the explosions and saw Dallas police officers all running in one direction. Parents ran to find their kids. Now, Cassie easily heard a loud *BANG!* that had only slightly registered before. She gasped and her skin prickled as she scanned for her son.

There! His red hair stood out in the sunshine half a head above the other kids he was with, laughing, oblivious to the sounds of gunfire. He was only thirty yards from her. She ran toward him, her short, out-of-shape legs pumping fast. Other moms and dads did the same, yelling the names of their sons and daughters.

The speakers on the stage screeched and crackled to life and a voice boomed over the portable public address system. "Hey folks, calm down! It was fireworks—firecrackers! Relax! Nothing's wrong! Just some cherry bombs!" The voice, a note of laughter in it, came from Ted Baier, this year's Band Master. "Everything's A-okay, folks! Just some kids havin' too much fun! Now drink some cold tea and cool off for a minute. We'll get started with our little program here pretty quick." The loud click echoed as he turned off his microphone.

Cassie had tried to stop in mid-stride but tripped and fell in the grass, scraping a stain onto her light blue pants and banging her right knee, the one that was already sore from a fall the week before. The only sounds she could hear over her thumping heart and her own heavy breathing were the flapping of the huge vinyl banner and the excited chatter of other parents nearby.

She swore to herself and looked around. A man came along beside her and helped her get up. To her left and right were other adults who had run from the line of tree-shaded picnic tables out into the sunny open area toward their kids, just as she had. They had all stopped and now stood still, looking around, breathing hard. A couple of the women were crying. Men cursed in anger and wiped their foreheads.

Cassie's light beige crepe blouse was stuck to her by sweat from the exertion and adrenaline. A drop of perspiration ran from her red hair down her temple and cheek. She turned and walked, limping slightly, back to the picnic table, sat down hard, and waited to catch her breath as she gazed across the field at Mark. He and his friends hadn't even reacted at first to the sound of the fireworks and were just beginning to look around, curious about what was going on and what Mr. Baier's announcement was all about.

Her reactions as a mom subsided as the journalist in her took over. Darn kids! And this gun-crazy society for being so violent that a couple of weeks before the Fourth of July, people would think first of gunfire instead of fireworks! Reflections on this would become a part of her article for the In Dallas section of Sunday's paper. The panic and fear. Both so totally out of place during a warm mid-summer band picnic in a public park.

She wiped her forehead with a paper towel, leaned back against the table and grabbed her red plastic cup of iced tea. The cold of the cup was welcome as she held it against her neck. Her breathing was just beginning to settle down.

The grass stain on her knee didn't yield to a dry paper towel. "Ever the writer, never the athlete, right, Cassie?" she muttered to herself as she straightened her leg and sighed.

Cassie's photographer, Larry, ran up to her table, set one of his cameras down and wiped his forehead with his sleeve. "Some idiots with cherry bombs. Thought it was the real thing for a second!"

"Yeah, same here. They catch 'em?" She shaded her eyes against the bright sky as she looked up at him.

"I dunno … hey, *crap*, I gotta get some water. See ya!" He grabbed the camera and was gone again, headed for the food tent.

The speakers screeched with feedback as Baier's voice boomed out again. "Well, that woke us all up, didn't it! Sorry 'bout that! After all, it's almost the Fourth! Hey, everybody, welcome again to the 19th Annual Texas State All-Star High School Band Welcome Picnic!" Scattered applause answered him as he smiled and looked out over the crowd.

"Beautiful day, huh?" He said as he looked down at some papers. "Okay! The Fourth'll be here before we know it. The band concert this year is right here in Klyde Warren Park, and that's comin' along mighty quick—so, young ladies and gentlemen, be glad we still have another week of rehearsal! And we're gonna want to be at our best, 'cause the Governor's coming this year!" Again, scattered applause, less than before. Mr. Baier turned and asked someone a question, then continued. "Okay. Now, for all you parents and host families, I know you've got a written schedule tucked away somewhere, but listen up. The schedule is gonna be different this week. Listen here so y'all are there on time on Monday!"

At that command, the crowd began to settle down and pay more attention. "We'll be starting this second week of rehearsals on

Monday—that's this Monday—at the same place as last week, up in Plano at that beautiful new Travis High School band building on Babcock Road." He cleared his throat and started to sing in a tonally correct but too nasal Bob Dylan imitation, "But the times, they are a'changin'."

He paused and chuckled as groans rose from the crowd. Cassie wondered how long he'd spent thinking about that little pun. Young people turned to ask their parents what the joke was, or didn't notice at all.

He cleared his throat and shrugged. "So, everything is one hour earlier than last week. Get your young people there on time, right at eleven—that's *e-lev-en* a.m.—or before, so we can start the practice. You can come and pick 'em up at 2:30—that's *two-thirty*—and go get ice cream or go swimmin'. Y'all got that? Eleven 'til 2:30 every day next week. Now have a great time. Eat some burgers 'n' hot dogs. We're fixin' to get the Mayor up here in just a minute to say a few words." Sparse applause ushered him off the makeshift stage as the frisbee and volleyball games resumed.

Cassie sighed. A chill shook her in spite of the muggy 100-plus degree heat. What if it had been a shooting? She shuddered and forced herself to think about something else.

Out on the field, Mark was kicking around a soccer ball with two other boys. She was happy for him. He had tried out to be in this band last year, but was edged out by a senior flugie at his school. Since Mark was a junior and the playoff had been a toss-up, the other boy had been given the spot. But this year, Mark would shine as first chair flugelhorn, where he deserved to be.

The afternoon wore on with more announcements and introductions, games, hamburgers, watermelon, iced tea, and sweat. By the time things were winding down and Cassie had gotten all the interviews she needed, she was worn out, ready for a cool shower. Her knee ached and she was angry about the grass stain on her pants.

Mark ran up to her. "Mom, hey, can they come home with us?" He motioned to the two boys running up to his side. "We want to jam some, you know?" She looked up at his handsome smiling face, glistening with sweat. He looked at her leg. "Hey, ouch, what happened to your knee?"

She gave his request a moment's thought. "I fell down. Yeah, they can come over. Let their hosts know—" She paused as they turned to walk away, "—and get their phone numbers!" Mark raised a thumb to say okay. Cassie gathered up her notebook and camera and eased herself up. The knee wasn't feeling too good. Larry, the photographer, had already left. His photos of the picnic would be in her email when they got home.

She started walking toward the parking lot. The three boys eventually caught up with her. "Mom, can we go up to Bone Daddy's for barbecue? You have to work on your story, right? It'll be quiet for you that way."

Always has an angle, she thought. "Yeah, I guess so."

"Can they spend the night?"

She looked at her son, almost said no, then remembered that for him, this two-week period was the pinnacle of his high school experience. "Okay. But I have to go in tomorrow morning and finish this piece."

"Cool. We'll just sleep."

Cassie chuckled and nodded. If they were planning to sleep, that probably meant she'd be hearing their music late into the night. She hoped the condo's thick cement walls could keep the neighbors happy.

They all climbed into her Explorer. The boys groaned at the heat inside. Cassie's thoughts turned to her article. The State All-Star Band picnic always got a big splash, since the DP was the major sponsor.

Ten minutes later, they turned off Main Street into the parking structure of Cassie's building. Tiredness washed over her as she parked and got out.

While they rode up to the eighteenth floor, she thought of how, and if, she would include the fireworks scare in her article. She felt a tinge of anger that some foolish kids would pull a trick like that and freak out everybody at the picnic. The investigative reporter in her rose to the surface for a moment and she started asking herself some of the questions that once drove her. Where'd they get the cherry bombs? Then, she chuckled to herself, realizing it was really no big deal. She smiled as she pictured headlines. "Boys Used Illegal Fireworks," and, "Fireworks Trigger Picnic Panic." Hardly enough to worry over.

The doors opened and Mark led to the left toward their condominium. Cassie caught up with them, inserted her key and let them in. Mark took the other two boys out onto the small patio to see the view. Cassie stood at the smoked glass wall and looked out, preferring not to go into the heat again. She enjoyed watching Mark point out some of the downtown Dallas landmarks to the other boys, whom she'd found out were from Galveston and the tiny panhandle farm community of Estelline.

The city was like an open furnace at this time of day, nearing Friday rush hour. Traffic below on Main Street was congested, and out toward the freeways to the east and north, she thought she could almost see the heat waves rising from the concrete. Belo Garden, eighteen floors below, was practically deserted, with one small group of kids playing in the fountain. It wasn't all that different from Brooklyn, where they'd once lived. Just more open. And a little less muggy, but not by much.

"Mom, we're gonna take showers." Mark said as they came back inside. She smiled and nodded and slid the patio door closed. The other two boys, Wayne and Jimmy, smiled at her. She gave Jimmy a pat on the shoulder as he passed by, his gray hat skewed sideways to look cool. A few seconds later, one of them turned on the shower, and Mark's flugelhorn sounded in his room, with his practiced Chuck Mangione-style tone.

She sat down on the couch. Her mind turned back to the article. Mrs. Wright, the *Daily Post's* publisher, would have to approve it. The all-star band was her pet project, founded years before by her husband Walter. He had died five years ago, and the paper had continued with his vision to celebrate Independence Day every year with a free concert put on by the best high school band musicians in Texas.

So, she had to make it sound important, probably more so than it really was. The photo coverage would help. Larry was good at getting candid shots of people having fun. That would be the slant of the article, she decided, as it began to take shape. Fun and dreams of the future. "So bright they had to wear shades."

She got up and opened the refrigerator to see what she could make for her dinner.

As a community interest columnist, she liked the easy pace of her job, but sometimes missed the urgency of hard news and investigative reporting she'd done for the *Times* in New York. It had been exciting, working for the Gray Lady years ago, but it was another life, and she was glad not to be there anymore. Here in Dallas at the *DP*, back where she started out in reporting almost twenty years ago, she could deal with happy subjects, ignore anything controversial and fade into the background. She sometimes wondered if this role really suited her, but she found it easy and rarely stressful.

She lay down on the couch and closed her eyes. She had decided on cold fried chicken.

The new band room at William B. Travis High School, in west Plano, twenty miles north of Dallas, was the perfect place for the band rehearsals. With a dedicated building beside the gym and separated from the rest of the campus and classrooms, the sound of the band was never a distraction. The new structure had a thick steel door in front and a large double cargo door in back, an excellent air conditioning system, and was almost completely sound-proofed. Even at full volume, a full 80-member marching band was barely audible from outside, and then only close to the building.

Pulling up at the curb beside the band room, Cassie opened the back of the aging Explorer so Mark could grab the bundles of papers. She had brought two hundred copies of the In Dallas section. On the front page were a half-dozen or so of Larry's photos and the beginning of her article, which continued through the first four pages. It was a long, splashy coverage and she was happy with it.

Mark pulled the papers out and dropped them on the asphalt. "Hey mom, Can I use the car tonight? To go up to Denton for a concert?"

She thought a moment. Nothing else was coming up. "Yeah. No problem. I'll be back at 2:30 to get you."

"Okay. Thanks. Love you!"

Her "Love you, too" was covered by the hatch slamming. She smiled to herself and watched Mark as he got some other boys to help carry the bundles up the concrete steps into the room. Her watch read 10:30. She just had time to hop onto the tollway and head for the DP building, down on Young Street.

"Thank you, Ma'am," Cassie said as she hung up the phone in her cubicle. Tom Hammond, her editor, was waiting for her and motioned for her to follow him. As they stepped into his glass-walled office, Cassie said, "That was Mrs. Wright on the phone. She said she appreciated the article and thought I did a good job on it."

"That's a pretty long-winded compliment, comin' from her," Hammond said, laughing. "She's a tough ol' lady!" he said, smiling. "But y'know, Cass, I don't disagree with her. That was a really fine article."

"Thanks. I might've put something extra into it because of Mark."

"Prob'ly so. That's okay. Hey, close the door and tell me some more about those firecrackers."

"Yeah," she said as she settled into a chair, "somebody was blowing up cherry bombs. Everybody thought it was guns. Scary."

"Yeah. You think it was okay to put it in the story?"

"Sure. Why not?"

"Mrs. Wright didn't care for it."

"Why didn't she say so just now?"

"I don't know, I'd talked to her already about it. 'Sides, ink's already dry! I could've pulled it out, but I thought it was a shot of reality. We all need that sometimes."

"Maybe. I just put it in 'cause it was part of the day."

"Mm-hmm. Don't worry 'bout it. So you took Mark up to rehearsal?"

"Yeah. He's super excited about this. His dream come true, you know?"

"I bet. He's really good on that horn of his, huh?"

Cassie smiled and nodded as Hammond walked around his desk and eased into his creaky chair. "I'm lookin' forward to that concert. Oughta be real good this year! You stay on top of it."

"Right. Thanks, Tom." She rose and turned to go.

"What for?"

"Supporting me. Much appreciated."

Hammond looked up at her and winked, then turned to his computer screen.

The editorial room was large, covering almost a full floor of the building. About eighty people worked in it. Cassie's cubicle was just like all the others spread throughout the hundred-foot-square room, each one's short walls covered with canvas-like material, with inside walls full of pins and scribbled notes. It held her chair, computer desk and work station, and a small set of shelves. On the back wall of her space, where she wouldn't have to look at them often, were awards from the New York Journalists' Association, a Pulitzer nomination letter from her Times nomination for the series on First Responders after 9/11, and her most prized piece of memorabilia, a photo of her husband John and New York City Mayor, Rudy Giuliani, laughing together at Station 51, two days before 9/11. It was the last photo she had of him.

On the wall, several feet above her across the walkway, a flat high-def TV screen showing World Network News flashed silently while white-on-gray captions tried to keep pace with the audio. The low hum of the room's constant background noise—faint clicking of computer keys, sometimes a murmur of conversation, the creaking of chairs and footsteps—conveyed a feeling of suppressed energy. Cubicle walls were low enough to reveal the top of most people's heads. Because she was barely over five feet tall, Cassie's head was usually hidden, and wouldn't have been visible at all except for her "big red bobble head hair," as the sportswriter across the aisle had named it once when he saw her animated way of talking on the phone.

She sat down to examine the mail. Some was fan mail for her

"Around Town" column—more was junk. It took only ten minutes to trash most of it and set the rest aside for later.

Her only assignment this week was to cover the all-star band's activities. She would have been following them anyway, since Mark was in it, so it was an enjoyable duty. She picked up a copy of the Sunday section, glanced at her picnic coverage, and wondered if including the fireworks had been the right thing to do. Tom was probably right; it could help keep people aware, though she wondered what difference that would make. She put it out of her mind and began researching the history of the band, which had been founded in the late 1990s by Walter Wright, founder and publisher of the paper.

Its members were the best young musicians from all over the Lone Star State. Each had gotten here by auditioning in person or on video, from as far away as Galveston, Amarillo and El Paso. They'd been practicing here in Plano for a week, preparing for their upcoming Independence Day concert in Klyde Warren Park.

She could understand Mrs. Wright's happiness that this year was going so well. The band concert had become extremely popular throughout the metroplex, and its performance every Fourth of July was one of the best attended local celebrations in Dallas. This year, Governor Hubbard would be there, so it would be bigger than usual.

She was excited for Mark. This spring, he had been selected for the All-Star Band and had received the John Philip Sousa Award from his instructor. It was given to a student who was the most dependable, musically accomplished and cooperative. Cassie smiled every time she saw the trophy in his room.

She thought about last year, when Mark had been disappointed that a senior had gotten the last flugelhorn spot. He'd been angry at the time, but she'd reminded him it was only fair and just. Her sense of justice and fairness was something she felt he had picked up. It frustrated her at times, but it also imbued her work with passion.

A glance at the clock brought her up short. Time had slipped away while she pored through historical photos of the bands and made notes on additional photos she wanted Larry to get during the week.

It was almost two o'clock. She realized she'd better get on the road to pick up her son, and she still needed to stop for gas.

TWO
JUNE 27, 2016. MONDAY.

The black Ford pickup, its dark tinted windows hiding the driver, rolled slowly to a stop on the hot parking lot asphalt, just twenty feet from the building. Inside, where it was cool, its driver leaned forward, clicked off the radio, and ran trembling fingers through his longish blond hair. Then he sat still, hands hanging on the wheel, and gazed at the band building for half a minute. He was enjoying the air-conditioned comfort of his truck before stepping into the swelter of midsummer North Texas heat. Finally, he slowly reached down, pulled the key and dropped it on the floor. It became quiet in the closed cab, but quickly grew warm, then hot.

He opened his door and hung one leg out. Nobody was in the parking lot that he could see. A few cars sat empty. All the band people were in the rehearsal. The place was empty and hot. Like he remembered it.

The only visible motion was from heat waves rising from cars, sidewalks and graying asphalt. Even the parched yellowed grass of distant athletic fields seemed to radiate heat.

The soaring, joyful notes of *The Stars And Stripes Forever* were faintly audible. During the softer strains of the bridge, a lone cicada off in the scrub was louder than the music.

He slid off the seat, closed the door and leaned against it. Anger welled up inside as his fingers absently pressed imaginary valves on his leg, fingering the notes of the second chair baritone part of this same piece that he'd played when he was in the school band three years ago here at Travis. His band hadn't had a nice big building like this one.

He bit off a hangnail and spat it out, thinking how he should have been in that all-star band in his senior year, but he'd been ripped off. His anger was under control though, now. This would fix it once and for all. He got his skullcap out and pulled it down tight over his ears.

At six-feet-two, he was as tall as the cab of his truck, but he looked shorter with his prominent belly and slumped posture as he scuffed around to the passenger side, opened the door and pulled out a battered brown baritone case. It was heavier than normal. He closed the door, set the case down and leaned against the truck. The damp cigarette he took from behind his ear didn't light easily.

He'd taken a couple extra of his pills that morning along with a can of his favorite energy drink. He thought they would calm him down, but instead he felt a mixture of confusion and excitement.

He enjoyed the entire cigarette, his last one. After a long last drag on the cigarette, he flicked the live butt into dry grass along the sidewalk beside the band building. Maybe it would light a fire. Not that it would matter. He hoped so. Anyway, life was bullshit.

Across the field, the cicada went quiet, as if anticipating what was about to happen.

Fifty-six members of the Texas State All-Star High School Band had just ended the John Philip Sousa march, heard comments from instructors, and were now playing the *Overture* from Star Wars.

The five instructors, all but one of them doing their first All-Star band, were still discovering their specific roles and settling in. Bret Welch, at twenty-five the youngest of them, stopped to help a student find a replacement reed for her clarinet. His daily task of unlocking the wide rear cargo door had been neglected in favor of more pressing problems as the rehearsal progressed.

At 2:10 pm, the young man walked toward the band room, his old-style, large baritone case bumping his right leg. Sweat ran down his torso inside the faded gold sweat shirt, its blue *Hawks* logo cracked and almost worn away. With his dark blue walking shorts, black athletic shoes and socks, he could have been a high school student. The brown *faux* leather of the case suffered new scuffs as he lugged it up the concrete steps.

He set the case down and paused to catch his breath before reaching for the steel doorknob. Then, after a few moments, he pulled open the heavy steel main door and bumped the case through. The loud strains of John Williams's popular movie theme struck him as a physical force and escaped for a few seconds, then were quieted again at the mechanical slam of the extra-thick door.

Bandmaster Ted Baier, conducting the climax of one of the themes of the overture, glanced to the side at the man, curious because he didn't recognize him, then looked back down at his score to finish the movement.

The young man quickly set his case down and opened it while surveying the young faces before him on the multi-level floor. Nearest were four girls playing flutes and piccolos. They didn't see him. Each one was alert, intent on their music.

All of the instructors were busy concentrating on the music and helping students in their sections, some looking over at him as he opened his case. They couldn't see exactly what he was doing as the case lid opened only partially, hiding what was inside. They assumed it was a baritone.

He attached the 30-round drum magazine to the Russian Saiga twelve-gauge semi-automatic shotgun, cocked it, and raised it.

By the time anyone recognized what it was, they were frozen by their fear and it was already too late.

The gun, heavy with its lethal load of thirty shells, each firing nine lead balls a third of an inch in diameter, began to jump in the young man's hands and the music died instantly, replaced by loud booms and the awful sounds of slaughter.

First killed was Ted Baier, the Band Master, taking almost a full twelve-gauge load of double-0 buckshot, each shot with its nine lead balls, in the shoulder and head. He died almost instantly. The music was replaced by screams but they were drowned out by the gun's explosions, one or two per second. They were deafening inside the room, but outside, less audible than a cymbal's clash.

It didn't seem real to the man pulling the trigger. It was as if someone else's finger was doing it, firing fast, holding the gun against its heavy recoil. He saw the awful results as if on his video screen at home. His hearing went away. He licked his lips and tasted a foreign, coppery tang, then realized it was somebody's blood. He didn't like it and tried to spit, but his mouth had gone dry.

One young man from the sax section first threw his alto sax at the shooter, and then charged toward him, but he tripped over others running from the gun and was shot as he tried to rise. A red-headed kid threw his horn case, but the shooter got him in the head. Most of the others ran toward the back door, which should have been unlocked, but wasn't. No escape existed. They didn't try to attack their attacker. Their numbers would have subdued him, but they tried to flee, and tripped and fell over the folding chairs, instruments, and each other.

He quickly used his first drum of thirty shells. Almost a third of the band was down. The rest were either cowering or trying to hide or run. The floor was slick, but he made his way back to his case for his second magazine without falling down. In ten seconds, a time of quiet except for crying, screams and yelling, and a few boys trying to throw instrument cases and chairs at their attacker, the second drum of shells was attached, the gun cocked, and the deafening explosions resumed.

To anyone standing beside the band building, the muffled explosions could have been a car backfiring two blocks away. Unnoticeable. But no one was there to hear. All of the sounds—of screaming and gunfire—merged, becoming a single cacophonous noise that barely escaped, reduced in volume like the joyful music it had replaced. The building, this day, was perfectly suited to its unintended use.

Near the back corner of the room, Bret Welch had run to unlock the rear door. Panicked young people did the same. They quickly piled up and buried Welch as they climbed over him, trying to open the door. He couldn't reach the top of the door to get the key into the lock and was overrun as young people were shot and fell on top of him and others who weren't shot. Forced to the floor, being crushed, barely able to breathe or move, he passed out.

After a few more shots, most of the sound inside the building had ceased. There had been almost five dozen shots fired from two circular thirty-round magazines. The barrel of the Russian Saiga shotgun smoked.

Somewhere, a random crying could be heard, but when he tried to reach the sound, the young man slipped in the slick blood on the floor and fell, then decided to stay there. It didn't matter. He was done. He slumped, sitting in a pool of dark crimson, and looked around. The only movement in the room now was from the overhead fan and him, shaking his head quietly and murmuring to himself. He tried to get up, slipping again and falling on his knee. He tried to use the gun as a brace to get up, then swore loudly when he burned his hand on the overheated barrel.

The big clock on one wall clicked softly over to 2:15.

It had been about four minutes since the music had stopped.

The young man walked to the front door, slipped again in a slick dark red puddle, and swore again. He swiped at blood and stinging sweat in his eyes.

Beside Mr. Baier's podium, in the cooled air now laden with acrid smoke and the horrible smells of violent death, the young man stopped, laughed, and then began sobbing and swearing. Then, he urinated on himself.

Outside, all still seemed normal.

Charlie Toms, one of the school's custodians, had just emerged from cleaning the girls' athletic locker room, around the far side of the main gym building. He pushed his yellow tool and supply cart around the corner toward the band room. Reaching a narrow strip of shade, he leaned against the building, mopped his brow and looked at his watch. Two-fifteen.

It seemed odd to Charlie that the band wasn't still playing. They never quit early, and this was a whole fifteen minutes early. He figured they'd either play some more or they'd come out soon. He enjoyed hearing their music, even though it was only barely audible if a wisp of wind blew it toward him from the air conditioning exhaust.

Today, the air was almost perfectly still, with occasional breezes between the buildings. At first, it didn't surprise him that there was no sound.

Some of the parents and hosting moms or dads were just arriving in the parking lot, some waiting in their cars to stay out of the heat and others getting out to talk. Under a dozen had gathered at this point. Nothing seemed out of the ordinary.

Charlie figured the instructors must be talking to the students. He waved at some parents he knew from school, who had just arrived and gotten out of their car to talk to another couple. The man pointed to the watch on his wrist, then shrugged and smiled. Charlie shrugged back.

Suddenly, with a loud clang against the steel pipe railing, the heavy band room front door burst open. Everyone turned toward it, expecting the members of the band to begin streaming out, laughing and talking.

But, they didn't. Instead, a tall blond man in blue shorts, a few years older than high school age, staggered out, his bushy blond hair a counterpoint to his oversized baggy gold sweat shirt, his face and the shirt splattered and smudged with dark spots. He slipped and fell halfway down the steps.

He could have been drunk, judging by his unsteadiness, but he held on to what he carried. The assembled dozen or so parents exclaimed a loud collective, "*Oh-h-h!*" Several of them began to hurry toward him, as if to help, then stopped in their tracks, frozen, as some realized he had a gun. He struggled to his feet.

One of the women who had rushed forward fell to her knees, and screamed as she recognized the gun gripped in his hands. Horribly loud and chilling, her panicked voice pierced the still, hot air.

As he regained his footing, the young man brought the muzzle of the gun to his own chin, a puzzled, frowning expression on his wet and blood-spattered face.

Everyone, Charlie included, was paralyzed. The same woman stood and screamed a single word—"*NO!*"—and the man's head turned toward her at the same instant as his hand jerked from recoil.

All other sounds ceased for a microsecond as the final boom of the shotgun echoed among the buildings. A spray of red mist shot into the air above the young man's head, hanging briefly against a rich blue sky until it dissipated and drizzled back down. The gun jumped from his hand and clattered down the steps, its large round magazine snapping away and landing beside him on the blacktop. He fell unconscious on top of the weapon as his own blood began to drip onto the asphalt.

A panicked jumble of screams and yells began. The parents stormed the steps, the screaming woman leading, stepping on the man's leg as she struggled to get up the stairs into the band room. She pulled the heavy door open, and then she began screaming again and didn't stop.

Right on her heels, more parents ran up the three blood-splattered concrete steps, only to begin screaming and crying anew when they saw inside the band room.

They tried to reach their children, but some soon pushed back out against the flow of others, unable to stand what they were seeing. All screamed and sobbed. A few, men and women, fainted. Many vomited, the leaders trying to escape the ghastly sight that had met them inside, spewing their stomach contents over the rails and the steps, some splatting onrushing parents and the crumpled body of the young man. Nobody noticed that he lay alive but unconscious in a dark red spot of his own blood.

More parents continued to arrive as the crowd grew in size and its vocal reactions grew in volume to a terrible, unified howl of panic.

A few adults tried to enter the band room and try to help, but they couldn't get in. It was no longer a musical place, but the scene of slaughter and death. Unmuffled sobbing and a few cries for parents could be heard inside the room. It was impossible to reach the few survivors without stepping on bodies.

Charlie Toms had finally managed to tap three numbers into his phone with gnarled and wildly trembling fingers.

"9-1-1, what is your emergency?"

He could barely hear her over the screaming and crying. Charlie, too, was crying, realizing what he was reporting, and his old, weak voice rose to a strained yell as he forced the words out.

"Travis High School! This is Charlie the janitor! We got a bad shooting! It's the band! Oh God!" He took a breath. *"Send help here! Send everybody here to help right now!"*

The 9-1-1 operator was saying something, but she couldn't be heard over the sounds of panic. Charlie dropped his phone to the ground. He couldn't hear the woman's questions and stumbled backward, sobbing, collapsing back against the rough stucco surface of the wall behind him. His ears were filled with the awful echoing chorus of crying and yelling that bounced between the gym and the band room. He could only look at the ground, braced by the building and his hands on his knees, and tremble and sob.

Newly arriving parents ran from their vehicles and tried to get into the band building. More cars continued to arrive, stopping in a jumble that would soon hamper emergency vehicles. A panicked group of over eighty parents and friends were now packed around the steps, all crying, screaming for help, fainting, trying to get inside the band room, many being held back by other crying parents. A few, with some experience in first aid, did what they could to find survivors. A few repeated Charlie's frantic 9-1-1 call.

It had been only half a minute since the last shot boomed the shooter's blood into the air. He still lay on the asphalt where he had fallen. Some people, unable to see his body on the ground in the close crowd, tripped over him or stepped on him. Those who thought he was a fallen band member tried to help and were themselves knocked down.

Charlie's stomach convulsed as the smell of death and gunpowder from inside the band room wafted to him. It returned him to the rice paddies, the killing fields of 1965 in South Viet Nam. Gun powder. Blood. Sweat. Vomit. Feces. Within another twenty seconds, the wail of multiple sirens and blaring klaxons seemed to be coming from every direction. But they were already too late—much too late.

THREE

JUNE 27, 2016. MONDAY.

"*Jeez!*" Cassie exclaimed under her breath as she hung up the gas pump. "Seventy-five *bucks*!" She hung up the pump handle and opened her door, pausing as she heard ambulances leaving the hospital across Babcock Road just west of her. Their sirens blared as they raced past the station.

In the distance, she heard more sirens approaching at high speed. At first, she didn't think they were unusual, since the Brookside Hospital emergency entrance was right across the road. She wondered idly if her friend, Linnie, was working in the ER today.

But now, she was hearing too many sirens. They came from every direction, north and south on the tollway and access road, and more heading east on Babcock past the hospital. All of the emergency vehicles—EMT trucks, ambulances, police and fire vehicles from Plano, Carrollton, Addison, The Colony, Hebron—turned onto Babcock Road toward the school. They barely slowed down on Babcock as they passed under the tollway bridge. She was puzzled for half a second, and then her mouth went dry and her stomach dropped.

"*Oh! God! No! Oh my God!*" She screamed as she leapt into the Explorer and screeched its tires leaving the pump. More police cars and ambulances with sirens screaming continued to blaze through the intersection without slowing as motorcycle units controlled the intersection for them. Ambulances and EMT fire engines with klaxon horns and warbling sirens forced traffic to open up or move over as they headed east under the tollway. Two ambulance helicopters passed overhead, low and fast.

Cassie's whole body was tense. She gripped the steering wheel so hard she almost couldn't steer.

They were all heading for the school.

She yelled at the traffic and pounded on the wheel, waiting for a chance, then decided to go anyway. They'd have to avoid her. She chose an opening in the stream of police cars, and was lucky to get a small gap, so she could join the line and get through the intersection. The old Explorer strained to gain speed. She ignored the bleeping siren of a fast-approaching ambulance and rode hard on a Plano PD car's tail.

Interrupting a police emergency pursuit didn't bother her and none of them would stop to write a ticket. She stayed on the cop's bumper until they were in front of the school, where she saw dozens of emergency vehicles jamming the driveways and streets. She swerved to the left onto the median strip, skidded to a stop, turned off the motor and ran across westbound Babcock Road toward the front of the school. Traffic had been diverted. She had her Dallas *Daily Post* press card on a lanyard around her neck, as usual, so she was allowed to get through the first police line already in place in front of the school.

She cried as she ran. Praying. Pleading. Ignoring the pain in her knee.

Rounding the main front building of the school, she had to slow down to a fast walk. Her legs were not used to running, and her knee was too sore from Friday's fall at the picnic. Her blouse was soaked.

Then she saw the band building, surrounded by ambulances and police cars, gurneys being hurried into ambulances. Sirens and klaxons blared as the vehicles escaped the jam to head for Brookside Regional Trauma Center, two miles west on Babcock Road. She could hear cries and wailing coming from the panicked crowd of people.

Beside the band building on the ground lay several shapes, human bodies, some already covered by yellow plastic tarps.

She froze and stared. Her mind fought what her eyes were seeing, screamed inside not to believe it, but she couldn't deny it. She sobbed and began to run again toward the band building.

A policewoman stopped her. She held up her press card and yelled, "*My son Mark! He's in there!*"

The woman pointed west and said, "If he's alive they'll take him to Brookside! *Go there!*"

Shocked by the words she'd heard and only now comprehended, Cassie stared at the woman and choked on a cry, ran back a few steps, then turned aside and vomited. She ran as fast as she could to her car, spitting and wiping her chin as she ran. She started the engine and bounced along Babcock on the median strip, found a turn-through and sped back west toward the hospital.

The Brookside Trauma Unit had gotten an emergency alert at 2:17 that casualties would be arriving from a shooting at Travis High School, two miles away. One of a dozen Level One trauma centers in the Dallas area, Brookside was the obvious choice. Helicopter ambulances had been dispatched and two were returning with patients.

The first casualty, brought in by EMTs, had just been wheeled into an emergency exam cubicle. As head of emergency neurosurgery at Brookside Trauma Center, Dr. Linnea Kennedy took the patient. He was overweight but not obese, over six feet in height, in his early twenties. A portion of the scalp on the left side of his head had been shot away. His left ear was gone, but his skull appeared to be intact and was confirmed by x-rays. The way it appeared he had been shot, it had only grazed the side of his head. A flap of scalp had partially covered the wound, with bits of gravel stuck around the area. The blood had clotted quickly because of dirt that had gotten into the wound and the quick clotting powder used by EMTs. He was no longer bleeding, but lucky to be alive.

Blood was instantly drawn for pre-surgical typing and screening. The technician hurried through a description of what had been done for him. Dr. Kennedy made mental notes as his gurney was hurried into a surgical prep room. His clothing showed heavy blood splatter, but she had no time to think about it.

His limp form was stripped and checked for other wounds, then sprayed with antiseptic, shrouded and transferred to a surgical gurney.

He was draped for surgery and wheeled into the operating room. Dr. Kennedy started her scrub. Expert nurses prepped the man, inserting IV's for fluids and terminals that the anesthesiologist would use, connecting monitors for blood oxygen and heart rate.

A minute later, Dr. Kennedy backed into the room, where three nurses and the anesthesiologist waited. She was gowned, gloved and masked as she entered, then approached the patient, nodded to the other doctor and said only, "Ready? Let's go."

Five seconds later, the anesthesiologist nodded to Dr. Kennedy and said, "You may begin, Doctor."

She looked toward the far wall where a large flat screen displayed three x-ray views of the patient's skull. It showed no fractures. She glanced quickly at the toxicology report on a second screen. No blood thinners or amphetamines present. One generic chemical—*chlorpenframine*—was hand printed on a line, with the notation "ETL"—extra-therapeutic level. She glanced at it only briefly and dismissed it. It was a common psychoactive prescription drug that would have no effect at all on what she needed to do.

She started the surgery, immediately finding some bits of red plastic and wadding from a shotgun blast embedded in the edge of his scalp where a large flap had been ripped away, along with some small bits of gravel. "Must've been close, but he's lucky," she mumbled, shaking her head slowly. She was glad his wounds weren't life threatening, but from what she'd heard on the ambulance channel before he arrived, he would be one of very few survivors.

The surgery on the young man lasted just eighty minutes. He was wheeled out of the surgery and into a recovery room, accompanied by two police officers. Dr. Kennedy watched as they entered the elevator and wondered why the cops were there, but it wasn't her concern. The patient would be sent up to SICU, the Surgical Intensive Care Unit, after leaving recovery. She expected him to be awake and communicative the next day. Her mask and other surgical garments went into a biohazard hamper as she left the surgery, stopping outside the surgery door for two minutes to record a quick verbal report before moving on to the next patient assignment.

One of the ER nurses walked up to her. "That was the shooter," she said under her breath.

"*What? Say that again?*" Dr. Kennedy cupped a hand over her ear and leaned over to the shorter nurse to hear through the noise of the intake and waiting room.

"That was the *shooter!*" the nurse repeated, this time much louder. People turned and looked, then scanned the hallway to see who she meant.

As the nurse's words sank in, Dr. Kennedy stood still for a moment. The first life she'd saved—the first patient she had worked on—was the killer. She closed her eyes and sighed a curse word, then shook her head and hurried toward the triage desk. "Who's next?"

The assignment nurse just looked at her with a blank expression and teary eyes. "There aren't any! Dr. Ryan has another head wound. Ten others already in surgery."

"Oh—oh my God!" Dr. Kennedy said as she understood what that meant—that less than half had survived. It was the first inkling she had of the enormity of the attack. Without another case to consider, her thoughts went to her friend Cassie's son, Mark. He was in that band.

She looked over the board and saw that one other patient had been admitted for a major gunshot wound to the head. Dr. Ryan was operating on him now. There was no name. He was on the board simply as "Trav #2." Ten others, numbered three through twelve, were in surgery for various wounds. Four more were on the board with "ER" beside their numbers, meaning they were being treated there and not going to surgery.

She went to the surgical recovery room to check on her patient. He was beginning to come out of his anesthesia, but she'd given orders to keep him unconscious until they could assess brain swelling from the concussion of the shotgun blast. His vital signs were stabilizing.

In her office, she listened to her recorded surgical notes and added the recovery information to them, then sent them for transcription.

When she came back to the recovery room, the other neuro patient was just being wheeled in from surgery. She met his gurney and was struck by the fairness of his young skin, his light freckles and the red hair that showed outside the large bandage covering half of his head.

Then, she gasped and her stomach twisted as she recognized him. *Mark Stevens.* She grabbed the chart and examined it. Her heart fell as she saw there was absolutely no chance he could live very long.

She fought tears as she left the recovery room and headed for the ER intake room. It was easy to spot Cassie by her red hair.

Cassie Stevens was hunched over her folded arms, rocking forward and back, crying and praying. Her diminutive form was almost hidden by larger people.

Dr. Kennedy walked directly to her and put a hand on her shoulder. "Cassie?"

Cassie looked up at her friend, her face streaked with tears, as if she'd just been awakened. Then she jumped up and put her hands on Dr. Kennedy's arms. "*Linnie!* Oh god, Linnie, is Mark okay? Is he okay?"

Linnea Kennedy put her arm around Cassie's shoulders and guided her through the hallway doors, then turned her around. Much taller than Cassie, she had to bend her knees to look into her friend's teary red-rimmed, blue eyes.

"Cassie, Mark is alive, but he's very badly injured. I'm so, so *sorry!*" She teared up immediately, her professional mask gone in the face of her best friend's anguish.

Cassie reached around Linnie's waist and fell against her, sobbing. Linnie patted her head as if she were a child, shook her own head and closed her eyes, trying to stop tears from forming.

"Can I see him? Is he going to be okay?"

Linnie didn't answer. "Cass, did you call Zach? Is he on his way?"

Cassie wiped tears from her eyes that were immediately replenished. "Yeah. He was up on Grapevine Lake. He's coming."

"Okay. They'll send him up to SICU when he gets here. I'll take you up there now. Mark is still in recovery for now and he'll be in a room up there in a little while."

34

"Will he be able to talk and—"

"Not now, Cass. We'll have to wait." She knew she was not giving her friend the full story, but what she did say was true. Mark wouldn't talk soon ... or ever.

Neither said anything for a few long seconds, as Cassie cried. Linnie put her arm around her shoulders and hugged her.

"He was so happy this morning," Cassie started. "He was going up to Denton tonight for a concert. He was—Oh, *dear God!*" she sobbed.

Linnie whisked tears away from her own eyes as she walked Cassie to the elevator and took her up to the waiting room next to the surgical ICU.

They didn't speak. There was nothing more to say, and Linnie didn't want to tell Cassie how serious Mark's injury was until her fiancé could be there with her. She seated Cassie in the waiting room and phoned the ER desk, leaving word for them to send Zach Barber up when he arrived. Cassie would need him with her when she was informed that her son was certainly going to die. Then she went to find Dr. Ryan, Mark's surgeon, to get more information on the surgery.

FOUR

JUNE 27, 2016. MONDAY.

To Kelli Tremaine, Travis High School looked every bit as bad as the triage scenes she had witnessed as a correspondent in Jerusalem. When she'd been transferred to the WNN station in Dallas, she'd never dreamed that she would see anything that would compare with the horror of bombed Israeli buses with dead children, but this was much worse.

She hadn't been able to get set more quickly because of the crowding of emergency vehicles, parents and other news crews. When they did set up, it was well outside the yellow-taped perimeter, nearer to the gym, so that the scene behind her as she spoke on camera would show the band room, parked emergency vehicles, silent but with lights flashing, and forensics teams searching for evidence.

"Okay, David, ready here." She said into her microphone, letting the studio know the shot was ready to televise. Seconds later, her camera man gave her the 3-2-1 and pointed at her.

The camera went live. "This is Kelli Tremaine at the scene of what could soon be confirmed as the worst mass shooting in the history of our country. The building behind me is the band room of William B. Travis High School in Plano, Texas, about twenty miles north of downtown Dallas."

To the camera, she appeared serious and professional, but not detached. Her expertise at projecting appropriate emotions had gotten her this job with WNN, but this time she didn't try to project anything. Her emotion showed. She continued with the facts, doing her best to remain apart from the inner fury she felt.

* * *

Zach Barber hurried to the ER reception desk, waited impatiently as he glanced at the blond WNN reporter on an overhead screen talking from Travis High, and finally got to approach the nurse at the counter. "I'm Zach Barber, my friend's son, Mark Stevens—"

"Yes sir." She checked a paper in front of her. "Okay, the surgeon said to send you up to the SICU when you get here—"

"The what? Where is that?"

She pointed to the side. "Surgical Intensive Care. Go through those doors, take the elevator, second floor, turn left and you'll see the sign."

Zach nodded his thanks as he hurried through the doors. Sweat beaded on his forehead as he punched the elevator buttons. He pulled his shirt tail and wiped his face, then tried to tuck it back in.

The elevator doors opened, Zach went to the right, then remembered the nurse's instructions and turned around. The room was right there. He saw Cassie and hurried in as she stood and put her arms around his waist. Her head hit his chest and she cried.

"Cass. What … I don't—"

"Mark … he was shot in the head," was all she could say through her tears.

"Oh god," Zach said as tears began to fill his eyes. They stood together, Cassie crying, until Zach spoke again.

"What is … is he okay?"

"No he's *not* okay. Linnie just—"

As Cassie said her name, Linnie walked around the corner. She took Zach's hand and squeezed it, shook her head slowly, and sighed. "Zach," she said, "I need to talk to Cassie in here for a minute."

He nodded and let Cassie go, looked around, and sat down. Across the room, a TV screen played.

"As I was saying," Kelli Tremaine continued, "We don't know much yet about exactly what happened here. There apparently are several survivors who are not seriously injured and who might be able to provide details later, but for now we only know that every other person in that building up to a little while ago is either deceased or has been taken to Brookside Trauma Center."

She paused to take control of her trembling voice and motioned toward the scene behind her. "When we first arrived here, this was more chaotic than it is now, but now all survivors have been transported. You can see, and hear, that sirens are no longer being used. David, the meaning of that is probably too terrible for me to say."

The shot flashed from her to a split screen, with a typical male anchor, handsome but grim, talking into the camera. "Kelli, thanks. I understand a custodian there at Travis High was present when it took place?"

The scene flashed back to her, holding her fingers against her ear piece to hear. She looked into the camera. "That's right, David. That would be Mr. Charlie Toms. I have him right here." She looked to the side, out of the shot. "Mr. Toms? Can you come and speak with me for a little bit?" She reached outside the frame and gently brought the old man into the picture beside her.

He was slumped, his head bowed, as the camera pulled back. His wrinkled, sweat-streaked dark brown face was drawn, making him look even older than his sixty-seven years. His khaki shirt was sweated through and dirty. He looked at the ground as Kelli put her hand lightly on his shoulder.

"Mr. Toms? Mr. Toms?" she waited as he looked up at her, then back down. "You were the first one to call 9-1-1, is that right?"

Charlie Toms nodded slowly and shrugged, still not looking up at her or the camera. She leaned down to try to meet his eyes. He looked up at her, then down again.

"Can you tell us what happened? I understand you witnessed the alleged shooter shooting himself, and then you called 9-1-1?" She held the mic close to the man's drooped head. He had trouble speaking, clearing his throat two times before his trembling voice would work.

As he looked up at her and began to speak, she held the mic close to his mouth.

"I never seen anything much worse ... My god it was, you know, one of them things cain't ever forget. Ol' Johnny comes bangin' out the door, there, and a lady starts screamin' and he just puts his gun up to his face and BOOM! Looked like half 'is head went up in the air, all red. Then I was callin' nine-'leven, cause I could tell it was somethin' real bad. *Real* bad." Tears marked trails down the old man's dust-covered cheeks as he told the story. He wiped at new tears with the forearm of his shirt, then looked blankly into the reporter's face again. "Sorry, Lady. I loved them kids."

At that, Kelli's voice caught. "It's all right, Sir. But wait, Mr. Toms, you said, 'Old Johnny,' didn't you? Did you know the man? Personally?"

Toms gave her a surprised look. "Well, yeah, I guess I do! Played in the school band right here at Travis, some years back, but Johnny was a good boy! Back then anyways! Used to hep me sweep up once'n awhile." He shook his head and looked back at the ground. A new tear fell from his eye as he lifted a trembling hand to try to catch it.

Sudden excitement was obvious in Kelli Tremaine's light blue eyes as she glanced into the camera. She leaned toward Charlie Toms. Her photographer slowly zoomed in to her and Toms's faces as she asked the next question, leaning down to look into his eyes again.

"Mr. Toms, do you remember ... can you give us his full name?"

Seeming surprised again, he frowned, a puzzled look on his lined, grey-whiskered face, so close to her perfectly smooth young complexion. This time, she stayed close, with the mic close to his lips to catch his words above the beat of news and police helicopters overhead.

"Well, o'course I can! It was ol' Johnny Hoff. He been around here some just lately. You know, while the band uz practicin'. Said hello to me last week."

Kelli Tremaine was visibly trembling as she listened, then asked. "And Mr. Toms, did you give this information to the police?" She pushed the mic close to him again.

"No, ma'am. None 'em's asked me nothin' yet."

She put her hand on his shoulder. "Thank you, Mr. Charlie Toms, custodian here at Travis High School. Sir, we are all *so* sorry about this." She held her hand on his shoulder for a moment as he nodded and turned away. She looked up from the man, took a long breath and continued talking directly into the camera.

"Well, you heard it. It seems that the perpetrator of this shooting, at least one of them if there were others, was unofficially identified here by Mr. Charlie Toms as a former band student named Johnny Hoff. That's not officially confirmed yet. We'll get more information on it as we go, but for now, what we know is that there are only a few survivors of this horrific attack."

She reached down and picked up a newspaper, then lifted it into the frame to show the headline. "And, David, in a horrible irony here, this joyful article about last Friday's big welcome picnic in Dallas, in the Sunday *Daily Post*, was written by the mother of one of the band members. That young man's status is not known."

She clutched the paper and turned to motion toward the scene behind her. "As you can see, they're raising screens behind me so that the area near the building will be hidden from view. We'll stay on it. That's it for now from Travis High School in Plano. Kelli Tremaine, WNN, Dallas."

The TV screen switched to the light-gray suited, tanned individual in the studio, with video from a helicopter high above the shooting scene still showing on a large screen behind him. The top of the band building, blue metal, stood in sharp contrast to dozens of yellow-blanketed shapes lying on the asphalt, some being moved on gurneys to vehicles. The screen didn't change as he sighed and shook his head. "More after this," he said, looking down at his papers. Two seconds of the copter shot at Travis High were followed by a silent, slow-moving 3-D chyron in the blue and gold colors of Travis High School, its lettering reading "Tragedy at Travis High." After a few seconds, it faded and a commercial began.

Zach had already turned away when the reporter held up the newspaper, trying to quiet the sick feeling in his stomach. He jumped up when Cassie and Linnie came back into the room.

"I'm sorry, Zach." Linnie said, touching his arm. He sniffed and nodded. "I know." He put his arm around Cassie's shoulders as she looked at the floor, not speaking, tears welling up. "Cass, I'm ... I don't know what to say."

She shook her head and turned, laying her head against his chest. "Just pray."

"Linn," he said, "are there many others? Injured, I mean?"

"I don't know. I worked on just one patient. Not certain, but I think there were about ten or eleven other surgeries."

"Oh, that's ... oh, no, god." He looked up. "Maybe they took some to other hospitals?"

Linnie looked into his eyes and silently, slowly shook her head. He squeezed his eyes shut and hung his head.

"Mark should be brought into a room here in a few minutes. Let me check," Linnie said, touching Cassie's arm as she turned to go.

On the television screen, now, a gaggle of reporters had assembled in front of a lectern with a uniformed police official speaking. In the background was the frame and canvas-draped screen erected around the band building; only the structure's blue roof showed above it.

He held the lectern and controlled a stiff but trembling chin. "I won't take any questions at this time. This is what we know. A single shooter attacked the band during rehearsal. He used a semi-automatic twelve-gauge shotgun found at the scene. We haven't officially identified him yet. Survivors have been admitted to Brookside Hospital; no word on their condition. The shooter was also admitted and treated." The man clenched his jaw after his last words and took a breath. When he raised his head, his eyes were red. "That's all for now. We'll have another press conference tomorrow. And do not bother the families with your ridiculous 'how does this make you feel' kinds of questions!" He turned away and ignored questions being called out.

Linnie came back. Zach held a supporting arm around Cassie's shoulders as they were led slowly around the corner toward Mark's room.

FIVE

JUNE 27, 2016. MONDAY.

A high mid-afternoon overcast lingered in Houston, about two-hundred-sixty miles south of Plano. Justin O. Richardson stood at the glass wall of his office looking out over the entry walk and expansive lawns of his company, Provachem Pharmaceuticals. He sipped vitamin water from a crystal glass and watched employees walk to their cars. He flexed his shoulders. They were a bit sore from an extra workout his trainer had put him through. Regular workouts in the club gym kept his 52-year-old body looking and feeling more like 42, and his carefully groomed short gray hair and clean-shaven tanned face perfected the well designed look his executive status demanded. It also kept his 29-year-old wife happy. That and his money.

His secretary opened the door of the large office. "Excuse me, sir, you need to see what's on TV. WNN."

Richardson turned slowly, nodded to her and picked up the remote control from his desk, pressed a button, and sat down at his desk.

The shot was from a helicopter circling a blue-roofed, beige building surrounded by emergency vehicles. Elongated spots of yellow—bodies covered with yellow plastic—were laid out near the building. Was this a drill?

Richardson's jaw tightened as he hoped, then realized, it wasn't a drill. People in white coveralls were busy removing the yellow-draped bodies to a line of vans surrounded by emergency vehicles. Bystanders were gathered outside a tape line. Some of them were lying down while being treated by emergency personnel.

The title below the picture read "Travis High School Shooting." Richardson's hackles rose and a sensation, not exactly a chill, ran through his body. He concentrated on the crawler running below the picture.

" ... *Travis High School in Plano Texas scene of shooting earlier today when lone gunman shot members of Texas State All-star Band and then himself ... Unknown number of survivors transported to Brookside Hospital two miles away ... gunman reported to have survived suicide attempt ... shooter identified as John Hoff, former student at Travis, survived attempt at suicide ... REPEAT BREAKING NOW ... ...A shooting in Plano Texas of high school musicians at William B. Travis High School in—*"

Richardson muted the TV and pushed the intercom button. "*Shelly!* Get me Tim Savage. *Right away!*"

"Son of a *bitch!*" Richardson pushed himself back in his desk chair and squeezed his eyes shut. He sat motionless and forced himself to become calm, using a procedure he'd learned from his yoga master. This time, it didn't work very well. *What will be the most productive course?* he asked himself mentally. Any problem can be dealt with if taken in logical steps. He considered options, then unlocked a lower desk drawer, withdrew a small older cell phone, and pressed a speed dial number.

The phone rang four times and went to voice mail.

Richardson clicked off, swearing to himself. He tried again.

The phone rang four times again. He clicked it off.

The interoffice phone buzzed. Richardson grabbed it. "Savage?"

The high-pitched voice of Tim Savage answered. "Yes sir?"

"I need you to find a name for me, see if this name was in the Brookside Clinical Trial. John Hoff. H-o-f-f. Find anything that sounds like that. *Fast!*"

"I'll get it, sir."

"I need it *now!*"

"Yessir."

Richardson slammed the phone down and glanced at the TV. A pretty blonde reporter was on camera reading from a notepad. From the camera position at ground level, the area around the building was hidden by canvas screens. He unmuted the sound.

"...four not seriously injured ... um ... they'll be released from the hospital." She flipped the page of her pad and looked back into the camera. "Twenty people were transported to the ER at Brookside Hospital. Four were pronounced deceased on arrival ... four others were treated and released. One was an instructor." She paused, looked at something off-camera, then nodded and continued, brushing hair out of her face, "I was just told the alleged shooter was one of those taken to surgery. His identity we have confirmed as John Allen Hoff, age 21, a former student at Travis. His current condition is unknown."

Richardson muted the TV again and drummed his fingers.

His phone buzzed. "Yes!"

"Tim Savage, sir, line one—"

He pushed the button. "Savage, *get* to it!"

"Okay, uh, a John Hoff was not in the clinical trial at Brookside. Nobody with a name like that."

"That was the bad one?"

"The trial? Uh, yes sir, the one XR failed."

Richardson didn't reply. He hung up and stared at the far wall for a moment, thinking about what to do.

He muttered obscenities to himself, then hit the intercom button. "Shelley! Get Winston and Bliss up here immediately. I don't care what they're doing or who they're with. I need 'em here *now*."

"Yes sir," she answered.

While he waited, he laid the cell phone on his desk. He turned to the TV again. The crawler had added information about four slightly injured survivors but nothing else had changed. His anger rose as he thought about why something this ridiculous couldn't have happened in three months instead of now. Such a useless, stupid thing! And the damn killer couldn't even put himself down without screwing it up.

Two men came through his door. Chuck Winston, Provachem's President, was slim, tall, dressed in a tailored pinstripe suit. His expression said he knew about the shooting. Behind him was a short man in shirt and slacks, March Bliss, the company's chief counsel.

As they entered and closed the door, the little cell phone buzzed on Richardson's desk. He took the call.

"Where were you? Yeah, yeah, fine. What? *Damn!*" he breathed. "Yeah. We just got the news. What did you find?" He listened as the answer came, then commanded, "You *will* hide it! Do you understand? … Good. What? My god, he's out of surgery? He's stable? *Shit! Hold on!*" He lowered the phone and looked at the other two men for a few seconds, his eyes narrowed. Then he spoke into the phone. "I'll call you. Wait for me but hide it first! This is *imperative*, Doctor!" He clicked the phone off, knowing for sure they would now have to go further.

He stood and looked at the others. "This shooting." He pointed at the TV. "We have a problem. The moron killer had XR in his blood. He's alive. I was hoping he'd die in surgery. He needs to." Richardson cut off their responses and told them what he had in mind. Five minutes later, they left his office. They'd told him he should just take care of it. They didn't want to know details.

As the door closed behind Bliss, Richardson closed his eyes and sighed. He always had to do the dirty work. They agreed with him, though, that this problem had to be suppressed immediately. They knew he would do what they wouldn't.

He trembled, realizing what this could cost. It couldn't come out in the news—his drug in the killer's blood. Why couldn't the little bastard have succeeded in killing himself? After thinking about it for a few seconds, he knew there was only one way to take care of it permanently. A quick plan formed in his mind.

His secretary answered the intercom instantly. "Shelley, get a pool car brought around front for me. Right away."

"A pool car? Okay. Yes sir."

Richardson opened his briefcase and withdrew another old cell phone. He entered a number on it from memory and waited, spinning his chair around to look outside and tapping his fingers on his knee as the phone rang.

It was answered. "Yeah, it's me. You in town? You're available? No? Dammit! I'll double your rates!" He paused for an answer, then, "Okay. Meet me in twenty minutes." He waited for confirmation, clicked the phone off, then leaned down, opened a cabinet and worked a combination lock. The safe door opened to reveal his Glock 30, an extra magazine with ten .45 caliber defense rounds, some files and a couple of envelopes. Richardson grabbed the gun and the fatter of the envelopes and glanced into it, slammed the door shut and spun the lock.

He looked out toward the circle and saw a robin egg blue and cream-colored Chevrolet Malibu sedan stop at the curb in front of the wide walkway to the building. He put the envelope and gun in his shoulder bag, and left.

"I'll be back in an hour." He didn't wait for a reply from his secretary as he breezed past her desk and entered the elevator. It took only a minute to reach the car. The driver opened the rear passenger door for him.

He shook his head. "Close it. I'll take the car."

The man nodded and mumbled something about "nice day," as Richardson got into the car and left.

He took the Sam Houston Freeway south to Katy Freeway, got off, and was waiting for Kardov when he arrived. The blue Provachem car wouldn't look out of place in the hospital lot, if anyone even noticed, since his Provachem sales reps were there often.

He hadn't seen the man in almost a year, since the last time he had hired him, and thought he might have a new look. What he could never change, though, was his extreme height and the uncertain way he walked, like he was learning to use stilts.

Richardson was surprised that the skinny Russian hadn't changed his appearance at all. He wore the same gray Tom Mix-style ten-gallon Stetson on his bald head, Levis, a wide belt with a big burnished copper buckle, and boots that added two more inches to his six-feet-five. With that height and the man's gaunt look punctuated by a white handlebar mustache, there wasn't much point in trying to be unnoticed.

The Russian removed the hat from his bald head as he grunted and folded himself into the Provachem car, stayed inside for five minutes, then got back out, stuffing the fat envelope Richardson had given him into his back pocket. He stroked his mustache and ambled away.

Richardson pulled the flip phone out of his jacket pocket and entered a number. The call was answered on the first ring.

"I need your attention to this. I don't give a *damn* if you're busy! You know what it'll cost you if you don't help me." He listened for a moment, then began to describe what would happen and how he wanted the situation handled.

While he talked, he watched the Russian, Kardov, as the man sat in his red Dodge truck and brazenly counted the hundred Benjamins.

"Of course you'll take care of it, won't you? And without delay. No mistakes, Doctor, or you *will* regret it!" He waited, then nodded as he heard the response and clapped the phone closed.

Kardov drove away. The whole thing would rely on these two men, and it made Richardson uncomfortable. He had never been sure of anyone other than himself, but in this, he had to depend on them. Still, too many people were becoming involved, with Winston and Bliss, and now two more. He almost wished he'd not removed his younger brother from the company's headship and had never heard of Kardov.

He watched others come and go, people with normal lives. His anger welled up as his thoughts went to all the places where this could have happened and not screwed up his life.

After a minute, Richardson started the car and forced himself to drive calmly toward the exit ramp. He turned on the radio and fought to control his anger as he heard reporters blathering nonstop with repeated detail after detail of this random event in Plano. One stupid kid went nuts and killed a bunch of other kids, and now that meaningless act threatened *his* whole future. "It's *unfair!*" he bellowed, and slammed his hand against the steering wheel.

SIX

JUNE 27, 2016. MONDAY.

Cassie grimaced at a sudden stab of pain in her knee. She rubbed it and glanced at the clock. It was 11:30 p.m. The small room was dark, lit only by the various machines and a dim lamp over the bed. For five hours, she'd been holding Mark's limp left hand, feeling his heartbeat, occasionally praying and crying. She thought of her husband, John, who had died on September 11, 2001, when World Trade Center Tower One had collapsed. She had never been able to say goodbye to him, never even had any of him to bury. She wondered which was worse, not being able to lay to rest the person she loved after he died, or holding his hand and watching as it happened, as she was doing now.

Zach had sat silently with her for the last two hours. The only motion was Mark's diaphragm rising and falling. The only sounds were the respirator and the muted workings at the SICU nurses' desk and a couple of people in the hallway. She turned toward Zach as he took a long, deep breath and let it out quietly. He patted Cassie on the shoulder and whispered, "Back in a minute," rose and entered the small bathroom. She watched him go and shuddered as the thought struck her. He was the third important man in her life. Would he die violently, too?

She looked around as he closed the bathroom door and noticed a tall, thin doctor with a white handlebar mustache standing outside the room tapping an electronic tablet as he looked down the hallway.

She released Mark's hand, laid it gently along his side, and walked to the door.

"Excuse me, Doctor?"

49

As she approached him, he barely raised his head from looking down at the tablet because he was over a foot taller than she was. His gaunt face was expressionless. He didn't speak. She was startled by the coldness of his eyes as he turned them in her direction.

"Um... can you check on my son? Just for a second? His IV looks like it's running out or something." She stepped aside to give him room to step past her into the opening of the sliding door.

He glanced into Mark's room, then turned to Cassie and said, "You will wait for me one minute." His voice was high, but dry, and almost a whisper, with a Russian accent. He walked unsteadily past the empty nurses' station, showed his ID to a man in a black suit, and entered a room down the hall to the right.

Cassie was still standing in the door when the tall doctor left the room, nodded to the guy in the suit, and walked past her just a few seconds later. She tried to smile at him and expected him to step into Mark's room, but he didn't acknowledge her or turn his head. He passed by, his head still down, not even glancing at her, his long steps unsteady and slow, looking as if his legs might collapse with each step. He disappeared around the corner.

Her face burned. She walked to the nurses' station, where the nurse had just returned.

"Did you see that?"

The nurse had just picked up the phone. "Ma'am?" the middle-aged woman said. "Hold one," she said into the phone, held it against her chest, then turned toward Cassie. "Yes, ma'am?"

"Did you see that doctor just walk by me like that? I asked him to look in on my son and he said he would but he just—just *left!*"

"I'm sorry, ma'am, I'll look in on your son. All of his vitals are displaying as expected, here." She pointed to the small monitoring screen in the console in front of her.

Cassie exhaled and shook her head. "But his IV is almost empty, so can you come *into* the room and just look?"

"Yes ma'am," the nurse said, telling the caller she'd call back. When she reached Mark's bedside, she replaced one IV bag, examined the monitors and gave Cassie a sympathetic smile.

"I'm sorry, Mrs. Stevens. It was his fluids, and he's not in any pain at all. I'll find out who that doctor was you talked to." She started to pat Cassie's shoulder as she said it, then pulled her hand back, smiled again and left the room.

Cassie turned back to Mark's bed, sat down beside his motionless body and wept.

Zach walked quietly back into the room from the hallway, paused as she looked around at him, then spoke. "Sorry, Cass, I had to make a phone call to get Woof taken care of. Saw you talking to the nurse."

She looked up at him, swiped at her tears, stood and put her arms around his waist. She started to tell him about the jerk doctor, but it didn't seem to matter. All that mattered was Mark.

"He's fading away, Zach." She finally said in a high, constricted voice, and began to sob.

He held her close. After a minute, she fell silent, patted Zach's chest, sat back down, and took Mark's hand. Linnie would be stopping in before too long, hopefully with good news.

In the hallway, Zach stared at Linnea Kennedy, who was just an inch shorter than his five-feet-eleven, and spoke so that Cassie couldn't hear. "So, it's certain? He's not gonna make it?"

She looked at him, reached out and touched his arm. "I'm sorry, Zach." She took a deep breath and let it out. "We're keeping him completely free of pain. He isn't suffering at all, but his brain function—"

He looked down and nodded. "Yeah ... thanks," then turned and walked into the room.

She took a deep breath and entered the room behind him. It was almost midnight. She had left Mark for next to last in her late rounds so she could spend some time with Cassie when she informed her that Mark was not going to live much longer.

Her last stop would be the room down the hall, to check on the man who had done the shooting—the man whose life she had saved.

* * *

Cassie came awake to the sound of an insistent beeping. It seemed as if only minutes had passed since she'd talked to Linnie. She'd cried herself to sleep leaning over on the side of Mark's bed.

At first, she thought she must be dreaming and the beeping was in Mark's room, and he must be in trouble. She shook herself into consciousness and gripped Mark's hand in both of her own, gazing at his face. But it wasn't Mark. He wasn't moving except for his diaphragm rising and falling. Same as before.

The beeping came from the door of the room down the hall that the tall jerk doctor had gone into.

People were yelling, "Code Blue-Room 3!" and "Crash Cart!" and other things. She realized something big was happening and looked at the clock. It was 2:05 in the morning. Zach wasn't there. Where was he? Then she remembered he had left because he had a meeting he couldn't cancel in the morning, and he had to take his schnauzer, Woof, to a kennel.

Cassie stood and gently laid Mark's hand and arm against his leg and walked to the door. She could hear excited voices coming from the room down the hall. Nobody was at the nurses' station or in the hallway except the guy in the suit, who was talking on his phone as he watched what was happening through the door.

Cassie watched from Mark's door and heard the sounds of subdued, excited voices giving commands, a clank of something hitting the floor. Nurses and doctors rushed into the room. Someone barked "Clear!" twice. Then it all suddenly stopped. After a few seconds of several people quietly talking in urgent tones, she heard one man's voice announce, "I'm calling it. 2:13 a.m."

All became quiet. The suited man looked up and stepped from the doorway into the room. The door slid closed. Half a minute later, it opened again. The first person out was a nurse. She strode across the dimly lit hallways to the console that faced the rooms and picked up a phone, talked quietly into it, hung it up and saw Cassie watching. She walked toward Mark's room, smiled at Cassie and touched her arm as she passed.

She looked at Mark and checked his monitors. "He wasn't

disturbed, was he?"

"No, why?" Cassie answered.

"Just making sure."

"I was asleep in the chair, there. The noise woke me."

"Yeah. Sorry 'bout that."

"What happened?"

"The patient there, he passed away."

"Oh! My gosh. One of the kids … who was shot?" She felt a lump forming in her throat.

"Nobody told you? The patient was the guy who did the shooting. The guy in the suit? He's FBI."

Tears sprang up in Cassie's eyes from the shock of finding out the killer was right there all along. "But Dr. Kennedy, she's a friend of mine, told me the killer was going to recover! I didn't know he was in *there*—"

"I shouldn't say any more, Mrs. Stevens. There'll be a little bit more activity, and then it'll get quiet again. I'm so sorry this all disturbed you."

Cassie was trembling. She nodded as the nurse turned and walked toward the FBI agent, who had stepped out of the room and was once again talking on his phone.

It was surprising to Cassie that the killer was right down the hall. From her experience in New York, she knew prisoners were often put in standard rooms, especially if they were unconscious. But it was still unsettling. She just hadn't thought about the killer.

It didn't bother her in the least that he was dead.

What was shocking to her was that the death next door was so undramatic except for a couple of minutes of activity. Would Mark's be the same way? Quiet? Routine? Would the world then just continue, even though the dearest person in her life had left it? No big deal, just another death on the ward? She knew the answer, and she hated it.

She wondered idly if the killer had parents. If he did, why didn't they ever show up here? Maybe they lived somewhere else and they were still traveling to get here? She wanted to know. Despite everything, she could feel the old drive to investigate rising in her. The old saying came to mind: *"Investigative reporters don't die, they just go off chasing the biggest story in all eternity."*

Why would he die, like that, when Linnie had said he wasn't that bad? Why did he do this in the first place? Was he a psycho? Or just a kid full of hate for some reason?

The questions wouldn't leave her mind. Why? Why did this happen? Why Travis High? Why that kid? Why would *anyone* do this?

She knew that everyone was asking the same questions as they had been after Columbine, Virginia Tech, Newtown, Aurora, Charleston, and all the others. Why? Why did people suddenly take a gun and kill? But there was almost never an answer. And certainly never a solution.

Not that it would help Mark, or her.

She turned back to Mark's room. His still, thin body lay in the bed covered and tucked under a light green blanket, his breathing driven by the respirator. She walked slowly to her chair beside his bed and collapsed into it. Her grief was a physically heavy load that forced her into a slump, her head down.

It was only ten minutes later when she heard the large elevator doors at the far end of the hallway opening. She walked to the door. Two young men in blue scrubs wheeled a gurney with stacked and folded blue sheets toward the FBI guy still standing outside the room, then turned into the room. The agent stepped in behind them and closed the door.

She couldn't get over the fact that it was all so routine. No big fuss. She remembered the death of her own mother, years before. She and her brother had stood, one on each side of the bed, each holding a hand. Then her mom had simply stopped breathing. Just like that. A doctor had stepped in, held a stethoscope to her mom's chest, and very quietly said, "I'm sorry, she's gone." The monitoring machines had only showed flat horizontal lines where a living heartbeat and respiration had registered only seconds before. And that was it. She had felt, odd as it seemed, a momentary connection with eternity.

Cassie came back to the present when the door to the room down the hall slid back open. One of the young men backed out, pulling the gurney, which now held a large draped body covered head to toe by the blue sheets. Pushing the other end, the other attendant followed, and behind him, the FBI guy. They all entered the open elevator. The doors closed on them as Cassie turned her attention back to Mark.

Linnea Kennedy awoke in her apartment to the ring of her cell phone. She looked at the phone's clock face as she picked it up—5:27 a.m. Less than five hours earlier, she had laid it on the bedside table and gathered her covers around her.

During her interning and residency in New York, five hours would have represented a welcome night's sleep. Now, as Head of the Neurosurgery Trauma Unit at Brookside, she was accustomed to six or seven restful hours.

She pressed the button to answer and managed to say something that she thought sounded like, "Hello."

"Hello, Doctor Kennedy, this is Doctor Bhavesh Krishnamurthy from the hospital." She would have recognized the distinctive Indian accent of Brookside's Head of Pathology without hearing his name.

"Yes, doctor. What is it?"

"I am calling to inform you of the death of one of your patients."

"Oh—?" She hated the way this man forced responses from people he talked with. Why couldn't he just say it all? "Please tell me the details, doctor!"

"Mr. Hoff has died."

Linnie's breath caught.

"It was a coronary thrombosis, probably as a complication of surgery."

"But I checked on him just before midnight. He was fine!" She knew this had no bearing on a sudden event like a blood clot traveling to the heart, but she said it anyway.

"Yes. He died at 2:13 this morning. I have seen your notes in his chart. It was not to be expected."

Linnie shook her head, trying to figure out why this happened when Hoff had been receiving heparin to thin his blood. It should have prevented this very thing.

Krishnamurthy spoke again. "Doctor, we have been asked to be available for a press conference at ten this morning. I will see you there?"

Even in her still sleepy state, she could detect an uncharacteristic trembling in his voice, but she didn't ask about it.

"Yes, I'll be there. Thanks." She held the phone and heard it go silent as Krishnamurthy ended the call. She would want to get there early to see what she could discover. She had never had blood clotting problems with a surgical patient and didn't expect it with this one.

John Hoff should not have died.

SEVEN

JUNE 28, 2016. TUESDAY.

Linnea Kennedy was surprised to find that her reserved ER parking space and two others were blocked by a TV satellite truck, its wheels held up off the asphalt by large mechanical stands. She swore to herself and considered banging on the door of the truck, but decided she didn't need the extra stress.

After searching the crowded parking lot, she finally found a space, with the added benefit of a bit of shade. At 8:30, the temperature was already over 85 degrees. She left the windows down a half inch and walked to the hospital's administrative entrance instead of taking the longer walk across the hot parking lot to the ER.

Once inside, she stopped to get her bearings. This was one of the largest hospitals in the Metroplex, and she had always made it a habit to avoid this busy part of it. Today, it was crowded, with media people and photographers carrying large video cameras on their shoulders. She recognized a few of the better dressed ones—the "talent."

"Dr. Kennedy!" She turned at the sound of a man's voice and British accent she recognized. He approached her from across the room, his perfectly styled salt-and-pepper hair and lightly tanned metrosexual complexion set off by a powder blue shirt, blue silk tie and medium grey Savile Row suit.

"Good morning, Dr. Chase," Linnie answered. Hospital Director Randall Chase, a man she disliked, was always the first to hold his staff responsible for anything going wrong, rarely defending them, and never taking responsibility if he could place blame elsewhere.

"Dr. Kennedy—Linnea. I am receiving quite a number of

requests from the press for information on Mr. Hoff." He looked around before continuing in a lower voice. "You are up to the minute on what has happened, yes?"

Linnie resisted the impulse toward sarcasm, wanting to say, "Yeah, the SOB's dead." Instead, she nodded. "I got a call from Dr. Krishnamurthy this morning about it."

"And what do you believe might have happened?" The man, shorter than Linnie, cocked his head sideways. His voice rose in pitch at the end of his sentence, a speech habit Linnie found annoying.

"I was told it was a coronary thrombosis."

"You had ordered heparin?"

"Absolutely. Of course." Out of the corner of her eye, she noticed a TV person she recognized edging closer to them. "Dr. Chase, I think we should go somewhere else to talk." She motioned with her eyes toward the reporter.

"Yes. Yes. Capital idea." He took her elbow and guided her toward an entrance to a room marked Staff Only. She resisted the urge to jerk her arm away.

Entering the room, he closed the door loudly behind them and his manner, as she had expected now that they were in private, made a sea change.

"What in bloody hell went wrong, Doctor?" He stood too close to her, forcing her to step back.

"The patient died, Doctor Chase. That is what went wrong. As I said, I don't know any more at this time. I just got here."

"I suggest you bring yourself up to speed before the press conference. I will ask you to address this."

"And, Dr. Krishnamurthy? He is Head of Pathology—"

"He will be there, but you were the surgeon. Dr. Krishnamurthy has completed the autopsy."

"Well, that's—*wait*, why so fast?"

"You'll need to check with Dr. Krishnamurthy on that. His department has also created another major bloody problem for us, I'm afraid! I will see you on the stage in the theater." He turned back toward the door, straightened his tie and put a pleasant smile on his face before opening the door and leaving.

Linnie stood still, stunned by what he'd said. Why in the world would the autopsy have been done so quickly?

Linnie walked the long hallways from the main building back to the ER wing, informed the desk that she was in the hospital, and stopped into her own office to check her messages. She turned on her computer screen to see if they'd been transcribed yet.

They were done. She pored over her report on the Hoff surgery, specifically looking for the dosage of heparin she had ordered. It was more than adequate; the kid shouldn't have thrown a clot.

Next, she opened his file and saw that the standard entries had been made. It was customary in the SICU for vitals to be recorded every fifteen minutes and signed in the computer. Nothing out of the ordinary had been recorded until the patient had begun having trouble at just after two in the morning. That wasn't so unusual, though, with blood clots. They didn't always provide much warning before they caused a problem.

Linnie was amazed, though, that the autopsy had already been done. It might provide more information. She clicked into her email. The autopsy report wasn't there yet.

She sat back in her chair and tried to put it all together. Her surgery on Hoff had ended at about 3:30. When she had checked on him after he was brought to SICU, at 5:30, everything was as she expected. He was still sedated, and would have been for the next eighteen hours. Her orders for blood-thinning heparin in the IV were being followed to the letter, or so the chart entries said. Everything looked normal. So, how could a blood clot form? She searched the files for the pre-surgical blood work, brought it up and examined it on the screen. Nothing was out of place that she could spot, but still it seemed to her like something was missing. She couldn't put her finger on it.

A deep frown creased her forehead. She stared at the documents on the computer screen for a few seconds, then clicked it off, grabbed a white coat and her ID lanyard, locked the office door, and left.

* * *

As Linnie approached Mark's room, Cassie was standing beside Mark's bed, head bowed, her eyes closed and her lips moving.

Linnie waited and reflected on their friendship. They'd met here when Cassie did a column on doctors who had been on duty in New York on 9/11, and how many of them were now working in the Dallas-Fort Worth Metroplex. It had turned out there were seven, and Cassie had hosted a get-together for them. The coincidence that amazed both of them was that they had met once before when Linnie worked in New York at University Hospital and Cassie worked for the New York Times and did her series on First Responders of 9/11. When Linnie had been offered the ER neurosurgery job at Brookside, she took it. They'd met again at Cassie's social gathering and had become the best of friends.

She walked in, slowly. Cassie saw her and dabbed at her eyes with a tissue.

She laid a hand on her friend's shoulder. "Cass, how are you doing?"

"Not very well."

"I'm so sorry, Hon. Have they been taking care of Mark?"

Cassie looked down at him, most of his hair and one eye completely hidden by the bandages, and fought against more tears. "Yeah, I guess. They've been real nice."

Linnie took a long breath. "He's not feeling any pain at all. You know that, right?"

Cassie nodded. "Mm-hmm. I've been talking to him, too. Can he hear me?"

"Somehow, I think maybe he can."

"I wondered last night if he heard me talking to the nurse about that doctor."

Linnie took a step back. "Who? Right! Of course, you were *here*! You saw what happened?"

"I was here for the whole thing. I was surprised it wasn't a bigger deal. The guy just died—it seemed almost, you know, so *routine*."

"I know." She waited.

"But I was talking about that doctor, the one who was here earlier. The jerk."

"What do you mean, *jerk*? What doctor?"

"The tall bald guy with the white mustache. He was here two or three hours before the other thing happened. Before midnight."

"Oh," Linnie said. "He wasn't—what, friendly? What did he do?"

"Well, he was standing in the hall outside Mark's room, and I just asked him to look in on Mark. He said he would in a minute. Then he went down there and went in the room."

"Hoff's room? The second one down?" She pointed down the hallway.

"Yeah. He told me he'd take a look at Mark but he came out and didn't even look my way when he left. He didn't even use the elevator. Went down the stairs, I think. He was a cold—well, just a *jerk*!"

"How long was he in the room, there?"

"I don't know, not very long—way less than a minute. Less than half a minute, really."

"Where was the nurse?"

"I don't know. I didn't see her. I think she was talking with Dr. Johnson in another room."

"What about the guard, the FBI agent?"

"I didn't even *know* he was an FBI agent. He looked at the doctor's badge and let him go in."

"So, this doctor went in Hoff's room and came out in just a few seconds? Did you see his name tag?"

"Huh-uh."

"Okay, Hon. Have you told anyone else about this?"

"No—well, just the nurse, last night."

"Okay, then don't tell anyone else, okay? I want to look into it. I'll find out who that doctor was and let you know."

"Okay."

"He'll be on the video cameras. Security can help me."

"Probably not, Linn. He walked with his head down all the time. His face won't show on any of them." She motioned with her head up toward the cameras in the hallway.

"Wow. That's strange." Linnie thought for a second. "Did you see any other docs, when it happened?"

Cassie nodded. "Yeah, Johnson, went in when the buzzers were going off." She shrugged and turned back to Mark.

"Hmm. Yeah, Johnson's a good guy. Cass, I've got to go right now. I'll be back after this press conference, okay?" She leaned over and gave Cassie a hug, laid a hand on Mark's leg for a second, turned and left.

Randall Chase, it was obvious to everyone in the room, enjoyed being the center of attention. In Linnie's mind, he was a narcissistic ass whose single best skill was manipulating others to get his way. She watched as he stood at the podium and bent the microphone down to his level.

"Yes, we have, at this time, eleven young people from the shooting in our care. They are recovering from surgery for their wounds."

"Will they all live?" A woman called out.

"I won't address that," he answered, and pointed to another questioner.

The man stood and spoke. "Dr. Chase, it's not yet clear, the exact numbers we are talking about. Can you go over how many were in the band room, how many were dead at the scene, and how many made it to the hospital—all those details?"

Chase looked down at papers in front of him. "These are the statistics from this tragedy. Listen carefully, as I will not want to repeat this."

Linnie thought she could have been mistaken, but she might have detected a glimmer of humanity in Chase. He took a deep breath and continued.

"In the band room at the time of the attack were fifty-six high school musicians and five instructors. And John Hoff. Twenty of them, one of them an instructor, and one of them the perpetrator, were transported to the hospital. Four of those, all young people, were pronounced deceased on arrival. Four of them, including the instructor, had only minor injuries and have been released. Of the twelve others we received, all were treated surgically. Three of them are still in critical condition. Eight others are in the hospital and in serious condition but stable. One of them died here in surgical intensive care at 2:13 this morning."

"He was the killer?" The reporter asked.

"He was."

Another woman stood. "Doctor, what can you tell us about his surgery. We understand he shot himself in the head and was treated for that?"

She knew it would come. Dr. Chase turned to Linnie. "Dr. Kennedy is Head of Neurosurgery in the emergency unit. Dr. Kennedy?"

Linnie could have sworn he smirked unpleasantly at her as they passed. She had always had the impression that he disliked her because she was over six inches taller than he was, she was beautiful, blond, and a competent woman. When she approached the microphone, she spoke slowly. Like her friend Cassie, she had a fear of public speaking, though not as deep a phobic dread as Cassie's. "I am Dr. Linnea Kennedy— "

"Spell it please?"

"L-I-N-N-E-A … K-E-N-N-E-D-Y. Mr. Hoff was the first patient to arrive. His injuries were not life threatening. There was major damage to his zygomatic bone—that's the cheekbone—and his left ear was basically gone. Hearing on his left side was no doubt destroyed. A section of the scalp on the left side of his head was torn away. After surgery, he was expected to recover fully except for his hearing damage. There was some concussion and expected brain swelling, and he was kept sedated to reduce the swelling."

"Then why did he die?"

"The cause of death, according to our pathology department, was a coronary thrombosis—a blood clot that traveled into his heart and caused a blockage that resulted in congestive heart failure."

"Heart attack?"

"Yes, basically."

"Isn't it customary to prescribe blood thinning drugs following surgery, just so that won't happen?"

"Yes. And the orders were that heparin was to be administered intravenously. He was correctly dosed."

"Was it? Were the orders followed?"

"Yes. The staff in this hospital is meticulous about following post-surgical orders."

"Then how *did* this happen?"

Linnie stared at the man. He was backing her into a corner. "We'll need to do more investigating before we can answer that."

Another man stood and spoke. "So, Dr. Chase, just to confirm, if only twenty people were transported, that means forty-two people were dead at the scene? Four instructors and thirty-eight band kids? And four more died in the ambulance? Forty-six victims, and the killer, dead?" Somewhere in the back of the room, a woman sobbed and left.

Linnie turned to Chase, who stepped up beside her and took over the microphone as she stepped back.

"Yes. It's very confusing. Twenty arrived, but four were deceased. Of the sixteen left, four were treated for minor injuries and released. Mr. Hoff died last night. Eleven students are currently in the hospital recovering from their wounds."

Another reporter rose to his feet with another question. "Who were the ones sent home?"

Chase continued. "I can't give you all their names because some are minors. One is an instructor, Mr. Brett Welch, who is local." The room was silent for a moment as people made notes.

Linnie left the dais as the questioning continued. When she reached the side door, she heard Mark Stevens's name. She looked for Dr. Ryan, Mark's surgeon, but didn't see him, then looked back in case Chase wanted her to speak again. He answered the question himself, then announced that there would be only one more question and chose a reporter.

"Dr. Chase, is there any reason to suspect that the surgeon or anyone else here had anything to do with John Allen Hoff's death? After all, he was known to be the killer, and—"

"My *god*, man! Certainly *not*! You are questioning the integrity of this hospital and its staff, and that is improper in the extreme! I would not give that question the honor of a reply, but it seems that I already have done. Your answer is an emphatic *no*—there is absolutely no reason to think along those lines."

He took a breath. "That will *end* this press conference. Good day. Please clear your equipment and trucks from our property quickly. Thank you." He glared at the reporter who had asked the final question and stepped back.

But Linnie, watching from the side door, had her own questions along the same lines.

EIGHT
JUNE 28, 2016. TUESDAY.

Randall Chase walked past Linnie. She stood and waited for the man she needed to see. Dr. Krishnamurthy, Head of Pathology, had been standing on the other side of the platform and came out last, shuffling along with his head lowered in his usual deferential manner as he allowed others to pass.

"Dr. Krishnamurthy," she said quietly. He paused but didn't stop, forcing her to fall in step with him and shorten her steps to match his smaller ones.

"Doctor," he said, greeting her in his usual hushed tone. His accent from having grown up in Jaipur, India, was still pronounced, and he had never gotten rid of his "head wobble."

Linnie liked the man, but she often felt he was not willingly sharing information with her. Until recently, he had called her "Linnie," but they had argued over a difference of opinion on a cause of death. It was never settled between them, and he had been overly formal ever since.

"Doctor Krishnamurthy," she said, "we really need to talk. I want to see the complete documents from your autopsy of John Hoff."

"I think the file has been sent to you." He said, continuing toward the elevators. She stepped into an empty elevator with him.

"No. I looked. Doctor, what was the cause of Hoff's death?"

He spoke without turning toward her. "You said it in the press conference, there. It was an embolism, as I told you. Nothing more was found."

They reached the second basement and the doors opened.

"I'll need that autopsy report, Doctor." She had the feeling he was not even listening to her. "And I would like to examine the body, as well."

"Oh, the written report of course. That is not a problem. But the body, it is already gone." He shook his head as he opened the door to the Pathology Department and let Linnie enter first.

"What? Why?" She stopped and spun around as he shut the door. "All right, then, I want to bring it back. I think I should examine it. Why was the autopsy done so quickly? Something is wrong here!"

"Not with the autopsy," he answered as he walked past her. "His was not the only autopsy; we are doing a large number of them to cooperate with the Coroner and provide information. I was under very much pressure to move quickly and there was no reason not to do so. His autopsy was more important to the authorities." He paused, looked down and shook his head.

"Doctor Kennedy, you will find this out soon enough, so I will tell you now." He looked at her and took a deep breath. "The tags on the body were somehow mixed up by one of my interns, and Mr. Hoff's body was sent to a crematorium early this morning. We were too late to stop it."

"What? My god, Krish! He was the *killer*! His body was evidence!"

"Yes, that is correct. It has been a terrible mistake and I will certainly be in the hot water for it, but his dead body could reveal nothing that was not shown in the documents. The autopsy had been completed. Nothing about it was out of the ordinary. Your surgery notes and records, and our completed autopsy, were all the Coroner and the FBI really needed. The body itself was superfluous." He sat down in his chair behind his desk and lowered his head.

She stood over him. "Doctor Krishnamurthy, this is highly irregular and you don't seem to be bothered much—"

"No, you are wrong, Doctor. I am very sorry, and I realize the magnitude of our error, but we have not ever before had a mass killer and dozens of bodies in my department at one time, and therefore something bad has happened. It is done, and I cannot change it now."

She stared at him.

"You're not telling me the complete truth, are you?"

"About what?"

"I don't know, Doctor. If I knew, I would ask you about it. Now please send me that autopsy report."

He nodded, clicked his computer mouse a few times, looked at her and stood. "Dr. Kennedy, it is all you should need. It has been sent to your email. It is really all you should need."

She looked at him, wondering why he seemed to be *asking* her not to need anything more than the report. "Thank you, Doctor," she said, forcing a benign expression. She started to go, then turned. "I'm sorry I was so difficult, there. I'm sure you are feeling badly already."

He nodded and walked around the desk. "Yes." He put his hand out to shake hers.

She thanked him, turned and left. She had pretended to back off, but she was angry. She reached her own office and finally began to get her mind around all the things that were wrong.

First, there was the embolism. Practically impossible, given the amount of heparin she had ordered in Hoff's IV, but there was no way to argue with it, even if it wasn't the real cause. The records showed her dosing was correct. Then, there was the fast autopsy, practically in the middle of the night. The Coroner's allowing it was not unheard of, since Krishnamurthy was a Deputy Coroner. But it was still extremely rare. Finally, the body being cremated by mistake? She didn't know for sure, but she doubted this happened very often, if at all.

An erroneous cremation? Perfect way to hide anything about a body that was out of the ordinary, and she was now convinced that something here was most definitely far from ordinary. Hoff wouldn't have died from his injuries and didn't die from a surgical or nursing care error. That left only one option, and it was strengthened by the mysterious "doctor" with whom Cassie had had words.

John Hoff was murdered.

Her incoming email included the autopsy report, and she already had the pre-surgical blood work report. She looked them over and saw nothing odd, but printed both of them to examine later. The absence of Hoff's body took away any time pressure, especially since it was already reduced to about a pound of bone particles and dust.

For now, she needed to visit Mark and see how Cassie was doing.

She had to force herself to leave her chair. A heavy tiredness had begun to settle on her. She hadn't yet allowed herself to process this whole event—especially not the certain impending death of her best friend's son—and she knew it was all beginning to hit her. She steeled herself to hold it off until later. For now, it was nearing noon, and she had to do early rounds. Patients needed attention and she had to be the strong, dispassionate surgeon everyone expected. She rose slowly to go and do her duty.

Mark's hand in Cassie's was warm but heavy, limp. The word lifeless crossed her mind, but she rejected it. He still hadn't made a sound or movement. The SICU daytime attending doctor, Dr. Levin, stood on the other side of the bed, quiet, waiting for Cassie. Zach stood beside her, his hand on her shoulder.

They had told her that Mark would not be able to live without the respirator. She had cried anew, though she had suspected it when they told her his bodily functions simply couldn't be supported by the portions of his brain that were functioning. They'd said it was the machines keeping his body going. His brain wave on the sensors, when they showed it to her, was a flat line. He was already gone, but she couldn't accept it.

A doctor had previously asked her if she would agree to his organs being donated. She had signed the forms to okay it, since everything except his brain and one eye were still perfectly intact; he could save or improve several people's lives. She had also signed the forms that relinquished custody and treatment of him to the hospital until he was delivered to a funeral home.

All that was left to do was for her to say, "yes," and leave. But now, at this moment, with Dr. Levin waiting, she couldn't. They would keep the machines going so that his organs could continue to receive oxygenated blood, and she simply had to walk away. She wouldn't be able to say her last goodbye, but had to simply walk out of the room.

She felt as if she was abandoning him. She couldn't do it.

"Mrs. Stevens," Dr. Levin said, "Please, take your time." His warm and caring smile, and kind eyes, gave her a moment's relief from the tension. He smiled, turned and left.

Cassie watched him go, thinking she would not be able to do this. How could she just buzz the nurse's station and let them know she was ready to walk away from her son so they could take him out and dismantle him? How could she just leave him like that, no matter how noble it was?

Zach spoke close behind her in a quiet voice. "Cass, you know that Mark isn't going to change. It's just a time when you don't have any more choices. His spirit is already with the angels. You have to let him go."

"But I can't!" she said, turning to him, then back to Mark. "How can I just—just walk away?"

Zach didn't reply.

Just at that moment, Linnie entered. She stood across the bed from Cassie, held out her hand and took Cassie's. Tears ran down Cassie's cheeks. There really was no choice.

Linnie said, "Cassie, I'm so sorry, so sorry," and fought her own tears.

Cassie released Linnie's hand, reached for a tissue, used it to dry her eyes and cheeks, leaned down and whispered something toward Mark's unbandaged ear, kissed his cheek, hugged him for a moment, turned and walked around Zach and out of the room.

Linnie looked at Zach, closed her eyes briefly, and shook her head. "Zach, go. Take her bag. I'll tell Levin Mark's ready." She gave Zach quick hug and watched as he left, then looked at Mark again, mouthed "Goodbye, sweetheart," to him, and walked out. She found Dr. Levin and told him that Cassie had left and they could go ahead with Mark.

When she reached the waiting room, they were gone.

* * *

Cassie stood at the curb and stared into the sky, tears hanging in her eyes. "I can't believe we just walked away—just walked out. I *can't*—"

Zach nodded. "I know, Cass. I know. I want to be here to support you. Just tell me what you need."

They left the shade of the sidewalk cover and Zach followed Cassie to her Explorer.

"Zach, I need to be alone and—"

"Really? Are you sure? That might not be the best thing—"

"It is the best thing for me right now. I'm going home and I want to be alone for awhile."

"Some arrangements have to be made."

"I know. I can only deal with this one thing right now and I have to be by myself."

"Well … okay. Whatever you need. You want me to come up later, bring food, you know?"

"No." She stood on her tiptoes and kissed his cheek. "Thanks. I'll call you."

She climbed into the Explorer, tried to give Zach a half smile, started the engine and drove away.

It didn't feel real. She couldn't really be going home, alone. Just, *alone*.

But she was.

The SUV seemed to drive itself. She didn't know how she had gotten halfway home, couldn't remember turning, driving, stopping, going, driving on the tollway.

She couldn't get control of her thoughts. She could only see Mark lying in that bed. Then her thoughts would jump to the operating room where they would take him apart and ship pieces of him in ice to other people.

Then she was almost home and she remembered she needed to

do laundry for Mark—

No. Mark will never come home.

The Explorer seemed to turn itself across traffic and into a strip mall and park crookedly.

Cassie turned off the engine and picked up her cell phone. She dialed the paper.

"Tom, it's Cassie. Mark has died. I thought you should know." She dropped the phone in the passenger seat, opened the door and walked into the liquor store. She came out with a bottle of vodka, got into the Explorer and was surprised thirty minutes later when it took her into the garage and seemed to park itself. She was mentally and emotionally functioning in an automatic mode, not allowing herself to think about the impossible present moment.

A few minutes later, the door to her condo opened in front of her and she walked through. The bottle was in her hand. She released the door behind her and jumped at its metallic *click* as it closed. She walked into the kitchen. Stood there. The place was empty. *Quiet.*

Possibly for the first time, the reality of this ending hit her.

She would never again hear the tones of Mark's flugelhorn.

She would never again hear him say, "*crap*," after a cracked note, then continue working until he nailed it.

She burst into tears and collapsed, sobbing, on the couch.

NINE

JUNE 30, 2016. THURSDAY.

Zach Barber's marketing consultation business was in a slump. He hadn't been paying much attention to it lately. Normally, he would have been traveling or writing, but for now, he was consumed by what had happened three days ago. His partner had understood and said he would carry the load for a while.

He looked at his TV, where the morning news was on, but his mind was three floors up, in Cassie's condominium. He'd taken Mark's clothes to the funeral home the day before. When he'd gotten back and knocked on her door, she had only said through the closed door, "Leave me alone, Zach, please. I'm okay." But he knew she wasn't.

He picked up his phone and called her again. Same message as usual. After her announcement, he just said, "I love you, Cass. Call me when you can."

Cassie's TV was on, but she was dozing. Her cell phone rang, waking her. She didn't look at it because she didn't want to talk to anyone. On the TV screen, the words, "Travis High Tragedy," appeared and faded to a group of people around a table. She found the remote and turned up the volume.

The moderator said, "Tell us, Alice Roberts, what is the goal of 'Moms Against Guns?' "

The attractive blond woman paused before answering. "Larry, MAGs wants to make privately owned guns illegal! Simple as that. Without all these three-hundred million private guns in our country,

75

the shootings could not happen!"

A younger man spoke up. "But, Alice, taking guns away—well, first of all it's a constitutional right to own a gun, and second it's just not even possible to remove them all—but taking guns away would just keep law-abiding, *legal* gun owners from—"

"Yeah, we hear that all the time. But almost all of the guns used in these kinds of killings have been 'legal,' James! And *most* of these people were not criminals to begin with! Regular gun laws don't touch them!"

"*That's* a valid point," the moderator said. He looked across the table. "Doctor Grace Doyle, what do you see as the central problem?"

The middle-aged woman raised her eyebrows, removed her glasses and took a breath. "Larry, there are *so* many variables. You know, James is right. You can't even *find* all the guns! But in this particular situation, not so *many* had to die, if the back emergency door to the band room had been unlocked, as it should have been. But that's not what happened. Of course, without access to guns, this kind of killing *couldn't* have happened, that's true." She looked at the others. "But the question is *not* what was used to do the killing, but why the killing was done. This young man, John Allen Hoff, had *just* been jilted by his fiancée. We call that a 'stressor.' *And* he had a history of disappointment with this particular band—he'd apparently missed an audition when *he* was in high school, right there at Travis, and not gotten a second chance—"

"But don't you also think," the young man, James, interrupted, "that there had to be something else? The shooting happened just this Monday, three days ago, and there's still a lot more to be discovered."

"Well, that's also true, James" the older woman replied, "But, just like with *most* of these tragic events, the killer is dead, so we'll never know for sure *what* his motive was."

"—if there can ever be an understandable motive for such as this," Larry Rivers, the panel anchor said, turning again to the camera. "That's it for today. Thanks for tuning in. We'll stay on top of this story and provide details as we get them. Remember, tonight, the special, 'Looking Past Travis High,' nine, eastern."

A silent montage filled the screen. It was a high shot from a helicopter, emergency vehicles' lights, people crying, a shot of Brookside Hospital's crowded ER entrance, large title letters in red that read "47 KILLED," then another screen showing the makeshift shrine display with mylar balloons, flowers, cards and flags.

"Forty-*eight* killed, dammit!" She started to throw the remote control at it, then stopped herself and slapped the remote down on the couch after clicking the TV off.

She rose slowly and walked toward the kitchen area. The condo was too tidy. Mark's sneakers would normally be over there by the entrance to the hall. No sweatshirt was thrown on the couch. It was the same in the hallway bathroom. Bath towels were neatly hung. The sink was clean.

She was plagued by pictures in her mind from the morning before, walking with Zach into the funeral home, hearing the salesman's voice as he described her options. Her thoughts had kept repeating: *The man is making big money off this shooting.*

All she was left with was the reality of the ending of the most important and only truly joyful part of her life. It would never be the same. She should have died before Mark did. Children shouldn't die first. The casket didn't matter. The music didn't matter. Mark's clothing, which Zach took back to the place after they got back to Cassie's condo, didn't even register. She tried, without success, to stay emotionally distant from the whole experience, as if it were a nightmare that she was forced to be part of, but could watch from the fringe.

She had been silent all the way home. Zach had wanted to stay, to give her some support or something, but she'd said no. She had gathered the clothes and ushered Zach out, changed clothes, and tried to will herself to die. It didn't work.

Now, suddenly, she became aware of knocking on the door. It had to be Zach, again. She opened the door.

He stood there, a sympathetic smile on his slightly pudgy face, and held up a bag from Jason's Deli, a block away down on Main Street. "You're probably hungry?" He said, not moving to enter.

She found herself glad to see him.

"I am, a little." She stood aside. "Come on in."

He walked past her and set the bag of food on the dinette table.

"Cass—" he started to say.

"Yeah, I know. Don't say it. What can you say anyway?"

He just looked at her.

"I guess I look like hell, don't I? Sorta feel like it." She ran fingers through her hair. "What's for dinner?" She looked into the bag. "I'm not very hungry."

"Did you eat anything today?" he asked.

"No."

"Well, hey, let's just pull this stuff out where you can smell it. Maybe that'll help." He started to unpack the salads and sub sandwiches.

"You're treating me like a kid."

"Sorry. I don't mean to."

She sat down heavily in one of the chairs and didn't reply. He got the food out onto the table, then put out napkins.

"Drink?" He looked into the refrigerator as he said it, pulled out a pitcher of tea and held it up with a water bottle. Despite trying to ignore it, he looked at the unopened vodka bottle on the counter.

"Tea."

"Ice?"

"I don't care."

They both sat down. Neither said anything, and neither touched the food. Cassie brought it up. "Tomorrow."

"Yeah." Zach looked at her and took a breath. "Cass, I know this is the hardest thing you've ever gone through and—"

"No, Zach, you *don't* know. You don't know what it's like to lose all the men in your life and to lose your only—"

"I mean—"

"*NO!* You *don't* know what it's like! Who've you ever lost?"

"Cass, please just—"

"Please what? Please what? Act like it's all going to be okay?

Please act like things are normal? Well they're not! They won't be for a *hell* of a long time, and that's a fact!" She stood, pushed her chair back with her leg, knocking it over.

Zach reached for her arm to steady her.

"Don't touch me, dammit! Just go home!"

"Cass, look, I'm going to miss Mark! You don't know how much—"

"You're gonna miss him? *Miss him?* Like he's gone to summer *camp?* God, you … you… Just get the hell out of here!"

Zach slumped. He walked to the door and opened it, turned and said, "I'll come up to get you tomorrow, Cass," then closed the door quietly and left.

Mark's memorial service would start in just over one hour. Zach finished tying his tie as he stared at the television. The reporter was somber, looking worn. "This will make forty-six funerals, forty-two of them for the best and brightest young musicians in Texas, and four more for talented, dedicated instructors, in just a few days," the reporter said as she finished her commentary, her black skirt and jacket in contrast to her light complexion and strawberry blonde hair, "and nine of them here in the Metroplex. It's hard to believe, impossible to accept. The President, Governor Hubbard, and everybody else have all issued statements and made speeches. It's clear that they all feel terrible about this, as we do, but their solutions are the same as before. They say 'gun crime' is to blame. In Texas, especially in Plano, as you can imagine, that isn't being very well received. This is Kelli Tremaine, WNN, outside the William B. Travis High School auditorium, in Plano."She looked into the camera until it switched back to a studio scene.

The anchor at the TV station began to talk, but Zach turned it off. He walked out the door, still not sure if he should go to Cassie's and then with her to the limo that would arrive, or if he should just go by himself. He decided he had to at least knock on her door and see if she still wanted him with her.

He approached her door and knocked. It was 9:55 a.m., and the limo driver was scheduled for 10 a.m. down on Main Street beside the building.

The door opened. "Zach," Cassie said, a resigned note to her voice, "I need you there today, and I know you want to be there, but after last night, I want you to leave me alone for awhile."

He was shocked by her cold tone but could only mumble, "Okay, Cass. I understand." He barely met her eyes as she walked past him and down the hall.

They walked out onto Main Street, where a black limousine waited at the curb. The driver said good morning and opened the back door. Cassie got in, slid over, and looked out the other way as Zach got in.

It was a quiet ride from downtown Dallas up to the school in Plano, twenty-five minutes away. Cassie didn't speak. Zach looked out his window most of the way, not wanting to add to Cassie's distress in any way. The one time he did look at her, she silently shook her head and said nothing.

Cassie wasn't sure she could make it through this. She wouldn't have allowed Zach to escort her, but she knew he would be an actual physical support if she needed it. She thought she might, as she had almost collapsed in tears earlier as she applied her makeup. She didn't think she could handle it alone. As for her and Zach's future, it was the furthest thing from her mind.

As they walked from the limo to the auditorium entrance, she let Zach take her elbow, and as they entered and walked down the aisle, she put her arm in his. When she saw Linnie along the aisle, halfway up from the front, she stopped and asked her friend to come to the front with them.

The auditorium was about half full—not as many people as for the mass memorial that had been held two days ago. People were worn down by the unending sadness.

Cassie didn't remember setting any of this up. Zach must have done it. A high school girl with a remarkably good voice sang a hymn. A man in a dark suit came to the podium, looked down at

Mark's closed casket, and began to speak. After a short prayer in which he echoed the song's message of acceptance and love, he began to speak about Mark and his music. It had all been said before in other services, but Cassie hadn't attended them so it was new to her and comforting in a small way.

Then, he began to speak more forcefully.

"We've all seen the news coverage of this tragedy. We've seen this same thing before, in other places, taking other people's children, some as young as four years old, like up in Newtown a few years ago. But age doesn't matter. Every one of these lives taken is a crime, a tragedy, a heinous and vile act, the theft of life and joy from families and friends."

He paused and looked out at the audience for a long few seconds. Then he spoke again, but more gently. Cassie's thoughts began to wander.

She didn't know how long she had been mentally absent, but she was brought back to the present when the preacher looked up from the lectern and demanded, "We *must* do something!"

"Beyond our mourning, *far* apart from our anger, each one of us *must* resolve to do what we can do, within our capabilities and from our station in life, to *stop* this kind of crime." He paused and scanned the room, then continued more quietly. "Otherwise, these will never be stopped. Every year, more innocent victims will die. We must each at least speak up and demand a solution!"

The last comment was met with scattered applause, out of place at a memorial service. The man finished talking, but in Cassie, his words had stirred something.

She just didn't know how to apply it to herself, or if she had the energy or courage, or could think of anything she could accomplish. Everything seemed unimportant now.

At the cemetery, the day was unusually cool for the beginning of July, with scattered billowing cumulus clouds in an azure sky. Now and then, a zephyr would whip through, creating a lonely whisper as it ruffled leaves on stately oaks. Cassie, Zach and Linnie stood close to one another as Mark's casket was held waiting to be lowered, Cassie stared without seeing, her mind still unwilling to accept what was happening.

The pastor said a few words of assurance, then led the group in The Lord's Prayer, and then it was over. Each of them placed a rose on the casket. Cassie kissed her fingers and touched the box, then turned slowly and began to walk away. The group of about fifty people milled around for a moment before making their way to their cars. Some of Cassie's friends from work stopped to hug her, including Tom Hammond, her editor.

Cassie didn't speak as Linnie held her arm and Zach followed on the other side. They walked away from the burial plot. Linnie steadied her friend and looked at Zach with a question in her eyes. He just shook his head in reply.

They reached the limousine. Cassie hugged Linnie. "Linn, can you take Zach home? I know it's a long trip but—"

"Sure, no problem, Hon. Will you be all right?"

"Yeah, I just need to think." She tried to smile, then turned and entered the limousine.

Zach and Linnie watched it leave, looked at each other, then walked to the car. They drove slowly through the curving byways of the cemetery to the exit, and headed for the tollway south to Dallas.

"So, what's going on?" Linnie asked.

"Long story, Linn. We had an argument. Well, not an argument, really. I said something that came out the wrong way, and Cass let me know. She's just really hurting."

"Of course she is. She needs your support more than ever. You love her, don't you?"

"You know I do."

"Okay, then don't let her go. Get on your knees if you have to and beg her to forgive you for whatever you said, but you have to be there for her. I don't want her to start drinking again."

"Drinking? What?"

"You didn't know? I'm surprised she didn't tell you. She told me about it a few months ago. It was back when her husband was killed. Mark was almost two years old. John was killed when Tower One collapsed on 9/11. You knew that, right?"

"Yeah."

"She couldn't handle it. She started drinking. But she's apparently not an addictive alcoholic, and she didn't drink long enough to become one. She got in a car wreck in Brooklyn and it brought her to her senses, I guess. Hasn't had a hard drink since, not that I know of. That's what she said."

"I hope it's still true. I saw a bottle of vodka at her place."

"Oh, *no!*"

"She never told me about the drinking. I didn't think anything about the bottle. It hadn't been opened."

"Yeah, people don't like to announce their weaknesses. You know? How much of the bottle was gone?"

"None! Like I said, it wasn't opened."

"Right. Right." Linnie glanced at him, thinking about it, as they arrived at the building on Main Street. "Zach, we really don't want her to start drinking again. It won't always be easy, but you just need to be there to support her. I don't know how you'd bring up the drinking, but we need to be behind her a hundred percent."

He nodded as she stopped the car. "Don't worry about that. A hundred percent, and then some." He opened the door. "Thanks, Linn."

She nodded as he smiled and closed the door. All the way back to Plano, she tried to think of something that might help Cassie.

As she was turning into her carport, she mulled over John Hoff's mysterious death, and Bhavesh Krishnamurthy and his monumental "mistake," and the germ of an idea came to her.

TEN

JULY 3, 2016. SUNDAY.

Linnie set down one of the bags she carried, and knocked on Cassie's door. She had called two hours earlier to be sure Cassie wouldn't be surprised. She also wanted to visit so she could see if Cassie had started drinking again. She hoped the vodka bottle was still unopened, but she had talked to Zach three days ago and a lot could have happened since then.

The door opened. Cassie looked much better than Linnie expected.

"Hi, Linn. Thanks for coming." She stepped aside and then closed the door, glancing at the grocery bags.

"You're looking pretty good, Cass! Feeling okay?"

"Yeah, I guess. Tired, sad, empty, angry...all that. You know."

"No, I don't know. I can't imagine."

"Come in. What's in the bags?"

"Just some stuff. Groceries and other things." She set one bag down beside the table and carried the other into the kitchen. "You mind if I just put these in the fridge?"

Cassie nodded and shrugged. "So, what did you and Zach find to talk about?"

As Linnie closed the refrigerator door, she noticed the empty vodka bottle on the counter but didn't comment. She walked over to Cassie and gave her a long hug. "Not much. He just told me that he had blown it and he wants to help you. He's a good man, Cass. Strong."

"He doesn't get it."

85

"Get what?"

"How it feels to lose the entire focus of your life, your only child." Her eyes began to fill, and by the time she reached the kitchen and a napkin, the tears were running. "It's *hard*, Linn!"

Linnie guided her to the couch and sat her down, then joined her and put an arm around her. "Cassie, you are strong enough to make it through this. You really are."

They sat quietly until Cassie stopped crying.

She turned to Linnie. "I'm not so sure about that." She blew her nose and took a deep breath. "Where do you think God is in all this?"

Linnie leaned back on the couch and shook her head. "I don't know, Hon. From what I've seen in hospitals caused by people's brutality, I don't know if God's involved at all. Where has he been for all of these mass shootings?"

Cassie sniffed and nodded. "So, where do you think the devil is in it?"

"Oh, *he's* all over it!"

"So, you can put him at the scene, but you don't think God's there?"

Linnie looked at her. "Like I just said, I don't know. Theology was never an interest of mine. Got any coffee I could make?"

"Yeah, but I'll get it."

While Cassie walked to the kitchen area, Linnie tried to overcome her puzzlement. Two days ago, she had seen a defeated, angry, understandably depressed woman, and today she was seeing a different one. She was aware of some recent studies that showed sadness often triggered elevated physiological response, often activating the body and brain in some ways, but it still surprised her.

"You seem to be getting on top of this a lot better. I have to ask this, Cass ... you haven't started drinking again—"

"No. I bought a bottle but I poured it down the sink last night. I thought I wanted it like before, but I don't want to be—anyway. I'm not drinking. And I'm not on top of anything, but I'm trying to put up a brave front and I want to try to do something. Just, something."

"Okay—" Linnie said, waiting.

"It's—I don't know—like there's nothing much to live for anymore. I just don't know what to do now, but I need to do something." She put coffee in a filter and into the coffee maker. "I have all the time in the world to sit and cry, and I'm doing plenty of that. But there's got to be something else I can do, maybe for the other families? I don't know. Maybe join a support group. I'll probably do that anyway, but I want to do more than that." She continued talking as she filled the carafe with water and poured it into the machine, then pressed a button. "You remember what that preacher said at the memorial service? How he said we each needed to find out what we could do about these things and start doing it, no matter what it was?" She opened the cupboard and got out two mugs.

"Yep. That was good."

"It really hit me. I have a platform, in the paper—I really do—I can use to say something. If I just had something to say."

"Yeah, you do have a platform there." They both sat down at the dinette table. "So, what's the next step?"

"I don't know. I don't have the slightest clue. All I feel like doing is sitting and thinking of Mark. But—" She looked out the window at the buildings nearby. "I don't know. I could write columns that say these things shouldn't be allowed to happen, but that wouldn't do a hell of a lot of good. Everybody feels that way."

Linnie agreed. She rose and poured them both coffee. She was still wary of Cassie's newfound strength. But she decided she would go along with it and tell Cassie why she'd wanted to visit her today. She took a long breath, looked at her friend and sipped her coffee.

"I've always hated it when people say, 'Things happen for a reason,' you know? It might be true in a novel, but not in real life."

"Mm-hmm," Cassie said, with a puzzled expression.

"I don't happen to think 'things happen for a reason' like they're part of a big cosmic plan. Sometimes people look at the outcome of a situation and they think, 'gee this wouldn't've happened if that didn't happen.' That gets a big 'well, duh' from me. There's cause and effect, you know? But sometimes people *are* in a unique position. We're in that position right now, and you can tell a lot of people all about it in the paper. Like you said."

"Linnie, what in the heck are you talking about?"

"Okay here it is in a nutshell. Ready?"

"On the edge of my seat, girl! Just *tell* me!"

"John Hoff shouldn't have died."

"Oh," Cassie shrugged. "Why would I care about that?"

"Cassie, he was murdered! Right there in his hospital room!"

"Well, that doesn't bother me either!"

"Okay, okay, but Cass, I think Hoff was under the influence of a drug and he was murdered to keep it a secret."

"So?"

"Okay, look. Try to keep an open mind, here. I know it doesn't bother you that Hoff's dead or that he was murdered. Doesn't bother me that much either, to tell the truth. But, it's the injustice of it." She leaned back in her chair and looked into Cassie's eyes.

"You know, you told me that when John died, the thing that made you so boiling mad was the injustice of his death. It was those people who attacked the towers just because their own hate-filled philosophy says they can kill people who don't believe what they believe. They had a horrible, wrong reason. It was unjust."

Cassie frowned and rubbed her coffee cup handle.

"Hoff killed your Mark, without a reason that makes any sense. But I think that the real culprits were the same people who killed Hoff."

"They told him to go crazy?"

"No, they didn't *tell* him to, but they killed him to hide a drug that was in his system. I think *it* was the reason he did this."

"What was it? Meth or something?"

"No, a legal *prescription* drug, an antidepressant, and there was nothing at all wrong with him taking it. Lots of people take it and drugs like it."

"Okay, Linn, I'm officially confused."

"Sorry, Hon. Here it is. They killed Hoff because of this drug in his body. Then they autopsied his body in the middle of the night, while it was still warm! Then they made what they called 'a terrible error' and switched his toe tag with a man who was going to be cremated first thing in the morning, so his body was burned to ashes just about eight hours after he died. My gosh, Cass, that *never* happens. What did it do? It destroyed *all* the evidence his body held."

Cassie just stared at her.

"They did it all on purpose, Cass!"

They both sat still while Cassie let it all sink in.

"Cass, somebody's hiding something, and they started hiding it right at the beginning. And I know *what* it is. I just don't know *why*."

"Linn, you know that tee shirt that says, *'You have obviously mistaken me for somebody who gives a shit?'* That's sorta how I'm feeling right now." She rose and rinsed her coffee cup. "You said they hid the drug right from the beginning. So, just out of curiosity, how do *you* know about it?"

"They made a mistake, and I saw the drug on the pre-surgery toxicology report, but they removed it from the report, so now all the proof of it's gone."

"What about the police and the FBI?"

"I told them all this when they interviewed me, and they think I'm a conspiracy nut and I'm trying to hide my own mistake. Besides, they feel the same way you do. They're glad Hoff is gone and they don't have to spend millions on a trial. They're looking into it, but not very hard. They think I killed him and Krishnamurthy cremated him, and beyond that—" She shrugged.

"Well, I'm glad he's gone, too."

"Don't think I'm too bothered by it. I'm not! But Cassie, *listen* to me! If what I'm thinking is true, we might have a shot at keeping these kinds of attacks from happening, at least some of the time. When somebody goes off and shoots a hundred kids at a rock concert next year, do you want to know you might have done something to prevent it, but you didn't do anything? What if, out there somewhere, there was somebody who had the kind of chance we have to shine a spotlight on the biggest reason for mass shootings, and they didn't do it? And Mark's dead because of it? It was your sense of justice and fairness that infuriated you when John was killed. I saw it! I *know* when you think about this, you'll see that this happened because somebody, somewhere, didn't *care* about this drug's bad effects. You want to put other moms through this when you might be able to help stop it? How fair would *that* be?"

At that, Cassie stopped moving. She sat still for almost a minute, then stared into Linnie's eyes, shook her head as her own eyes became red rimmed, rose and walked down the hallway. The toilet flushed, but Cassie didn't return right away. When she did return a few minutes later, she sat and leaned toward Linnie. "Okay. So, who killed the killer?"

Linnie realized there was a different note in her friend's voice. She sounded a little bit like the investigative reporter Linnie had known.

"It was that tall doctor you talked to. I *know* it! When he went into Hoff's room, I'm convinced he injected a coagulant into Hoff's IV. Took him five seconds or so. It counteracted the heparin Hoff was getting. It caused a clot in the lungs after a couple of hours and it killed him when it reached his heart. It looked like a normal post-op occurrence, but it wasn't."

Cassie's eyes narrowed. "So, I asked for help … for my son … from the man who murdered the murderer of my son?"

Linnie nodded her head, her lips pinched.

"The *bastards*! The dirty bastards! Okay, Linnie, I want to look into it, but if it turns out to be nothing, I'll leave it alone. 'Cause I don't *care* that Hoff's dead. Okay?"

"Okay. It's *not* nothing, Hon, and you'll start seeing that pretty quick." She paused. "But, Cass, you need to know that if you investigate this, it could change the course of your life. You have to be ready for that."

"Linn, with what's happened in my life, it's already changed forever. If this adds to it, then so be it. Show me."

Linnie looked into Cassie's eyes, nodded, then reached down beside the table into the bag she had set there and pulled out the first of several books.

ELEVEN

JULY 5, 2016. TUESDAY.

Because she was still deeply fatigued and depressed, when Cassie first started looking at the books her friend had brought, she could read only a few pages before falling asleep. But they had eventually piqued her interest and her anger.

Naturally, after every mass shooting, the internet and TV flared up with commentary, pro-gun and anti-gun, battling about the "reason" for such attacks. But as Cassie read, she began to realize the reasons for the attacks were more complicated and probably had as much to do with financial gain as with firearms.

She stood and glanced over the books on her table. *Pharmageddon. The Emperor's New Drugs. Pillaged. Talking Back To Prozac. The Broken Brain. Let Them Eat Prozac. Anatomy of an Epidemic.*

Pillaged, the most recent of the books, was open to the first paragraph of the Foreword, by Dr. David Healy, a man she'd learned was a Professor of Psychiatry in Wales and author of twenty major books in the field of psychopharmacology. She read the paragraph again and was newly angered, as she had been when she'd begun to grasp it all during her last two days of study.

"The question of whether antidepressants or other psychotropic drugs can cause suicide or homicide or other serious adverse effects in those who take them in the hope of preventing suicide or homicide is more than just a story of adverse events. It is one of the central issues of modern medicine and modern healthcare."

To Cassie, the simple clarity of those two sentences seemed to sum up the horrible irony of what had just happened to the members of Mark's band, all the families, and possibly even to John Hoff. Evidence wasn't absolutely conclusive, but the circumstantial evidence added up quickly. Very quickly.

She had begun to formulate an article for the paper and was on the verge of writing it. First, she needed to talk to Linnie some more about the drugs. Her friend was coming over again for dinner in a few minutes.

Her doorbell sounded. Was Linnie early? She looked through the peeper and opened the door, unsure of what to say.

"Zach!"

"Cass, hi. You look great. Sorry to just show up." He raised his hands. "Can we talk?"

She hesitated, then nodded and opened the door for him to come in. She realized her anger at him was gone.

He walked in and stood, almost reaching for her, then backing off. "I need to apologize—"

"Wait, Zach." She held up her hand and took a deep breath. "You might have said something stupid, but I overreacted. I'm sorry too. I know what you meant and I know you loved Mark like your own son."

Zach looked at her, then down at his feet. When he spoke, his voice was constricted. "Thank you. But I felt terrible. Still do. I'm sorry."

"All right, then let's just try to move on. We can move on together."

He nodded.

She hesitated, then moved slowly toward him and put her arms around his waist. His enveloping hug made her relax and take a deep breath.

"Zach, a lot has come up since Sunday. It's from Linnie. You have to see this."

He glanced across the room at the table where several books and

Cassie's laptop were open. "What?"

"Okay, I'm going to give you the short version and then show you some stuff. Okay?"

He nodded, looking at the books strewn on the table top.

"Okay. Linnie thinks—no, that's wrong. She *knows* that Hoff was *murdered*. Somebody did it to hide a drug that was in his system that made him go crazy and attack the band." To her surprise, her voice caught, making her realize she couldn't set aside her loss so quickly.

"Cass—"

"No, it's okay. Really." She took a breath and continued. "I think she's right. I never told you about that fake doctor, a *jerk*, that I talked to that last night in the hospital. He actually murdered Hoff! Linnie said he must have put a chemical in Hoff's IV that made a blood clot form, and it killed him. Then, they did the autopsy really fast, and somebody made a so-called 'mistake' and sent Hoff's body to be cremated the next morning!"

"You're kidding! How do you know all that?"

"Linnie. I think she's right. It's the only explanation that fits. They did it to cover up the drug Hoff was taking, but there's no proof of it. The police don't care. I don't know if they're investigating at all. They're blaming it on Linnie and an error in dosing the blood thinner!"

"Oh my gosh! That's—that's incredible! But what's all this?" he asked, waving a hand over the half dozen books in front of them.

"This is some stuff Linnie left for me to read about these drugs. They're the reason Hoff was killed! It's the drugs, Zach! *Prescription* drugs!"

"But why's she getting *you* into this stuff?"

"I think she wants me to try to expose it to people. Write about it."

"But what about the gun thing everybody's talking about. Guns are the problem, aren't they?"

"Obviously every shooting is done with a gun, but I read on this one website—" she turned to her computer and clicked a tab on her browser. "—Mother Jones. Here it is. This is one of the most anti-gun websites you can find *any*where, and they created a big spreadsheet of all the mass shootings, seventy-two of 'em, since 1982. They found that more than half of 'em were done by people being treated for mental illness. And probably more of them were on antidepressants! It's really incredible."

"But you've *got* to be mentally damaged to do something like this, right?" he said.

"Well, probably. But Zach, most of the time, these days, if you even talk to a shrink about depression or anxiety, you're prescribed a drug. That's just how they do business now! And it's the drugs that are the problem!"

"Wait, the cure's the—?"

"Here," she said, picking up the *Pillaged* book from the table, "Read that very first paragraph. It's the whole truth in a nutshell."

The doorbell rang. Cassie went for it. "That's Linnie. She's coming over and—" her words were lost as she reached for the doorknob. "Hi, Linn. Uh-oh. I forgot the food."

Her friend shrugged and walked through the door as Zach turned from the table. "Hey! You two've made peace? That's great!"

"Yeah, we have," Cassie answered. "I was just showing Zach some of this stuff. It really is amazing how we've been played for fools."

"I knew you'd get something out of it. So you think I might be right?"

"Yes, I do. But I've got some questions. I'm sorry I forgot to make anything to eat."

"No problem. I knew you would have questions. Hey, let's just go out."

It was the first real meal Cassie had had in over a week. She could only eat a small part of it. They finished quickly.

"Hon, you need to get your strength back up," Linnie said, when they'd settled around the table back at Cassie's condo.

"Yeah. I know. But let's get back into this stuff now."

Linnie looked at her for a moment, then spoke. "Okay. I want to give you some more detail that isn't common knowledge."

Zach and Cassie nodded.

"It's about the hospital. We have some amazing equipment. It's *fast*. When I get into surgery, even with an emergency patient, I already can see the results of a blood analysis that shows if there's anything in his blood that might cause trouble. They flash it up on a video screen I can see before I even start the operation. There was nothing in Hoff's blood that affected the surgery, but there was something on the screen, and this is what it was. I finally remembered it last night."

Cassie perked up. Zach gave them both a puzzled look.

Linnie wrote a long word in block letters on a tablet and turned it toward them. Then she said it. "*Chlorpenframine ETL.*"

"What is it?" Zach asked.

"The chemical name for a prescription drug—an SSRI antidepressant brand-named 'Pefrexa XR.' "

Cassie's sharp intake of breath grabbed their attention. "It's one of those drugs!"

"That's right, Cass."

"So," Zach asked, "was this the kind of drug that paragraph was talking about?" He motioned toward the *Pillaged* book.

Cassie nodded.

"What was it, *SSI?*"

"S-S-*R*-I. Selective Serotonin Reuptake Inhibitor," Linnie said. It's the class of drugs most associated these days with treatment for depression."

"Hmm," Zach uttered, frowning.

Linnie continued. "Yeah. Okay, look. This drug was shown on a video screen in the operating room when I started Hoff's surgery. So chlorpenframine was in his system. And it said 'ETL'— that means 'extra-therapeutic level.'"

Zach said, "Uh, I'm a little confused."

Linnie took a breath. "Sorry, Zach, I'm just hurrying through it. So, Pefrexa XR—chlorpenframine—is a new SSRI on the market. Just got approved and released in January. Cassie, you've been looking into the books and websites I left, right? So is it beginning to come together for you now?"

Cassie looked at her and nodded slowly, knitted her brow, then whispered, "Oh my gosh. It's true! This is proof!"

Linnie sat back in her chair and folded her arms. "It's not proof, except to me. I know what I saw."

"Proof the guy was murdered?" Zach asked.

"No, just proof the drug was there."

"But, can you get a copy of that report you saw?"

"That's the problem, Zach. On the paper copy, somebody's taken the chlorpenframine off. There is no proof except up here." She tapped her temple.

Cassie frowned. "Linnie, this is reminding me of that Wisbacker thing in one of the books."

"Yeah. It was *Wesbecker*, and I agree."

"What's that?" Zach asked.

Linnie leaned forward over the table. "It's a famous trial in the pharmaceutical world. Joseph Wesbecker was prescribed Prozac, one of the earliest SSRIs. Then he murdered several people. His family filed a lawsuit against the drug manufacturer, Eli Lilly & Co. It went to trial, but Wesbecker's family lawyers were paid an 'early settlement,' like, *during the trial*, and they didn't present all of their evidence. The jury found the drug company not liable, not guilty."

Zach started to say something, but Linnie held up a hand and continued.

"The judge in the case thought something was not right, so he did some investigating on his own. It went all the way to the Kentucky Supreme Court, but the judge was eventually allowed to change the official verdict, making Lilly liable as the family had claimed. But that took awhile, and by the time a new verdict came out in favor of the plaintiff, over a hundred-fifty other cases waiting to be filed against Lilly had all given up! It's all public record."

"But this Hoff thing wasn't Prozac, right?"

"Right. This was another drug from another company. Different, but the same type of drug. It has the same kinds of adverse effects—major effects that patients rarely know about until after they happen." She sat back in her chair. "So, what do you think a company would do to save billions in future profits?"

"Just about anything," Cassie finally said in a flat voice.

"That's right. And murdering a murderer of forty-six people might not be investigated very actively, *especially* if it can be laid in the surgeon's lap."

Zach looked at her. "So, you think the manufacturer of this drug made this happen—*murdered* John Hoff—to save their own corporate butts?"

"Right. We just have to find a way to prove it."

TWELVE
JULY 14, 2016. THURSDAY.

Justin Richardson's eyes followed the rhythmic movements of his young wife's red bikini and her perfect skin as she swam laps under the warm Houston sun. He enjoyed these rare serene moments with a nice whiskey sour in his hand and a gentle breeze coming across the pool from the long, perfectly manicured expanse of green behind his home.

Since the shooting, he hadn't heard much except the political clamor for gun control. The usual crap, just like after Virginia Tech, the worst until now, and Newtown, the worst emotionally, since innocent toddlers had been murdered. Even he had given in to some sorrowful moments over that one. Roseburg, Oregon, the most recent before this, had him thinking he would be glad to leave this business, because someone was soon going to put two and two together.

But guns and major mental illness always caught the blame. He smiled to himself, thinking of the head guy at the NRA, trying to make the point in the media that guns weren't the problem, while everyone else said they were. And besides, the man pleaded, if over twenty thousand federal gun laws already on the books would just be enforced, there wouldn't be a gun problem. So, when pressed, he admitted there *was* a problem, but it was actually a law enforcement problem and that the laws weren't being enforced or the crimes prosecuted.

Richardson leaned back in the chaise. It didn't matter to him who got blamed. He didn't know for sure what was to blame for the other shootings, but in this one, he was just glad he'd gotten them through it.

Besides, every one of these repeated sham arguments always came to naught, and nothing was ever done. Politicians would prattle on about the need to remove a certain kind of semi-automatic rifle, trying to demonize it as an "assault weapon." Next, the NRA and other gun organizations would mobilize their membership to write and call their senators. It would reach a crescendo, fail to get cloture and be voted on in the Senate, and then trail off as the news cycle hurried on to something else. The special interests would continue their battles, but the press always moved on. For his part, Richardson didn't give a whit about the gun issue, except that it provided a scapegoat. But, a scapegoat that never paid the price.

Another patsy was violent video games, though he agreed that they actually were part of the problem. But, hell—what could they expect when they put out lifelike violent first-person shooter video games where a kid learned to shoot people and get rewards for it? Add that together with doctor-supplied drugs like Provachem's, that dulled his emotions, made him not worry about consequences and even think he was just dreaming. Then give him access to a high capacity semi-automatic weapon of some kind. What the hell did they *think* would happen? He kept his own guns locked safely. Even the Glock he had handy at his bedside was in a biometric safe that opened only to his own fingerprint. He had a smaller gun, in a separate biometric safe, for his wife. They were both expert shots.

But the press and the pols almost always missed or ignored the prescribed drugs in the equation. He, Winston and Bliss had almost felt like raising a toast the day before. The two of them had at first bridled at his removing John Hoff, but they'd agreed there was no alternative. It had gone smoothly as far as he could tell. Kardov was an expert and, in Richardson's mind, almost worth his fees. They were paid grudgingly, nevertheless.

He loved watching his wife, Alisa's, beautiful body move through the water, sunlight glinting in water droplets on her wet fair skin, and her buttocks flexing under the thin red fabric. When they left here in a few months, maybe moving to the south of France, or Tuscany, he could have moments like this all the time instead of during rare stolen afternoons away from the office.

Thinking about the company sale and his plans gave him a tinge of anxiety. He pulled the burner phone from his pocket and dialed.

It was answered immediately.

"Good afternoon, Doctor. I haven't heard anything. By my lights, that's a good thing, but I'm calling to see that all is well at your end."

He waited a few seconds, listening, as he watched his wife emerge from the pool and pick up a towel.

"You think she'll present a problem?" He listened again as Alisa squeezed her long blond hair in the towel. "You are certain of that? No record?" He mouthed a kiss to her as she continued to dry off. She smiled and walked slowly toward him.

"Oh, no. That's not going to happen. Have you forgotten about your family? No, I'm sorry, but you are in this for the long haul." He paused, then said, "I don't care what you think, Doctor! I am in control here, and that's it."

He listened for a minute. "You will stay ahead of things there and keep me informed, yes?" He nodded as he heard the response he wanted, then clicked the phone off.

Just as he held out his hand to his wife, the other phone buzzed in his pocket. He looked at it. *Kardov.*

"What." Richardson answered. He had learned long ago not to use names during his phone calls with these people, even on his burner phones. The one time he had identified himself, when he had gained control of Provachem after his brother's unfortunate sudden demise, he had almost been charged with murder. Only an incompetent detective, a realistic district attorney and a very large political contribution had saved him from it.

He listened to the Russian's voice, a mix of Moscow and Texas that would be comical if the man weren't so vicious.

"Yes, dammit. I have it! I'll be at the hospital. Thirty minutes—no—ninety minutes." He snapped the phone shut and looked at his wife, who was eyeing him curiously. He wouldn't admit it, but he was genuinely afraid of the Russian. He often wished he hadn't used him for his brother's accident. But he was efficient, and now he was useful once again. Richardson knew he could be more or less trusted as long as he was being well paid. He also knew to never cross the man.

His wife, her slender body still mostly wet, had reached behind her as he was talking to Kardov and unfastened her red bikini top. She smiled and removed it, then walked slowly over to him and straddled his extended legs on the chaise. He easily put everything else out of his mind.

Kardov's flat statement in his ridiculous nasal voice irritated Richardson. "I am telling you the agent was not a problem. He let me in."

"Did anybody see you? What about a nurse, or—"

"Nobody. No nurse. Nurse was in another room."

"Okay. Nobody saw you at all except the guard."

"Maybe some sad little woman from another room. She was nothing."

"Who was that?"

"How can I know? She ask me to look at her son. That was all."

"Can she identify you?"

"*Nyet!* She looked very bad herself. I think she will not remember."

Richardson reached down for the envelope with fifty-thousand dollars in it and stopped as he saw Kardov's tenseness and his hand moving toward his other side. "It's just the damn money. You think I'm stupid?"

"Many people are stupid. I keep safe from them."

Richardson shook his head and handed over the cash. "Fifty," he said.

"This is not all of it. You are playing games with me, Mister?"

"Not at all. I'll have the rest next week. I still want you to be available for awhile."

"That will be okay, but retainer now will be ten more to keep me around."

"What the—" He started to complain, then realized the Russian had the upper hand. The smug smile on Kardov's face gave him an uncomfortable chill as the Russian's cold blue eyes glanced at him.

"You are smart man, Mister," Kardov said as he left the car.

Richardson fumed and swore to himself. He looked across the expansive concrete parking area toward the top floors of the hospital, a hundred yards away in the hot Houston sun.

This time, rather than waiting for Kardov to leave, he waited only long enough for him to walk away between two other parked cars, then started the engine and headed for the exit ramp. Looking in his rear view mirror, he could see the man walking to his truck and wished he would never have to see him again.

THIRTEEN
JULY 15, 2016. FRIDAY.

When Cassie awoke on Friday morning, her first coherent thought, the same as it had been for two weeks, was that Mark was gone. He would always be gone. She had no flashes of memories of him, of happy times, of anything—just emptiness. She didn't want to leave the bed, but she had to use the bathroom. As she walked, the feeling of loss began to turn into anger.

So, Hoff had been murdered. Not that it bothered Cassie. She probably could have killed him herself for revenge, in the right circumstances. That someone else had done it didn't even make her blink.

But the reason it was done, to hide someone else's crime? That raised the old anger she had always felt toward people who took advantage of others. At the *Times*, she had been known as a reporter who wouldn't let go of an issue like this, as the dogged pursuer in the interests of justice. Now, if what Linnie said was true—and everything Cassie had read pointed toward it being true—she realized she was back in that same track again. Her old self would have gone after the people responsible for Hoff's murder, found out why they did it, and seen them figuratively hanged. But would she do that now? Would she go after them?

She thought she probably should, but she wasn't sure anything mattered that much anymore.

It wasn't as if Mark would benefit from it. Or any of the other kids or instructors, or even the murderer himself.

But she knew she would. Maybe others, too. She'd always had a strong sense of justice. Every time she took and retook a Myers-Briggs test, it always indicated her sense of right and wrong and strong desire for just outcomes. She didn't particularly want to pursue whoever did this, but she had to, because they needed to be exposed, and nobody else would do it.

She left the bathroom and walked slowly into Mark's room. Was there a spirit? A presence? Or her imagination? It felt to her as if he was there with her, that he was waiting for her to act, like he used to do when he was ready to leave for band practice and she was lagging.

She knew she had to find out who did it and why, and expose these people who might have murdered a killer to hide something else. It was a matter of justice. Whoever it was, they had to pay.

"Mark," she said to the empty room as she almost started crying from her rising emotions, "I promise you, Baby, I will find out why you were killed and I will make the bastards pay for it!" With that, she broke down, closed the door and sank down to sit against the wall in the hallway.

The support group in the church's basement was just getting started when they arrived. Zach said, "Wow. Not many people."

"Yeah. Kinda surprising. Maybe not that many from the local area?"

"Maybe," he answered. They found places in the circle and sat down. Of the ten people there, Cassie noted that it was mostly women. She counted six. They were all just getting seated.

"Well," a tall man said, walking into the center of the group, "I'm glad to see all of you here. In case you walked into the wrong room, this is a support group for the victims' families from Travis High School. I'm sorry you are here because of the reason for it, but I'm glad you're here, too, because we all need support. I'm Jacob." He had a calm, assuring manner.

He walked to one of the chairs and sat. "Just so you know, I'm not a psychiatrist. I'm an experienced counselor, I guess. My daughter was murdered in the terrorist shooting at Fort Hood in 2009, so I know some of what you're all feeling. I'd like us introduce our-

selves. Just say whatever you want, even if it's just your first name."
He turned and motioned to the woman beside him.

The woman fidgeted, then spoke. "I'm Jan. My daughter Carlie played flute." She paused, started to say more, then shook her head and looked at the man beside her.

He nodded. "Our daughter hid in a bass drum case. She's sort of small. She survived. I'm sorry." Tears filled his eyes, then he continued. "She's in the hospital and might still lose her leg. My name is Kenneth." He looked at Cassie, who was next.

Her nervousness almost kept her from being able to talk. She finally blurted, "My name is Cassie. My son was—"

"You're the newspaper lady!" a woman opposite them said.

"Yeah," she said, nodding.

The other woman didn't say anything else, but Cassie noticed that others in the circle seemed to be paying more attention to her.

"I lost my son, Mark. He played flugelhorn. This is my fiancé, Zach." Cassie's eyes filled. She hated saying the words, confirming the finality of it. Zach raised a hand off his lap but didn't speak.

Others introduced themselves, saying much the same things, until they got back around to the facilitator, who repeated that his name was Jacob. "I want each of you to say whatever you want to say, within limits," he said. Then he opened up the floor.

"Well, I guess we're all in 'bout the same situation," a man named Charlie said. "We've lost our kids, 'cept for Kenneth over there, 'cause some little son of a bitch was able to get a damn automatic shotgun, and—"

"Hey wait a minute!" A woman called out.

"No, I ain't finished! We oughta all get together and go to Congress and tell 'em to get rid of the guns! I can't bring Tim back but by-damn I can try to keep this from happening again!"

The other woman spoke up. "I'm not done either! What the hell do you mean, get rid of the guns! The gun didn't do this. And it wasn't 'automatic.' That crazy son of a bitch did it and he's dead! He can rot in hell. Sure he will, too!"

The woman beside Cassie cried and said, "But it will just keep happening if there are so many guns! It'll just keep *happening*!"

Others instantly chose sides and joined the fight.

"Hold it! Hold it!" the leader, Jacob, said, his hands outstretched, coming to his feet. He stood and walked to the center again. "I didn't lay down the ground rules. I'm sorry about that." He reached up and stroked his chin. "You know, when my little girl, Ellen—Ellie—was murdered at Fort Hood, I had the same emotions you folks are talking about. I wanted a new law so that military on a military base were required to wear their sidearms.

"Right now, after the Chattanooga attack last year, that's getting some new energy. But, you know what?" He stopped and looked around the group slowly. "You know what? We're not here to try to find who to blame and certainly not to argue about guns. There's enough of that on TV. We're just here to support each other. What can we do to help? Now, I hope I've talked long enough so that some emotions could cool a little bit. Let's go ahead and take an early break. Get some juice or coffee. Donuts over there, too. Then let's come back and think of the real need we all have, not the revenge we want." He smiled around again, and walked out of the circle.

The two people who had argued walked out the door. Cassie and Zach went to the coffee urn. As they turned away from the table, Jacob stepped up to them.

"Hello," he said, shaking both of their hands. He looked at Cassie. "That lady said you were a newspaper reporter?"

"Yeah, more or less. More of a columnist these days."

"Which paper?"

"DP—Dallas *Daily Post*." She sipped her coffee. "Why?"

"Just wondered. The *Morning News* came out with an article on John Hoff and I wondered if you had anything to do with it."

"No. I haven't really been back to work since—" she was going to say "the day it happened," but her throat constricted and her eyes filled.

Zach put his arm around her shoulders. "I saw that article. It put a lot of blame on that instructor, Welch, for not having the cargo door unlocked. I didn't think that was fair. This was such an unimaginable thing. How hard that must be, especially since he survived."

"Yeah," Jacob said. "I didn't like their slant on the whole thing. They seemed to blame the school, and the instructor, and the complete lack of security and all. Everybody but the kid, Hoff."

"What about drugs?" Cassie asked. "Nobody's bringing that up."

"You think he was on drugs? None of the articles or TV have said that. Your paper didn't."

"No, but there's more to come out about it."

Jacob took a step back. "Really? Now, that's interesting. There was some press about Hasan at Fort Hood and his drugs, too." He turned and noticed people were looking impatient and returning to their seats. "Hey, we better get started again. Nice talking with you!" He smiled and turned toward the circle of chairs and called the meeting back to order.

This time, things went more smoothly. One man still argued that guns were to blame, but Cassie was surprised when Zach spoke up.

"I know you need to blame something. We all do, but the question here isn't what did this guy do the shooting with. It's *why*. Why did he do it?"

The other man said, "Yeah, maybe." They spent most of the next hour sharing about their kids. An hour later it broke up. Cassie felt better just knowing that she wasn't alone in the world, and she was proud of Zach for speaking up.

That was the question that was burning in Cassie: *Why?* Even if drugs were involved, as Linnie seemed to know for sure, that couldn't be the only thing, could it? So, why did Hoff do it?

On the way home, she turned to Zach. "Zach, why do you think Hoff did it?"

"Well, it was the drug, wasn't it? Wasn't that what Linnie said?"

"More or less. I was just thinking about it. Millions of people take those drugs and they don't go kill people."

"Yeah, millions of people drink too much and they don't all cause wrecks. We all know alcohol is still dangerous."

"That's different. This is more like if people get drunk and go looking for a way to cause a wreck."

"That can't happen very often though, you think?"

"Neither does this." She waited until they pulled into the parking garage.

As the elevator doors closed to take them up, Cassie said, "I think the drugs are the main problem, but it can't be *just* the drugs."

"Okay, but how're you gonna to find that out?"

"I'm going to try to meet with Hoff's parents."

Cassie left the shower and went back into her bedroom to dress. She noticed the shine of her stainless steel revolver in her underwear drawer and reached for it. She put her fingers around the rubber grip and pulled it out. It was heavy, but she liked handling it. She gingerly opened the cylinder and removed the seven cartridges with their grey-tipped bullets. She noticed the hammer lock key in the bottom of the drawer, something someone told her she should use. But someone else had told her if she ever really needed the gun, she would need it fast. That made sense to her, so she'd never locked it.

She clicked the cylinder back into place, cocked the hammer and pressed the trigger. So little effort it took. At the range, the explosion and recoil it released at first startled her until she got used to it. This was a Smith & Wesson, model 686, with a plus sign after the number. She dry-fired it a couple more times, aiming it from the braced stance she'd learned.

Years ago, her dad had taught her to shoot a .22 rifle and his Colt six-shooter. He'd apparently bought this gun for her mother, who never even mentioned that she had it. Cassie had found it in her mom's dresser drawer after she died. Her mom had never fired it.

Zach had been shooting off and on, so he took her to a local range where they took lessons together. He hadn't thought he needed them, but he was surprised and slightly angry that though she'd only shot a little bit, she shot as well as he did. The instructor said it was something about men thinking they knew what they were doing and women not having any bad habits to overcome and being willing to follow directions.

Zach knew she had the gun. He had asked her if she wanted him to keep it for her, for awhile. He was afraid she might end her life with it. She said no, she wouldn't use the gun anyway, when the patio was there. She could just fall off and everything would end quickly and not leave a mess inside. Now, here she was, holding the gun, but without any thought of firing it.

She had given suicide some thought at first, but her pragmatism had taken over. She decided it would be the easy way out, not much different from what John Hoff did—trying to take his own life to escape. But he hadn't succeeded, and someone else had taken his life away, hadn't they? Why? There was that little questioning word, again. Every statement about this seemed to end with, "But, why?"

The gun went back into the drawer, its seven cartridges reloaded. She went out to the dinette to review the notes she'd been making and then sent a text to Linnie. She was so loaded with information that she didn't know where to go with it. Her friend could help her focus if she had some time available.

Her phone buzzed in her hand. Tom Hammond's name showed on her screen.

"Hi Tom."

"Hello Cass. How're you doin'?" The kind voice and drawl of the lifelong Texan was a welcome sound.

"I'm better. Thanks." She sat on the edge of her bed. "How are things down there?"

"We're okay here. People're more than ready to fill in, so you can just take all the time you need. Mrs. Wright sends her prayers, too."

"Thanks."

"Honey, I've got some bad news. You know Bret Welch, the young instructor who survived?"

"Yeah ... ?"

"Yeah, he was found in his garage this morning. Hanged himself."

"Oh no! Oh god, Tom!"

"Yeah."

"Survivor's guilt?"

"Well, prob'ly somethin' like that. Maybe even worse in his case since he should've had the exit door unlocked. Tough to imagine what he was goin' through."

Neither said anything for a few seconds.

"Hey, you take as much time as you need, okay? I gotta go. But we're all thinkin' about you down here."

"Thanks, Tom. I'll get in touch soon." Cassie turned on the TV.

"... heard the President," a reporter was saying, "announce that he is going to ask Congress to appoint an ad hoc committee to study and come up with recommendations for new gun laws to try to prevent shootings like Travis High School. He also mentioned the ripples from the tragedy, including the apparent suicide just this morning by hanging, of 25-year-old Bret Welch, the only surviving instructor from the Travis attack. Charles?"

"Thanks, Jim South, from the White House. We have a statement by the father-in-law of Bret Welch, until this morning the sole surviving instructor, who was found dead in his own garage early this morning." He looked to the side and his picture was replaced by a film clip of a man talking in front of some church steps, surrounded by reporters.

The white-haired, bearded man took a long breath before speaking, his head down. "We know only that Bret, if anything, cared too much. He was absolutely dedicated to his job. He loved the kids he worked with, and they loved him. He was my son-in-law ... a fine man. We haven't planned his services, but they will be for the family only, and we ask for your courtesy to honor our privacy."

"What is your name again, sir?"

"Raymond Butler. Thank you." He started to turn away from the microphones when another voice called out.

"Did Bret Welch feel responsible for too many kids dying? He could've saved some if he'd done his job, isn't that right?"

Exclamations of dismay at that question rippled through the reporters. The older man froze in position and stared into the crowd, then put his head down and turned away, walking up the steps to the church. Other questions were called out, and as if to separate herself from the offensive questioner, one woman called out, "God bless you and your family!"

Welch's father-in-law, his head down, gave a small wave without turning, and entered the church.

"Well," the anchorman said into the camera, "as you saw there, people have mixed reactions to Bret Welch's death. We'll have a panel here to discuss this and the overall issue of mass shootings after this break."

Cassie muted the sound as her phone buzzed again. It was Linnie's text, saying she could come over at about four. Cassie texted "ok" back and went to get her laptop.

She felt compelled to make some more detailed notes, to write her own thoughts about all that had happened. It was part of her healing mechanism, as it had been after her father's death, and her mom's, and John's, and now Mark's. She wasn't confident that it would help this time; the weight of her grief and anger this time might be too great.

As she opened her laptop, the panel discussion resumed on the television screen. She unmuted it.

"But on the other hand, Robert, you have to admit that if guns really caused these kinds of killings, there would be even more of them, right? I mean, there are over three hundred million guns in this country, and only a couple of mass killings a year? If it's prevalence of guns causing the shootings, there should logically be more of them, right?" The woman turned toward the anchorman and the person she was addressing, waiting for a response.

"Kelsey, you're a great spokesperson for the gun crowd, but get off that illogical claptrap they feed you. There are plenty of shootings, and you know the FBI doesn't label it a 'mass' shooting unless four people die in the event. Take a look at the Brady Campaign website! But, the problem isn't the guns, themselves, it's what they make possible! That kid couldn't have killed forty-plus people in a few minutes with a knife or a bow-and-arrow, or even with his pickup truck. It was his semi-automatic illegal Russian Saiga shotgun that made it possible, and his thirty-round drum magazine—*two* of 'em, in fact! I won't argue with you: Guns don't kill people: people kill people. But people could kill a hell of a lot less people if they didn't have *these* kinds of guns!"

The woman glared at him, started to speak but yielded to another panel member, a younger man. "But there's no way to prevent random acts like this. Besides, if the gun was illegal already, what good does another law do? And the school was a 'gun free zone!' *Ha!* This kid Hoff was just like most other mass killers—no record of violence, no police record, no major mental health issues, and no indications of any violent intentions—except he apparently liked violent video games, but lots of people do and they don't go out murdering! Hoff was just another young man on the street and we can't question him because he's dead like most of the others. So, without taking away all guns, how do you keep someone like him with no history of violence, from going off the deep end? How do you even know about him? And we can't—meaning 'it is not possible'—get rid of all the guns. It just can't be done!"

"Well, then," the woman said, "there's no reason to talk about it, is there? We obviously can't prevent it or solve it!"

Her opponent's response was interrupted by the anchor. "Plenty of reasons to talk about it, panel, but I'm afraid we'll have to leave it at that for now! Thank you all. This is Charles Jenson, WNN, New York. I'll return after this short break."

The graphic "Tragedy at Travis High" appeared and was accompanied by ominous bumper music. Cassie clicked the TV off and looked back down at her computer screen, navigating to her own paper's website. The main news page showed a headline about Bret Welch's suicide. She read it and closed the laptop, then lay back and closed her eyes.

FOURTEEN
JULY 17, 2016. SUNDAY.

It was a typical North Texas beige brick ranch house with a high roof and two mature oaks in front. The street was quiet except for a lawnmower a few doors away. It didn't look like a place where a mass murderer would be bred. Local and national media had long ago abandoned the site, as the Hoffs had never shown themselves and only once spoke to the press, and that was a short request to help them maintain their privacy. The information they had given the police had made it into the media, so it was all second hand. Cassie was surprised that they agreed to meet her.

She took a deep breath and grabbed her bag. She had checked the recorder the night before and made sure it had fresh batteries. It was good for four hours.

Nervousness overcame her as the doorbell rang. She shivered from the tension, then shook it off. There was plenty of reason to be apprehensive about this, but she steeled herself.

Footsteps approached the door. It opened, and Cassie stood face to face with the mother of the person who had murdered her son.

The woman was not remarkable looking. Her hair had once been blond but now was going gray. She wore a drab green dress, belted at the waist. She was slim and had a pleasant enough face, with laugh lines radiating from her eyes. As she looked at Cassie across the gulf of the open front door, tears sprang to her blue eyes.

"Ms. Stevens?" She said, and a tear spilled down her cheek. "Forgive me, I'm so sorry. Please come in." She stepped back.

Cassie made herself step through the door and into the house. A generous entryway had doors to the left and a long hall to the right, and opened onto a large living room with vaulted ceiling, fireplace, and a sliding door out to a shaded patio.

From around the corner, a man appeared. He was tall, balding and graying, with a bluish plaid shirt stretched over a generous belly.

"This is my husband, Thomas."

Cassie nodded and said, "Hello." It didn't seem quite right to shake his hand.

"My name is Christine."

Cassie did extend her hand to Mrs. Hoff. "I'm Cassie Stevens. Mark Stevens's mom." Tears escaped from her eyes, taking her by surprise.

The other woman's tears ran also. Each of them almost reached for the other to offer comfort, but stopped.

Cassie recovered first, pulled a tissue from her pocket and dried her eyes.

"Mrs. Hoff," Cassie forced herself to say, "I want you and Mr. Hoff to know that I don't hold you responsible for this. I just want to try to understand. I want to find some reason why." At that, a fresh batch of tears descended. She quickly dabbed them away, straightened, took a deep breath.

"Let's all just sit down," Thomas Hoff said. Cassie was surprised at the gentleness of his voice.

As they sat, the Hoffs on an overstuffed flowered sofa, together, and Cassie in a nearby matching armchair, Mrs. Hoff said. "Would you like some coffee or tea, Ms. Stevens?"

Cassie thought about it for a moment, weighing the incongruity of being offered refreshment in the home where her son's murderer grew up. She decided it would help the situation become more tolerable.

"That would be nice. Ice tea, sweet, if you have some."

Christine Hoff rose with only a nod and a slight smile and walked into the hallway.

Thomas Hoff seemed to be halfway staring at Cassie. After a long few seconds, he spoke, a constricted note to his voice, looking directly at her, but through her at the same time. "We never even knew he had a gun."

She didn't know what to say so she answered with a small nod. As she struggled with the difficulty of this whole event, Mrs. Hoff reentered the room carrying a tray with three tall glasses of ice tea on it.

Christine Hoff set the tray on the coffee table, got a coaster from a drawer, and placed Cassie's tea on it. She handed Cassie a napkin.

This was such a surreal experience, Cassie began to observe it as if she was outside looking in. Here were three people forced together by an event caused by the couple's son, who killed the other's son and almost four dozen other people, for no discernible reason.

And Thomas Hoff's statement still hung in the air, begging for a response.

Christine Hoff sat down after serving her husband and herself. Still silent, she sighed and smoothed her dress across her lap.

Cassie had never before been in such an uncomfortable situation, where everyone was equally ill at ease and not knowing what to do or say. She finally spoke.

"Mrs. Hoff—may I call you Christine? Please, you can call me Cassie."

For the first time, a slight smile on Christine Hoff's face began to break some of the tension. She nodded and said, "And call my husband Thomas."

He nodded slowly in agreement.

Thomas spoke again and repeated, "We never even knew he had a gun." It was said with a tone of apology and astonishment, same as before.

Cassie could see that these people were still devastated and felt responsible. She began to feel sorry for them, thinking what she would be feeling if she were in their shoes.

"I know, and I think every one of us who lost someone knows, that you aren't responsible for what John—what happened."

Christine answered. "I wish everyone felt that way." She took a long, halting breath and thought for a few seconds. "I want to show you something." She rose and disappeared into the hallway, returning with a framed 8x10 photo, and handed it to Cassie.

She looked at it, and there was the smiling face of John Allen Hoff, in between his two parents, with the front of this house in the background. He was taller than either of them, by more than half a head. All three looked happy. She felt a rise of anger inside but fought it down. She set the frame on the coffee table turned so it would only face the Hoffs.

Christine looked at it as she talked. "That was the last happy picture we ever got, one of the last happy moments we ever had!" Her husband nodded and stared at the photo, his arms now folded and supported by his bulbous belly. "That was before he started taking the damn drugs! The reason he was smiling, he'd just came from the doctor. He was upset, had been for almost a month, because his girlfriend had run off with another kid and took Johnny's engagement ring with her. Wouldn't give it back!"

Cassie looked at her and shook her head.

"Johnny got over bein' mad at her, we thought, anyway, but he was so sad, you know? He'd come over here for dinner—he had his own apartment in Plano near his job at the muffler shop—and it used to be he'd eat plenty. He was a big kid. But, awhile ago, he more or less quit eatin' much of anything except candy bars when he got real hungry."

"Wouldn't even eat mama's rump roast." Thomas mumbled, still fixed blankly on the photo. "Used to, he'd eat the whole thing if we let him."

"So, he finally went to the doctor. Went to a doctor over at Brookside somebody recommended. That picture was right after his first appointment. He had a prescription with him. We were talking to a neighbor out in the front yard when Johnny drove up. The neighbor had a camera with him and he said, 'let me take your picture.' While he was lining us up out there, Johnny leaned over towards me and said, 'I'm gonna be okay Mom.' Then, the neighbor told us to act like we liked each other and we all laughed. We were feeling like things'd be okay. Johnny was, too, that day."

Her husband nodded, reached up with one hand and self-consciously swiped a tear away from his right eye.

Mrs. Hoff continued, "Johnny came in and we had some tea, then he went to get his drugs. He said this doctor, a psychiatrist, not a real doctor, had talked to him for about twenty minutes and wrote out a prescription. He gave him a little sample box. Johnny popped one of 'em in right here. I even still have the box somewhere."

"Oh? May I see it, if it's handy?" To her surprise, Thomas Hoff patted his wife's knee, rose with a grunt and walked into the hall. He returned almost immediately with a small robin egg blue and cream-colored box, open at one end. He handed it to Cassie and sat back down, grunted as he reached for his tea, drank a few swallows, put it down, then settled back in his seat. He said, "We didn't tell the police and the federal people we had this." He never met Cassie's eyes as he spoke. "Told 'em he was seein' that head doctor, but I 'magine they found out all about the drug anyways."

Cassie held it in her hand and looked at it. In dark blue, bold letters, the name "Pefrexa XR" stood out. Below the name, in smaller but also bold type, was the chemical name, "Chlorpenframine." Below that, "Oral 25mg." A paper sticker had the name of a doctor. This sample box proved he had at least sampled the drug.

"There were two pills in there," Christine Hoff said. "Johnny took one and said he was supposed to take another one in the morning. He told us both before he left, said, 'I'm gonna be okay. Don't worry.' Seemed encouraged, like, just because he thought he was getting some help."

"Well, then, what happened?"

"That was about the end of March, sometime like that. He started out okay, but then we started noticing Johnny was gettin' kind of, you know—sullen. He argued with us about anything we said but didn't talk much other than that. He said he wasn't sleeping very well." She looked at her hands in her lap and sighed. "We didn't know what to do. It didn't seem like the pills were good for him, really. He got to where he didn't come over anymore. Used to come over every Monday and Thursday night—"

"We used to watch football in the fall," Thomas Hoff interjected.

"—but he just stopped coming over. We called him and asked if he maybe ought to go see the doctor again, and he just said he'd called and the doctor told him it would take a few weeks for the pills to work and he should just wait. And he told him to take two pills at a time, instead of just one." She stopped and reached for her tea.

Cassie did the same, glad for a break in the narration.

"That was just a week before it happened. We never did talk to Johnny again, then."

"Wasn't really our Johnny no more. Not no more," Her husband said, never looking Cassie's way, never moving his head at all, just staring at the photo.

Cassie was beginning to feel a great sympathy for these people. They had no control of any of it, and seeing their son first emotionally demolished by a woman's rejection, then becoming a mass killer who had been driven into madness by a drug that was supposed to help him—it must have been awful.

"Tell me, Christine, did you ever talk to Johnny's doctor?"

"No. I found that box from those pills there, and called to ask some questions, but they wouldn't talk to me. They said they couldn't because of privacy laws. I told them I was his mother and I could bring identification and everything, but the woman said they couldn't talk about him to anybody unless he signed a form about it." She sighed. "That never happened."

"What about now? Can you see his records now?"

"Huh-uh. They say they aren't available. That's all they say."

Cassie looked at the sample box in her hand. Inside was a tightly folded, lightweight paper. She pulled it out and unfolded it to its full size of four inches by over a foot. The type on it, in one column on both sides, was half the size of the regular text type used in their newspaper—too small for most people to read without bright light and reading glasses. At the top was the 'Black Box' warning she'd seen on PDFs at the FDA website, noting the danger of suicidality, suicidal thoughts and actions. Somewhere in the document, there would also be cautions about changing dosage without consulting the doctor, as well as suggestions for weekly follow-up visits and cautions for family members to closely watch the patient's state of mind. From what Cassie had read, too many doctors seemed to think SSRI drugs were not nearly as dangerous as they had proven to be in some people, especially young people under stress. Like John Hoff.

"Did you ever read this?" she asked.

"No. I didn't know it was important. The drug was given to him by his doctor so I figured it had to be safe."

"Do you know if Johnny ever read it?"

"Doubt it," Thomas Hoff said, recrossing his arms. "John didn't read much." The man seemed, mentally and emotionally, to be somewhere else entirely. Cassie wondered if he was like this all the time, or if he would be the next Hoff family member to go to a doctor and be prescribed a drug that might as soon destroy his life as improve it.

Mrs. Hoff sighed. "The doctor called one day. You know, after. Said he wanted to see if we were okay. I just told him of course we're not doing okay!" She burst into tears and sobbed. Her husband just shook his head slowly, reached out one arm and put it on her shoulders. It seemed awkward, like it was something he wouldn't normally do and didn't quite know how to do.

"We went up to Johnny's apartment, you know, to get his things," Thomas Hoff said, still not meeting Cassie's eyes. "The FBI people told us it was okay by then, y'know, to go over there."

"Mm-hm," Cassie said.

"They came over to see us after they went to his place. Told us they found his video games and all that. We didn't know he was watchin' all those kinds of things."

"Like what?"

"Oh, Grand Auto Theft and some military thing, The Call of Duty I think. There was one named Super Columbine-something and some others. They asked us if we knew he had them but we didn't. We didn't know he was watching those kinds of videos."

"Did you know what those were?" Cassie asked.

"The FBI told us what they were. I heard since then they were pretty violent games. They didn't let us have 'em."

Thomas Hoff said, once more, in his same tone of unbelief, "We didn't even know he had a gun."

Cassie tried to stick to her conversation with his wife. "Do you think they were harmful to John?"

Mrs. Hoff looked at her. "I suppose they could of been. We didn't know he had 'em and couldn't of done anything about it. He was grown."

They fell silent.

"Didn't even know he had a gun," Thomas said again, in that same dead tone, then raised his eyebrows and moved his head with a small shrugging gesture. Cassie thought the man was either already using some kind of drugs, or he was just still severely depressed and in pain.

Christine Hoff wiped her eyes and nodded her head. She drew one corner of her mouth up in a resigned expression, and shrugged.

Cassie waited a moment before speaking again. "You said his fiancée had broken their engagement and wouldn't give back the ring?"

Mrs. Hoff frowned and nodded.

"Was John more or less, um, 'happy' up to then?"

"Yeah, he was. Before they met, he was just a big kid. Didn't raise too much hell. Didn't drink much, at least as far as we could tell. Just a normal twenty-one-year-old, 'til after she dumped him. That was when he got the drugs from that doctor."

Cassie suddenly realized she still hadn't asked the question that burned in her mind.

"Mr. and Mrs. Hoff, you know John was aware of the all-star band being here, right?"

"Oh, he sure was. He almost got into it his senior year."

"I know. Tell me, Christine, do you know if he read the article in my paper about the big welcome picnic down in Klyde Warren Park?"

"What?" she answered, "John read a newspaper? Lands no, I never saw him read one. He didn't much care about the news."

They continued talking for another half hour, and by the time she left, Cassie felt differently toward John Allen Hoff. She was relieved to know that he almost certainly didn't read her article. Her general attitude toward him had also changed.

Johnny Hoff wasn't just a crazed killer, a racist, a "hater." He was given a drug he shouldn't have been given, and in his situation, after the trigger of his fiancée dumping him, it somehow drove him to kill. And to "relax," he played video games that rewarded him for killing people. Another piece of the puzzle. But nobody knew the whole picture before it happened, so Hoff, like so many of the other mass killers, at Columbine, Virginia Tech, and others, had no one to help him through it. No one, that is, except the shrink, whose best answer for him was to prescribe the pills. She would need to interview that psychiatrist.

Her newspaper article was beginning to take shape in her mind, and she found herself anxious to get back to work.

FIFTEEN

JULY 19, 2016. TUESDAY.

So, Cassie thought, John Hoff must have been one of the unlucky few whose reactions to the drug included acting out the violence he'd become skilled at by watching his FPS murder videos. Skilled and desensitized.

She snorted at her own thought—that Hoff was unlucky. But, that could be the best way to explain it. People were different, and he was obviously one of those whose brain put together some things in different ways than most others. In this case, when he was under stress, it led him to kill people, emboldened by the drug at the same time as he was emotionally blunted. She couldn't hate him as much as she had at first, but she couldn't pity him and she didn't care that he was dead. Her feelings were mixed up. She tried to change her mental subject, picked up her phone and pressed a speed-dial number.

"Tom Hammond," came a gruff answer.

"Tom, it's Cassie."

His voice softened. "Hey, Honey, how're you doin'?"

Cassie chuckled. Like a favorite uncle, he called her "Honey" often. "Thanks, I'm doing a lot better. Say, Tom, I want to do a story on the shooting."

"Well, you must be doin' better! Sure you're up to it? You ready to get goin' again so soon?"

"I'm not all the way back. That'll take a long time, but I've discovered something I can't ignore and I want to strike while the iron's hot, you know?"

"Sure, tell me what it's about."

"It's about why John Hoff attacked the band."

"Whoa! You know some things nobody else does?"

"Maybe I do. I want to write it and then meet with you and Mrs. Wright. Should I go ahead?"

"Well, I need to be sure you're onto something that's real. Just tell me a little bit about it."

She took a deep breath, tried to organize an "elevator pitch" that would encapsulate it and make Hammond want to read it. "Okay. John Hoff was on a drug. It showed up in his pre-surgical blood work. He also played a lot of first person shooter video games. He was driven to do this killing by what the drug did to his mind. Oh, and we are pretty sure he was murdered, too." She instantly wished she hadn't added the murder part.

"Well, okay, but that's not news. People on drugs like PCP and Meth do crazy things all the time—but wait! Murdered? And who is 'we?' "

"Tom, this is a prescription drug. "

"A legal drug? Really?"

"Yeah, prescribed to him by his doctor."

"Well, if that's true, there's maybe somebody out there that doesn't want this story told."

"*Exactly*! And that's why we think somebody murdered John Hoff and cremated him within just a few hours." She waited for that to sink in, picturing the expression on Holland's face—that calculating, excited look that he got when he thought a story could be a real scoop. She wasn't disappointed.

"Murder of a murderer? Okay, Cassie. I want to read it. Better be good, though. You write up a draft and bring it in here tomorrow morning at ten. I'll set up a talk with Mrs. Wright. She has to decide. If it's good, we'll get it on the front page of your section on Sunday."

"You got it. Thanks, Tom, I'll see you in the morning." She hung up the phone with a temporary pleasant feeling. Hammond had called Sunday In Dallas "her" section. She liked that. And he forgot to ask again who the "we" was. She was glad, since Linnie might not want to be pulled into the whole thing. Not yet anyway.

Just before three the next morning, the article was finished. It was much longer than her usual 800-word columns, at about fifteen hundred, but Tom had told her they'd run it on the section's front page, so it deserved the extra length.

She read it over quickly, hoped she hadn't gone too far with it, and printed it.

Cassie walked into the building's staff entrance and was greeted by a sympathetic word and handshake from Toby, the security guard behind the counter. She went up to the editorial floor. When the elevator opened, she realized Toby must have called ahead of her, because practically everyone on her floor was standing. A brief flurry of applause—for what, she wondered, being a victim?—and then many of the women rushed up to her. Some cried, which brought tears to her eyes. Struggling to keep her composure, she endured their sympathy as long as she could, then looked up to see Tom standing at the end of the row just past her cubicle. She said she had to meet with him and excused herself. She noticed as she passed her own cubicle that numerous lavender and blue sympathy card envelopes, and a flower arrangement, covered her desk top. All of the co-workers she passed smiled and said something as she went by.

"Wow," she said as she walked into Tom's office. "I wasn't ready for that."

"Yeah, but y'know they all just love you Cass. We all do."

She couldn't speak for a few seconds, then just said, "Thanks."

"You want some coffee or somethin'?"

"No, I'm okay." She reached into her bag and pulled out a paper copy of the six-page article and handed it to him.

"I talked to Mrs. Wright. She's not sure she wants to go down this road, but she agreed to read it before she decides." He sat down beside Cassie in a side chair and started reading.

THIS PRESENT MADNESS
By Cassie Stevens

It goes without saying that a mom or dad can never be prepared for the kind of thing that happened at Travis High School on June 27. We dare not even think of it. Doing so acknowledges our inability to prevent it. And yet, it has happened, again, and again, and again.

We've all been almost destroyed emotionally, our lives changed forever in one of the worst ways imaginable. But we've also been led during our grieving to demand answers to the two questions that always follow these horrible acts:

One: Why?

Two: Can it be predicted and prevented?

Everyone clamors for answers after every such shooting, but are there any? What could make any person do such a thing? Knowing why might salve a drive for some kind of explanation. But it won't reduce our pain.

To most of us, it doesn't seem possible for anyone to be so pointlessly evil. But it happens. Regularly. Can such events be prevented? The standard knee jerk reactions, always just band-aids on a mortal wound, will never suffice, so misguided are they. If we can't prevent them, all that's left is to combat them. But combat what, when nobody has a profile of the next killer? After all, most of them are—pardon the word—so *normal*.

Political leaders and speakers, doing their show, bring to my mind The Bard's lines, reminding us that, "...All the world's a stage/ And all the men and women merely players;/ They have their exits and their entrances,/ And one man in his time plays many parts, ..."

And the politicians all play their public parts—some well, most badly—but always at least appearing to be "doing something about it," so we'll be quieted until the next attack comes. But perhaps, for our congressmen and senators, the more descriptive quote from Shakespeare is found in Hamlet: "... Life is a tale told by an idiot, full of sound and fury, signifying nothing."

I question the politicians' efficacy more than their sincerity. I have to believe they would act quickly if they found a real solution, if for no other reason than that it would guarantee their re-election. (Cynical? *Yes*.)

The truth, we all know, is that none of the measures they routinely suggest, like more so-called "gun-free zones," will ever work. They're all directed toward guns—not the damaged human mind that chooses the gun. They think a new gun law will help? Last time I looked, it was already illegal to murder people, but it happens daily.

No law will stop a person from acting evilly.

The politicians all attack crime—gun crime. But there's a problem with that: It is not even "criminals" who do these shootings! Check the statistics:

Out of over seventy-two mass killers in the last three decades, over nine out of ten had no criminal record, no history of violence, and no history of treatment for mental illness. Most of them were young, and came from intact families in middle-class homes (in the old sense of that term). Over two-thirds were white. Only one was female. These are facts.

Two more facts: Most of them were taking at least one *legally prescribed* drug of a specific type—an antidepressant known as an "SSRI," shorthand for Selective Serotonin Reuptake Inhibitor. (Just go ahead and Google it by its initials.)

Secondly, many of them in the last few years enjoyed playing violent first-person video games. (Those are the kind where the player is looking over the barrel of a gun and shooting people, and is rewarded for "good shooting.")

If this isn't "madness," I don't know what is!

We all know that depression, anxiety, and other problems of the mind run rampant in our society. They always have, always will. And since the 1980's they have no lack of prescription drug treatments.

Beneficiaries? Sometimes, the patients. But most of the time the sellers of these über-popular and mega-profitable drugs. They are the pharmaceutical giants, and they are the most profitable companies on the planet.

Yes, of course there is such a thing as depression, from mild to major, and the pills pushed by Big Pharma help relieve it for some people (only slightly more effectively than the placebos they are tested against). But, for a small percentage—and this is something you can read for yourself in the complete FDA "label" of these drugs—antidepressant meds like this lead a small percentage of patients not to a successful reduction in depression, but to an act of suicide or violence. Such might have been the case with John Allen Hoff. There are rumors that at the time of his attack, John Allen Hoff was under the influence of an SSRI antidepressant.

This was actually the case in many of the seventy-two mass-shooting attacks like this in the last 35 years. Factual evidence, though called "anecdotal and unscientific," is plentiful; most of the time, the shooters were taking these specific psychiatric drugs.

Often, the drug makers will blame the mental illness, itself. But another interesting fact is, these people had lived quite awhile with their mental illnesses, but they didn't go murdering until they started taking the SSRIs. That fact should be difficult to explain away.

The drug makers might also say, and have said in so many words, "Certainly, when such a tiny percentage of patients go off the deep end, we don't want to scare off the many who might be helped by these drugs." Maybe that argument deserves consideration. But they'd better not use that one on me or other victims' families.

Some people's mental states are improved through these drugs. But research in the drug makers' own clinical trials has shown it is only slightly better than the improvement gained from placebos. Is that worth a few dozen lives in mass killings once or twice a year? (And many "regular" murders, wife beatings, and assaults could undoubtedly be added to those dozens. They just aren't readily available as statistics.)

I think regulatory measures could and must be adopted that could at least reduce the numbers of patients who suffer extreme adverse effects. And we could stand more control of direct drug marketing to physicians and patients, like those ads on TV. (It's the income from these ads that explains why print media and network news will not implicate prescription drugs in these killings.)

It all depends on how much we care. When other "news" takes over the cycle, do we still care? Those of us who've lost loved ones ... we do! Call us a special interest group if it'll help.

We must find voices with ideas to control the bad effects while maintaining the good. We should be looking not at "gun control," but instead, "drug control." Or maybe a little bit of both? (After all, guns are already regulated and "controlled" in specific ways; the Second Amendment is not un-infringed. Why not cross-reference gun background checks with antidepressant-prescription databases?)

Because we are hopeful idealists, we keep looking for the good in people and in companies. But, for now, I am like Gen. Yamamoto's sleeping giant, awakened and filled with a terrible resolve. I will find a solution and fight to see it implemented.

In the meantime, we Moms and Dads, families and friends of the forty-six murdered kids, all the injured kids, and five dead teachers, are forced into grief and sorrow, to say goodbye to the joyful melodies of their lives and hear instead only the dirge that accompanies our tears. We all grieve together and pray for one another.

Thank you to all who have expressed your caring for my loss and that of so many others.

Email me with comments: cass@cassiestevens.net

"Cassie," Hammond said, lowering the paper and removing his glasses when he finished, "I don't see how we can print this. I don't see any way she'll go for it." He pointed upwards with his reading glasses. "Besides, it could open us up to a lawsuit."

"From who? No drugs or companies or video games are named!"

"Well, I just—"

"Tom, the world has to start discovering what I've found out."

"But Cass, you're not the first one to say these people are mentally ill. People've been sayin' that for years."

"It's not just the mental illness, Tom! It's the treatment for it! It's a reaction to these damn drugs! It's what they do to some people! It's for sure some 'regular' murders come from these things too!"

"Yeah, but what's the percentage?"

"Overall? I can't say." She fixed him with a stare. "But, for me and some others here, it's a hundred percent!"

Hammond looked back at her and let out a long breath. "I'm sorry, Cass. That was insensitive. Okay, let's go see what the boss has to say. It's her call anyway."

As they entered her office, Rachel Wright rose and walked around her desk. To Cassie's surprise, the publisher held out her arms and gave her a brief hug, then stood back. Her eyes were red.

"Cassie, my dear, I am so, so very sorry about your wonderful son. I feel like we've all lost a dear member of the family."

"Thank you, ma'am," Cassie said, her throat tight.

The old lady motioned them to seats. "You know, I have reacted in different ways at different times to this. I have had tears, and rages, and I've been unable to sleep many nights. But I know all that is only a small part of what you have felt. I just want you to know that this newspaper will do whatever we can to help you through this."

"Thank you again, ma'am."

Hammond leaned forward and offered the sheaf of pages. "Here's the article Cassie's asked us to consider."

"What do you think of it, Tom?" The publisher asked.

"It's well written, of course, in her editorial style. But, ma'am, you should read it before I say anything."

She raised her reading glasses, put them on, glanced at Cassie and Hammond, and started reading.

From the woman's narrowing of eyes, deep breaths, and glances at the two of them, Cassie could easily tell when she read certain parts of the piece. After a few minutes, she lowered the pages, took off her reading glasses, and looked up to her left at a large formal painting of her late husband, Walter L. Wright, hung on the wall. After a few seconds, she turned to Cassie.

"A newspaper can't afford to guess at things, you know. But we can't be cowards, either. Hell, my Walter wouldn't have shrunk from a controversy. He'd call a skunk a skunk, and I know that's how you work, too, Miss Cassie!" She stood slowly, paced for a bit, then sat back down and fixed her eyes on Hammond. "Now, tell me what you thought about this."

He took a deep breath. "I don't see how we can publish it, myself. It's gonna bring a lot of negative feedback. That's a big bear we'll be wakin' up."

"Who do you mean?"

"The pharmaceuticals. They'll be on us like flies on sugar, and you know that's a fact."

Cassie started to say something, but Mrs. Wright held up a hand to stop her, then settled into her chair and stared at the pages for a few seconds. Then she slapped at them with the back of one wizened hand.

"We will run it! Now, I want to get some feedback, so I'm going to make a couple of phone calls. All right with you, Cassie? But, we'll run it on page one of the Sunday In Dallas section. Tom, you take it over. Get some of Larry's best pictures of the picnic, the band, and the crime scene—those telephoto shots that show the yellow blankets and emergency vehicles, if we have them."

"Ma'am, are you sure—"

"Tom, I am sure. Like I said, Walter wouldn't have backed down from stirring up a hornets' nest and I won't either. This band was his and this newspaper's happiest achievement, and we've not only lost it for this year and maybe more, but we've lost one of our own dear ones and all those young people and instructors. We're going to say what needs to be said. We're a newspaper and we're going to act like one!"

She turned to Cassie. "You understand, I'll get some fact-checking done on this? And maybe another article to go along with it?"

"That is absolutely fine with me, ma'am. I've soft-peddled some of it, but there's more to come."

"Okay, then. I don't know if I'd call this a soft-peddle approach, but let's get to work." She stood and put out her hand again. "Cassie, thank you, and again, I'm so sorry for your loss. Let me know personally if I can do anything to help you."

A minute later, they left her office and entered the elevator. Hammond looked at her as the doors closed. "This is gonna be a heavy week around here," he said. "You ready for it?"

She looked at him. "I'm ready."

SIXTEEN

JULY 20, 2016. WEDNESDAY.

Justin Richardson stabbed the intercom button. "What."

"Sir, there's a Mrs. Rachel Wright on line two for you. Calling from a newspaper in Dallas?"

"Who the hell is—," he answered, then remembered. Rachel Wright, the lively old crone widow who published the Dallas *Daily Post*. "Okay, thanks." They'd met when both were honored as "Texas Stars of Business," two of the ten most successful business owners in the state. He recalled that her little daily rag was the main sponsor of the state all-star band. But how was this connected? He sighed and wondered what she might want, tried to put a genuine smile on his face and picked up the phone.

"Well, hello, Rachel! It's been awhile since the Texas Stars banquet last year. How are you?"

Her old but vigorous voice caused him to hold the phone away from his ear. "I'm well, Justin, and you?"

"I'm doing well also. Wonderful to hear from you."

"I know you're a busy man, but I have a huge favor to ask. You know about the all-star band attack here, I'm sure. Horrible. Our hearts are sick. One of our columnists, Cassie Stevens, lost her son in that attack. She's just brought an article to me that pins part of the blame for the attack on drugs like those your company produces— SSRIs, I think they're called?"

Richardson came to attention, but he tried to sound casual. "Yes ma'am, we produce two of those types of products. Why?"

"I want to send you a copy of the article, more of an editorial, that I am going to run on the first page of our community section

135

this Sunday. If possible, I'd like you to provide a matching article as counterpoint. I wouldn't have called, knowing how busy you must be, but I don't know anyone else remotely connected to these drugs, and I think I can trust you to be honest. We don't want to go off half-cocked here. When you read it, you'll know what I'm looking for. It's sure to be a controversial piece and I know you'll be able to speak well for your industry. What do you think?"

Richardson had to take a breath to tone down his response. This could be a problem, or an opportunity to nip negative press in the bud. "It must be quite a piece! But yes, I think I can help you with this, always happy to defend the good guys, you know."

"Well, I don't know if it's good or bad guys we're dealing with, I just want this to be balanced and I remember you struck me as a fair-minded man. The only thing is that I will need your article—a thousand words or so— before five p.m. today. Can that be done?"

"Hmm. Not easy, but I think so. I wouldn't want to miss this opportunity," he said, sincere honesty in his voice. "Send it to my email address—jr@provachem.com—and I'll reply to it with the article before five."

He said goodbye and hung up the phone while he turned on his computer screen. His mind was already racing, trying to figure out who to get to write the article. A couple of favorite ghostwriters came to mind. He told Shelley to contact both of them and get a call back to him right away.

Did he need to include Winston and Bliss? His quick decision was negative. They had almost kept him from getting to Hoff quickly, but they'd been wrong. That was working out just fine. And they'd just want to edit or put in their worthless opinions, taking extra time. He needed to make this move quickly.

An item, "dp_article," popped into his private email. He opened it and read the attached article. As he read, blood crept up to his face and his anger rose.

The intercom buzzed. Shelley had one of the writers on the phone for him. He calmed himself before picking up the phone.

"Hello, Chris. If you're available to drop everything and work today, I'll make it worth your while." He waited and heard what he wanted. "Good. I'm sending you an article that will appear in a Sunday paper in Dallas, and I want about a thousand-word factual rebuttal. I'll pay you a thousand dollars to get it done in three hours and back to me. If it's a good put-down of the writer, I'll add $500. Know what I mean?" He listened. "Yeah. Can you do it? Certain?" He was gratified to hear a positive response. After he gave her a few more specifics, he hung up and forwarded the article to her. As one of the ghostwriters Provachem used for research articles to be "peer reviewed," she knew as much as Richardson about the drugs and their side effects. Probably more.

Now, he had to wait. He thought back over everything he knew about how Hoff had been handled at the hospital. He was tempted to call up there, but he resisted the urge.

Cassie was encouraged. Being in her cubicle at the newspaper office also helped. It was good to be out of the condo where she could re-alize life still existed. She wanted to do a sidebar to the article. She wasn't sure if she could handle it, but it would ideally be something about John Hoff's life, from his parents

Mounted on the wall above her, the TV carried an image of that reporter, the blonde on WNN who had made the story her own, near the Travis High band room. Cassie plugged in her ear buds.

"…been almost four weeks, now, since this location became na-tionally known as the site of the worst school shooting in U.S. histo-ry. Now, as you can see, it is quiet, still cordoned off, with a couple of Plano PD cruisers sitting at the entrances to the parking lot, and some overall-clad CSIs still working in the scene." She turned her head into the wind to keep hair out of her face.

"The pain this has brought throughout the state of Texas, and the many calls for more gun control even here, where gun rights are simply taken for granted and accepted, has begun to die down a little bit as other stories grab most people's attention. But here in Plano, and in many other towns and cities in Texas, where the music of tal-ented high school musicians was suddenly silenced, it might never die down. This is Kelli Tremaine, WNN, in Plano. David?"

The scene changed to the studio where a somber young man said only, "Back after this."

As the commercial began, Cassie disconnected. Her mind went back to the big question again. Why? She was convinced that antidepressants combined with violent video games, in a small percentage of patients, caused these shootings. She knew from what she'd been reading lately that there were probably several people on the editorial floor with her who were beginning, taking or trying to withdraw from antidepressants. The pills were apparently prescribed almost willy-nilly to anyone who answered a doctor's or psychiatrist's questions in certain ways. They all used the book she'd read about, the "DSM-Five," The *Diagnostic and Statistical Manual of Mental Disorders*, a book that provided interview questions about symptoms. If a person described what they were feeling, and answered the questions just right, a specific mental problem would supposedly be identified, and most likely a drug would be prescribed.

She had an idea for an excellent sidebar, and she knew who could help her find someone to help with it. She picked up the phone to try Linnie again.

Justin Richardson began to read through the first page of his article. He expected it to be right on-point, but it would have his name on it as CEO of Provachem, and it needed to strike a balance between respect for an investigative viewpoint and disdain for the writer's maudlin prose, while not ignoring the fact that she had lost her son and would therefore be granted a great deal of sympathy. But that didn't mean her facts had to be accepted as correct, even if they were.

When he got to a passage about Scientology, he actually laughed. "Over twenty years ago, when now well known pharmaceuticals were helping people stricken with depression to get on with their lives, others like this well intentioned but badly informed writer came out against drugs in general, claiming that their 'Dianetics,' some kind of memory regression, was a better treatment than drugs developed under rigorous FDA requirements. They were woefully wrong then, as she is now. We don't know if she is a Scientologist, but her words are eerily similar to theirs."

He liked the way the writer harkened back to the popular drugs from the late 1980s and early 90s whose effectiveness were known worldwide. Though his own Pefrexa was a better formulation, it was good to be linked with other successful products of the same type.

Richardson dialed Rachel Wright, let her secretary know he was sending the article, sat back and played with a rubber band. The slight smile on his face as he anticipated the article's effect began to fade. He would turn back to company business, but first, a call up to Plano was needed.

Linnie's recommendation was to see someone at her hospital, and now, less than an hour later, Cassie stood outside his office in a near-by building.

"Cecil M. Thomas, Psy.D., M.D.," the placard on the door read. Cassie opened the door and walked into the airy, open waiting room. At the far end, past rows of chairs, an attractive receptionist smiled and stood. Two other people, a couple, glanced at her as she passed, then resumed their magazine reading.

Cassie leaned over the counter and said in a low voice, "Cassandra Stevens. I have an appointment for a consultation." The receptionist asked her to take a seat. Five minutes later, a door opened and a young woman was ushered back into the waiting room by a tall middle-aged man whose kind smile seemed reassuring. The woman, Cassie guessed to be in her mid-twenties, clutched a small box in her hand, robin-egg blue and cream colored, like the one at the Hoffs'.

Cassie was ushered into the office of the psychiatrist. He rose to greet her, holding out his hand. "Hello Ms. Stevens. It's a pleasure to meet you. May I offer my sincere condolences for your loss." His resonant voice was soothing and his smile and warm two-handed handshake comforting.

She was somewhat surprised that he knew that her son had been a victim. Her main impression was that the man was a caring individual who probably wanted to be a help to her. Most likely an effect he'd practiced to perfection.

"Thank you, Doctor Thomas. It is pretty hard."

"Yes, I'm sure of that. Would you like to have a seat? Can I get you some coffee? Tea? Water?" He stood until she answered, then sat down as she turned them all down. "How can I help you today?"

The simple, open question made Cassie quickly rethink her reason for coming, which was originally to get him to interview her and prescribe some kind of pill, like the Pefrexa XR she'd seen in the previous patient's hand.

"Well—" she said, and started crying.

Before she could search in her bag for a tissue, the doctor placed a box of them on the desk in front of her.

"Take your time," he said.

She dabbed a couple of times, shook her head and looked at him.

"Doctor, since you knew who I was, you must also know I'm a columnist for the *Daily Post*." He nodded. "I have an article coming out this Sunday that puts forth a possible reason for John Hoff's attack on our kids. It's about SSRI antidepressants that are prescribed too easily and have dangerous side effects, and it mentions violent video games. They could have been part of the reason."

The doctor, his hands tented in front of his chin, nodded and smiled. "I know that all of us are desperate to find an answer for why this was done, but there aren't any simple answers. There never are."

"But what about the fact that so many of these rampage killers were taking prescription drugs and the young ones seem to favor first-person shooting video games?"

"Yes, there's that. Many of them were. Yes, I believe FPS games are a factor. From a mental health standpoint, they're a mistake in the entertainment industry, but they're hugely profitable—"

"Like the SSRIs," Cassie interjected.

"uh—and, you know, there might be more like John Hoff out there than we can imagine. But with the human mind there's rarely just a single or even twofold reason why anybody does anything. It's especially true with violence."

"Can you explain that a little more?"

He smiled, leaned forward and put his elbows on his desk, hands clasped. "Of course, but I need to ask you a question first. Are you here because you need help dealing with the loss of your son, or are you here to interview me for your newspaper? I need to know if I am talking to you about your loss, or talking theoretically about the killers. It changes my approach, as you can certainly understand, being a writer. So, who is my audience?"

Cassie smiled at the disarming personality of the man. "How 'bout both?" she answered.

He smiled. "Okay. Let me address the wider question first. What could make a person do what John Allen Hoff did? Or Cho at Virginia Tech? Or Alan Lanza in Newtown? Or Holmes, in Colorado? Charleston, Chattanooga and Roseburg? There are always multiple answers, and they're rarely the same. Just take four of those—Hoff installed mufflers, Cho was a student, Lanza had Asperger's syndrome, and Holmes was a graduate psychology student. The other three looked like anti-religious and other motives. See, their reasons were probably as different as their lives seemed to be. It's pretty clear they all took some sort of medication, but we don't know exactly what kind, and if we did, we couldn't draw a straight line between the meds and the murders. We'd need to thoroughly investigate each killer's life, medical and mental background, relationships—all that. And most of them are dead, so we can't talk to them. We would still never arrive at a good answer."

"Why not?"

"Because the human mind, separate from but comprised of all the perceptions of the brain, is so complex in itself. The history of an individual and his emotions are mixed in. His personality. And, then, there's the micro health of the brain, itself. Take twins, raised as identically as they are genetically identical. Suppose one of them is dropped on her head at eighteen months of age and a slight injury occurs, but is never discovered. Her brain will likely in some way be different from her sister's, and because of that her mind might be, also. She might react differently to certain kinds of situations, and different medications. And while on certain medications, she might have different reactions than are generally expected. Or, not! You see, with the mind, there are just no easy answers."

Cassie sighed. "Mm-hm, that's pretty obvious."

"Yes, and since the killers are almost always dead following their crimes, we have no opportunity to find out what was in their mind."

"Yes, I mention that in my article. What do you think about the general SSRI issue?"

He looked out the window for a moment. "You've actually hit on something that is quite perplexing to some in my field."

"Why just 'some?' "

"I don't know how much you've researched this. You probably didn't look into it until, uh—how should I say this—?"

"Right. Not until after the shooting. Actually not until last week, but all I did for about five days was read and study about it. Half a dozen books."

"Crash course. Then, you've probably read some of Dr. Healy, and maybe Kirsch's metastudies? Robert Whitaker?"

She was surprised. "Yes, all of those, actually, and some others. They were brought to me by a friend who's a neurosurgeon."

"Dr. Kennedy? Linnea? Excellent surgeon! We've talked about the biophysical model of depression." He looked at his hands and smiled. "Okay, then. So you've been steeped in the theory that SS-RIs are evil, that they cause people to do things they wouldn't ordinarily do, having no remorse, being emotionally blunted, ignoring consequences. All that. And you've discovered the artful ways the drugs are marketed?"

"Yes, pretty much," she answered, but she couldn't be sure from his tone how he felt about them.

"I've read those sources as well, and they are quite convincing in many ways."

"But, I thought you were going to argue with them?"

"Why?"

"I just did."

"Well, I didn't say I was in their court, but I can understand their point of view. Still, there are other points of view, too. Have you considered that the medical doctors and psychologists who believe the brain can become imbalanced, really do believe it, while the Big

Pharma approach is something like 'give the expert doctors what they want, and a huge profit is also okay with us.' " He paused and smiled, shaking his head slightly. "But then you have to ask, 'Which came first, the pill or the problem?' Big Pharma isn't squeaky clean; they're all in business for only one reason, and that's the duty to their stockholders to produce a profit. But they aren't completely bad either. But mention public health and the greater good? They talk about it, but they secretly laugh. Their greater good is their financial bottom line."

"Doctor, you sound like a politician. You're disgruntled with both sides but all you do is ask questions. Don't you have an opinion? I mean, do you have an opinion?"

"Okay, then. I have read the same books you have, plus many more. I'm basically on the fence. I'm not convinced that SSRIs 'cause' any particular acts of violence, even though people in clinical trials for them have exhibited suicidal and homicidal ideation—thoughts—that they never showed before, and even though there are known adverse effects mentioned in their labels. It simply hasn't been conclusively proven to me that there is a causal connection to this kind of violence."

Well, even if it's on one out of a thousand, what the FDA calls 'rare,' that's a lot of people thinking about suicide or homicide."

"That's true. It's a shame we can't ID them, isn't it?"

"Yes, but maybe we could, with better follow up from doctors."

"Maybe." He stood and walked around his chair, then turned back to her as she spoke.

"Let me ask, do you use the DSM in your practice?"

"The Diagnostic and Statistical Manual? Of course. Every psychiatrist I know does, and many doctors. Why?"

"Does it really work like an interview, where you ask the patient questions about their lives and come up with a diagnosis from their replies?"

"Sometimes, yes."

"Do you prescribe for patients based on those interviews?"

"Sometimes, yes."

"Well, let me ask a specific question. When I was waiting, a young lady came out and I noticed she was holding a small box, a light blue and cream-colored box, that looked like a sample of pills—?"

"I can't comment on that. Sorry."

"Can you tell me if that little box was something she got here?"

"Can't answer that either. Could've been cough drops she had with her, or gum, you know?"

"It looked like a sample box of Pefrexa XR to me." She looked directly into his eyes. "I saw a box just like it in the home of John Hoff's parents. Just yesterday. It had your name on it."

He stopped all movement and stared at her for a few seconds, then rose and looked down at her. "Mrs. Stevens, it seems we've gotten a bit sideways here. I don't much like to be ambushed and confronted in my own office like this. I think your consultation is over."

"Well," she said, standing and picking up her bag, "I'm sorry, but confrontations are part of my business. I appreciate you giving me your answers."

She could feel his angry glare as she stood and walked out of his office.

SEVENTEEN

JULY 23, 2016. SATURDAY.

Saturday afternoon was always a quiet time in the newspaper office. One of the mail boys wheeled his cart into the break room where Cassie was standing, politely listening to Erin, the *DP*'s perky website director, telling her something about the online paper. The mail guy brushed by them and laid a stack of Sunday In Dallas sections on the break table.

Cassie glanced down at it, anticipating her article's treatment, and almost choked on her coffee.

First, she froze, then yelled: "What the—hell?" She put her coffee down hard and scooped up the section, opened it and stared, horrified, at the full-page, two-sided layout.

Her article, retitled, from her original "This Present Madness," to "Do Drugs Spur Shooters?" was on the left. Her lead paragraphs had been eliminated and a new section inserted. A single, large aerial photo below the headline, tightly cropped top and bottom, showed the blue roof of the Travis High School band room surrounded by yellow-shrouded bodies, emergency personnel in white kneeling here and there.

She felt sick to her stomach.

On the right was another article, whose headline was, "Drug Maker Says No," and the byline under it was, "Justin Richardson, CEO, Provachem Pharmaceuticals, Inc." A Time magazine-type photo of Richardson in a gray suit, with a typical chemical lab and people in white coats working in the background.

She started reading the article, her anger building with every word.

"Entering 'SSRI' in Google will return almost seven million results. Many people know of these prescription drugs, partly through misleading articles such as the one on this page. The fact that Selective Serotonin Reuptake Inhibitors have been implicated in some of the tragic mass shootings in past years is thought by some to be 'proof' that these beneficial drugs 'cause' such horrific attacks on innocent victims.

"But this is easily proven wrong. There have been hundreds of millions of prescriptions of SSRIs since they were introduced in the late 1980s. But we've had under one hundred mass shootings, and not all of them were done by a person being treated with an SSRI.

"If we are to accept circumstances as evidence, and align coincidence with causality, this one bit of numerical information should tell us, the problem is not with the drugs, but with the original diseases suffered by these people. Unfortunately, the human mind is still unfathomable in its extremes, and no one can say what inner demons drive the small number of people to do these things.

"It has long been agreed in the pharmaceutical academy that a precise chemical balance is needed in the synapses of the brain, where the neurotransmitter serotonin and others do their miraculous work. But they sometimes simply malfunction. We do not know exactly why. One theory is that the illness itself—depression—causes the imbalance, while another is that the imbalance causes the depression. That may be a 'chicken-and-egg' puzzle, but it is important to understand that the chemical imbalance is a malfunction we can treat. SSRIs are prescribed for no other reason than to restore the proper chemical balance to the brain. When that balance is reached, the prescription is normally adjusted downward until withdrawal from the drug is complete.

"Unfortunately, it is also known that certain individuals will not respond as hoped to the benefits of SSRI drugs or any psychotropic drugs. These individuals do not necessarily become spree killers, as the *Daily Post* writer has intimated; indeed, many of them merely move with no ill effects to another form of treatment or to another pharmaceutical product. SSRIs are basically benign."

Cassie began to tremble as she realized that this reasonable-sounding counterpoint was calmly dismantling the entire emotional thrust of her own article. People would see this and believe it, even though, so far, it hadn't disproved anything she said in her own article. The mere impression of serious scientific thinking would win.

She could feel her face burning as she continued reading more of the same unruffled statements from the Big Pharma side of the question. It sounded so authoritative, so valid, that she felt defeated.

Then, she read this at the end of the article:

> "Over twenty years ago, well known SSRIs and other psychiatric pharmaceuticals were already helping people stricken with depression to get on with their lives. But groups and individuals like this understandably angry but badly informed writer came out against drugs in general, claiming that their 'Dianetics' (some kind of memory regression), was a better treatment than drugs developed under rigorous FDA requirements. They were woefully wrong then, as she is now. We don't know if Mrs. Stevens is a Scientologist, but her words are eerily similar to theirs. A religious view should not be allowed to question medical science that is based on evidence from multiple controlled clinical trials and then affirmed by years of successful treatment.
>
> "We offer our deepest condolences to Mrs. Stevens and the families of all the other young people and instructors who were lost in the tragedy at Travis High School. This is something beyond understanding, and we, like Mrs. Stevens, still search for the knowledge and insight that might help us prevent it. But we must declare that when all is taken into account, any fault of quality pharmaceuticals prescribed by medical doctors is simply nonexistent."

As she dropped her arms and let the crumpled paper fall in her hands, she looked around the break room and realized she had been saying what she was thinking as she read. Three people at separate tables looked at her as if she were a bomb about to explode. Her face was already burning, her breathing shallow and quick. Tears of fury ran down her cheeks.

She stood and left the room, not knowing what to do or who to yell at.

Just as she turned the corner and entered the editorial room, Tom Hammond almost bumped into her.

She was barely able to stop herself from yelling in his face.

"Cassie, you know, I wanted to tell you about that—"

"This is bullshit, Tom!"

She threw the crumpled pages on the floor toward him and knew almost every eye in the huge room was looking her way.

"Cass, you need to come in my office and talk about this! Right now." He took a breath. "I mean *right* now!"

She glared at him, then turned and led him into his own office. When he entered and closed the door, she was pacing, arms folded, her breathing heavy and her cheeks wetted again by more tears. She was angry at herself for the tears but couldn't stop them.

"Cassie, I didn't know about this either. Mrs. Wright—"

"Who does she think she is!"

"Well—" he chuckled in spite of the situation.

"I know. I know. That was stupid. Tom, why did she do this! What the hell? Huh? When did she tell you?"

"She got an article from that guy and sent it down to me. I was told not to talk to you about it because you would want to change your article."

"Damn right I would've!"

"Yeah." He stepped toward her and pulled out one of the chairs. "Here, sit down and let's talk."

"I need to talk to Mrs. Wright. I'm gonna quit."

"She's out of town this weekend, Cass. You'd just get yourself fired anyway."

"I said I'm gonna quit!"

"Well, Cass, you can do that right here if you really want to. We'd sure miss you, and it would be a big mistake. And you know it."

Cassie sat down and Hammond sat down in another chair next to her. She was fuming, deep in thought for a couple of minutes.

"The guy made me sound like a frantic mom ready to blame anything just to find a reason for my son being murdered. And that slap about Scientology! Where in heck did *that* ever come from? I've never even known a Scientologist!"

"Yeah. Me neither. That was a low blow. But Mrs. Wright gave me strict orders to edit the piece only for grammar and syntax. It was perfect, by the way. I doubt he wrote it himself."

"Well, you know, I've got to respond to it. If I don't people will think I'm in that cult or whatever it is."

"Yeah, and I believe Mrs. Wright would want you to refute that part of it, if you can."

"Of course I can! That's the easy part, but I'm gonna do more than that. He might think I'll fade in to the shadows, Tom, but I won't!"

"Yep, I thought you would be ready to fight. Tell you the truth, Cass, I'm glad to see you fightin' back. You need to."

She stood and looked at him as she grabbed the doorknob. "So, why did she call him, in particular?"

"She knows him from that Texas Stars thing last year. Remember?"

She opened the door and walked out into the editorial office. In response to the looks she got, she just rolled her eyes and shook her head. Knowing nods came back, and the room went back to work. After fuming for a few minutes, she called Linnie and asked her to come over for dinner Sunday afternoon so she could rant to friends.

"So," Zach said, "what about the article? Did you know they were doing this other one from that company?" Zach set his tea glass down, rose and took Cassie's and Linnie's dishes off the table.

"No. When I saw it, it hit me like a truck. I just about lost it right there in the office. Actually, I did lose it."

"How so?" Linnie asked.

"Well, I guess I overreacted. Anyway, Tom, my editor—a good guy, by the way, sort of like a second father to me—was told by the publisher that he shouldn't tell me about it 'cause I would've changed my article."

"Would you?"

"Well, yeah, Linn! Of course! But now, since the guy pretty

much said I must be a Scientologist, I can come back at him on that and include some facts."

"You're not going to put in that we know Hoff had Provachem's drug in him when he attacked, are you? I don't have any proof of it—"

"No, I was going to take a different tack. I'll wait 'til you get the proof, if you can, and then we'll see what Mr. Justin Richardson has to say."

"Okay, but remember, the drug being in his system wasn't a crime, and nobody has proven beyond a doubt that SSRIs cause these attacks."

"You sound like that shrink, Dr. Thomas."

"Just being careful, Cass. If you go off naming Provachem's drug as a cause, they could sue us for something, I'm sure! They have a whole quiver of legal arrows ready, and that's why nobody has made a concerted attack against them or any other drug company on that issue. Except for individual lawsuits with special circumstances."

Cassie sighed and looked at the floor. Zach reached over to Cassie's hand and took it in his. "So, Cass, besides that, how are you feeling?"

She took awhile to answer. "I don't know. They say there are those five stages of grief, and I suppose there are. I don't know if I fit that, though. I've felt guilty a couple of times in the last few days that I wasn't depressed and crying. When I think of Mark, now, I can get that way—" she stopped as her throat constricted "—see?" She let her tears form and dried them with her napkin. "But, I'm so determined to find out more about why that guy Hoff did this and why somebody killed him, I'm more driven by that than by feelings. Does that make sense? Am I a cold woman? I did love Mark more than anything!"

Linnie shook her head, reached over and patted her on the knee. "We know you did, and so did he. That's not an issue. And there're no rules for grief. Those five stages might be the usual things people go through, but there aren't any timetables or requirements. Everyone handles grieving in their own way, so don't think you're, like, 'doing it wrong' or anything like that."

Cassie nodded. Her cell phone rang. She looked at it and frowned.

"Hello?" she listened to the voice at the other end and her face took on a surprised look.

"Carlos! Or should I call you Senator Rivas? My gosh it's been years! Decades!" She pointed at the phone with an astounded expression.

Linnie and Zach looked at each other and shrugged.

"Thank you, Carlos. It has been difficult, but I have wonderfully supportive friends and I'm doing okay, I think." She paused and listened for half a minute. "Yes, I know you're probably pretty busy. Go ahead," she said, walking away toward her glass wall and looking out over the early evening cityscape. Ten minutes later, she hung up the phone and turned to Linnie and Zach, who had quietly cleaned up the dinner table and packed the dishwasher as they tried to hear what Cassie was saying.

"That was Senator Carlos Rivas! He wants me to testify in front of a Senate committee in September!"

"Wha-a-at?" Zach said, imitating a sitcom character.

Cassie smiled. "Yeah. Amazing, huh? I met Carlos during our college years when we were both interns in Washington DC. Linnie, I think I told you about him, but I don't know."

"Wow. Tell us about it now!"

"He has an online clipping service, I guess, and he got something today about my article and that other one, from the online edition."

"So what's his connection with it? Why'd he get it?"

"He's on the HHS oversight committee and he's ranking member on the subcommittee that oversees the FDA."

"Yeah?"

"They're going to hold a hearing on mass killings. Guns, drugs, the whole mess. Apparently people are asking a lot of questions, just like I am."

"So, when is the hearing?"

"Not 'til September when they're back in session, but I'm not doing it."

"What? Why not?" Zach asked.

"You know I can't handle public speaking. I took a 'D' in college because I couldn't force myself to just walk out on the stage and read a speech! And *that* audience was all friends! It ties me up inside, Zach. I just can't do it."

"Well, how did you leave it?"

"Carlos said thanks and to think about it and call him if I change my mind." She laughed. "Like *that's* gonna happen!"

EIGHTEEN
JULY 27, 2016. WEDNESDAY.

Wednesday already, Cassie thought, and drummed her fingers on her desktop. The newsroom was pretty quiet this time of day. She wouldn't be able to talk with Mrs. Wright until the publisher returned from vacation on Friday. She sat in her cubicle, idly reading the marching crawler on the TV screen above her. The President had said he would issue a four-point letter of intent regarding firearms laws. Just more political mud, she thought. The Mayor of Plano had announced a special weekend of band concerts put on by area high schools in honor of the all-star band. Various lawmakers had written op-ed columns or made speeches.

Her Sunday column needed to be written and submitted. She wanted to bring up the Scientology thing Richardson had hinted at, but wasn't sure how to do it. She couldn't just come out and say, "I'm not a Scientologist, and I'm not against all psychiatric drugs!" A bare statement like that would just sound defensive and wouldn't prove anything. Some people would probably think, wrongly, that Richardson couldn't have said that unless it was a fact. But there had to be a way to approach it that would weaken his case at the same time it strengthened hers.

She reached into her bag and pulled out a book, *Anatomy of an Epidemic*, opened it and looked through her notes, underlines and dog-eared pages. It occurred to her to search the index.

And there it was, *Scientology*. She turned to the pages that contained it and was soon immersed in the perfect source material for her column. And, as she read, an idea for the perfect slant popped into her head.

153

The mail boy, Ricky, arrived with a small bundle for her and laid it on her desk. She exchanged a few words with him and picked up the bundle, the usual mix of press releases, a couple of fan letters, and one plain business envelope that caught her eye. It had a name, "Tim Savage," but no return address. The postmark was from a non-local zipcode, on Monday.

She debated whether to open it, but she was caught up in her idea for the next column and would need to get it into the mill today. She folded the envelope and stuck it in her bag to read later.

The story of how the drug companies and quasi-public interest associations came together sounded to her like one of the outstanding marketing ploys of the century, and she hoped she could expose it and explain it so people would see how underhanded it was. She wished the *Daily Post's* readership of almost a quarter-million was a hundred times larger. This story needed to be exposed.

Three hours later, she had a draft of the column ready to send in. She printed and read it.

SSRIs and ALL OF US
By Cassie Stevens

I was surprised when my own article in last week's paper was rebutted by the CEO of a big pharmaceutical company. Who was I and our little daily paper, that the CEO of a Big Pharma company would bother to talk back? Did I strike a nerve? Had Mr. Justin Richardson ("JR") been piqued to the point of defensiveness?

In any case, I am glad JR chose to respond, because it has incited me to make this into a series of columns. I'd originally intended to do just one article on the subject of SSRIs and their implication in mass shootings. But Big Pharma doesn't want even a bit of light shone into its tight, dark community.

Today's article is a history lesson, a lesson in marketing brilliance and luck. It's about the four points of attack the psychopharmacology and biopsychology folks assembled in order to create the public's belief that SSRI antidepressants actually work as they claim to treat depression. (They never use the word 'cure.') Added to those four points, luckily for them, was a fifth influence that came out against the biopsychologists and by doing so, to their delight, helped them succeed.

Here's a brief timeline. (If you'd like to read more detail, and references, see *Anatomy of an Epidemic* by Robert Whitaker, and *Pharmageddon* by David Healy.)

It was 1951 when Congress gave doctors the privilege of prescribing drugs. This monopoly, extended to medical doctors and psychiatrists, defined the perfect market population for pharmaceutical companies. It took them twenty years, but they eventually stumbled on the seed of their success: they didn't necessarily need to change the public's mind, just doctors' minds.

In 1974, the American Psychiatric Association (APA) formed a task force to find out how important pharmaceutical-company support could be. Then, in 1980, they germinated an idea. Why not let pharmaceutical companies sponsor scientific symposiums to fulfill continuing medical education (CME) requirements for medical doctors and psychiatrists?

Within a few years, by 1987, the APA actually spoke of the drug makers as "partners in industry," and formed a PAC to lobby Congress. The PAC was funded by the drug companies.

This informal partnership let the drug makers legitimately train and pay speakers from leading medical schools to tout the benefits of their products at APA conventions. Academics and practicing professionals were (and still are) paid thousands of dollars per speech to tell their fellow psychiatrists that drugs were the answer to mental illness, primarily depression. The lecturers were termed "thought leaders," and those who rebelled and didn't toe (and speak) the company lines found themselves relieved of the opportunity, status, and extra stream of extra income Big Pharma had provided.

In another medium—medical and psychiatric journals—these "thought leaders" had their bylines placed along with other professionals on supposedly peer-reviewed articles that had actually been crafted by company-paid ghostwriters. These were note scientists, but technical writers, hired by the makers of whatever drug the article dealt with. The bylined professionals (and peers) usually had little or no input to the articles. Currently, some of the major journals are taking steps to curtail this practice.

The National Institute of Mental Health (NIMH), in the mid-1980s, began to back a new principle of biopsychology. It was spelled out in Nancy Andreasen's *The Broken Brain* (1984), and was the theory that depression was a disease resulting from a specific chemical imbalance in the brain. Andreasen claimed that it could now be treated and controlled, in the same way diabetes could be controlled by insulin. That her theory was never proven, didn't matter. (Note: To this day it still has not been proven.) But everyone was on the gravy train. It was political correctness, of a type, before that term was ever invented.

To backtrack a bit, another supportive player entered the scene, the National Alliance for the Mentally Ill (NAMI), an organization founded by two Wisconsin moms in 1979 and dedicated mainly to disproving the Freudian theory that mental illness came from bad parenting. The chemical imbalance theory was perfect for their purposes. NAMI's following grew quickly as people joined, tossed Freud aside, and adopted the "disease theory" of depression and mental illness.

For the other three, the APA, Big Pharma, and NIMH, the addition of NAMI provided a needed moral component. After all, nobody cares more than a mom, right? The "four-part harmony," as Robert Whitaker terms it in his book, was all on the same page, and their music was a moderate hit.

However, over twenty years of research at that point still had not proven their theory that depression, for example, was caused by a chemical imbalance in the brain. Those same twenty years of research, on various drugs in scores of studies and clinical trials, had in fact shown that the drugs were only a scant few percentage points better than placebos at treating (not "curing") some mental problems. And even those few percentage points could easily be explained by the fact that a placebo effect was also present when the actual drugs were being administered. (Placebo effect is the positive change resulting from a patient's expectation that the treatment will work or is working.) Even NIMH researchers had stated in print: "Elevations or decrements in the functioning of serotonergic systems per se are not likely to be associated with depression." In other words, more or less serotonin wasn't truly certified as a cause of depression. Never has been. (In fact, drugs increasing and drugs decreasing serotonin, in separate clinical studies, had been shown to affect depression to the same degree. Placebo effect?)

Clearly, the bio/psych coalition still needed something to help sell their biopsychology claims to doctors, those trusted individuals who could distribute their products to the medical profession and to us.

So, imagine their glee when, out of the blue, a major antagonist entered the story—a "common enemy," as it were. A religious sect. "Scientologists," a group founded in the early 1950's by a science-fiction writer named L. Ron Hubbard, whose theory was that our world was originally populated by souls who had come here from somewhere out in space. The Church of Scientology had, in 1969, helped establish an association of their own to fight the drug makers: the Citizen's Commission on Human Rights (CCHR). The group came out publicly against the scientific claims of the APA, NIMH, NAMI and PhRMA (Pharmaceutical

Research and Manufacturers of America), now at www.Phrma. org.

As Robert Whitaker writes in *Anatomy of an Epidemic*, "At that moment, Eli Lilly and all of psychiatry had achieved a public relations victory of lasting importance." The scientific-sounding groups came out on top. When an organization that believed disembodied alien souls founded our race came out against the coalition's supposed science-based theory, the latter was the obvious choice.

Fluoxetine, under Eli Lilly's brand name Prozac®, sold a billion dollars worth in 1992, despite the fact that, in 1991, an FDA Advisory Committee heard hours of testimony linking fluoxetine to suicide. A national Prozac® Survivors Support Group had even formed in 1990. Videos of Senate hearings are still available on YouTube. One, from 1991, is an example of the FDA's lack of response to real-world individual problems and its reliance on advisory committee members who are paid by the drug companies. *(https://youtu.be/Om2J9g-ssKo)*

But, thanks to CCHR and their blundering attacks, the drug folks and the doctors who supported them were the winners.

From that point on, in the medical establishment and the public's minds, the future of biopsychiatry, the medical model of mental illness including mental health through drug treatment, was secure. Even with all its warts and inconsistencies, all the research showing clinical trials to be biased, journal articles that were faked, deaths in trials hidden and mislabeled, etc., the view that Big Pharma had the right answers was secured in the public mind.

And that's how it still is, today. That's why JR made a thinly veiled insinuation that I might be a Scientologist: to discredit me, at least in this context. By the way, for the record: I'm not, never was; I don't even know anyone who is a Scientologist. Not that it matters. But that's how Big Pharma rolls: "Don't debate the facts, just discredit and destroy the messenger." It's a familiar ploy these days.

Send me your reactions: cass@cassiestevens.net.

Cassie went back to the paper's editing system, made a few changes, crossed her fingers and clicked submit. Mrs. Wright might protest, but if Tom Hammond approved it, it would be printed before she returned.

NINETEEN
AUGUST 1, 2016. MONDAY.

The hospital cafeteria buzzed with lunchtime business. Linnie had just finished reading Cassie's article.

"It's good, Cass. *Really* good."

"But Linn, I'm still amazed at all of this! How come it's not better known?" Cassie said.

Zach nodded until he could chew and swallow his bite of turkey sandwich. "No kidding, this stuff is unbelievable! I was reading about their marketing strategies, and, tell you the truth, they are geniuses! My gosh, it's taken some time, but they have the whole world thinking their drugs are the only answer! Incredible!"

Linnie reached for the pepper and held it over her salad as she answered. "Yeah, and maybe you read that in countries where depression cases are just as numerous, but they don't have these 'beneficial' drugs, the depressions pass in a few months. They aren't debilitating for life, the way they are here. It's like the old days."

"What do you mean, 'the old days?'" Cassie asked.

Linnie peppered her salad and smiled at a passing colleague. "People've always had depressions. They didn't always report them to their doctors. Maybe people were tougher then—I don't know—or maybe they just thought it was nothing a doctor could fix—but they got over their depressions and moved on. Oh, I'm sure a few didn't get over them, but if you accept that over ten percent of our population has depressions that should be treated, like the AMA says, then it was probably about the same before SSRIs came along."

"Why is that? I mean, why do people not just get over it now?"

"Well, first of all, depression is real. But now patients are told it's medical and then prescribed treatment. Their depression is rec-

159

ognized by their doctor, and a drug is prescribed. They expect to get better, but a lot of people don't, and the drugs cause additional problems. They're told the side effects are from the disease, not the drugs, and often the doctors increase the dosage, change the drug, or add another drug. Like, when an antidepressant causes anxiety, they'll prescribe a tranquilizer to offset it. It's called 'polypharmacy.' Pretty soon, they're taking several drugs to treat other drugs' side effects, and no one knows if it's the disease, or the drug! Sometimes it lasts for life, and makes their life shorter."

"Jeez," he said, shaking his head.

"Yeah," Linnie said. "Read *Dying For A Cure* if you can find a copy. Amazing story. It's all too common."

"So, what's the link with that and the shootings?" Zach asked.

"Nobody has established a perfect, direct connection, like, 'Take the drug and you go shoot somebody.' Huh-uh. There's just a certain amount of statistical correspondence, I mean, like the coincidence of SSRI drugs and the shootings in most cases."

"Tough to nail down, huh?" Zach said, laying his napkin down.

Linnie continued. "But, these kinds of mass murders aren't the only things that happen with antidepressants. A lot of so-called accidents and drunk driving incidents are connected, too."

"Really? Like what?" Zach asked.

"One example. Remember the crash that killed Princess Diana?"

"No! Really?"

"Yes. Really. Her driver had therapeutic levels of fluoxetine and high alcohol content in his blood. Three blood tests with the same results."

"Oh my gosh!" Cassie said, her eyes wide.

"That's right, Cass. It came out in a few journal articles at the time, but in the popular press, the driver was just called 'intoxicated.' Thing is, SSRIs potentiate the effects of alcohol."

"What? 'Potentiate?' "

"Yeah, the drug increases the effects of the alcohol." She set her napkin down. "SSRI's are implicated in the rise of autism, too. There's a statistical connection."

"No!" Cassie said, frowning.

"*Yep*. Several studies have proved the link to autism, but the news media is so in love with their Big Pharma ad money, they won't touch it."

Cassie leaned back heavily in her chair and shook her head. "Just keeps getting deeper, huh?"

"Sure does. So keep writing about it! Your article was excellent. I wish I could've seen Richardson's face when he read it!" She frowned for a moment, then said, "Cass, there's something else you should write in an article."

"Tell me," Cassie answered.

"Have you run across the 'Learned Intermediary Doctrine' in your reading?" She waited as Cassie shook her head. "Okay, it's in one of David Healy's blogs. Just search for it on davidhealy.org."

"Well, tell me what it is, briefly."

"Okay, but I've got to get back to work pretty soon. Okay, uh, basically, it's a legal thing that protects drug companies from being sued for adverse drug effects, in most cases."

Cassie stared at her and sighed.

"I know. They're slick. This legal principle basically says that the doctor is a 'learned intermediary' between the patient and the drug company, and he or she is the one who can be held liable for a patient having a reaction. So, sometimes, the patient can sue the doctor but not the drug company. They *say* that they warn the doctors, but you show me a doctor who has time to read and research those forty-page drug labels, and I'll show you one without many patients. Anyway, look it up on Healy's website."

"I will," Cassie said. "My god, it's all so hard to digest!"

Linnie leaned back in her chair. "Yeah. Speaking of digestion— Zach, how did you like our hospital food? Not bad, huh?"

"Too healthy for me," Zach said, smiling.

"Ha!" Linnie laughed as she stood. "You guys take care, okay? I'll talk to you soon." She patted Cassie's shoulder as she left.

Cassie watched her go, then turned to Zach as they both rose from their chairs. "She's a great friend. Don't know what I'd do without her."

Zach smiled and nodded, put his arm around her shoulders and walked her out.

They swept onto the tollway back to Dallas as Cassie enjoyed the air conditioning in Zach's Lexus.

Her cell phone rang. "Hello?" she answered, not recognizing the number. She listened for a few seconds.

"Mr. Richardson! This *is* a surprise!" Cassie said as she gave Zach an amazed look. His eyebrows shot up.

Cassie listened, then said, "Really? Okay, I think tomorrow might be possible. What time would we be picked up? I'd like to invite a friend, a doctor, to come with me." She was shaking as she said it, but her voice sounded calm.

"I'm looking forward to it. Goodbye."

She clicked the phone off and looked at Zach. "Can you believe that? He's asking me to tour his company tomorrow!"

"You're kidding. Is that a good idea?"

"Heck, I don't know. Sounded like he wanted to be friends, or something. You know?"

"Right. Don't think so. Probably Sun Tzu, you know, 'Keep your friends close and your enemies closer.' If he does want to make friends, it's so you'll go easy on him in your column."

"Yeah." She looked out the window at the Dallas skyline ahead. "Oh, I've got to call Linnie and see if her schedule is open tomorrow!"

She dialed the phone and got Linnie. They talked for a few minutes.

"She's going to see if she can get someone on call for her tomorrow. She didn't have any surgeries scheduled. I hope she can go."

"Hey, I could go with you if she can't."

"You gonna be a doctor for a day?"

"You could explain it."

"*Ha!* Right!"

TWENTY

AUGUST 2, 2016. TUESDAY.

They landed at Houston International after a two-hour flight in the Provachem Gulfstream V. A Mercedes limo picked them up beside the plane and they rode silently for most of fifteen minutes from the airport to the Provachem campus.

Just as they came in sight of the buildings, Linnie leaned over to Cassie and said in a hushed voice, "Oh, by the way, while I was doing research last night I discovered something really interesting." Cassie looked at her. "Ready for this? One of Pefrexa XR's Phase Three clinical trials was done at my hospital before I got there. At Brookside."

"Really!"

"Yep."

Cassie looked at her, wondering what it might mean, and shook her head.

The flags of the United States and Texas flew from tall flagpoles in rose beds that extended along the sides of the long walk in front of the main building.

A tall, dark-haired thirty-something woman dressed in a perfect robin egg blue skirt suit with cream colored silk blouse arrived beside their car, a tablet computer clutched in her arm.

"Hello," she said as the driver opened their door, smiling, "I'm Charleen Garrison. I'll be helping you with your tour today." Her slight Texas accent was charming.

"Hi, I'm Cassie Stevens and this is Dr. Linnea Kennedy. We're here to see Mr. Richardson today—"

"Yes, thank you Mrs. Stevens. We're going to show you a short film about Provachem, and then I'll accompany Mr. Richardson

163

with you on a tour. Please follow me."

She turned and walked back toward the three-story glass façade of the main building, slowing her pace so as not to outdistance Cassie and Linnie. When they entered the building, a security guard had them sign the guest register. He gave each of them visitor's badges to wear.

Ms. Garrison waited, then asked them if they needed to stop in the ladies' room. When neither did, she ushered them into a side hallway, walked before them and opened a door with a sign that said, "Theater."

It was similar to screening rooms in movie studios, complete with plush carpet, five rows of eight deep leather seats arranged in tiered rows. She ushered them into the second row.

"Would you like some refreshments while you watch this? It's about fifteen minutes long."

"I'd like a bottle of water," Cassie said, and Linnie nodded that she'd have the same.

As the room grew dark, Miss Garrison brought each of them a cool bottle of Evian water, a crystal glass, and a napkin, smiled, and left.

The screen brightened, showing the same plane they'd just flown in taxiing to a stop. The door opened, steps were lowered, and Justin Richardson came down them, speaking as he walked, looking into the camera. His slim physique and tanned face made him look younger than his 52 years.

He rested one hand on the rail and looked into the camera. "Welcome! I'm Justin Richardson, Chief Executive Officer. Here at Provachem, we have a mission. It's a mission that's important to all of us, because we care about you." He stopped walking and the camera slowly zoomed in on his rugged face, providing a dramatic buildup for what he was about to say. His expression was disarmingly sincere.

"At Provachem, it is our quest to help every person who has ever experienced depression, and their loved ones. Come with me and see where we begin the process."

The professionally produced film took them into the main buildings, through the labs, and showed clips of trials, FDA inspectors, and ended with people's personal testimonies of how Provachem's drugs had helped them.

The lights came up in the room. Ms. Garrison came in and got them, and after a short elevator ride, they were ushered into Justin Richardson's opulent office.

He came hurrying around his desk and covered the fifteen feet to the door quickly. More handsome than he had appeared in the movie, he had a ready smile and friendly, engaging eyes. They never guessed that a half-hour earlier, he had been cursing to a subordinate about Cassie's column and was spitting mad and wishing the limo would crash with them in it.

He reached out and took Cassie's hand in both of his. "Ms. Stevens, Cassie, it is truly a great pleasure! Please call me Justin."

He turned to Linnie and said, "And Dr. Linnea Kennedy—'Linnie,' if I may? It's an honor! I am very glad to meet both of you. Please, take a seat and let's get acquainted. Do you mind if we use first names? Please call me Justin."

"Thank you, Justin," Cassie said, seating herself in a white leather chair and watching as Linnie was seated. She seemed suddenly stiff, somehow, in her manner.

"Can I get you something to drink? Water, coffee, tea …?"

"No, thank you," they both said, almost in unison.

He took a seat and looked directly at Cassie. "I won't mince words, Cassie. Your columns, especially yesterday's, were rather shocking. I believe you planted a couple of zingers there for me, didn't you?"

"Possibly. Mr. Richardson. I was doing my best to get across my true feelings about products like yours."

"Well, another zinger!" He laughed, then became serious. "Cassie, I am aware of your loss, and I realize that I can't begin to imagine how it feels. I understand your anger, especially if you thought that young man was taking a prescribed drug like the ones we produce." He leaned back in his chair and appeared to relax. "But, it is also clear that there are a number of things about this business, this industry, that you don't yet know, and I want to help you understand them while we're together today." He looked at Linnie and continued. "You would know, Dr. Kennedy, being a neurosurgeon, that the brain is a complex many-faceted organ, with mysteries we're still trying to unravel."

"Yes, it is that," Linnie said, but her closed body language reminded Cassie she was bothered by something. "I'd like to get to the point with a question to start. Tell me, uh, 'Justin,' exactly how your Pefrexa XR differs from Alexira Pharmaceuticals' Orensafam? And any of the other SSRIs? Please tell me how yours is different and why that's better, as you say."

"Well, Linnie," he scooted to the edge of his seat and leaned toward her, and Cassie noticed that she stiffened when he said her name. "You know, obviously, that SSRIs keep serotonin from being reabsorbed from the synapse as quickly as they are when the brain is, uh, 'sick.' That's the 'reuptake inhibitor' property. The difference between Orensafam and Pefrexa XR has to do mainly with the stage of reuptake when they work. Pefrexa XR works earlier and longer in the synaptic gap than Orensafam does. And I'm sure you know we couldn't have gotten a patent without substantial differences in our molecular structure."

"But, their effect is virtually the same?"

"No, ours is actually different. I would call it 'more active,' but that's probably not descriptive enough. To tell you the truth, Doctor, I am going to have you ask that question of one of my research neurochemists in a little while."

Linnie didn't respond, but turned toward Cassie. Her eyes held something—an irritation?—that Cassie couldn't figure out.

"But, Cassie," Richardson said, "the main thing I would like to accomplish today, and I hope it's your goal as well, is to reach some kind of an understanding so that you can be more accurate in your writing about what we do in this industry, and why."

"We'll see about that," Cassie answered. "But can we begin the tour now? I'd like to talk while we walk. And maybe you can fill me in while we go as to exactly how my writing has not been accurate? I'd love to hear that!"

"Certainly," Richardson said with a smile, missing or ignoring her sarcasm. He walked to the office door, leaned his head outside and then ushered the two women out. The statuesque Ms. Garrison led them all to the elevator and pushed the button.

The tenseness Cassie had expected during this visit didn't seem to be present—at least, not from Richardson. She wasn't warming up to him, but he wasn't irritating her, either. She decided that he was either not really bothered by what she had written, or he was as good an actor, or manipulator, as she'd ever seen. Maybe he was a sociopath, particularly skilled at ignoring and overcoming negative feedback from others. But as they walked and talked, his obvious pride in his company was genuine, and with good reason. It was a prosperous competitor in a tough and highly profitable industry.

But she couldn't figure out why Linnie seemed so tense, almost protective and defensive with everything she said. She wanted to ask about it, but didn't get a chance. Richardson seemed to notice too, but went ahead with his monologue about the company.

They walked down the same hallways and saw the same working labs that had been featured in the movie. Richardson even fell into the same rehearsed speech. After they'd seen a number of labs, Cassie spoke up. "Tell me, Justin, where were your clinical trials done on Pefrexa XR?"

Richardson smiled at her. "Our final one was done up in Oklahoma, at the university hospital. But one trial was done at Brookside, actually," he said, with a nod and slight bow to Linnie, "where you work, right Doctor?"

"Mm-hm," Linnie answered, distracted by something she was looking at in one of the labs. She turned to face him. "That one was unsuccessful, wasn't it, Mr. Richardson."

"Well, yes, it was. The CRO decided to end it because there were some irregularities." He turned to Cassie and continued. "We have the trials done by CROs—Contract Research Organizations. It's the standard procedure. We provide them with the parameters and primary goals we'd like to see, and they assist us in designing and conducting clinical studies to try to prove them."

"And your people aren't involved?"

"Well, I wouldn't say they aren't involved. Of course, we monitor the projects constantly and stay in touch with the researchers. And, as you know, the FDA has to approve the entire planned series of trials and methods before we can file the IND."

"IND?" Cassie asked.

"'Investigational New Drug' application. It outlines everything we propose to do to test the drug in each trial phase, and the FDA offers suggestions for the studies. After the IND is finalized, the FDA sits on it for quite a while—please excuse my sarcasm—and then gives the go-ahead. Years of complex trials follow. The CRO conducts them, but while they're going on, we monitor everything. After it's finished, we prepare the New Drug Application and they see the results of all the trials. It's all very closely watched all the way through."

Linnie spoke, "Yes, we know that. You said they see the results of all the trials, but that's not really the case, is it? In fact, I'd bet that the trial you abandoned at my hospital was never submitted to the FDA. Was it?"

Richardson looked at her, not smiling. "Well, no, actually. I mean, no, you are absolutely wrong about submission requirements. We are required to submit all of our trials, even the negative ones with accompanying explanations. But we must submit at least two trials where our product is more beneficial than the placebo we use as a control. And, Doctor, we pay dearly for the clinical trials. They're expensive, so naturally we like to see successful results. Regarding who pays for the FDA's work of checking the trial and doing the approval process, we actually pay the FDA's costs for that, too." He turned to Cassie again, and seemed to let go of the hard edge he'd been showing Linnie. "Under the first President Bush, '41,' the FDA was falling on hard times, so he allowed the agency to accept funding from drug companies for the approval process. 'User fees,' they're called. It's all legal and above board, and it pays for a big part of the FDA budget."

"So, your company pays the bills for the government regulatory agency that approves your products?"

"Well, yes, in a manner of speaking, Linnie. But I assure you, it is the standard practice in the industry."

"That doesn't sound like a good thing, either! 'Standard practices' in industries are usually there to benefit the industry, not the consumer. And the FDA certainly seems to favor pharmaceutical companies' wishes and welfare, don't they?"

"Just how do you mean that, Doctor?" He and Linnie were obviously conflicting for some reason, and Cassie could only listen and try to figure it out.

Linnie stared at him. "I believe the FDA is a little too fond of the money from Big Pharma, if I may use that term—" Cassie watched as Richardson's eyes narrowed, but he quickly faked a smile and tilted his head. "—I'm thinking of a memo that came out of the FDA some years ago." She looked directly into his face as she asked.

Cassie could only watch and marvel at her friend's tenacity. She clearly had a point she wanted to make, and she was going to force Richardson at least to address it.

He nodded, but looked away from her and waved a hand in the air. "I don't know, Doctor. There are many thousands of memos."

"This one made some waves; I'd be surprised if you are really not aware of it—from trials of one of your competitors?"

Richardson's eyes were riveted to Linnie's.

She continued. "The FDA had made a decision that results of clinical trials where the drug failed to beat the placebo should be kept from patients and prescribers of the drug. It was their official position and they knew it amounted to hiding important results from patients or prescribers. That might sound great to a drug maker, Mr. Richardson, but as a doctor, I would want to know if a drug failed to be better than a sugar pill."

Richardson, stepping back from Linnie, shook his head. His slight smile had become a frown of puzzlement.

Linnie pressed on. "But the writer of this memo was basically an early whistleblower, of sorts. He thought the patient and the prescriber should know that this drug—any drug—failed to prove effective in some of the clinical trials, but he was overruled by the FDA's upper echelons. And, he happened to be the Director of the FDA's Clinical Psychopharmacology office. You've not heard his name? Dr. Paul Leber?"

As she took a breath, Richardson looked at her, his eyes, even with hers, now cold and without courtesy. "That wasn't our product. So what is your point, Doctor?"

Linnie looked him directly in the eye. "No, that drug wasn't your company's drug. It was citalopram, another SSRI. But, I thought you said you were not familiar with the memo?"

Richardson turned away from her with a look of cold anger, but he quickly changed it to a more benign expression. The blood vessels in his tanned temples were throbbing. He held up one forefinger, stepped away and spoke to Ms. Garrison, who got her cell phone and made a call as she walked away down the hall. Then he turned back to Linnie.

"Doctor Kennedy, it seems you have a bone to pick with me, but I just want to show you the quality of our plant, here. Can we put off the debate until after the tour?" His voice was friendly enough, but his body language was aggressive. To Cassie, he seemed like a man who was not accustomed to being challenged.

Richardson opened the door to one large room where offices lined the walls, and cubicles filled the center area. The only sound was a low buzz of conversation from people on telephones. As they walked, he explained, "This is our CRO Liaison section, where we keep tabs on what's happening in various clinical trials. They're working hard up here because we have a new MAOI product that's soon completing Phase Three trials. We expect to file the final application on it within a few months." He continued down a long row of offices and cubicles.

As they passed one office, Cassie noticed a name plate on the door where an overweight fiftyish man with a graying crew cut talked on the phone. The nameplate read, "Tim Savage, Director." He looked up as they passed, and Cassie thought she saw a glimmer of recognition on the man's face, but she smiled and didn't acknowledge it. His name seemed familiar, but she didn't know why.

She was beginning to say something about it to Linnie when Richardson said, "I'm sorry, lousy timing!" He reached into his vest pocket and pulled out his cell phone. "Can you excuse me for a moment? I have to take this."

As he walked away, Cassie turned to Linnie. "I didn't hear his phone ring. Did you?" She forgot about Tim Savage.

"Ha—no. Could've been on vibrate."

"Yeah. Could have."

"What's going on here, Linn? Are you okay? You seem kind of worked up with this guy."

"Yes, ma'am, I am. I'll tell you why later. But, just don't trust him or anything he says."

"Okay. I won't, didn't anyway."

Richardson walked back toward them. Cassie noted that Ms. Garrison had joined them once again. Richardson spoke to her, then turned to Linnie and Cassie. "I am very sorry, but I must bring this to an early close. I have a minor emergency to attend to. You're welcome to stay and have lunch in the executive dining room; I had planned on it, but I can't be there. You're welcome to come down again, soon, in the jet—"

Cassie looked at Linnie, then said, "I think we'll just head back to Dallas. I hope your minor emergency gets taken care of." She smiled and held out her hand.

"Thank you, Cassie. I look forward to your next column—interesting stuff! And Linnie, I'm sorry we couldn't continue our talk, but perhaps we'll get another chance?" He shook her hand as he spoke.

"I hope so, Justin." None of them missed her challenging tone.

Richardson hesitated, then smiled, nodded and spoke to Ms. Garrison, who pulled out her own cell phone and ordered their car to meet them at the front entrance.

They took the elevator and emerged at the side of the huge lobby. "Do you need to stop before we get you back to the airport?" She gestured toward the ladies' room.

"No. Thank you, Ms. Garrison," Cassie said. "I've watched you and I am amazed at your skill at seeming aloof while you hear every word that's being said. You're very good at it."

The woman smiled. "I believe your car is arriving outside."

The plane accelerated and leapt into the air. Both of them relaxed while the flight attendant offered them a snack and drinks. Cassie opted for a bottle of beer, while Linnie ordered a glass of white wine.

Cassie spoke first. "I'm surprised he didn't say anything specific about the column."

"He's absolutely a confirmed narcissist. He probably didn't even think of it. Besides, I'm afraid I didn't give him much of a chance. Sorry 'bout that."

"Yeah. What was that all about? You had a burr under your saddle almost from the beginning back there with Richardson. What was going on?"

She took a sip of her wine before answering in a hushed tone. "You know how he called me 'Linnie?'"

"Yeah, we call you that. I had an Aunt Linnie, once. So what?"

"You're right, sweetie. But only you and Zach call me that. Nobody else but you and my family have ever called me that. One other person I can think of, until we had a serious professional disagreement, ever called me 'Linnie.' Dr. Krishnamurthy, our head pathologist, the guy who did the middle of the night autopsy when he shouldn't even have been in the hospital, and then let Hoff's toe tag get switched with a cremation case."

"Well, that's interesting!" Cassie sipped her wine.

"Yeah. You know what it probably means, right?"

Cassie's mouth fell open as she inhaled sharply. "That Krishnamurthy knows Richardson? Do you think—?"

"I don't know for sure, Hon, but he might be involved, I'm sorry to say. I was a little bit suspicious, after what happened to Hoff. We're just gonna have to find out!"

TWENTY-ONE
AUGUST 2, 2016. TUESDAY.

Linnie left Cassie at her building and headed to the hospital. Traffic was light for a change going north on the tollway, and she was able to think. First, it was clear to her that Krishnamurthy was somehow connected to Richardson. And that meant that his autopsy results couldn't be trusted. She didn't know if she should talk with Randall Chase about it, or not, though it took only a few seconds for her to decide against it. Chase would not want the bad publicity, in the interest of "protecting Brookside Hospital's good name." The press wasn't curious, and the police weren't either. The papers and media had accepted Krish's story and termed it an "innocent but serious error." It has cost Krish his Deputy County Coroner standing. She thought that was probably good enough for Chase. Better a stupid mistake than an unlawful act, at least for the hospital.

But the second thing was, why in heaven's name would Krishnamurthy be helping Richardson, anyway? She'd discovered that Krish was involved during his residency in the failed clinical trial for Pefrexa XR at Brookside, but that wouldn't mean he would ever cross paths with Richardson at all. She was mystified and angry.

She soon turned into her parking space near the ER entrance of the hospital and went in. The admissions board showed she wasn't needed in a scheduled surgery at any point, though an emergency could always come in. As she approached her office door, she noticed that the light was on inside, and didn't think she had left it that way. The door wasn't locked.

She opened it slowly and saw immediately that her computer was out of position and the screen was on, but blank. Her skin prickled. She peeked around the door, then stepped in and looked around the room to make sure nobody was there. She went to the keyboard and entered her password. But when she hit return, the blank screen reappeared. Nothing happened. She tried again and got the same result. She pulled the door shut and walked to the nurse's station.

"Terrell?" she said as she approached the desk.

The young attendant, still in training, turned to her. "Yes ma'am, Dr. Kennedy?"

"Did you see someone go into my office?"

"Oh, yeah. The IT guy was here. He needed to look at your workstation for regular maintenance, so I let him in."

"Did he have credentials?"

"Yes ma'am. Had a photo and all that. Probably can see him on the videos." He gestured toward the cameras in the hallway.

"When was that?"

He looked at the wall clock. " 'Bout a hour ago." His face took on a worried look. "Did I make a mistake?"

"No, not at all. Thanks." She walked slowly back to her office, opened the door, held it for a moment and then decided she should do her rounds first. Three patients would be expecting her. She thought about calling the IT department, but that could wait until later.

Rounds took longer than expected. She looked at her phone—three-fifty. As the elevator doors opened at the second basement level, she hurried down the hall to the IT office and was gratified when the doorknob turned.

The department manager, a rotund and dour man with black-rimmed glasses, looked up from a large sandwich and a pile of potato chips on his desk.

"Hello, I, uh, need to find out about my computer?"

"And, you are—?"

"Linnea Kennedy, from ER." She held out her ID badge for him to examine.

"Okay, doc. What's the problem?"

"Someone came to do maintenance on it, and now it's blank. It just doesn't do anything."

"Did ya try to reboot it?"

"Well, no. But—"

"Okay." He picked up a clipboard. "Nobody's been doing any maintenance today, Doc. Sorry." He looked down at his sandwich.

"My nurse told me there was a guy with credentials, so he let him in."

"Well, he wasn't from here."

Linnie just stared at him.

"I don't know what to tell you, Doc. He wasn't from here and I don't know who the guy might've been. So—"

"So, you don't care, do you?"

"Well, I can't do anything about it. I think you oughta call security."

She stood and stared at him.

He stared back. "Look, Doc, I don't know who that was. I've got a lot of work here, if you don't mind." He looked down at his sandwich again, then started to reach for it.

"Yeah, okay. I—okay." She was perplexed, but she realized now that her computer's hard drive had been tampered with by someone. But, why? She left the office and headed for the elevator.

It would have to have something to do with Hoff. What else could it be? And, who? She entered the elevator, stood looking at the floor for a few seconds, then blocked the closing doors and went back to the IT area.

The man looked up again from the unbitten sandwich in his hands as she opened the door again.

"Hmm?" He grunted and spoke. "What now?"

"You keep copies of documents, right?"

"Sure."

"I need a printed copy of the pre-surgery blood and toxicology report on a patient."

The man set his sandwich down, sighed and rose slowly, walked to another desk and sat down in front of a computer screen and keyboard. "Okay. This one of *your* patients?"

"Yes. His name is John Allen Hoff. Date of the surgery was June 27."

"Oh, yeah, *that* guy. Gimme a second." He tapped a few keys, peered at the screen then turned to her. "You're Doctor Kennedy, right?"

"Just like a few minutes ago." She held out her badge so he could see her photo.

He pressed a key. "Okay. Printing." He reached over and took several printed sheets and handed them to her.

She flipped to the last sheet, where any additional information such as drugs in the blood would have been recorded. All the lines there were blank.

"This is the only copy of this?"

"Don't know, doc," he said, sighing and glancing over at his sandwich. "Lemme look." He typed some more and looked at her. "That's the original copy. No others."

"How about the same patient's autopsy report?"

"Date?"

"June 28."

"You want it printed too?"

"*Yes*, please," Linnie answered, trying to maintain her patience.

The printer spat out eight pages. Linnie accepted them. "Thanks for your help."

"Sure," he said, sitting back down and turning his attention toward his sandwich.

She put her hand on the doorknob, then was struck by an idea. "Say, do you by any chance keep copies of surgery videos?"

His impatient answer came back. "Yes, we do. Every one of them."

"So you'd have June 27? John Hoff's surgery?"

"Like I said. Every one of 'em."

Nervous excitement rose inside her. "Can I get a copy of it?"

"I'll send it to your workstation."

"Uh, not working, remember?"

"Oh. Okay," he grunted as he went back to the other desk, reached sideways and opened a drawer, pulled out a small metal flash drive and inserted it into the computer. He typed a little bit, clicked his mouse, and looked at her. "Okay. 'June 27. Hoff, JA Surgery.' Uh, you want both the files in the folder?"

"Both? Oh my gosh, that's right! *Yes!* Both of them!"

He gave her a frown, shook his head slightly, clicked the mouse, leaned back in his chair, and waited. While the videos copied to the flash drive, he looked again at his sandwich on the other desk.

"Okay. Done. Here," he said, pulling the small drive from the USB slot and thrusting it toward her.

Linnie reached out and took the little drive. "Thank you! You don't know how helpful this will be!"

He faked a smile and nodded as she turned, opened the door and left. Her excitement began to grow as she turned toward the elevator, and she laughed out loud when she heard the dead bolt click on the IT door. She could picture the man lovingly reaching for his sandwich. She couldn't help but picture the traitorous overweight lab technician in the movie, *Jurassic Park.*

She got her laptop computer from the trunk of her car, returned to her office and locked her door. The computer started up quickly and she inserted the small drive, copied the videos to her hard drive, and pulled the flash drive out and stuck it in a pocket.

She opened the files on the computer. The two videos were labeled as *HoffJohnA_01_06.27.16_LKennedy.mp4* and *HoffJohnA_02_06.27.16_LKennedy.mp4*. She had completely forgotten that a second video, a static overall shot from behind the surgeon of the surgical team working, was always recorded, beginning when the surgeon entered the room. Randall Chase had ordered all surgeries video recorded following a costly suit the previous year.

She opened the first. It was the surgical field with everything draped except Hoff's head. It didn't show what she wanted to see.

She hoped against hope as she opened the second video, and there it was. She gasped as she saw it.

"*Busted!* Ha! *Ha!*" she exclaimed at the computer screen, her fists raised in victory.

She dialed Cassie's number. No answer. She trembled as she left a message. "Cassie, it's me. I know it's gonna be late, but I'm coming to your place after work tonight. Get Zach there too! Don't worry, it'll be worth it. I'm bringing a little flash drive with me—or should I say 'the smoking gun.' I'll be there a little after ten."

She checked the time. Just after four-thirty. She thought about calling, then decided that if Krish was there, it would be best to surprise him.

Her office door locked, she grabbed some printed pages, hurried to the elevator and pressed the button for the second basement.

This time, she bypassed the IT door and walked quickly to the Pathology Department.

Doctor Krishnamurthy didn't see her enter. As one of the other doctors glanced at her, she pointed toward the department head's office and walked in. When he turned toward her, he frowned.

"Hello, Doctor," he said, standing as she entered.

"Doctor Krishnamurthy," she started, "I had my office computer vandalized today."

"Oh? Oh my!" he answered, motioning her to a chair and sitting back down behind his desk.

She shook her head and stayed standing. He rose to his feet again.

"Yes. They erased my computer hard drive or something."

"Oh?" he said, tilting his head, "That is a shame. But they have copies, do they not, in the computer department?"

"Yes, they do. I've just come from there. Doctor, would you look at this pre-surgery blood screen report and tell me if you think it is complete?"

He accepted the two sheets of paper she thrust toward him, looked them over and met her eyes. "Yes, they are complete, if I remember correctly."

"Nothing missing that should be there?"

"No, nothing missing."

"What about the 'chlorpenframine ETL' notation that was originally included there?" She pointed toward the papers in his hand.

"No, I think you are misremembering something, Doctor. There was no other substance found in this patient's blood."

"Oh, but I must argue, Doctor! There most certainly was a notation that chlorpenframine was present on the original report."

"I am sorry, but you are mistaken. This *is* the original report, here in my hand."

Linnie was amazed at what a brazen liar the man was. She wished she could read faces better, but she didn't need to. She knew he was lying.

"Doctor, I want to know what your connection is to Provachem Pharmaceuticals."

Krishnamurthy appeared to lose his footing for a second and leaned over with his hands on his desk. When he laid the sheets of paper on the desk close to her, his hands trembled. His voice was shaky. "I have had only the connection to a clinical trial for one of their drugs, when I was a resident some time ago."

"You don't know Justin Richardson?"

"Who? Oh, yes, he is the president of the company? Yes, I think that is his name. No, I do not know him."

She had known he was definitely lying about the blood report, and she knew that he had to be lying about Richardson.

"Doctor Krishnamurthy, why did you switch those tags on John Hoff's body?"

"Oh, my goodness, Dr. Kennedy, you are going much too far now. It was an error. Nothing more. I do not know what it is you are trying to imply."

She could have sworn that his dark Indian complexion had changed. Was some of the color leaving his face?

"Krish, how could you do this? I went to the IT department, and now I have on my laptop computer two videos of John Hoff's surgery. One of them shows the live camera feed of the tox screen you sent to me for the surgery—the real original blood report, including your tox lab's notation of 'Chlorpenframine ETL.' "

He stood still, staring at her with a shocked look.

She turned toward the door, then turned back. "Doctor, if I were you, I would call a lawyer. Have a nice day." With that, she gathered the printed pages from the desk, spun on her heel and left.

Late rounds took longer than she expected. It was already ten-thirty. Cassie and Zach would be waiting for her. She considered calling but knew they wouldn't mind the wait when they saw the video.

After leaving a voice mail for the security people, she turned out the light, shoved her laptop into her shoulder bag, locked the door, and walked to her car. It was a warm, pleasant evening, so she opened the windows and let the air blow around her. She felt light, relieved, knowing she could now clear her name and probably provide enough evidence to get the police and FBI interested.

She had just pulled out of the hospital lot. A tenth-mile away, a stalled truck on the narrow onramp to the tollway stopped her.

Her door was yanked open. *"What the hell!"* She yelled as an arm reached in and grabbed her by the lapel. All she saw in the orange light of the high interchange lighting was a tall, lanky man's body, and a glimpse of a large white mustache in a skeletal face. Then she shrieked as a spray of something hit her eyes, stinging, burning.

"Help!" She tried to yell but couldn't get the word out as she tried to breathe through burning nostrils and lips and wipe away the stinging goo from her eyes. She felt a sharp impact on her neck, and another on her head. Not quite unconscious, she felt herself being pulled out of the car, and another heavy strike to her head. Then, she was falling, and blackness overtook her.

She never felt the rear tire of her own car as it rolled over her forearm.

TWENTY-TWO

Cassie looked at the clock. Just past eleven. She shot a worried look at Zach and dialed her cell phone. "Dr. Kennedy, please?"

"Dr. Linnea Kennedy? Who is calling, please?"

"This is Cassie Stevens. I'm a friend of Dr. Kennedy." She heard the phone muffled for a second, then a man's voice came on the line.

"Hello, this is Detective James Matlin, Plano PD. Who am I speaking to?"

"*Detective!* My name is Cassie Stevens! Dr. Kennedy is my friend! What's happened?"

"Ms. Stevens, there's been an incident, and Doctor Kennedy is here in the hospital."

"What was it? An accident?"

"No ma'am, she was carjacked. She was found about an hour ago on the tollway onramp."

"*Oh, my god!* Is she okay? I'm coming to the hospital!"

Cassie jumped up and got her shoes and bag. Zach had heard her on the phone. He was ready with the door open.

It was eleven-thirty when they turned into the parking lot. Cassie saw that Linnie's parking space was open and took it. At the reception desk inside, a nurse named Ellie, who Cassie knew, recognized her and motioned her over.

"Is Dr. Kennedy here? Is she okay? What happened?"

The nurse took a moment. "I know you're a close friend, but don't tell anybody I told you. She was carjacked and beaten, and her car is gone. She's unconscious.'

"Oh! Oh no!" Cassie shrieked. She started to cry.

"Can we see her?" Zach asked.

" 'Fraid not. Not tonight anyway. She's in surgery. Y'all sit down out there and I'll let you know when the doctor comes out."

Cassie wiped her eyes and leaned on Zach. "Oh, god, Zach, if she's not okay I'll die. I can't *stand* any more of this!"

"We have to wait. We just have to wait," he answered as he guided her to a chair.

Minutes later, a man approached them as they sat. "You know Dr. Kennedy?"

They both looked up and nodded.

"I'm Detective Matlin, Plano PD," he said, holding out an ID with a photo that accurately depicted his bulldog face. "You're friends of Dr. Kennedy?"

"Yes," Zach said, "you spoke to Cassie, here, on the phone."

"Right. I was close to the hospital, so I took the call. I can't tell you much, but this just looks like a random carjacking. Nice car, late at night, a woman alone. But, still, do you know of anyone who might've wanted to hurt Dr. Kennedy?"

Cassie dried her eyes. She didn't want to say anything she couldn't back up, even though she suspected that Richardson was behind it. "No. She never mentioned anyone she'd had a hard time with. She's a brain surgeon, who'd want to hurt her?"

Matlin shook his head and shrugged. "There was a witness—he was in the car right behind her. Hospital employee. Called it in and talked to me a little bit when I got here. Saw the whole thing. Good thing, too. She could've been run over by somebody else since she was in the middle of the ramp. But he said the truck that was blocking the onramp started up and drove away while the attack was happening; sounds like it could've been a setup, you know? Said the guy came up to the driver's door. Real tall, skinny, had a white mustache. Walked kinda unsteady like his knees didn't work so good."

Cassie looked up at him.

"Someone you know?" the detective asked.

"No, maybe, but I don't think so. I don't know who he is but I might have seen him before. I don't know. Everybody seems tall to me."

"You don't know a name?"

"No. I don't. I wish I did."

"Why d'you—where do you think you've seen him?"

"I'm not sure. Maybe here at the hospital when my son was here." A catch in her throat made her realize with a stab of guilt she had momentarily not thought about Mark. "I thought he was a doctor, but I don't know who he really is at all."

Matlin frowned. He stared at her, then relaxed. "Okay, you need to give me your contact information, okay? In case something else comes up."

"Sure," Zach said, and told him their names and contact numbers.

"Here's my card," the detective said. "If you think of something else, you let me know. I'll be in to see Dr. Kennedy after she's awake." With that, he walked away, spoke to the nurse, Ellie, and then left.

Cassie sat and shook her head slowly, her eyes closed.

Two hours later, Cassie had fallen asleep. Zach woke her when a surgeon in scrubs walked out. He talked with Ellie for a moment, then came over and introduced himself as Dr. Hellem.

"She's alive, but she has had a head injury, concussion, laceration to the skull and a serious epidural hematoma."

"What's that?" Zach asked.

"It's a result of the trauma to her head. It's a buildup of blood between the skull and the outer membrane of the brain."

"Will she be okay?"

"It's too early to tell. We put her into a coma—"

"Oh, god! A *coma*?" Cassie whispered.

He nodded. "We did a small craniotomy—an incision in her skull to drain the blood and relieve the pressure—but we won't know anything for sure until tomorrow at the earliest. We think she got in here quickly since it was a hospital worker who saw the attack and called the ER direct, and that can make all the difference."

"So, she might be all right?"

"I can't say right now. We'll have to get the brain swelling reduced. We'll monitor her closely. She'll be in an SICU room within about three or four hours, then ICU after that."

"Why so long?" Zach asked.

"She's still in surgery. The car's wheel ran over her forearm; the nerves in her arm and hand might be damaged. "

"Oh, *no!*" Cassie said, her eyes tearing, "Her career, her work! It'll *kill* her if she can't do surgery anymore!"

Hellem looked at the floor and sighed. "Dr. Kennedy's a gifted surgeon and we're all doing everything we can. I'm sorry I can't give you more information." He tried to smile, then turned and left.

"Those sons of bitches!" Cassie hissed at the floor. As she leaned over, Zach put his arm around her shoulders. She trembled with anger as her tears fell. "That guy with the mustache. He sounds like the same guy I saw—that last night—" She dropped her head into her hands.

"Cass—" Zach started, but had nothing to add. He waited several minutes.

She gasped and sat up suddenly. "*Zach!* We've got to find her clothes. Linnie always stuck little things in her pockets! She said she had a flash drive. She would've—oh, gosh, Zach, maybe she stuck it in her pocket—?"

"But they won't let us go through her pockets! Where would her clothes be anyway?"

"I never thought I'd need to know this, but they brought some of Mark's clothes—" she stopped and took a deep, halting breath "—Mark's clothes to the room in the SICU and put them in a cabinet beside the closet, in a plastic bag. Maybe they'll do the same thing."

Zach nodded. "Maybe."

Cassie walked to the counter and spoke to Ellie. It was a five minute conversation, but at the end of it, Cassie turned to Zach and motioned for him to follow her to the SICU waiting room.

Thursday's sun was just rising when they brought Linnie into the SICU room. Cassie was glad it wasn't the same one Mark had been in. Zach had slept but Cassie hadn't tried. She wondered what the "smoking gun" might be that Linnie had talked about—a video of the fake doctor in Hoff's room?

The nurse told them they could go into her room for just a couple of minutes. Zach rubbed his eyes as he tried to wake up. Cassie took his hand and led him around the corner into the same area where she had spent the worst two days of her life. The heavy hopelessness returned, but this time mixed with fuming anger. When they walked into Linnie's room, Cassie could no longer contain her emotions. She broke down and sat on a chair beside Linnie's bed. It was just like the room had been when she was with Mark, twilight with only a dim light panel above Linnie's bed, her slim body covered with the same light green blanket, the same machines providing dimly glowing numbers and lines.

Linnie's right arm from shoulder to fingernails was wrapped in a large bandage, immobilized. Around her head was a dressing somewhat smaller than Mark's had been, but still shocking in its similarity to his. Cassie winced. She could hardly believe this.

As soon as the nurse left, Zach stepped across the room and opened the drawers and cabinet beside the built-in closet. There, at the bottom of the closet, was a large clear plastic bag with a bundle of clothing—Linnie's charcoal gray pantsuit and shoes.

"Cassie," he said.

She turned and looked toward him.

"You search, Cass. I'll go ask the nurse some questions."

Cassie nodded and knelt down beside the closet, wiping away tears. As he walked out, she opened the bag. The pants of Linnie's suit had no pockets. The jacket was at the bottom and felt gritty with gravel and dirt from the road. It had a breast pocket and two small side pockets. She searched them all.

Nothing.

She slumped in despair and began to put the clothes back.

Then she remembered. Men's suits, she knew, always had an inside pocket. Maybe... She reached into the small jacket and felt around. There it was. A tiny pocket that held a wadded-up tissue. She pulled the tissue out. Nothing else was there.

She sighed and gave up. It was too much to hope for anyway.

Zach coughed and cleared his throat. She stuffed everything back into the bag and closed the closet. She had hardly made it to Linnie's bedside when Zach and the nurse walked in.

"You'll need to leave, now. If you'll give me your contact information, I'll give it to Dr. Hellem."

Cassie slumped. She didn't know what to do now. Linnie had been her rock, her guide. She couldn't lose her now to these bastards.

Zach put his arm around her shoulders to comfort her and his gesture made her eyes fill again. Linnie's tissue was still in her hand. She raised it to her eye to dab away a tear and felt something small and hard inside.

A chill went through her as she unwrapped the tissue and found a thin black metal object not much larger than a thumbnail—a tiny metal USB flash drive.

They hurried home, but it was still almost an hour later when they reached Cassie's condo. When they plugged the tiny drive into Cassie's laptop, they found only two files on it. Zach was angry after they watched the videos. "Movies of John Hoff's surgery? What does this have to do with anything? They almost killed Linnie for *these*?"

Cassie was exhausted and puzzled. "Let's watch 'em again," she said, and clicked the file name for the first one. It was simply a view straight down from the ceiling to the operating field, showing Linnie's and the nurses' hands working on Hoff's head wound.

"Yuck," Cassie said and opened the second video. The view

from above and behind the surgeon showed Linnie's general motion, but obviously concentrated on the movements of the three surgical nurses. The operating field was not visible. The rest of the room seemed dark by contrast because of the brightness of the surgical lighting. On the far wall, a sliver of the bottom half of a video screen was barely visible.

"*Wait* a minute!" Cassie said, standing suddenly as the video continued to play. She paused the video. "Wait just a minute!"

She hurried over to her dinette table where papers and files were scattered. Among them was the large envelope Linnie had given her. She pulled out the contents, looked it over, and came back to the couch.

"What?" Zach asked. "What?"

"Look at this," Cassie said, restarting the second video. Her eyes brightened as the video continued to play. "Look! Right there! It only shows for a couple of seconds." She rewound the video and clicked *play*, then froze it. She pointed to the bottom of the screen on the wall.

"*Look!* It says 'chlorpenframine ETL!' Just what Linnie said! Look at this paper. It's the same report that they're supposed to be showing on that screen! The drug's not on the printed copy!"

Zach looked at the paused video, squinted, then looked at the paper. A glimmer of understanding began to appear.

"Zach, this is the drug Linnie told us about, remember? She couldn't prove it, but *this* proves it!" She let out a fast, deep breath. "Hoff had this drug in his blood when he came in for surgery, which means it was there when he attacked the band! This 'ETL' means 'extra therapeutic level'—that's what Linnie told me."

Zach just looked at her.

"Zach, don't you get it? This is Provachem's drug! This is Pefrexa XR! This is why they murdered Hoff and incinerated his body so fast! To hide the drug! Linnie had it right all along."

Zach fell back in the couch and mouthed the words, "Oh, wow!"

Cassie took a screen shot of the video frame showing the handwritten notation "chlorpenframine ETL" and saved it under the name "smokingun.jpg," then printed it, closed the computer and fell in a slump. She leaned over on Zach.

"Thank you, Linn! You *did* it!"

"Amen to that," Zach said.

"Oh god, Zach, I hope she'll be okay."

Zach nodded silently.

Cassie thrust her fist in the air. "And Mr. Justin Richardson, you crooked SOB, you are going *down!*"

TWENTY-THREE

AUGUST 4, 2016. THURSDAY.

The printed screen shot and the final toxicology and autopsy reports sat on Mrs. Wright's desk. She had listened to the entire story.

"This is from the video done by the hospital? Not edited at all?"

"Yes, ma'am. And I wouldn't know *how* to edit it. Would you like to see the entire video? Or both of them? I have them right here." Cassie held up the flash drive between two fingers.

"No, I don't think so. If you know for a fact that this is legitimate, that's enough. But what do we do with it?"

"Yeah, Cass," Tom Hammond said. "All it proves is there was a drug in John Hoff's system and that's not a crime. It doesn't prove anything."

"To me, knowing what I know, it's a motive for murder."

"What, Cassie," the publisher said, "to have a prescription drug in his blood would give somebody reason to murder him? I certainly think that's a thin theory!"

Cassie looked at the small drive in her hands. "Somebody went to a lot of trouble to keep this information hidden. Has to be a reason for that. I think after the police and maybe the FBI hears the whole story, I think they'll be interested!"

"But, Cassie, I don't think just having this information proves anything. And it *could* have been just an error in the lab, not getting it right in the first report." The old lady finished with a gentle smile.

"Look," Hammond said, nodding, "the only fact we know is that your doctor friend got carjacked right after she left work. The police are workin' on it, right?"

"Yeah," Cassie said.

189

"Well, they oughta find out somethin', anyway. They'll find her car, most likely, unless it's already in Mexico bein' made ready for resale."

Both women looked at him.

"Well," Mrs. Wright said, standing, "I don't think we can accomplish anything at this point. Stay with it, Cassie, and let us both know if you find out more." She turned away from them, then turned back. "Cassie, if this is true, then I made an error by asking Justin Richardson to do a companion article to yours. But it was my call at the time, and I felt—still feel—that I can trust him. But if I was wrong …"

"Ma'am, I don't think it matters now. If he's involved, we'll find out how. I'll keep looking."

She nodded. "Yes. Please keep me informed."

Cassie thanked her and left, Hammond going with her.

They got into the elevator before Cassie spoke. "Tom, I know this is just what Linnie called it—'the smoking gun.'"

"Aw, Cassie, this is just circumstantial evidence. You don't even have anybody to pin a murder on even if this *was* a smokin' gun! Nah, I think the old lady's right. This is nothin' by itself."

"By itself, yeah! But add that Hoff died in the hospital when he should've recovered, and autopsied while he was still warm? And then he was cremated by mistake? And Linnie being carjacked?"

"Well, maybe you're right. But you need to go investigate before we make this public, and we oughta wait for the police up in Plano."

She frowned at him and turned to go into the restroom. To her it was another piece of the puzzle. If the carjacker was the man she talked to in the hospital the night Hoff died, and if the carjacking wasn't a coincidence committed by a man who just looked like him—unlikely—then she still had a big question. How did they know Linnie had that video with the very evidence they had to hide?

When she got to her cubicle, she didn't know what to do. She was already within hours of her deadline. She had to do a column and had nothing ready. She opened her laptop and searched her notes on some of the books Linnie had provided and found a document that was much too long, but could be divided.

She began to work on it and within two hours, was rereading it before she sent it over to Tom Hammond.

THE CONSUMER AS QUALITY CONTROL
By Cassie Stevens

Do drugs cause violence? Is that a stupid question? Are you thinking, "Of *course* they do!"

However, you might be thinking of meth, PCP and other illegal drugs. Or maybe even alcohol.

But, you might *not* be thinking about prescription psychoactive drugs. Antidepressants. Doctors and psychiatrists routinely prescribe them to help patients cope with mental and emotional problems. These drugs are prescribed for depression, anxiety, schizophrenia, ADD, ADHD, bipolar disorder, etc. Their primary purpose is to affect the chemistry of the human brain.

But these drugs will have differing results in different people. Make no mistake, they affect us just as much as "street" drugs can. Their major points of difference from street drugs are that they are purer, and their dosages are better controlled. But, safer? Not necessarily so. (About 100,000 deaths per year in hospitals come from adverse effects of prescribed drugs. It's now accepted as the fourth leading cause of death in hospitals.)

You might ask: Prescription drugs, though, do go through a testing process, don't they? Aren't they certified "safe and effective" by the government before they can be prescribed? The best answer is, "Yes, but..."

Allow me to quickly describe the high points of the entire drug approval process, from discovery to prescription.

Once a new compound is discovered or created that might become a treatment for an illness or condition, the company files an "IND" (Investigational New Drug) application with the FDA. If that's approved, the drugs are tested by pharmaceutical companies under FDA rules. In "Phase One," they are first tested on animals. If they pass, they're tested in "Phase Two" on paid human volunteers to establish proper dosages and identify common side effects. After that, two "Phase Three" clinical trials (with the drug simply proving itself "better than a placebo") must be successfully completed. These include people with and without the illness the drug is supposed to treat. More than two trials may be conducted to get two successful ones. Eventually, if the drug company has demonstrated to the FDA that the tests were on the level, and the drug is shown to be both safe and effective to treat (not cure) the illness or condition, the FDA may accept an "NDA" (New Drug

Application) which, if approved, allows the drug to be marketed and released for doctors and psychiatrists to prescribe. Completing these steps can take years and cost over a billion dollars, and some drugs don't make it.

FDA approval, when it comes, powers up a marketing machine that has been continually fine-tuned since 1980. (See my previous column for a complete timeline.)

Pharmaceutical companies enjoy great benefits: Their products have the backing of our most trusted government agency (FDA), and their products are prescribed only by the medical establishment, made up of our trusted doctors and psychiatrists. Because of this, pharmaceutical companies are, by extension, trusted more than most other types of corporations; we buy and ingest their products almost without question when they are recommended by our doctor. But is our trust deserved? Please consider the following, particularly regarding the psychiatric drugs.

Let's start at the beginning, with the drug testing process.

The drug company's goal is to get its drug approved and on the market as quickly as possible. In this pursuit, it designs the tests and trials, and screens the people to be tested. When the trial results are good for the drug company, to get approval in most cases, they only need to show that the drug works marginally better than a "placebo," which is basically a "sugar pill" given to some of the test subjects who think they're getting the actual drug.

Often, the drug being tested is only *slightly* better than the placebo, that is, "a little bit better than nothing." Sometimes, it is only better by a tiny amount, like less than one patient out of ten. Theoretically, a phenomenon called the "placebo effect"—the patient's belief that he or she is being helped—will operate to the same extent for the placebo and the real drug, so there is no net gain or loss for either of them. But when a patient is actually feeling a change, the placebo effect can be highly magnified. This means a lot to drug makers, who rely partly on feedback from patients to gauge their product's effectiveness.

Now, if the drug company, through the Contract Research Organization (CRO) they hire to actually do the trials, comes up with just two trials showing its drug being "better than nothing," it creates and files its NDA, an extremely long and detailed application. The FDA's Center for Drug Evaluation and Research (CDER) begins to make its judgment.

Drug companies have been known to play fast and loose with results of clinical trials, too. Misreporting adverse effects is known to happen frequently. Surprised? You shouldn't be. (Just think of the potential profit involved.)

Now, how about the FDA approval process? The legal mission of the FDA is to approve drugs that are proven "safe and effective," and their further stated mission is to do it fast, which in government terms translates to "under twelve months." In their zeal to give a verdict quickly, the FDA trusts the drug maker to "tell the truth" in letter and spirit. For example: The FDA requires that the drug "pass" the tests, and that any Adverse Drug Reactions (ADRs) in clinical trials be recorded and reported. But there's the rub: some of the ADRs get "reclassified" by researchers, so they won't appear as a negative result. Suicidal thinking, for example, that had never been displayed by a patient before taking the drug, will often be called "emotional lability" (meaning emotions that are unpredictable and changeable), and the patient will be shown as a "drop out" from the trial. Ditto with suicidal, homicidal or violent ideation (thinking) or actions.

Because trials are short and don't use "real world" subjects (varied ages, varied physical conditions, taking multiple drugs), it is well known that, at most, 50% of the adverse drug reactions are discovered during the trials. Additional ADRs are then discovered by you and me, the "real world" quality testers, the patients who are prescribed these treatments during the new drug's first several years. (But, as with a new car, there can be problems! According to Dr. David Healy: "Drugs do a hundred different things but in a trial everyone is guided to ignore the ninety-nine other things and focus on just one thing—does this drug work for whatever it is *the company* is interested in." [Emphasis added])

Actual clinical drug trials normally last only a matter of weeks—ten weeks being an unusually long trial—so they simply don't reveal long-term effects, when in fact these drugs may be prescribed for lifetime use and often create a long-term dependency. Tests in controlled trials don't show what happens long-term, or how withdrawal, increase or reduction of dosage will affect a real patient. They also don't reveal effects on people with multiple diseases, or on people taking several drugs (termed *polypharmacy*). Even when the bad effects are major, they are left for unsuspecting "real world" patients (you and me) to experience and try to report. This is the case even though many psychotropic drugs are prescribed for an indefinite period, often for life. The extended use makes these drugs some of the most lucrative products of all. Conversely, this also explains why very few firms produce antibiotics. And why not? Simply this: Antibiotics *cure* illnesses, and their short-term usage doesn't yield enough revenue. Antidepressants, on the other hand, create dependency, and very high profit, for a long, long time.

Please send me your impressions: cass@cassiestevens.net.

Cassie finished her edits right at deadline and clicked the "submit" button. She could have provided references and footnotes but decided not to this time. She leaned back in her chair and thought about her situation. Here she was, a columnist for a small daily paper in a large metropolitan area, taking on one of the most powerful industries in the world.

It was foolish. She knew, from the many books she had read and the information she had found on the internet, that her task had been tried by others. But she was driven, compelled by a sense of— what? Duty? Fairness? Desire for revenge? Something to stave off her grief?

Nobody had ever prevailed to any great extent. Even in court cases. She thought about the Wesbecker trial Linnie had told them about and that she'd read about, where Eli Lilly & Company was sued, but their lawyers gamed the system and won, which kept other cases against them from being filed.

If that company would go to that length to win, what would Provachem do to her? And if they murdered Hoff, why wouldn't they come after her, too? After all, Linnie was in a coma with an injury that might end her career.

All this was done to protect a company whose drug might have had a hand in her son and dozens of other innocents being murdered.

No matter how she looked at it, though, she couldn't imagine that someone would do all of this when they couldn't be held responsible for what John Hoff did, even if he was taking their drug.

For now, the important thing was to fight the battle. Fight it to win. She might not, but she would fight anyway. She had to.

The office was quiet. Only a few people were working at this time of day. She decided she would go home, leaned over to pick up her bag, and saw the corner of a letter-sized envelope sticking out.

A wave of chills hit her when she made the connection. This was the connection to the name, "Tim Savage." The man she had seen at Provachem. Now she knew why he had looked at her as if there was some kind of recognition. She pulled it out and opened it.

It was a good thing she hadn't read it before they had met with Justin Richardson.

TWENTY-FOUR

AUGUST 4, 2016. THURSDAY.

"You're *sure* you got everything?" Richardson demanded.

"All but her."

"Dumped the car?"

The Russian nodded slowly, his blue eyes squinting against a bright Houston sun on the concrete parking lot.

Richardson took a deep breath and stared out the window. He had no idea whether the surgeon, Kennedy, had shared what she knew with her friend before Kardov got to her. He was pretty sure she hadn't gotten the actual video out.

"You will be paying me now." Kardov said. It wasn't said as a request.

Richardson looked at the man. As he reached down beside his seat to get the envelope, Kardov tensed, as usual, ready to draw his concealed gun if needed, or maybe a knife. In the envelope were five thick stacks of hundred-dollar bills, a hundred in each stack.

"Easy goes it, there," Richardson said, holding up his right hand. "Here's fifty. I might have another job in Dallas for you, so I want you up there again tonight."

"This is half. You owe more."

"I know," Richardson said, "but I don't have it right now. Don't worry, you'll get it. I have to be careful."

"Yeah, you *do*, Mister," Kardov said, nodding slowly. "You got to be very careful with me."

"Look, I don't like to be threatened—"

"You don't like? Don't *like*? You are a paper pusher with too much money. *I* don't like be used like a dog! You will pay me tomorrow, here, all of it, or *I* will do something. You understand, mister big executive?"

Richardson glared at him, but then looked away and nodded. "Okay. We'll do it your way. I'll meet you here the day after tomorrow, same time. I'll have the other fifty."

"Plus ten more for the waiting."

Richardson gritted his teeth, knowing this man could easily destroy him. Finally, he muttered, "Okay."

"Yes. That will be good. It is much a pleasure having your business." He laughed, opened the door, got his long legs out, stood and slammed the door. The envelope was quickly stuffed into his shirt.

Richardson spat out a string of curses as he started the car and slowly left the parking lot.

When she got home, Cassie had read Savage's letter again, then called Zach. He could help her decide what to do.

She opened the door and gave him a quick hug, then walked to the couch and picked up the letter.

"You need to help me figure out what to do about this—how I can use it," she said as she handed it to him.

He looked at her, raised his eyebrows and began to read.

"Mrs. Stevens:

I work at Provachem Pharmaceuticals.

First of all, please accept my deep condolences for your loss. I can't imagine your pain. These things should never happen to anyone. I'm so sorry.

The day of the shooting, I got a telephone call from Justin Richardson asking if John Hoff was in one of our Phase III clinical trials of Pefrexa XR, about two years ago. It was conducted through Brookside Hospital in Plano. (P-XR was approved and went to market in January of this year.)

Later that day, I heard about the shooting and the name of

the man who did it, John Allen Hoff. That gave me chills.

Your column mentioned Adam Lanza and Newtown. My cousin lives in Newtown and has a friend who lost her little boy in that shooting. We've talked about the drug angle a lot since then. I'm sick of being part of this. These drugs really are dangerous. I wish the world knew the truth.

I am very sorry about your son and all the other kids who were murdered. Please accept my heartfelt condolences.

Sincerely, Tim Savage"

"Wow, Cass. This is amazing. You think it's important?"

"Maybe. I don't know. I actually saw this guy during our little tour. He looked at me like he knew me but I hadn't even read the letter yet and didn't remember why his name was familiar."

"Well, this is good, right? The guy works for Provachem! You think he might have some info you could use?"

"I don't know."

"Well, it's a start, anyway, right?"

"Maybe. Maybe this guy's just a real feely type. The only thing he says in here is that he's 'sick of being a part of this.'"

"Of what?" he asked, walking to the couch and sitting.

"Like—heck, I don't know what. Maybe this company does more than the normal payola to politicians and bureaucrats. Maybe that's what he means?"

"Or maybe he knows something that could really help you?"

"Yeah. Maybe. Everything's a 'maybe.'"

She walked to the couch and sat beside him, taking the letter. "There's something else, Zach."

"What?"

"It's separate from the letter. That shrink I interviewed? He was Hoff's psychiatrist!"

"No!"

"Yeah. Hoff's mother told me. He was the shrink who prescribed

Pefrexa to Hoff!"

"Geez." He thought for a few seconds and took the letter back from her.

"When was this sent? There's no date on it."

"It was a real mailed letter. Here's the envelope. The postmark was July first."

"And you're just getting around to it? How come?"

"I stuffed it away and forgot it. So much sympathy mail, I just thought it was another one."

"Hmm. So, you told your bosses about the video?"

"Yeah."

"You gonna tell 'em about this, too?"

"I don't know. I probably ought to, but they were pretty 'ho-hum' about the video, so—"

"Really? They thought it was no big deal?"

"Well, they didn't think it was a smoking gun, like we did."

"Do they know about the whole thing? The way Hoff died, the fake doctor, all that stuff?"

"Yeah."

"Jeez. Cautious to a fault."

"Yeah. Remember, Mrs. Wright knows Richardson and even had him write that rebuttal. She probably wants to avoid anything that might give him a reason to sue her."

"He couldn't sue her just because his drug in a murderer's blood was made public, could he?"

"I don't think so. I don't know. But, Zach, I can't get up in her face about this! She's my boss and if I get fired, I lose my whole platform. I want the public to know about this!"

Zach fell silent for a moment, then said something almost in a whisper.

"What?" Cassie said.

"I said, 'There is another way.' " He turned and looked at her.

"What?" she asked.

"Call your Senator friend and tell him you'll testify. Lot's more coverage there than the *Daily Post* gets."

She looked at him and started to speak, but then stopped with her mouth open. Then she closed it and shook her head. "I *can't*, Zach—you know that! I can't speak in public!"

"Well, then, I guess you'll have to persuade your publisher to let you off the leash. You're letting your fear control you, Cass. That's not good."

Cassie frowned and sat up, turning to look at him. "*Dammit*, Zach."

"Dammit, what?"

"You're right. It's *not* good."

Zach had left to take care of Woof, his schnauzer. She had asked him to return and stay with her because she couldn't stand the emptiness of the place. Not that he was a substitute for Mark, but she was beginning to realize she wanted him in her life permanently. They slept in the same bed, but they didn't engage in any intimacy. She was glad Zach was understanding and supportive.

It was 5:30 a.m. Cassie had awakened at five, as usual these days, with the same shock of reality that woke her early almost every day. She sat down at her dinette table with her laptop open in front of her. Her well was dry. She had nothing to write, no thoughts that she wanted to share.

Zach had put his finger on her current minor problem. He'd said she was "afraid of being afraid," so she didn't want to accept what could be a rare opportunity for a journalist, to speak to a Senate committee about an issue that burned in her soul.

Just picturing taking an oath in front of a panel of US Senators, then sitting and answering their questions, gave her a chill and sick feeling. But she knew that her articles weren't reaching many people, and now, she had nowhere else to go with them. She had told the truth about the sham of the Big Pharma marketing scheme. She had exposed the inadequate testing of drugs prior to FDA approval. All she could do now was hope people would look into the issue for themselves. It was a matter now of quitting or barging ahead.

The larger issue, even bigger than the murder that took her own son, was the problem of prescription antidepressants. They were being marketed as a benign treatment that reduced the symptoms of depression and anxiety, yet in some people, they caused the exact opposite reaction. And sometimes resulted in violence and even death.

But aside from that, was she a coward in a situation that required real courage? She had asked that same question of a politician in a column some months ago. It came to her mind now, in regard to herself, and she decided to write her way through the dilemma, as she had done since she was ten. What was *she* willing to do to get these people who wanted to hide the real reason for Mark's murder?

She started typing.

COURAGE?
By Cassie Stevens

Many acts require courage. Risking one's life for others. Standing up for our rights. Fighting an attacker. Entering a burning building. Standing up to a bully.

And, there is the courage of going against one's own phobias, knowing that the fear will not subside and will likely become greater. This is a dilemma I, myself, now face. I've overcome certain things in my life and am still at war with others, but this fear of speaking in public is a phobic fear I've always had.

I've heard that the fear of public speaking is the number one phobic fear. (Number two is dying.) It's called *glossophobia*, and it affects 75% of women and 73% of men in the USA, according to the National Institute of Mental Health. So, that's basically three out of every four people.

Why has this even come to mind? Please bear with me while I tell you a story.

I recently received a telephone call from a man I met in during my college years, too many years ago. We were both interns in Washington, D.C., the same summer. He was a political science major and I was in journalism. We ran into each other in the coffee shop in one of the senate office buildings and he told me he was studying at John Brown University, a tiny high-quality Christian school in Siloam Springs, Arkansas.

Carlos was one of sixteen students who came to John Brown University as a "Walton Scholar," his whole college education paid for by the Walton Family Foundation. He had stood out in his city of Matehuala, Mexico, and at JBU became an outstanding student, a student council officer and a star in student plays. Imagine my surprise when, after not having talked with him for about two decades, he called me not long ago! He had worked for four years in Mexico and applied for US citizenship, was eventually naturalized, gone to law school, and had run for a school board in Arkansas, then mayor, then, boldly, for the U.S. Senate!

Carlos—now *U.S. Senator* Carlos Rivas (D-AR)—is the ranking member on the Health and Human Services oversight committee, and is on the FDA oversight sub-committee. He called me from his office in Washington, DC, to ask if I would speak before the subcommittee. You might ask: About what? (That was what *I* asked.)

He wanted me, as the mother of a victim of the Travis High School shooting and a journalist who has brought up a controversial angle on one of the possible causes of such shootings, to speak to the committee as a member of a panel on antidepressant drugs and their role in these tragic attacks.

I summoned as much grace as possible and gave him a firm "no." He remembered that I had always avoided speaking in front of people; we had talked about it quite a bit during that long-ago summer, as our friendship grew. He couldn't understand not only why I feared it, but why he so much enjoyed it. Neither could I.

But when his clipping service dutifully sent him clips of articles mentioning the FDA and antidepressant drugs, my first piece and the rebuttal to it from Provachem Pharmaceuticals were both included. Others followed, and Senator Rivas thought I could provide a unique point of view.

But what does a little woman from Texas tell U.S. Senators? Not just about my loss, which you know about, but also about the subject I've been writing about for the last few weeks?

I've lately realized, as you probably have, that U.S. Senators as a rule are either misinformed or heavily biased about certain subjects, sometimes depending on the state of their reelection funds. I think prescription antidepressants is one such subject. I've decided *this* little woman is going to attempt publicly to blow the lid off of it.

Lately, I've been writing a lot about SSRI drugs—antidepressants that have been sold to the world public as an effective treatment for depression, but that often do not work and create many well-known side effects. Those are listed in the FDA labels for the drugs, which are available to read for every drug on an FDA website at *www.fda.gov/drugsatfda*. Here's a short list of some of those side effects, in case you don't want to look for them: sexual dysfunction, insomnia, weight gain, weight loss, mania, akathisia, aggression, hostility, violence, emotional blunting, deperson-alization, disassociation, suicidality, homicidal ideation (thinking), increased depression, nervousness, … and others.

I write my way through dilemmas. That's what I'm doing here.

And, it has worked, despite my glossophobia. Still fearful, I will call Senator Rivas when I finish this, and I will accept his invitation to speak out about the problems I've had through this ongoing grieving process and about my newly gained knowledge of antidepressant drugs. I hope you'll tune in and watch on CSPAN-2. I'll be the nervous short lady with big red hair at the panel table who looks like she's afraid of the microphone.

Thoughts? Send 'em! *cass@cassiestevens.net*

Cassie could hardly believe, after mulling and writing for over two hours, that she was committing publicly to speak in front of a Senate Committee. How would she ever get through it? A nauseous chill overtook her as she pictured herself facing the senators and photographers with their long lenses pointed at her.

Before she could change her mind, she did a quick read-through of the column, fixed a few things, and sent it to Tom Hammond's staff email address so he would see it first thing in the morning.

She dialed the number Carlos Rivas had called her from and got the voicemail for his office. She left a message for him that she would like to accept his invitation to speak to the committee, and she would talk to him later.

To her column, she added a note for her editor: *Tom — no matter what I say tomorrow, don't let me back out of this. — Cassie*

TWENTY-FIVE

AUGUST 14, 2016. SUNDAY.

Linnie was to be brought out of her coma this morning. Cassie left Zach asleep and hurried to get to the hospital. It was a quick trip early on a Sunday.

She watched as Dr. Hellem stopped the flow from one IV bag and opened the tube from another. He was a pleasant man, narrating what he was doing and why. Linnie would no longer be getting the *propofol,* the drug that kept her under. She would come back to consciousness at her own pace. The doctor had told Cassie not to be alarmed, but that patients sometimes experienced vivid nightmares as they emerged from coma. Hellem left the room, putting the nurse on standby to call him instantly when Linnie began to stir.

Cassie sat in a chair beside Linnie's bed and found a magazine to look at. It was somewhat surprising to her that regular, everyday things were still happening. Hollywood was still pinpointing their ten sexiest men and women stars. Weight loss, getting in shape, sexual prowess, how to know "real" love—all those were still well covered. She turned a page and saw another article, this one titled, "Depression: Is There An Escape?"

The first sentence grabbed her: "For three decades, psychiatrists have been selling us dangerous drugs as the 'go-to' treatment for depression."

"Well I'll be darned," she said to herself, and kept reading. The one-page article continued, exploring various SSRI drugs in a superficial way and telling about some of the usual adverse effects like sleeping problems, sexual dysfunction, loss or increase of appetite, nervousness, and so forth.

And, near the article's end, where it could make a memorable point, was a paragraph that Cassie stared at:

> "The solid link of these drugs to violence cannot be argued away; they have been implicated in school shootings for years. Travis High School, in Texas, when the whole story is told, will probably be added to the list. With no record of violence or illegal drug use, John Allen Hoff was an unlikely killer. That is, until prescription antidepressants started 'repairing the chemical imbalance' in his brain."

Cassie didn't know where the writer had gotten her info, but she was right. And there it was. Without apology or moderation, the bold statement that she had yet to make in her own columns. She was at first indignant, but then realized it was her own fault for not wanting to get too far out front. She made a silent pledge to remedy that.

Zach had taken a sleeping pill the night before after watching a late movie. He'd told Cassie about it as he got into bed and asked her to let him sleep when she left for the hospital, since Linnie wouldn't know if he was there anyway.

His sleep was interrupted by a rustling sound out in the kitchen area of Cassie's condo. Morning light filled the bedroom. Looking at the clock, knowing it wasn't Cassie out there, he quickly came awake, shook his head and stepped out of the room. He looked out, down the hall into the main room and froze as he saw the elbow of a male arm with a long dark blue sleeve.

It wasn't anybody he knew. He froze, but quickly realized he couldn't stat there.

Adrenalin moved him. His heartbeat became audible inside his head. He broke out of his paralysis and moved back into the bedroom as quietly as he could. He didn't want to give away his presence. Whoever it was out there thought he was alone. Zach wanted to keep it that way until he could figure out what to do.

Call 9-1-1? No. Too much sound. In the quiet condo, it would be heard.

He shook his head again to try to wake himself more, stole further into the room and tried to think. He felt vulnerable in his underwear. Going out and confronting the person didn't sound good to him. But waiting for the guy to come into the room didn't either.

He quickly tiptoed to Cassie's dresser, where she kept her .357 in her underwear drawer. He eased the drawer open, dug around and saw the black rubber grip and short stainless steel barrel of the revolver. He froze as the muzzle dragged on the drawer bottom, thinking the scraping sound might have been heard. Apparently, it wasn't.

He picked up the gun, slowly pressed the cylinder release and checked. It was fully loaded, not with .357 magnums, but with .38 Specials with gray rubber-looking tips. He clicked it shut as quietly as he could, laid his trigger finger alongside the frame above the trigger as he'd been taught, made sure of his two-hand grip, held the gun in front where he could raise it quickly, and looked back toward the door. He could hear faint sounds from the other room of papers being shuffled. It didn't sound like the person was trying to be quiet; he obviously thought the place was empty.

Zach had long ago decided that he didn't want to shoot anybody, and that was the way he was thinking now. But at the same time, an overwhelming fear gripped him. With what had happened to Linnie, and the other things like Hoff being murdered, he figured the person in the other room had to be connected in some way. And he would probably attack Zach. He tried to overcome his fear, and failed.

His hand trembled. He pressed back against the wall inside the bedroom and squeezed his eyes shut, taking big breaths, trying to force himself to calm down. Maybe he should just hide?

After a few seconds, he moved and looked out down the hall again, holding the gun down in front, his grip ready. The hammer was cocked back so only a light touch on the trigger would be needed to fire. Until he was ready to shoot, he kept his finger off the trigger.

The man wasn't visible. He didn't know who it was. It might

be anyone, or it might be Linnie's carjacker. He would bet that was him, because he was supposed to be tall, and this guy looked very tall. And if it *was* that guy, he wouldn't leave Zach alive.

He felt a drop of sweat run trickle down behind his ear.

He stepped slowly out into the hallway, still holding the gun in both hands pointed at the floor in front of him. He suddenly wished he had gone to the range more often and practiced as his instructor had urged. He could have taken a defensive pistol course, but he didn't do it. "Real life" had taken over, and there never seemed to be enough time to go to the range and shoot the gun, then come home and go through the hassle of cleaning the thing.

He hoped to be able to surprise the intruder. He got to the middle of the hall, and there the guy was. It was the man, obviously. His back was turned to Zach as he rifled through a stack of papers on the dinette table. He was tall and wiry. He wore a gray cowboy hat, which make him seem even taller.

Zach didn't know exactly what he should do at this point. A cool breeze from the air conditioner found its way into his boxers; it made him feel extremely unprotected. Despite all that, he pointed the gun, readied his finger alongside the trigger, and yelled as loudly as he could.

"Freeze!"

The tall man did exactly as he was told. His hands instantly stopped moving. He even seemed to stop breathing. Zach's hand began to tremble. The man turned his head around toward Zach, revealing part of his white-mustached face and his right eye. He was definitely the guy Cassie had described.

"Now what, Mister?" the man said, in a high foreign-sounding voice. What was it, Bosnian? Russian? Whatever.

Zach didn't know what to do next. He wished he had called 9-1-1 before confronting the guy, but it was too late now.

The man spoke again. "You want me just stand here Mister?"

"No! Turn around! *Slow!*" Zach was glad his voice hadn't cracked. It irritated him that his voice trembled, while the intruder's voice didn't. His heart pounded in his ears. He kept his attention on the man's hands. They had always said, *watch the hands*.

The man turned, his hawk nose and bony, pale face looking thin beneath the large felt hat.

"*Slow!*" Zach yelled again.

"You got it Mister," the man said, and turned his face fully toward Zach. His right hand was on the back of a chair and his left hand was slightly raised.

The cold grey-blue eyes held a hint of humor. *Incredible*, Zach thought. *What the hell's humorous about this?* In any normal situation, he would have actively avoided even meeting this guy's eyes.

Now what? What should he do? He hated that he was hesitating.

Then, though he didn't even realize he was perceiving it, he saw the man's right shoulder rise, then his elbow and forearm moved quickly. The next thing Zach knew, a dining chair was tumbling toward him and the man was rushing him right behind it. It was a reflex. His eyes shut tight as he fired three times, the horribly loud *Bang!Bang!Bang!* sound of the gun strangely muffled in his ears, as if it was far away. Before he knew it, the chair had hit him in the hands and his head and he fell back into the hallway. He was sitting down, almost on his back, leaning to his right against the wall. But he still held the gun.

The man had taken cover around the hallway corner. Suddenly, another chair came flying around the corner and hit Zach in the knee. He pointed the gun and fired three more shots. *Bang!Bang!Bang!* Big mistake, he thought. All of them had missed. He was panicking. The ringing in his ears was now terribly loud. *Shit!*

Then, the man came walking around the corner. Zach couldn't believe it. The asshole was actually smiling! He was moving slowly, deliberately, but walking unsteadily and straight toward Zach.

He spoke. "That made six shots, mister underwear cowboy six-shooter. So sorry but you are finished now!"

Strange, Zach thought, the guy is grinning at me! All he could see was the man's face and chest; everything else was dark as if he was looking through a tube. He pointed the gun at the man's chest, now only a few feet away and above him as he bent down and the long skinny arms starting to reach down toward Zach, a big knife in one hand.

He heard the guy's strange closed-mouth laugh, and then he pulled the trigger again. The gun's final *BOOM!* drowned out everything.

Zach's aim was bad and he flinched, anticipating the gun's recoil. The S&W 686-Plus's seventh shot struck the man not in the chest, but at the base of his neck. The Glaser Grey Safety Slug, as it was designed to do, entered cleanly and then fragmented, releasing two dozen small steel pellets that each traveled its own course, tearing and puncturing as they went, none exiting the neck.

The tall man's stunned expression—or the complete lack of any expression—was the last communication he ever issued to the world, as he fell partly on top of Zach, but dying so quickly he didn't even know it, his thin, wiry neck broken and his brain stem destroyed by hydrostatic pressure.

Zach scrambled back away from the man's body, which quivered once, then exhaled. The stink of the man's waste filled the air as his body completely relaxed and he defecated and urinated in his pants, and was completely still except for a couple of nerve spasms.

Zach vomited. He hadn't eaten in over twelve hours, so only a small amount of fluid came up, stinging his throat. He retched again. He tried to stand up and couldn't. He dropped the gun on the floor and scrambled backwards along he wall.

Finally getting his breath, he began to shake uncontrollably. The adrenalin that had fueled his actions, still running in his veins, was now at its height. His heartbeat was fast and heavy. His skin was sweating, but cold. The hallway seemed to turn dark.

He shook his head, trying to clear it.

The dead man was still there, the chair, the gun, blood dripping into a small spot on the carpet, but only slowly because his heart had stopped instantly. Zach let out a loud groan, almost like a sob but full of anger, not sorrow, and rolled over face-first on the floor. He let go a loud stream of angry curses at the man and at the air, realizing what had just taken place.

Still shaking all over, he crawled into the bedroom, found his cell phone and dialed 9-1-1. He could barely talk as he tried to tell the operator he had just shot a man to death. Then he cowered beside the bed and dialed Cassie's cell number.

* * *

Linnie took a deep breath and her arm jumped spastically. The nurse had called Dr. Hellem as soon as the monitors showed Linnie's respiration increasing.

As the doctor came into the room, Cassie asked, "Why is she frowning and grimacing and all that?"

"Like I said, people sometimes have nightmares when they're coming out of a coma. We don't know why, for sure. Some say it's because of things they've heard or sensed while they were in coma."

"Gosh, that's amazing."

"Uh-huh," Hellem replied as he checked the monitors and took Linnie's pulse manually. "Mrs. Stevens, I'd like you to leave the room for just a few minutes, please."

Cassie nodded and walked out into the hallway. Her phone buzzed in her pocket. The screen showed it was Zach.

Good, she thought, *Zach's awake.* She pressed the button to answer and took a breath, but stopped at a sound she'd never heard before. It was a primal groaning, deep, low and loud.

TWENTY-SIX

AUGUST 14, 2017. SUNDAY.

"Zach? What's—"

"*Cassie!* Cassie, oh god, you need to get home. I *shot* that guy with your gun!"

She froze, her mouth open. "*What?* You shot—?" Her voice was loud in the quiet hallway. She turned away from a nearby couple, who were staring at her. In a more hushed voice, she said, "You did *what?* I don't understand! *What* guy?"

"He was gonna kill me! I *shot* him, Cass. He's in the hallway!"

She almost fainted and fell back against the wall. "Did you call the police? What happened? Good grief Zach! Are you all right?"

"Yeah I think so. Police are on the way, I gotta call a lawyer. Oh shit. *Shit!*" He coughed and groaned. "Just come home!" The line went dead. She couldn't believe it and blinked her eyes tight, trying to make sure she had really heard what he said.

She walked unsteadily back into Linnie's hospital room as Dr. Hellem looked up. His slight smile disappeared as he saw how pale she was.

"Mrs. Stevens, are you—"

"Doctor, please tell Linnie, if you can, I'm sorry I wasn't here. There's been a shooting at my house, and … " Her voice trailed off as she turned and left the stunned doctor standing, staring.

The elevator stopped.

It was the smell, first. She was repulsed by it as soon as the elevator doors opened. The door to her condo, under twenty feet from the elevators, was open, but she couldn't imagine that the awful smell was coming from it. As she walked nearer, hearing voices from inside, she realized the horrible odor came from her home and filled the hallway.

She grimaced and stuck her head around the corner and looked inside.

The man was lying on the floor in her hallway.

A uniformed Dallas police officer confronted her, his hands out. "This is a crime scene, ma'am. Please back away."

"But this is my home!"

"What is your name?"

"Stevens. Cassie Stevens."

"Wait here," the cop said and turned to speak with a detective. They both walked back to Cassie.

"Mrs. Stevens? I'm Detective Conn. You're the owner of this condominium?"

"Yes, I was at a hospital with a friend and—Zach called me! What happened?"

"Do you know that man over there?" The detective turned and Cassie saw Zach, sitting on a dinette chair in his green boxer shorts, his head in his hands.

"Yes! That's Zach—Zachary Barber—he's my fiancé! He was here and he called me and told me—" She realized she shouldn't say what he told her.

"Told you what, Mrs. Stevens?"

"He said I should get home right away. There was a man—"

"Cassie?" Zach's voice sounded weak.

"Detective, can I come into my home and talk to Zach?"

The man looked around to where the Crime Scene Response people were working. " 'Fraid not. Not 'til they're done."

"But this is my home!"

"Ma'am, a man was killed in here today and you can't come in until we're finished. Now, just let me get your contact information." He opened the notepad in his hand and listened as she gave her name and cell number. "It's still a crime scene. You can't come back in 'til it's been processed. That'll be sometime tonight. Maybe tomorrow."

"What about Zach?"

"Yeah. He'll be going downtown with us to talk for awhile. I need to get your statement about him, too. Let's walk down the hall a ways and get away from this stink."

"It smells like, uh, poop!"

"That's exactly what it is, ma'am. It happens a lot of the time when people, well ... you know." He motioned down the hall past the elevators and took her elbow. Cassie cast a glance back toward Zach as they left the doorway.

"So, are you okay, Hon?" Tom Hammond asked, laying his hand on her shoulder as she sat down in his office. "The news guys're workin' up the story. You want to make a comment for it?"

"No," Cassie uttered, glancing back through the glass walls at the regular Monday morning crew beginning to fill the editorial floor. "My god, Tom, I still can't believe it. I can't get over how bad it *smelled*. At least the detective told me how to find a crime scene cleaning company. Who knew they even existed?"

"Yeah. That's somethin', huh? How's Zach?"

"He's doing pretty well. They questioned him for about five hours and I went and got him last night."

"They gonna charge him with anything?"

"I don't know. They didn't tell him. Fingers crossed."

"Hmm," Hammond grunted as he sat down at his desk. Cassie folded her arms and gazed out at the editorial room. "So, did you find anything out about the guy?"

"Nothing. He was the guy from the hospital, for sure. I think I convinced the detective I don't know who he was. Actually, I don't."

"You think that was the thing to do? Not tellin' who you *thought* he was?"

"What do you mean?"

"I mean, maybe they needed to know you'd seen him in the hospital when Hoff was killed?"

"I don't know, and I'm not completely sure it was the same guy."

Hammond gave her a look that indicated he didn't completely believe her. "Well, you sure you're okay?"

"I'm fine. This kind of thing's becoming my 'new normal!'"

"Ha, yeah, let's hope not. You said your friend, Dr. Kennedy, came out of her coma?"

"Mm-hmm, but other than that it was a pretty bad Sunday."

"To say the least. You have a place to stay?"

"Yeah. I'm staying at Zach's 'til they clean my place."

"Okay. As long as you're safe. If this guy was the same one that hijacked your doctor friend, he was prob'ly lookin' for that video again, right? Or your computer. Think they'll try again? Send somebody else?"

"God, I hope not! I just want to find out who was giving him orders. I know it's Richardson."

"Yeah. But how do you find out without even knowin' who he is?"

"Good question. And my answer is, I have no idea." She gave Hammond a shrug, rose and left his office.

When she reached her cubicle, that question was still in her mind.

With everything they knew, the main link between all these events was still that *chlorpenframine* drug and the video that showed it. And she knew beyond a doubt that everything that had happened was connected to Provachem and Richardson.

And Tim Savage might know something.

She pulled Savage's letter out of her bag and reread it, then dialed her cell phone to call Provachem's main number.

"Tim savage in CRO operations, please." She was glad for Richardson's prideful tour.

"Tim Savage," a quiet, high voice answered.

"Mr. Savage, this is Cassie Stevens from the *Daily Post* in Dallas."

"*Oh!*" a pause. "I'll call you back." The line went dead.

She looked at the phone, exasperated, then sat and waited, aimlessly shuffling papers on her desk, wondering if he really would call back. Ten minutes later, her phone buzzed in her hand. An unknown number showed on the screen.

"It's Tim Savage," that same high voice said when she answered. "I'm in my car now."

"Mr. Savage, I have your letter here. I appreciate your sympathies, but, why did you really write it?"

The line was quiet for a few seconds. "I thought you must have thrown it away or something and I'd never hear from you."

"I've been preoccupied."

"Yeah. Of course. Sorry."

"So, why the letter? And why couldn't you talk from your office?"

"I just guess like I said, I'm sick of it all and I wanted to tell somebody. And the office walls have ears around here."

"Sick of all *what*?"

"This whole industry. The drug industry."

Cassie waited a few seconds. "Did you know the surgeon who operated on John Hoff was carjacked last week? And the man who probably did it broke into my home yesterday?"

"Oh, crap. No! Did they get him? Who is he?"

"Don't know who he is. He's dead."

"Oh-h, fu—uh, sorry. But you don't think all that was connected with *us*, do you?"

"By 'us,' you mean Provachem?"

He waited before answering. Then, "I don't know. I really don't."

"Mr. Savage, do you know who he was? A very tall, thin man with a white mustache and a Russian kind of accent?"

"No—I don't know anybody like that."

"Do you think your boss, Richardson, hired him?"

"What? Oh, jeez—I hope not. No. I don' t know."

Cassie waited, hoping he would say more. He didn't. "Okay, so, if I don't identify you as the source, what are you willing to tell me about your company's drugs?"

"Look, I can't be giving you that kind of information. It's confidential. I signed a contract. Besides, there's nothing about our drugs that's not in the records at the FDA."

"Then let me ask my question again." Her voice had an edge to it. "Why did you write that note in the first place?"

"I don't know, now. I guess I just wanted to say I was sorry. Look I need to go."

"Wait! I have one question that I hope you'll answer. Why would your CEO be mixed up in this?"

Savage answered too quickly. "I don't know. I have to go."

Before Cassie could say anything else, Savage's phone went silent.

TWENTY-SEVEN

AUGUST 16, 2016. TUESDAY.

"I need to apologize, Dr. Thomas." Cassie looked at the man across his desk. "For not being up front with you before."

"Yes, well, forgive and forget, as I tell my patients. It's healthy. Before we go any further, Mrs. Stevens, I need to tell you, since you used up your free consultation, you will be billed for this visit. That's okay with you, isn't it?" He rose and closed his office blinds against the low morning sun.

"I guess that's fair," she answered.

"All right. Now, how can I help you today?" He sat back down and leaned back in his chair.

"Honestly, Doctor, I'm not sure. I was coming here as a newspaper reporter, but suddenly it seems as if it's all so confused now."

"All what?"

"Well, my life. I feel like I'm a little boat being tossed in a big storm. Things keep happening to me that I can't control or even deal with. My best friend was carjacked, almost killed. My fiancé shot a man who broke into my home. Mark was murdered—" Her mind filled with a rush of pictured memories of Mark at home, watching TV, eating, and playing his horn, mixed with an image of his still body in the bed where she left him.

She had the impression that she was hearing a muffled voice, "Mrs. Stevens? Are you all right?"

The voice was far away. She felt dizzy. The room went dim. Then darkness and nothingness.

"Mrs. Stevens? *Mrs. Stevens!*"

217

His voice was coming from somewhere. It sounded far away again. She opened her eyes slowly and realized she was lying on a couch.

"I called your fiancé. He should be here soon," Dr. Thomas said. "You fainted. Do you feel all right? Any headache at all? Do you know what day this is?"

"Uh, I feel fine. It's August, uh, August 16?"

"Can you look at me and smile?"

"Huh?"

"Please, just smile for me."

She tried to smile. He tilted his head to look at her face straight on.

"Mm-hmm. Here, have some water." His receptionist, standing beside the couch, handed him a glass of water. He helped Cassie turn and sit up so she could drink some of it. "Can you raise both of your arms for me and hold them up?"

"Why?"

"Please. Just a quick check."

"For what?"

"Stroke."

"I've never had a stroke."

"Yes, well, most people haven't until they have."

She handed him the glass of water and held her arms up. They stayed up. He uttered a doctorish "Mm-hm," seemed satisfied, took her hands and put her arms down.

He reached behind him, pulled one of the side chairs close, and sat down opposite her. "Mrs. Stevens, you've been under an inordinate amount of stress in the last few weeks. I'm surprised this is the first time it's affected you. Is this the first time you've fainted?"

"Yeah, it is."

"I'm going to suggest that you see your doctor and maybe do something to help you relax. Stop being a detective for a while, maybe?"

She looked at him.

"I think you're trying to take control of a world that you can't hope to control, like you said in an article awhile back. Like you said, we have no control, really. And you've been hit with a lot."

"You read my article? Have you kept reading them?"

"Yes, I have." He leaned back in the chair.

"And?"

"And what," he said, chuckling. "You want a grade or something? They were thought provoking."

"Gee, thanks," Cassie answered. "Uh, how long was I out?"

"About eight minutes."

"Well, then, I still have some paid time left. Can we continue what I came here for?"

"Honestly, Cassie. This is a freebie, and I think I've given you the best advice I can. Get some rest. Let go of things for awhile."

"I can't do that." She twisted and sat up straight, with his helping hand.

"Well, I'm going to kick you out of my office again," he said, smiling. "We can continue at another time if you really want to. I understand that you think you have to find answers, but—"

"But I have to know why it happened! I haven't gotten a good answer yet!"

A knock on the door was followed by the receptionist peeking through and pushing it open. Zach hurried in.

"Cassie! Are you okay? They said you fainted—"

"Yeah, I'm okay." She reached up, took his hand and introduced the two men to each other.

"I better take you home," Zach said.

"Get her to rest, if you can," Dr. Thomas said. "Cassie, I wish I could provide that answer you're looking for. I hope you find it. For now, just take care of yourself and call me if you need to talk again. I'd prescribe a tranquilizer, but you probably wouldn't trust it."

"You got that right," she said, not smiling.

"That was a joke," Thomas said, with a wink.

"Oh. Not very funny, Doc. Don't give up your day job," she said without a hint of humor. She thanked him and they left.

Cassie felt good after a long night's sleep. She had taken a couple of non-prescription sleeping pills and slept late while Zach took an *Über* car to retrieve her car from the psychiatrist's office. Now, she poured a cup of coffee and sat down in Zach's living room as she waited for Tom Hammond to get back on the line with her.

"Sorry, Cass. What were you sayin'?"

"I was just saying I've tried to call this Tim Savage again, but now his cell number goes straight to voice mail. I call his office and they tell me he's not in. I can't leave a message because it might get back to Richardson."

"Yeah, Cass," Hammond said, leaning back in his desk chair, "that's a tough situation. You think the guy's taken off on a sudden 'well-deserved vacation?' "

"Ha. Could be. I just don't know what to do next."

"You know where he lives?"

"No. No idea."

"Hmm." She heard the phone muffled again, then he came back. "So, they're cleaning your condo? The police get anywhere with who that guy is yet?"

"Nothing."

"But he was the guy you saw go into Hoff's room."

"Yeah. I'm pretty sure of that. Looks like him."

"But you can't prove it."

"Right."

"Rock and a hard place, huh?"

"Yeah. Say, I'll be in to work tomorrow. That okay?"

"Yeah, that's fine. Do what that shrink told you. Get some rest."

"I will. I told you, I'm fine. I was just—I don't know."

"Well, take care of yourself."

She clicked off and tried to think of what she should do. It didn't take long to decide. She left Zach a note and took his car keys.

* * *

"Hi!" Linnie said as Cassie walked into her room.

"Oh, you're awake! This is a beautiful sight!"

"Yeah, I'm sure," Linnie said, smoothing her hair.

"Really! You're *much* prettier with your eyes open and smiling, girl!"

"Well, I hope so!"

"No, seriously. We were worried."

"Yeah, thanks Cass. I'm going to be fine. Trust me, I'm a doctor." She smiled again.

Cassie gave her a doubtful look. "Okay. So what have they told you?"

"They'll release me in a few days. My arm and hand will need more surgery."

"Is it—did they say—?

"Did they tell me how serious it is? Yeah, they did. It'll take some rehab, but I should regain full use in a few months. I'll be able to operate again. In the meantime, I can do some writing: typing will be a good dexterity builder. Got a real typewriter I can borrow?"

"Good! I'm so glad. And, yes, I'm sure the paper has an old Remington somewhere." Cassie breathed.

"Great." She patted the bed beside her, inviting Cassie to sit. "Okay, so *I'm* going to be fine. So tell me about *your* world lately. Miss Rip Van Winkle here, you know. No news, good or bad."

"Well, let me see. I decided to testify for the Senate committee, and—"

"Really! Really? That's a huge step for you!"

"Yeah. It's the right one. I'm a big girl. A big scared girl!" She laughed.

"When is it?"

"Early September, right after their summer break."

"It's going on my calendar. I might be on the operating table getting this arm fixed, but... So, what else?"

"You didn't see *any* news?"

"No—what?"

"A guy broke into my condo and Zach shot him and killed him."

"No! Oh my *god*, Cass! What happened?"

"It was the same man who faked being a doctor that night, skinny face like a skeleton, and a big white mustache—" She stopped as her friend's eyes suddenly filled with tears and her face turned red. "Linnie? Are you okay?"

"Cass, I haven't been able to remember," she said after a moment, sniffling between words, "but when you said that, I pictured him! It was that guy who hijacked me. The same guy. Really tall. Skinny. Pale face, prominent zygomatics and a big white mustache! And he's dead? Oh, god." She shook her head and blew her nose.

"Wow, Linn! That detective, uh, Malden? *Matlin!* He talked to me in the hospital the night you were attacked. We need to tell him, and the cops in Dallas too. This'll get Zach off the hook for sure!"

"What? How?"

"Has the detective been in to see you?"

"No—I don't think he knows I'm awake and—"

"I'm calling him." Cassie pulled her phone from her purse and fished for the business card. "Ah! Lieutenant Joe Matlin, Plano PD." She dialed the phone and got voice mail. "Detective Matlin, this is Cassie Stevens. I'm calling about the carjacking of Dr. Linnea Kennedy last week. She's awake and she remembers what the attacker looked like, and he is the same man who broke into my condo in Dallas yesterday. You can find him in the Dallas County morgue, but if you'll contact Dr. Kennedy and call Detective Conn in the North Dallas Division you'll get even more information. These crimes are linked and I know— Dang it! It cut me off!"

"Well, you gave him a lot of information. He'll call me. But Cass, is Zach okay? What in the world happened?"

"Zach got my gun, thank God! The way he told me the story, the guy thought Zach had a regular six-shot revolver. It does look the same from a distance but it's a seven-shot gun. The guy thought he was safe and Zach killed him with his last shot."

"That was the only shot he hit him with?"

"Yeah. Zach's no trained shooter. He was lucky that the guy was only two feet from him. He couldn't miss, shot him square in the throat."

"Oh, wow." Her eyes were still tearing.

"Yeah. But the problem is, the guy didn't have any I.D. on him. They're thinking Zach knew him, or something, and took all his identification off his body after he shot him. He didn't, of course, but he couldn't prove that. Now maybe he can."

Linnie dabbed her eyes and shook her head. "Wow."

"No kidding. But, that's not all, Linn. This pretty much proves that everything is linked to that drug!"

"You *found* it! You found the video?"

"Yeah! It was in your jacket in a tissue. It took us awhile to figure out what was so important about it, though! Then we spotted it."

"Yeah, and if it's linked to that drug, then it's linked to Richardson." She leaned over closer and whispered. "And Doctor Krishnamurthy."

Linnie looked at her without smiling. "Cassie, it's not really for me to say, but doesn't this tie the knot on the whole thing? Hoff was disposed of to hide the drug, right? And now we have proof the drug was there. Doesn't that tie Provachem to the whole thing?" She paused, searching Cassie's expression. "I mean, there's no way to prove Hoff attacked the band because of the drug. Not for sure. All we know is that the drug was there and it looks like they got rid of Hoff's body to hide it."

Cassie was silent, but frowned and nodded. "Yeah, but they hid the drug for a reason. We just don't know what that is. I just wish the cops would take it more seriously. I want to get Richardson 'cause I think he's behind the whole thing. It's not over 'til it's over, and we haven't put the noose around his neck yet."

"But we will, Hon. We'll figure it out."

All the way back to Dallas, Cassie thought about Linnie's last statement. She'd said they'd get Richardson. But how?

TWENTY-EIGHT

AUGUST 17, 2016. WEDNESDAY.

Zach had come home with bad news the night before. They were charging him with second-degree murder. It had tipped Cassie into a new gloom. She awoke early, momentarily confused that she was at Zach's place, and then remembered everything. Zach had still been up when she went to bed the night before. She didn't know when he got in bed, but she thought it was probably late. Now, he snored as she rolled off the bed

She sat motionless for a few minutes staring at the wall, then scribbled out a note to Zach, dressed quickly and left. She wasn't sure where she was going, but she knew she needed a change of scene.

Nothing was working. Didn't the good guys *ever* win? Richardson, the SOB, seemed untouchable. The tall man, the fake doctor who'd killed Hoff, was dead and they couldn't identify him at all. He got what he deserved, but had murdered Hoff and almost killed Linnie, and he got shot only when he made a third attack. Nobody in this was paying for their crimes, except John Hoff and the Russian. In Cassie's mind, they both got off easy.

She cranked the key of the Explorer and squealed her tires, left the parking garage onto Commerce Street, took a left on Fields, then another left on Main. It was the route she usually took to the newspaper office, so it was a series of absent-minded turns, but this time she turned right on Griffith instead of left. When she passed Klyde Warren Park on her left and remembered the fun they had all had at the welcome picnic, she knew where she would end up.

It was a peaceful morning in the cemetery in Allen, just north of

Plano. A gentle breeze blew from the south and carried the scent of freshly mown grass. The new sod on Mark's grave was now almost perfect, blending into the grass around it except for one strip that hadn't greened up like the others. She sat down in the grass beside the stone. Nothing's perfect, she thought, as she looked at Mark's monument. Tears rose and ran down her cheeks.

Mark Tobias Stevens
Beloved Son
May 20, 1999 – June 28, 2016
His Music Ended Too Soon

During the thirty-minute drive up here, Cassie had thought of nothing but those things that were going wrong. She knew inside that Richardson was certainly in charge of this conspiracy, but she didn't know how to get to him. He was a powerful man, CEO of a fast growing drug company. Provachem had released that new drug, the one Hoff was on, a few months ago, and Richardson must know something about it that he *had* to keep hidden. But it wasn't the first time someone on a prescription antidepressant had gone on a murderous rampage. Richardson's company wouldn't be in any more jeopardy than the others, would it? Especially if the doctor had to take the blame.

And now, even though with Linnie's video they could prove that Hoff had the drug in his system, Krishnamurthy could just claim it was a mistaken analysis that had been corrected. Krishnamurthy wasn't stupid, and as long as he claimed it was a mistake, there was no way to prove otherwise. Not yet, anyway.

But they weren't trying to prove the drug caused Hoff to attack, even though Cassie thought it certainly was. The whole thing now was that the tall mustached man had murdered Hoff, and Krishnamurthy had autopsied him immediately, he claimed, because of all the autopsies waiting to be done at the hospital, and his body had been cremated "by mistake" the next morning. Too many mistakes. Not like Krishnamurthy, if Cassie could believe his reputation—unless it was purposeful and he was involved in the coverup. But he was able to claim that with all the stress and all the extra work, these mistakes had simply happened, and even though they were hard to believe, they couldn't be disproven. She needed to show the *why*. She needed to find a motive.

She sat beside Mark's grave and started humming the tune of a hymn, *Going Home*. It was one of the few she even remembered. Mark had often made fun of her singing voice. The lump in her throat grew as she remembered his voice, his jokes about her "shower voice," always followed by a hug and, "Just kidding, Mom. You know I love ya, right?"

This was the closest she would ever be to him again, unless heaven was real and they both ended up there. She imagined he'd be playing his horn in a heavenly band. If there was a band. If there was a heaven. She even wondered sometimes lately, how God could allow these kinds of things. But that wasn't a question she could answer.

What she possibly *could* do was find a way to link Justin Richardson to the murder of John Hoff and Linnie's carjacking. And her break-in. Why would anyone in that man's position risk everything he had built just to eliminate a kid who went off his rocker on Provachem's new antidepressant drug? And then continue to attack? It was obvious, at least to her, that he had to have a big reason to avoid any real connection. So far, he had succeeded, except for what she had hinted at in her columns.

She remembered some of the things she had read about how far some drug companies went in order to keep their drugs' reputations unsullied. She knew there must be something else—something they just hadn't thought of.

As she sat and listened to the late-summer sounds that her son would never again experience, she began to burn with determination she hadn't felt since Linnie had first told her about these drugs. Now Hoff, whose attack might have been caused by a reaction in his brain that he didn't expect and couldn't control, had been erased, just as he had erased so many others. Somebody knew why.

A name popped back into her head. *Tim Savage.*

She was certain he knew more than he had told her before. Maybe he would answer a call this time.

She pulled her phone out of her pocket, found his name and tapped it. The call went straight to voice mail.

"This is Tim Savage. I can't answer right now. Leave your message and number and I'll call when I can. Thanks."

"Dammit!" Cassie said out loud, before the beep sounded. This time, she had to be sure he would call her back.

"Mr. Savage," she started in a flat, firm voice, "This is Cassie Stevens, I'm preparing an article for the paper that ties your boss to the coverup of Pefrexa XR in John Hoff's blood and the murder of Hoff, and your name and letter will be mentioned unless you can talk me out of it. Call me back before noon tomorrow or your name will be in the paper. That's my deadline and I'm serious." She ended with her cell number. If anything could do it, that would.

She sat there beside the grave for a few minutes, wondering exactly what she could tell Savage if he called her bluff. What she'd told him was an empty threat. The letter didn't prove anything, and Savage being "sick of it all" was of no value.

She rose to go, saying a quiet goodbye to Mark.

She decided to drop in on Linnie on the way back down to Dallas. Her friend had been moved to a regular room. When Cassie walked in, Linnie was talking with a distinguished looking well dressed man. Neither of them looked very happy.

"Hello?" Cassie said as she knocked lightly on the door frame and leaned into the room.

"Ah, a *friendly* face!" Linnie said. "Cassie Stevens, meet Dr. Randall Chase, our hospital director. Dr. Chase was *just* on his way out."

"Pleasure," the man said, nodding to Cassie as he breezed past her.

"So that's the guy. Kind of uppity?"

"Yeah. *Kind* of! He was just telling me they've reinstated my surgery privileges, but he didn't believe it was the right decision."

"But, you can't do surgery yet?"

"Yeah, I know. And he knows, and he wasn't particularly sympathetic about it, either."

"Ass."

"Yep. But he doesn't deserve this much attention. How are you doing?"

"Up and down, Linn. We've hit a wall. You know, it just seems like these people in power get away with things and we don't have much to say about it and can't punish 'em."

"Hmm. You know who called me this morning?"

"No. Who?"

"Krishnamurthy."

"Really? What about?"

"He seemed to feel genuinely sorry about everything. He even said so, but he said something else that was interesting. He said these words: 'I wouldn't have helped, but...' and that was it."

"What was he talking about?"

"I think he was actually talking about hiding the drug and making his big 'mistake' that got Hoff cremated. I even asked him, but he backtracked. He said he didn't mean that the way it sounded. Said he was talking about Chase and my suspension. Someone's making him do this stuff. He's too much of a mouse to risk his career this way on his own."

"So he must've been forced to do what he did," Cassie said, and sat down heavily in the chair beside the bed. After a few seconds, she said, "Well, we're right back to the beginning. Richardson. We can't prove anything."

"Don't give up yet. We're closer than we were." Linnie was silent for a few seconds, then, "Didn't you say you had a letter from that guy at Provachem?"

"Savage? Yeah. I've been trying to get him on the phone—"

"Well, I think Krish might know the guy because he was involved with the Pefrexa XR trial that failed, the one they ran here through Brookside three years ago."

"Really? If he does know Savage's name, Linn—" She jumped up from the chair and walked back and forth. Her mind was churning. "Wait a minute! If we can convince Krishnamurthy that Savage has told us about his connection to Richardson, maybe the doctor will come clean, *if* he's really involved."

"Cass, that's a great idea. But, how?"

"Let's get Krish up here in your room and tell him we know more than we do, and throw Savage's name into it."

"Okay. And if you tell Savage that we've flipped Krish—"

"Flipped?" Cassie laughed, despite herself. "You sound like somebody in a cop show!"

"Well, I've been watching too many of those in the last few days."

"Okay, let's do it. Can you call Krishnamurthy?"

Dr. Bhavesh Krishnamurthy stepped into the room and appeared to be surprised when he saw Cassie. He stopped. "Excuse me, Doctor, I didn't know you had a visitor. I will come back."

"Oh, no, Doctor, please stay. Mrs. Stevens is here to take part in our consultation."

The smallish Indian man, his black hair and dark skin in high contrast to his white coat and starched white shirt, looked at both of them, seeming unsure.

Cassie stepped toward him and put her hand out to shake his. "I'm Cassie Stevens, a friend of Linnie's."

"How do you do," Krishnamurthy said. He let go of Cassie's hand quickly, reached up to the antiseptic gel dispenser near the door, and coated his hands, then put them back into his coat pockets. "Dr. Kennedy, you said you wanted to consult. I am quite busy at the moment and—"

"Yes, that's correct, Doctor. I wanted to consult on the status of

John Allen Hoff."

Krishnamurthy looked at both of them, puzzled. "But that patient is … he is gone."

"We know. That's the point, Krish." Linnie fixed a stare at him.

"I am afraid I don't understand what you are wanting of me."

"My friend, Cassie, works for the Dallas Daily Post, and she received a letter we think would interest you. It was sent to her by the director of the CRO office at Provachem Pharmaceuticals, and—"

Krishnamurthy's body slowly stiffened. He took a half step backwards toward the door.

"—Wait a minute, Doctor. You should stay and hear this. Cassie?"

"Doctor Krishnamurthy," Cassie started, putting on her best interviewer frown, "Mr. Tim Savage—you may know that name—wrote to me recently. It has made me think that you must have had some contact with him during the Pefrexa XR trial here three years ago?"

"Uh, I am not sure. I have had contact with very many people. I must go now since this is—"

"Krish," Linnie said, "we know that you're involved with this coverup. We know you hid the toxicology results that showed chlorpenframine. We still have the video. The guy who carjacked me didn't get it and he's dead. He was the same guy who ducked into Hoff's room that night. We know that Justin Richardson has to be behind it all, but we don't know why."

The Indian doctor was slightly shaking his head and inching toward the door as Linnie continued. "Wait a minute, doctor! We just don't know why you would help him. You aren't a criminal! Whoever tells us the truth first is going to get off the easiest. The police and probably the FBI are already on it. It won't be long before they call you. Please help us here, won't you? What is Richardson using to make you do these things?"

Cassie looked at him. "You know, I lost my son at the high school. I'm not going to stop looking until I've made the public aware of everything."

Krishnamurthy was frozen in place. He stared at the floor without moving. Then, "My parents ... in India ... I cannot—" Then he turned and hurried out the door and down the hall.

TWENTY-NINE
AUGUST 17, 2016. WEDNESDAY.

When Cassie got back to Zach's place, he was gone again. She looked for a note but didn't find one. No text or missed calls on her phone, either.

She didn't know what to do with their attempted confrontation of Krishnamurthy. There really was nothing to do. He hadn't given them anything except the one small clue when he said the words, "My parents in India." Cassie had no idea what that could mean, but she knew Krishnamurthy was under pressure, and it must have something to do with his parents.

For now, though, she had to get her column finished and sent to Hammond. She picked it up at the end, quickly typed an ending paragraph, printed it and sat down to read it.

THE REST OF THE STORY
By Cassie Stevens

We now know some things about the Travis High School shooting that took my son, Mark, and forty of his fellow musicians, plus five instructors.

1) John Allen Hoff, the shooter, known to be an emotional and disturbed young man, was under the care of a local psychiatrist who had prescribed Pefrexa XR, an SSRI antidepressant drug made by Provachem Pharmaceuticals. The psychiatrist, who spoke off the record, was not aware of the information in the next point.

2) An "Extra-Therapeutic Level" of chlorpenframine (Pefrexa XR) was found in John Allen Hoff's blood when he attacked the band. There is proof of this. Hoff had exceeded the recommended dosage; this is a well known danger with these kinds of drugs. Suddenly changing the dosage makes the adverse drug

reactions become more likely and more severe.

3) Hoff's favorite video games were "First Person Shooters," such as *Grand Theft Auto*, *Call of Duty*, and *Super Columbine Massacre*, which were found in his things following his death.

4) Hoff's self-inflicted gunshot injuries were not life-threatening, yet he died mysteriously less than twelve hours after a successful surgery.

5) Within another twelve hours, John Hoff's body was autopsied and cremated "by mistake." Highly suspect, in this reporter's opinion, and the responsibility of Dr. Bhavesh Krishnamurthy, Head of Pathology at Brookside Hospital.

6) Final pre-surgical and autopsy toxicology testing documents report no drugs in John Hoff's system. That is, the final, *edited* official documents reflect this test result. However, clear evidence exists that shows that the first analysis of Hoff's blood did, in fact, show an "extra-therapeutic level" of chlorpenframine (Pefrexa XR, from Provachem Pharmaceuticals) at the time of surgery, about thirty minutes after the end of the attack. The disparity between these toxicology documents has not yet been explained. Was the final documentation edited to hide the drug?

7) The neurosurgeon who operated on John Hoff at Brookside Hospital, seven full weeks after the date of the attack and only hours after gaining access to the videos of his surgery which proved Pefrexa XR was in Hoff's blood, was carjacked and almost killed. In an effort to remove and destroy the video evidence, her laptop computer was stolen. The original video files, that same night, disappeared from the Brookside mainframe computer. Only two people at the hospital knew of these videos: The IT supervisor, and Dr. Bhavesh Krishnamurthy, Head Pathologist and Deputy Coroner, who had approved the inaccurate final-draft pre-surgery toxicology report, autopsied Hoff's body immediately after his death, and "mistakenly" sent Hoff's body to be cremated.

8) A man—apparently the same man who carjacked the neurosurgeon—only a few days later, broke into this reporter's condominium in downtown Dallas, probably searching for the flash drive containing the videos he missed in the carjacking incident. (Why I had them—and I did—is another long story.) Those videos, clearly showing the presence of chlorpenframine in John Hoff's blood during his surgery, are now in safe keeping. The man was shot and killed during that break-in. (This same man was identified as the individual who posed as a doctor at Brookside Hospital in the Surgical Intensive Care Unit, where this reporter's son and John Hoff both lay recovering, or trying to recover. The man was seen entering John Hoff's room two hours before Hoff died. How do I know this? I was the person who saw and spoke

to him, face to face.)

So, do you think we might have a case? Not just a case against a drug company in civil court, but also a strong criminal case against the individuals as accessories and conspirators who did their best to mastermind all of the following: the murder of John Allen Hoff as he lay recovering from surgery in his hospital bed; the carjacking and assault of Dr. Linnea Kennedy, Hoff's surgeon; attempted burglary of this reporter's home, and assault, and accessory to murder (death occurring during commission of a felony). Who knows what else?

Who could have masterminded these actions? And why? I have my own opinion, and I have my own answers to both questions. I don't have clear evidence … yet. But factually, and opinions notwithstanding, there is only one common party in all of this, soon to be unmasked.

We are committed to helping law enforcement authorities bring to justice the principal actors and conspirators in these crimes. Plano and Dallas police departments are involved, along with the FBI.

Helpful comments? Email me: Cass@cassiestevens.net

It was a little on the long side, but she knew that when Hammond read it, he would want to print it. Of course, Mrs. Wright would need to approve it as well. Some of the language in the piece might have to be softened; the legal department would make that ruling.

Cassie debated whether to make it clearer that in her opinion, the "one common party" to all the occurrences was Provachem's CEO. She wanted desperately to drop Justin Richardson's name into the mix with a hint at his probable involvement and a reference to Tim Savage's letter, but she voted herself down. All the lines of evidence would lead to him, eventually, so she didn't need to try him in the paper.

Then the idea struck her. It could break the whole case wide open.

She highlighted a few lines and printed a copy of her text, grabbed it and her keys, and left.

THIRTY

AUGUST 17, 2016. WEDNESDAY.

Regular afternoon rush hour traffic had built up on the North Dallas Tollway. Cassie called Linnie and told her what she was doing, so when she walked into her friend's room, Linnie was in a wheelchair waiting to go, with a brand new green hospital bathrobe and pink fuzzy slippers.

"Cassie," she said, "this was a stroke of brilliance."

"Think it'll work?"

"Hope so!"

They left the main wing of the hospital, took an elevator down, traversed the main hub, then another elevator down, and eventually arrived in the hallway where the hospital's huge Pathology Department was situated.

When the door to the department opened, they saw through a large glass window that Dr. Krishnamurthy was sitting at his computer, his back toward them.

Cassie pushed Linnie's chair silently on its rubber tires, and as she scuffed her heel on the floor, Krishnamurthy turned. He looked puzzled.

"Hello Krish," Linnie said.

Before he could say anything, Cassie walked to him and held out the printed pages of her column.

"What is this?" he asked.

"Please read the highlighted portions, Dr. Krishnamurthy."

He shuffled to the second page, and read quickly, his eyes growing wide. He looked up at Cassie. "But, you cannot—"

"Can't what, Doctor? Can't cite facts? You did release the final autopsy report, and the tox screen, and you made the mistake that got the body cremated immediately. Only you and I knew Linnie had the videos of the surgery, and she almost got killed!" She stood over him, fists on her hips.

Linnie spoke. "Krish, you need to help us. Whatever it is you're hiding, it's all going to come out anyway."

"Do you want this article to be in the paper on Sunday?" Cassie demanded.

He leaned back in his chair, slumped and tossed the pages on his desk. "He has hired somebody in India, in my parents' city of Jaipur, who has made serious threats, and he has somehow arranged to keep their visas from them. I haven't seen them in years. I am afraid for their lives."

"When you say, 'he,' who do you mean?"

Krishnamurthy looked up at Cassie before answering and took a deep breath. "I mean Richardson."

"Justin Richardson, CEO of Provachem?"

"Yes."

Cassie turned and looked at Linnie. "Well, that nails it, right?"

"I'd say so." She rose from her chair and walked over to her colleague. "I'm sorry, Krish. Sorry all this happened." She laid her free hand on his shoulder, but he didn't respond. "Did you get all of that?" she asked Cassie.

"Still recording," Cassie said, holding up her cell phone.

Krishnamurthy shook his head slowly. After what seemed a long time, he said, "I am sorry too. I am very regretful about everything. But I knew nothing about what was going to happen to the man, John Hoff. I was called after his body was brought to my department and told what had to be done."

"Who called you?" Cassie asked.

"I don't know. It was a man with something like a Russian accent. He said, 'This is from Richardson.' I remember that, oh very clearly. He said I must do the autopsy of John Hoff's body and have it burned immediately, or I would pay the price. He said I would be called later but I must be sure not to fail. It was something like that."

He put out one hand and played absently with a paper clip on his desk, staring at it and slowly shaking his head.

"Cassie, let's talk for a minute," Linnie said, motioning toward the office door. They walked out into a hallway that led to the labs. "Cass, what do we do with this? We need to go to the police, right?"

"Yeah, but not right away. We ought to tell him to just stay put, maybe get a lawyer and wait for awhile. I want to try to draw Richardson out. We still don't know why it was that important to hide the drug. Do we?"

"No. Not really. Good point. Okay, this is your deal, Hon. I'm here if you need me."

They walked back into Krishnamurthy's office. Cassie gathered up her pages. "Doctor, I'm going to remove these references to you from the column. You won't be in any danger from Richardson and your name won't be involved. Not yet. But we think you should get a lawyer, right away, and then just wait. Don't go to the police and certainly don't tell Richardson anything about this!"

Krishnamurthy nodded, his expression blank, and stood as Cassie wheeled Linnie out of his office and toward the elevators.

"So, what's the next move?"

"I've got to edit him"—she pointed backward with her thumb— "out of this column and get it to my editor. Then, I'm not sure. I'll call the cops too, and play them this recording." She got Linnie back to her room. "Thanks Linn, I'll let you know what's happening. I've got to get going."

"And keep me in the loop on Zach, too, okay?"

"Absolutely!" She leaned over and hugged her friend. "Thanks! 'Bye."

She knew what she needed to do. She reached Zach's condo at about six, made the changes to her column she'd promised Krishnamurthy, and sent it to Tom Hammond.

Next, she dialed Zach's cell number. No answer. She left a message for him to call her. They hadn't had a chance to talk in any detail since he told her they were probably going to charge him. She thought of calling the detective, Conn, and see if he had followed up and maybe talked with Matlin, but she didn't want to alienate him. Besides, if her next move against Richardson worked out, she might have more to tell him.

If the ploy they'd used on Krishnamurthy worked, it should have worked on Tim Savage. But he hadn't responded to her phone message.

She decided to try again, but this time dialed his office phone.

"Tim Savage."

She didn't speak for a second, surprised as she was to hear him answer.

"This is Cassie Stevens, Mr. Savage. I—"

"I'll call you in thirty minutes." He hung up.

She forgot to exhale for a moment, then relaxed. Would he call her or not?

She jumped when her phone rang in her hand.

"Hello this is Cassie."

"Cassie, my dear friend, it's Carlos Rivas."

"Oh, Carlos! Senator!"

He laughed. "Cassie, it will always be Carlos for you. How are you?"

"I'm much better, thanks. And you?"

"*Estoy bien!* I am well, thank you! But Cassie, I can't talk now. I wanted to be sure you would put the committee hearing on your calendar."

"Yes, absolutely!"

"It will be held on Tuesday, the thirteenth of September. My people will brief you the day before, so you should arrive on Sunday to be rested. Is that good for you?"

"Absolutely, Carlos, I will be ready."

"My office is in the Russell Building. I'll give you more details by mail. Oh, and Cassie, I apologize, but you will be receiving a subpoena. Senator Rosen-Lee, the chairwoman, thought it best."

"Oh, okay. Do I need to make a statement or will they just ask questions?"

"Ah, yes. You should do a statement, which you can read to the committee and have entered into the record as well. It should be no more than about five or six minutes long, but it should make all the points you want to make and give us items to ask you about."

"Okay, I'm nervous, Carlos! *Really* nervous!"

"I understand. I have read your column, and I can assure you, some of the committee members have the same fear of public speaking, believe it or not!"

"Okay, if you say so."

"Yes. Thank you Cassie. I'll see you in September."

"Okay, and Senator—Carlos—thank *you*! I never dreamed I would have this opportunity."

They said goodbye and Cassie's mind started reeling. She could hardly believe she was actually going to appear. Her stomach had begun to churn just talking about it. She wondered idly if anyone had ever thrown up in a committee hearing and chuckled to herself.

A while later, the door opened and Zach walked in. He was smiling. "They're not gonna file charges!"

Cassie hurried over and hugged him.

"It was your call to Matlin that did it. He called 'my' detective down here. Didn't they call you?"

"No, nobody did!"

"Wow," he said as he walked to the refrigerator, "I thought they would've. I guess your phone message was enough, huh?"

"Guess so! This is the first good news we've had in a long time!"

"They told me not to leave town, that the FBI would probably be involved and want to interview me."

"Wow Zach. I'm waiting for a call from a source, but—" Her phone rang. She looked at it, raised her eyebrows toward Zach, cleared her throat and answered with as calm a voice as she could muster.

"Thank you Mr. Savage for calling me back."

"I don't like being threatened."

"Well, it was more like a statement of the inevitable. I'm investigating your company and your CEO, and you've given me inside information on it. I have to mention where the information came from."

"You don't have to mention *who* it came from, do you?"

She knew she didn't have to divulge her sources, but hoped he wasn't well versed on that part of investigative reporting. She decided to skirt the issue. "If I don't provide it, it won't be credible. But, if you give me the whole truth, I'll try to keep your name secret."

Savage didn't respond right away. She could hear him breathing, and knew that whoever spoke first at this point would lose. She waited, picturing him sitting in his car, probably a nice late-model Jaguar or something, or maybe he was a minivan guy.

"Okay," he said quietly. "I've got a deal for you. If I give you information that you can verify independent of me, can you give me your word you'll keep my name completely out of it?"

She knew she was on the verge of something. "Maybe, but it depends. I can't agree until I've heard it and verified it. And I can only agree for myself. Law enforcement might be another matter."

She looked across the room at Zach and held up crossed fingers. He gave her a thumbs up, to which she nodded.

"This is the whole thing. Richardson is about to sign a buy-out to an Irish pharmaceutical company, Intrinshire, PLC. They call it a merger, but basically they're taking over this company. Richardson will probably walk away with a hundred million. Several other executives will get a big payday too."

Cassie couldn't reply immediately. This was better than she had expected. She finally spoke, "Spell that name for me, please so I'll know if I wrote it down correctly?" She hadn't been writing, but wanted an excuse for not responding for several seconds.

Savage spelled the name. "It's one of the biggest pharmaceuticals in Western Europe."

"Really. I haven't kept up with them," she said, trying to put sarcasm into her voice.

"You check this out, Mrs. Stevens. It will give you a motive for everything Richardson's done."

"Why don't you tell me what he's done?"

"I don't know directly. But I think he's involved with your situation up there. I've read all of your columns. If our drug is part of a giant scandal like the Travis High killings, Intrinshire will pull out for sure. They want Pefrexa XR now because they're convinced it'll be bigger that any SSRI ever produced."

Cassie's mind raced with the implications of the merger information. She only said, "I'll check all this and call you back."

She clicked the phone off and held up her hand to Zach to wait, opened her laptop and typed furiously, getting down everything Savage had told her. She knew in her gut that it was all true, but she would check it just the same. Then she sprang up and gave him a big hug. "Zach, we've got him!"

Her phone rang again. She leaned back over the couch and grabbed it. The screen showed Linnie. "Hi, Linn, guess what!"

"Wait, Cass, wait! *Krish is dead!*"

THIRTY-0NE
AUGUST 17, 2016. WEDNESDAY.

Cassie squeezed her eyes shut and grimaced, sitting heavily against the back of the couch to steady herself. "Oh no! What happened?"

"Pretty sure it was suicide, but nobody's saying much."

Cassie just sighed and didn't answer. The victorious feeling she'd had after talking to Savage quickly evaporated.

"Cass, did we push him into this? God, I couldn't handle it if we did!"

"No, Linn! We just made him face what he'd done. If he took his own life to avoid dealing with it, we aren't responsible. He did things he was ashamed of and when he thought he had to face the music, he couldn't handle it. I'm so sorry it happened."

"I just can't see it that clearly. I feel awful."

"Well, I do too. I'm sorry for him and for his family, but, good grief, Linnie, we had no idea he might commit suicide!"

"Yeah. Maybe so. I just have to work through it. I see death frequently, but—" She didn't say anything for some time. "So, uh, what was it you were going to tell me?"

"Not so happy about it, now. I wish we could've told Dr. Krishnamurthy what I just found out. He might've known, but—" She sighed. "Well, first of all, Zach isn't being charged, so that's good. The two cops must've talked to each other, and they told Zach the FBI is looking into it. That's great news, but that's not the big news." She looked at Zach, who was nodding.

"The major news is, Tim Savage just told me Richardson has a big merger or buy out deal going with a pharmaceutical company in Ireland. It's almost settled, I guess. Said he'd probably get *millions* of dollars. It's a huge motive!"

"Yeah. Good work, Cass." She fell silent for a few seconds. "Look, I'm sorry I'm not more excited. That really is good work. I can't wait to read about it in the paper. I'm just all messed up about Krish. We had our differences, but he was one of the few people here that I could almost call a friend, you know?"

"I understand, Linn. I'm really sorry."

"Me too. Talk to you later."

Cassie clicked off and put the phone down. She looked at Zach, tears welling up in her eyes.

"Krishnamurthy committed suicide. I didn't get to tell you yet how we put the screws to the guy today. Linnie feels guilty. *I* feel guilty, too."

"Oh man. Damn, that's really bad. What happened today with him?"

"We told him everything we know. But he could have gotten off easy. Good grief, Richardson was practically holding his parents prisoner in India! He was afraid they'd be killed if he didn't do what Richardson wanted. And Krishnamurthy didn't kill anyone; he just falsified some records and probably switched a toe tag."

"Yeah. Sucks. It all sucks," he said, walked over and put his arms around her. "Look, Cass, you need to get away from all of this stuff for awhile, you know? This has been your whole life for what, two months now?"

She gently pushed back from him. "But I'm so close to exposing Richardson! The column I just sent in lays down some hints about him, his company, but I want to write one more that'll put him away."

"Vengeance isn't healthy, Babe. You must know that."

"You're probably right, but it's what I've got right now. His damn drug probably caused all of this. And other drugs like it have caused killings, too! I can't let that go. I have to get him for that— for Mark."

"Yeah, I understand. I'll just be glad when you're all done with this Richardson character."

"You and me both. It won't be long, now. One way or the other."

*   *   *

She awoke early the next morning. The day before had been long and hard. Cassie had hated voting down Zach's idea to go out and celebrate, but she was just worn out and didn't feel like there was really anything to be happy about. As they lay in bed, talking, she had fallen asleep while she was telling him about Carlos Rivas calling and the appointment she had in Washington less than three weeks away.

When she became aware that she was really awake and the sun had just come up, the specter of her appearance in front of a U.S. Senate committee made her toss the covers off and get up. She dreaded it because she knew from experience that when she was facing a group of expectant listeners, she always froze and felt sick. The possible saving grace in this instance was that she would have a prepared statement to read from, a statement of her own, that might ease her entry into it. And she'd have a friend on the panel. She feared it, but she welcomed the chance to speak out. She might be able to give the American public some new information—those who bothered to tune in or read about it. And the politicians who really didn't care so long as they could look sympathetic might get information that might wake them up to the madness in their midst.

She left the bathroom and plodded into the kitchen, started the coffee and looked out to the west, where the long early morning shadow of their building was hidden in others that extended almost all the way to the freeway interchange.

What could she write, what could she say, that might have some impact? Maybe she should make it a story format? Stories usually worked, but would they work on a bunch of US Senators who were facing the usual budget crisis plus a load of unresolved issues at the beginning of a new session?

She wondered if Carlos had made a mistake, scheduling her for the first meeting of the subcommittee this session. But, she didn't know anything about how these committees worked. Maybe this committee wouldn't meet again soon and this would be the only chance? Or maybe they just had to strike while the iron was hot.

Either way, she had to make it good.

With that thought, she poured her coffee, sat down at the counter, and started making outline notes on her laptop.

THIRTY-TWO
AUGUST 19, 2016. FRIDAY.

Cassie handed the pages and a thumb drive to Hammond. "This is for Sunday, September 11. I want Richardson to read it the day we fly to D.C."

"This is mighty early, Cass! Why didn't you send it by email like usual?"

"I wanted to watch you read it. Go ahead, Tom. I need to see your reaction. And I know Mrs. Wright and the legal department will take forever with it so I wanted to give them plenty of time."

Hammond looked at her, raised his heavy eyebrows, put his glasses on and started reading.

It didn't take long for his reaction to show. He dropped his hand with the pages into his lap and shook his head. "You know, the old lady'll never go for this. I mean, this guy's somebody she knows, even if he did sorta use her with that rebuttal article. Besides it could put the paper in jeopardy of a big lawsuit."

"Maybe, Tom, but you haven't even reached the good part yet!" She chuckled.

"Oh. Great." He donned his glasses again and continued reading.

He read to the last of the pages in his hand. "Cassie, this is convincing, but you don't have any evidence of all this stuff." He frowned. "Do you?"

"Well, not real hard proof, but lots of circumstantial evidence. But what do you think Mrs. Wright will say about it?"

"She'll give it to the lawyers before she says anything. You know they'll shoot it down."

"Maybe, maybe not. Besides, she has the final say-so."

"Yep. Do you want to make any changes? Like, here, for instance, you say, here, 'Justin Richardson has been identified to this writer as the likely leader of a conspiracy to hide the presence of Pefrexa XR in the blood of John Allen Hoff by arranging for his murder and disposal of his body. Not only that, but the person who provided that information, the late Dr. Bhavesh Krishnamurthy, Head of Pathology at Brookside Hospital, also stated that Mr. Richardson had kept Krishnamurthy's parents under threat of harm in Jaipur, India, for several years. In this writer's opinion, Justin Richardson is a man who should be investigated.' This is for sure?"

"Yeah, that gets to the point, huh? I've got audio of Krishnamurthy telling us about it." Cassie said, a twinkle in her eye. "Don't you see, Tom, this guy has to be punished. If we don't expose him, he's got enough money he'll just buy his way out of any legal actions. The thing is, he's trying to sell his company; this will probably stop it."

"Yeah, but he's not goin' to prison just because of what we might print. He can still use his money in the legal system." He shuffled the pages again. "And what about this, where you say: 'And what would be the motive for his trying to hide Pefrexa XR in the blood of a rampage killer?' " He read aloud quickly, mumbling the words.

" 'A bit of background here: John Allen Hoff had been prescribed a psychoactive SSRI drug, generically known as chlorpenframine, and branded "Pefrexa XR," a brand of Provachem Pharmaceuticals, in Houston. It is a legal drug, hugely popular since its release in January of this year. Hoff took it under prescription, then apparently increased the dosage on his own, either on purpose or by mistake. The Travis High School shooting followed.

" 'But the real story begins in the middle of the night at Brookside Hospital, in the Surgical Intensive Care Unit. While this reporter's son lay dying in one hospital room, John Allen Hoff lay recovering from surgery just two rooms away. His suicide attempt had injured him, but not seriously, and his surgery was a complete success. His neurosurgeon at Brookside, one of the best in Texas, had no worries about his recovery.

Then, in the late evening, a man posing as a doctor entered Hoff's room. The FBI guard examined his forged credentials and let him into Hoff's room. The nurse was out of her station, in another room doing her job.' "

Hammond paused and looked at Cassie, his eyebrows raised and eyes narrowed, then continued, shaking his head as she nodded.

" 'This reporter actually spoke to the man, thinking he was on the Brookside medical staff. He didn't respond except to say to wait for him. He then entered John Hoff's room and emerged almost immediately. Almost three hours after that, John Hoff died of a pulmonary embolism—a blood clot. Everyone was surprised by his mysterious death, because Hoff's IVs contained plenty of heparin, an anticoagulant. But the actions of Dr. Bhavesh Krishnamurthy, Head of Pathology at Brookside and also a Deputy Coroner at the time, were absolutely astonishing. The autopsy on Hoff was performed by Dr. Krishnamurthy within hours of death, and the body of John Allen Hoff was sent for cremation early the next morning. A pretended mistake in the pathology lab—the switching of toe tags on the corpses—was blamed for it.

" 'Was this incompetence or malfeasance? *Neither one.* The pathologist, Dr. Bhavesh Krishnamurthy, was being directed to carry out these actions. Who directed him? According to the doctor's recorded statement, it was Mr. Justin O. Richardson, CEO of Provachem Pharmaceuticals, the maker of Pefrexa XR. Tragically, shortly after telling this reporter and one of his own colleagues the whole story, Dr. Krishnamurthy took his own life.' "

"My gosh, Cassie, this is quite a story! I don't know—I just don't know."

"Yeah, but Tom, we need to get the story out there. I still don't know if the FBI's taking it seriously."

"Well, I wonder why not. 'Sides, they might be. Have they talked to you?"

"No. I don't know—I think they wrote off Hoff's death as a medical error and I personally think they didn't really care because of what he'd done. The Dallas cops have wrapped up my break-in and the shooting. Plano cops have stopped working on the carjacking because they figure it's either unsolvable or it was the guy Zach shot. The Dallas detective told Zach the FBI's looking into things, and I've given them the recording of Krishnamurthy incriminating Richardson and the Russian. But nobody's talking to us or the public. They probably all think I'm a conspiracy nut and Linnie made a surgical error that cost Hoff his life!"

"So you think an article like this'll tie it all together for 'em?"

"Well, yeah, I guess that's what I'm hoping."

"Didn't your last article do that?"

"Sort of, but it didn't name Richardson or tell why he was doing these things."

"Okay. You want to go see Mrs. Wright with me about this?'

Cassie nodded.

"That's what I figured." He leaned back in his chair. "Y'know, I can see the connections with Richardson, and all that. But it's still iffy to blame the drug. It's a little bit like a drunk driver killing other people in a wreck. You can blame the alcohol, but the person who drinks the alcohol knows things like that happen."

"Yeah, but the difference here is that Hoff *didn't* know what could happen, and he was one of those people who really needed to know! Richardson knew the danger was there. I'd be willing to bet that that's why they canceled the first Brookside trial, because there were too many of these kinds of effects."

She thought about it silently for a few seconds. "Who knows, Tom? But the main thing is, he *was* on the drug when he attacked, and Richardson wanted it hidden. The crime we're looking at now is why Richardson had Hoff murdered right away, and now we know *exactly* why"

"Okay. Why'd he want it kept hidden?" He looked at the pages he had and shrugged.

"Here's the last page of the article. A kicker." She handed him a page she'd been holding.

Hammond read quickly, then sat back in his desk chair. "Are you kiddin' me? This is for real? You've verified this?"

She nodded. "It's for real."

"Richardson's company is being taken over by this Irish company? How'd you find out?"

"A department director at Provachem."

"You're kidding."

"Nope—guy wrote me that he was sorry about Mark and he was tired of the crap in the company, so I sort of leveraged him to tell me more to keep his name out of the paper."

"And how'd you verify it?"

"Our business guy, Dumas, is a wizard. He dug it out for me. The merger contracts are set to be signed soon. He said he talked to an analyst he knows who's an expert on Irish corporations and knows people on Intrinshire's board. They're apparently a little bit apprehensive, but they're going ahead with it because Pefrexa XR looks like a real mega-blockbuster. But this bad publicity would be a definite deal breaker, and that's Richardson's motive for doing all this to keep the drug hidden. If no merger, then no multi-million payday for him."

"Cassie, this is as good a job as you ever did for the Times! Really puts the icing on the cake!"

"Thanks, Tom! Feels good to be doing some real investigative work again."

"Okay. So, I'm calling Mrs. Wright. Let's go see her right now if she's available. You ready?"

"You bet. I'm totally ready!"

Cassie opened her door, expecting to see Linnie. Instead, a well-dressed, attractive young woman smiled and said, "Hello. Is Cassandra Stevens here?"

"I'm Cassie Stevens."

"Thank you," the woman said, holding out an envelope. "You've been served." She turned and walked toward the elevators.

"What?" Cassie said, taking the envelope. She glanced at it and remembered that Carlos Rivas had said she would receive a subpoena. It was an otherwise unremarkable oversize business envelope with her name and address, and inside it was a regular business envelope, again with her name and address. The return address had an embossed seal and the words beneath it in gold: "United States Senate, Washington, D.C."

She turned to Zach. "It's official. I got my traveling papers!" She handed him the inside envelope. He held it up and started to tear it open. "No! Let's not tear it. I want to open it neatly."

"Oh," Zach said, laughing, "Neatly! Okay, no problem." He walked around the counter, got a large knife and sliced the envelope open at the fold. "Perfect."

Cassie took it and pulled out the document inside. Her presence was required in the Russell Senate Office Building, Room H-100, on Tuesday, September 13, 2016, at 8:45 a.m. "No big deal, I guess. They do these all the time."

"Maybe you expected a plane ticket, or a smiley face?"

"Ha! Right."

Another knock sounded at the door. Cassie opened it to see her friend, Linnie.

"Hey there, Cass!" Linnie said as she stepped in and gave Cassie, then Zach, hugs, with her uninjured left arm. "The place looks, uh, exactly like it did the last time I was here!"

"Yeah," Cassie said, "You'd never know a death happened here."

"Yeah, well, I wouldn't. You're right. How does it feel, being here?"

"Feels okay for me, but Zach—"

"Yeah, I bet." She turned to Zach and patted his shoulder. "Are you dealing with what happened okay?"

"Pretty much. I sometimes have some bad dreams, mainly about what if I hadn't got the guy with that last shot. And I wonder if he had anybody who misses him, you know?"

"Yeah. That can be rough."

Cassie took Zach's arm and laid her head on his shoulder. "He did go to a shrink his regular doctor sent him to. She talked to him for about a half-hour and lectured him how guns were dangerous, then gave him this."

She reached across the counter and produced a small robin egg blue and cream-colored box with bold blue lettering that read, *Pefrexa XR.*

THIRTY-THREE
SEPTEMBER 11, 2016. SUNDAY.

Cassie pressed against her seat back, pushing it to a slight recline, and glanced out the window. The view from seat 5A of the Airbus A320, was a distraction. She usually loved gazing out the window when flying, but on this flight she had wanted to go over her notes and mentally rehearse her statement. She held the pages of it in her lap.

She was nervous. It was good that they were arriving on Sunday. It would give her a chance to acclimate to the pace and feel of Washington, D.C. She'd been here as an intern in college, and several times when she worked in New York for the Times, but those were years ago.

Beside her, Zach chuckled as he woke from a short nap and saw her holding the text of her statement. He cleared his throat and pointed. "You could probably do it from memory by now."

"Maybe," she answered with a smile.

"They'll want to hear it when they do your prep meeting tomorrow, don't you think?"

"Yeah. I suppose they will." She sighed.

"You okay? Cass, this is what you were shooting for, even with your columns—to get the word out about these drugs. So, why the long face?"

She chuckled, recalling the silly joke about the bartender and the horse. "I'm not sure. It's just—I don't know if I'm up to this."

"What, speaking to a Senate committee? I think you are."

"No, not just that. I'm really nervous about it but I think I can do it. I have to. It's just this whole thing of trying to get them to see how much they can affect the problem—or how much they're will-

257

ing to do something."

"Well, they're a Senate committee! Don't they have power?"

"Maybe they do, but they're part of the reason why these drugs are so widely accepted … why the public thinks they're 'good' drugs. Like, you know, the SSRIs for depression—they seem to work for some people and the side effects are minor so they're easier to handle than the depression. But for some people, they can be dangerous. Nobody knows who the next John Hoff will be. A grade-school kid? A teen? There's a ton of variables."

"Yeah. Sounds like it."

"And I'm just a little mom of one of the kids who were murdered, and I happen to have a newspaper column that's made some waves, but look at who I'm up against! One of the biggest industries in the world. Close to a trillion dollars in sales every year. So, hurray for them, they're making tons of money. But some of the people who take their drugs will have the same negative reactions they've been having for years, because they're the same drugs. Some young person like John Hoff will take Pefrexa XR and kill people because of it."

"Well, then that's the message you have to deliver! At least you get to have your say in public, and you're probably gonna put Richardson away for good. Besides, everything important in history was started by one person with a mission."

"Okay. But I think the days are gone when movements can really be started by a single person. Things are too big now. Hell, they could just have me killed and be done with it, you know?"

Zach said nothing. He just looked at her, concerned.

"Well, they could."

"Yeah, but now you've made yourself visible enough that they would be stupid to do that. It would be investigated."

"Lotta good that would do. I'd still be dead, wouldn't I?"

"Yeah, maybe you're right Cass, but if nobody blows the whistle because the enemy is so huge, then they're guaranteed to win! You know what I mean?"

"Yeah, I do. I'm going through with it—I just don't know how much it'll accomplish because it'll be buried in the Congressional

Record or someplace and nobody will see it unless they do a heavy duty search."

"We'll find out, I guess, won't we?"

She nodded and tried to smile, but couldn't.

The heavy Monday morning traffic around the Russell Senate Office Building added to her nervousness. Zach had consulted the map, and he seemed to be in control, so she just held on to the armrest and closed her eyes, wishing they'd taken a taxi instead of their rented car. Finally, they found the entrance to the underground garage and parked.

"Ready?" Zach asked as he pressed a button to stop the engine.

"I guess," Cassie answered, sighing.

It was just before ten a.m., when they'd been instructed to come to Senator Rivas's office. They took the elevator to the second floor, stepped out and looked both ways to locate his office number. The long hall was decorated by captioned historic photographs. It was full of people, all hurrying to get somewhere. Some smiled and nodded, but most were moving fast, preoccupied with their own thoughts. Most reminded Cassie of the White Rabbit from *Alice's Adventures in Wonderland*. She chuckled to herself, mentally reciting the rabbit's rhyme.

"What?" Zach asked.

"Oh, nothing. Just a silly thought."

"Okay," he said. "You don't seem nervous at all."

"I guess I'm not, now that we're here. I thought I would be, but this is just a briefing with Carlos's staff people, right? Besides, a good night's sleep works wonders."

"Yeah, sure does." He smiled and stopped in front of a door with a Rivas's name on a brass plaque beside it. "Here we are!" He reached out and opened the door.

The office wasn't extremely large, but it was nicely appointed. An attractive young woman at a desk in the front office rose and smiled. "Mrs. Stevens? Mr. Stevens?"

"Not quite yet," Zach said, and smiled. "I'm Zachary Barber, and this is Cassie Stevens."

"It's a pleasure to meet both of you. I'll tell Senator Rivas you've arrived. Please have a seat. There's a coffee machine and full selection over there for you, if you'd like, and bottles of cold water in that small refrigerator." She pointed in the direction of the refreshments, then smiled again and walked down a side hallway.

They sat, eyed the coffee machine, and decided against it. Zach stood and looked around the office, examining the various photographs, most showing Carlos Rivas shaking hands with various well-known elected officials.

Having seen enough of them, he sat back down beside Cassie, who was examining something on her iPad.

"I wonder which room we'll be in tomorrow?"

"Well, it's at the Capitol, isn't it?"

"Nope. Apparently, it's right here. This building houses several committees."

"Really? I thought those committee rooms you see on TV were in the Capitol building?"

"Guess not. It'll be in one of the rooms here, Carlos told me."

Just then, Carlos Rivas, his starched white shirt with rolled-up sleeves, emerged from the hallway where his secretary had disappeared earlier. They both stood as he hurried toward them with a wide smile.

Cassie rose and started to shake his hand, but he enveloped her in a big hug instead. "Cassie, it has been so many years, but one would not know it by looking at you!"

"Oh, brother, Carlos! I mean, Senator." She blushed. "You are as charming as ever and even more handsome."

"*Carlos*, always, dear friend! It is truly wonderful to see you, and to meet your fiancé. Zach? I am Carlos Rivas." He extended his hand to Zach and bowed his head slightly.

"Senator, Cassie said I would like you, and she wasn't wrong!"

"Thank you, Zach. The feeling is mutual, I assure you."

He took both of Cassie's hands and put a more serious look on his chiseled Hispanic face. "My friends, you are here and ready to expose the truth! This will be a momentous occasion. I believe it might shake up some people here!"

Cassie smiled at his enthusiasm. "I hope so, Carlos. I really hope so." Zach nodded in agreement.

Rivas turned as his secretary approached. "This is Ruthann Littleton, without whom I could not function. I'm very sorry, but I must meet with some other members for tomorrow's hearing. We will be meeting in one of the larger rooms on the first floor." He put a hand on Cassie's shoulder. "I'm so glad you could be here. If you will follow Miss Littleton, she will take you to a conference room where you will meet with my staff. Zach, you are welcome to be there, as well. I hope to see you after the meeting, but I am not sure."

"Thank you, Carlos, for arranging this!" Cassie said, still thinking that here in his office, in this magnificent building, she should be calling him "Senator Rivas," or at least, "Senator."

He bowed slightly to Cassie and said something in Spanish, then smiled at both of them, shook Zach's hand quickly, nodded to Miss Littleton, and strode back into his private office.

The secretary motioned toward the door and led them back into the hallway, where they joined the flow of foot traffic again. "Busy place, isn't it?" Zach said.

"Yes sir, it is. But, it's a bit more busy today because of the hearing tomorrow." She continued in more hushed tones. "A lot of the people today are lobbyists. They've been coming to our office all day."

"Because of the committee meeting?"

"Partly, but they're a constant feature. Here we are." She stopped and opened a door into a room where a twenty-something woman and a middle-aged, distinguished-looking man sat at a conference table. Both of them rose as they entered. "Jim, this is Mrs. Stevens and Mr. Barber. This is Jim Stanton, Senator Rivas's Chief of Staff, and Janeesa Davis, our Communications Director."

They shook hands all around as Miss Littleton left, locking the door as she closed it.

"Please, have a seat," Stanton said, pulling a chair out for Cassie. "We're glad you could be here."

"Well—" Cassie started to say, with a slight laugh.

"We know, you were subpoenaed," Janeesa Davis said, her bright smile in her light African-American complexion revealing dimples. "But, you know, as a friend of the committee, your subpoena isn't considered the same as, for example, the one that was sent to Mr. Justin Richardson."

"Richardson? *He'll* be here?" Cassie said, stiffening.

Stanton's eyebrows rose. "The senator didn't tell you?"

"Uh, no. He didn't! My gosh, this is—"

"Looks like a shock. Maybe that's why the senator sent you a subpoena."

"You mean, I would've had a choice without it?"

"Basically, yes, of course."

Cassie looked at Zach and took a deep breath. He patted her shoulder.

"Well, then. Miss Davis—" Cassie began.

"Please, call me Janeesa."

"—Janeesa. Will Justin Richardson be briefed the way you're briefing us?"

"No," Jim Stanton answered. "We don't consider him a 'friend' of the committee, like you are."

Janeesa nodded and smiled as he said it.

"That's good news, anyway," Zach threw in.

"Okay. Nuff about that. For this meeting, let's stick with first names, if that's all right. We have a lot to do. Can I get you anything before we get started? There's water and a glass for each of you here, so help yourself. But, anything else? Coffee? Juice? Sandwich? Anything at all?"

"No, thanks," Cassie said as Zach shook his head.

"Okay, then let's dig right into it," Janeesa said, and opened a binder notebook that appeared to hold newspaper clippings of the All-Star Band shooting, other stories from the national press about gun control, and all of Cassie's columns. She pulled out a page of notes and spoke. "Now, Cassie, I have to ask this to begin with. Are you sure you firmly hold the opinions you expressed in your columns?"

"Yes, I certainly do!"

"Please, don't be offended by our questions. We need to know beforehand how you will respond to some of the questioning you'll get from the other, uh, 'unsympathetic' senators on the committee. They won't all be friendly, and if you don't stick to your position on these things, we might end up having no effect at all." She smiled.

"Well, okay, Janeesa, I get it. Yes, I am extremely firm on the views my columns expressed. Not only that, but in the month since I got the subpoena, my good friend, Dr. Linnea Kennedy, who is a neurosurgeon and who operated on the killer, has been further educating me in the finer points of what SSRI drugs really do and don't do in the brain, so I'm ready for any questions they will throw at me."

"She knows her stuff," Zach added.

"I'm sure that's true," Stanton said. He leaned back and let Janeesa take over the meeting.

Janeesa continued. "Have you watched committee hearings on C-Span?"

Cassie and Zach nodded, Zach raising his eyebrows as he did.

"Kind of boring aren't they? You probably noticed that each senator, when he or she gets the floor, tends to make a small speech to set up a question. They do that to be sure their own constituency and the media will know their position before they even say anything."

"I've certainly noticed that," Cassie said.

"One of the things you need to remember is that these people are, first of all, politicians. Their little speeches are also designed to disarm you, to make you understand their point of view, to humanize themselves, to appear friendly to you, and so forth. By the time they get to their question, if they ever do—" she rolled her eyes "—their question might've answered itself, and they might leave you very little time to say much."

"But—" she smiled again and paused for effect, "—you can make your answer longer than their grandstanding speech or their question. They are limited by time, but your answer isn't. So, when they ask their question, even though the Chair might say, 'The gentleman's time has expired,' or something like that, *your* time hasn't expired. You can extend your answer a reasonable amount even if the Chair says something that interrupts. Just politely tell her you need to continue and finish. You are the 'star of the show' when they're addressing you."

"Never thought about it that way!" Cassie said, leaning back in her chair and smiling at Zach.

Jim Stanton spoke up. "That's really how it is, now. It's a game, really. It seems like a courtroom in there, and the committee chair is like the judge, but it's more like a kabuki drama. These people usually don't really care what happens. They're on a committee, they're putting in their time and getting noticed, and they're playing to the C-Span camera. The issue at hand isn't of much importance."

"Are you really that cynical about it?" Zach asked.

"Sometimes, yes sir, I am. Have you noticed that, after all these hearings that are held, almost *nothing* ever happens that you can connect with the hearing? The Executive resists the Legislative at every turn. Very little gets done. That's why the public—well, you know."

Cassie and Zach didn't react right away. Then Cassie spoke up. "Mr. Stanton, Jim, I didn't come up here to be some kind of a showpiece, like a victim they can parade for the media and say they're all so sorry I lost my son. There were forty-six other families who lost their sons, daughters and husbands, brothers, sisters—families with that ultimate loss, and the others with their lives severely affected forever. And the reason I'm here is to try to wake these people up to—to this *madness* that lets drug companies pull a fraud on all of us!" She looked at both of them and then lightly pounded her fist. "I won't settle for a damned show!"

She put her hands flat on the table, straightened her arms and pushed back, then leaned forward toward both of them. "Look, you two are nice people, but you both seem to have an attitude of this just being a form of public theater or something. Is that all it is? Really? If it is, then I don't want any part of it!" She glared at them.

Jim Stanton and Janeesa Davis were silent. Then, Jim spoke

softly.

"Mrs. Stevens, you are absolutely correct. In every way. I'm sorry, but the only show that's going on is this one. We approach every friendly witness with this same 'act,' if you will, just to see what your level of commitment is. Ma'am, you are clearly, potentially, one of the best witnesses we've brought before a hearing in a long time. I'm sorry to say, we've been manipulating you, and we've found over the years this is the only way to bring out the commitment and fire in a witness. Will you forgive us?"

Cassie stared at each of them in turn, then let out a silent whistle through pursed lips. "Pretty effective. Pret–ty *danged* effective!"

Janeesa reached across the table and laid her hand on Cassie's. "Thank you, ma'am. I'm glad you aren't too offended. Mr. Barber—?"

"Sneaky, but like Cassie said, effective." He took a deep breath and let it out. "Now what?"

Jim Stanton took over and began explaining the entire process of the hearing, what would be happening behind the scenes, how they should address the Senators, and so forth. Following that, they got into questions about Cassie's responses to committee members, the protocols she would need to follow, such as not addressing the other witnesses directly and staying respectful even when disagreeing or arguing.

Cassie was asked to read her prepared statement. She read from her iPad, making changes as they went along, to strengthen and shorten some sentences.

"Cassie, no criticism here," Janeesa said when Cassie had finished making a last change, "but can you read it with a little more, um, *fire*? Just like you will tomorrow? We want the members to pay attention. Maybe a little faster, too?"

Cassie looked at her, adjusted herself in her chair and picked up the iPad. She started reading again:

"Good Morning, Madam Chairwoman and Distinguished Members of the Committee:

"My name is Cassie Stevens. I write a column for the Dallas

Daily Post newspaper. My son, Mark Stevens, was murdered in the Texas All-Star Band massacre in June. Forty-seven people died during or from that attack. The killer was murdered in his hospital room, and an elaborate coverup followed.

"John Allen Hoff, with the SSRI antidepressant drug Pefrexa XR, in his blood, shot almost two full 30-round magazines with his semi-automatic twelve-gauge Russian-made shotgun. That provided about 540 lead balls, nine per shot. But the weapon he used does not matter. And this young man himself, who was probably unaware of what he was really doing, is not the issue— except for what his attack helps to illustrate.

"Hoff had no criminal history and he was not a violent person. In these ways, he was similar to over 60 other rampage killers, out of over seventy since 1982. He was also taking a legally prescribed antidepressant drug. In this too, he was similar to those other killers.

"This is a rare effect of antidepressant drugs on certain individuals—of wanting to commit violence, suicide or homicide. It has been observed for decades. It is acknowledged by drug makers and the FDA in their *complete* printed drug labels.

"As you might know, these are 'Selective Serotonin Reuptake Inhibitor' drugs, also called SSRIs. There are several brands available. The one John Hoff took was Pefrexa XR, made by Provachem Pharmaceuticals.

"The C D C says these legal brain altering drugs are used by eleven percent of Americans. *Eleven percent!* But over *half* of these people *have not seen their prescribing doctor in a year!*

"According to a 2008 study, over 60% of patients take SSRIs for two years or more. Over 14% take them for *ten* years or more.

"These drugs are most often prescribed for depression. In most of the people who take them, they cause only minor side effects. In most patients, they *sometimes* even help to control or treat the problem.

"But in a few individuals, the drugs cause *violent* side effects. The FDA classifies as 'rare' an adverse side effect that occurs in less than one patient out of ten thousand, but more than one in a thousand. Some of the adverse effects so classified in FDA-required labeling, are 'suicidal,' 'homicidal,' and 'violent' thoughts or acts.

"In 2013, the top five SSRI antidepressants accounted for over 148 million prescriptions, in the United States alone. This is the most recent year for which this information is published.

"Think of this: If such effects are *only as rare* as one in ten thousand, that *still* puts 14,800 people at risk for suicidal or violent thoughts. We become upset when just one of them becomes a mass killer. As we should!

"And those who *don't* become mass killers? They might just be our 'routine' wife beaters, murderers, and military and civilian suicides. It is likely that a high percentage of violent crimes and suicides, if they were fully investigated using blood testing as a means of discovery, might implicate antidepressant drugs.

"I propose to you that the 'partnership,' as the FDA and the pharmaceutical industry have referred to their relationship, must be ended. The FDA's drug approval process is detailed, yes, but it is not as stringent as it should be. It's too 'pharmaceutical friendly.' Also, the approval process is paid for by the pharmaceutical companies. 'User fees' is the term they use. If *ever* there was a conflict of interest, this certainly is one!

"Big Pharma is arguably the most profitable industry on the planet, *four to five times more profitable as a percentage of its revenues than the big oil companies.* Some of their hundreds of billions in annual profit could be used for research to make these drugs, and their handling by the medical profession, better and safer. Here are some ideas:

"1) Pharmaceutical companies could do research into why and how the rarest adverse effects happen. They admit they are present, as does the FDA. For example, why are males the spree killers in 95% of cases? Does testosterone potentiate the adverse violent effects of these drugs? Or does estrogen moderate them? It's worth examining.

"2) The FDA advisory committees are populated by consultants paid by pharmaceutical companies. It's a perfect setup for corruption. This should be questioned and investigated.

"3) In their final clinical drug trials before FDA approval, which only last a few weeks, subjects are monitored on a weekly basis—but—in the real world following FDA approval, doctors and psychiatrists prescribe the drugs and often don't even see the patients again for a *much* longer period. Certainly, a mandatory shorter time before the second appointment is in order. Also, long-term use is not covered by FDA trials. Consumers are the testers and they are suffering for it.

"4) Doctors must be better educated about the drugs, and not by the pharmaceutical companies themselves, as is the current practice in Continuing Medical Education symposia. And, certainly not by the drug company sales reps, which is also currently done and sometimes the only 'education' doctors get on drugs.

"5) Prescription records and gun purchase records could be matched. They could be flagged if in the same homes. Gun owners could be matched with participants in drug trials. Locked, unloaded storage of the guns could be required. This does not violate the 2nd Amendment in letter or spirit. *This one measure* would have prevented the Sandy Hook massacre in late 2012. We have the technology: the computer, IBM's 'Watson' can compare 250 million pages of data in fifteen seconds. Let's use it!

"We routinely accept that 'street drugs' cause violent behavior, but when it is these 'legal, FDA-approved' types, designed to change the brain, we deny it.

"These drugs are frequently involved in violence, but because of the ad money they provide, any mention of them is actively avoided in news reporting. It's the same in politics, while a convenient scapegoat—the gun—is blamed, and even attacked as a *cause!* That's beyond ridiculous, and I know all of you are intelligent enough to know it. I also know that many of you are already aware of these fact. That's where the huge Big Pharma lobby enters the scene, isn't it?

"The presence of Pefrexa XR in John Allen Hoff's blood was intentionally concealed, and it was uncovered only because of a vigilant and persistent neurosurgeon. Proof of this has been provided to law enforcement authorities.

"Big Pharma goes to great lengths to protect the reputation of their drugs, and thereby their profits. This keeps the public unaware of the damage these drugs are doing.

"John Allen Hoff had a right to seek treatment for his depression. But the treatment he received took away my son's and forty-six other victims' right to life. Which of these rights should be the higher priority? I urge you to take action to protect the American public.

"Thank you, Mr. Chairman and Committee Members, for the opportunity to appear before you today. I am ready to answer any questions you have."

Stanton asked, "Mrs. Stevens, have you ever considered becoming a speech writer?"

Cassie smiled at him and shook her head.

Janeesa closed her binder of clippings and notes. "That was excellent, ma'am! Now, I need you to send a copy of your statement to my email, and you can do it from here. It's jdavis@rivas.ussenate.gov. Okay? Well, is there anything else you want to cover?"

Cassie tapped an icon, typed the young woman's email and the send button. After the iPad's whoosh sound-effect, Cassie looked up and took a deep breath. "No, I'm just ready for a late lunch and a nap, to tell you the truth."

Jim Stanton smiled and tapped his cell phone, a minute later, a knock sounded and Janeesa opened the door. They said goodbye, and Cassie accepted compliments and encouragement from them.

Miss Littleton walked them to the elevator. "I'm sorry, but Senator Rivas was called to a closed committee meeting to prepare for tomorrow's hearing. He asked me to convey his great thanks and apology for not spending more time with you, and said he'll contact you later." She shook their hands, told them where to go the next day and exactly when to be there, and ushered them into the elevator.

Both of them were quiet on the way down to the parking level beneath the building. They walked out of the elevator and headed for their car without saying anything. Then, as Zach opened the door for Cassie, he said, "You know, you really are going to be one great witness tomorrow. I don't think they really get it, how good you'll be!"

"Thanks, big guy." Cassie answered, kissing him on the cheek before she sat in the passenger seat. "I hope you're right!" But as Zach walked around to his side of the car, a fear struck her.

Justin Richardson would be sitting at the witness table with her.

THIRTY-FOUR
SEPTEMBER 13, 2016. TUESDAY.

Only a slender crack of blue-gray between the drawn blackout curtains showed any indication that a new day was approaching. Cassie grabbed her iPhone to look at the time: 4:53 a.m. She held the phone in her hand and settled back into her pillow. Zach still snored beside her.

After returning to the hotel, they had grabbed a quick lunch and Cassie had sunk into her nap. Then, with most of the afternoon gone, they decided to walk beside the reflecting pool on the national mall and enjoy being in the nation's capital. It became a quiet evening, typical for early September.

"Hard to believe it's been almost twenty years since I walked here. I've changed more than this has," Cassie said.

"Yeah. A lot has happened."

"Some good, some so bad I can hardly handle it."

Zach hadn't responded, but lifted her hand in his and kissed it.

Now, she thought about him, lying there beside her. They both assumed they would marry, would not try to have children or adopt any, and continue with their careers. It had made her think, lately, wondering if her life was supposed to have any larger purpose, or should she just go along with the "flow" that seemed to be carrying her?

She jumped when her phone buzzed. It was a text from Tom Hammond. When she looked at it, she leapt off the bed and turned the light on.

"*Zach!* Look at this!" She rocked Zach's hip back and forth to wake him up. "*Look* at this!"

"Wha? What is it! 'S too early!" She could barely understand him, but it didn't matter. As soon as he got his glasses on, she thrust the phone in front of him. He held it and squinted at the screen for a few seconds while she laughed and thrust her fists in the air. He finally got it. "Is this for real? No kidding?"

"*Yeah!* Look at that beautiful headline! 'Below Radar Provachem Merger A No-Go.' *Woo-hoo!* Look what Hammond wrote! 'CASS YOU DID THIS' " She grabbed the phone and whirled with it in her hand.

"But Cassie, he's *still* going to be at the hearing, right?"

"Yeah, he will be, but I'm not afraid of him now!" She sat on the bed and laughed again as her breathing calmed. "*Wow.* So that's our business headline for the day we have this hearing. Can you believe it?"

"So, the merger's off. Won't that make him hopping mad?"

"Probably. I'm going to enjoy watching him try to keep his cool in front of the panel and the cameras."

"Jeez, Cass, when he hears your statement, with his drug in it, he might totally lose it and attack you!"

"Ha! If he does, you're right behind me. You're bigger than he is and you already took out his hit man!"

"Yeah. Not exactly a *good* memory."

"Right. Sorry. I've got to call Linnie and get online and read this whole story!" She leaned over the bed and gave Zach a big hug and kiss with a laughing grimace from their mutual morning breath. Laptop under her arm, she started tapping on her phone and disappeared into the bathroom.

The large hearing room in the Russell Senate Office Building would have filled early if the hearing involved a high-ranking or famous witness. Today, it was less than half full when Cassie and Zach entered. Most politicians, for the big hearings, preferred to make a grand entrance from the back that could be caught by the media. But today, no politicians were even there yet. Cassie looked around at Zach, behind her place at the witness table. The whole setup gave her a chill and made her stomach do a cartwheel.

Soon, the senators and aides began to flow in and in a few minutes all were seated, arranging their papers and glancing up at the audience and witnesses.

"This hearing of the Health and Human Services Oversight Committee will come to order," the Chairwoman said into her microphone. She rapped her large gavel twice. The sparse audience began to find seats.

Zach leaned forward and patted Cassie's shoulder. "Go get 'em!" he said, loudly, but for all except her, his voice was covered by the shuffling of feet and murmuring of people taking their seats.

Five placards were set at the table. Cassie's read, "Mrs. Stevens." Three other people were seated at the table, each with a similar placard. Beside her was the Deputy Commissioner of the Food and Drug Administration, Mrs. Renata Reyes, dressed, as Cassie was, in a dark suit with a light silk scarf. They had introduced themselves, both amiable enough, but Cassie noted an unmistakable air of—what was it—disdain? Superiority? Civil servant hubris? She couldn't put her finger on it, but she could feel it.

To the right of Mrs. Reyes was Michael Landry, CEO of Alexira Pharmaceuticals, a direct competitor of Provachem. Beside Landry, Richardson was also provided a seat, but he wasn't in sight yet. She wasn't surprised. The news of his failed merger couldn't have been easy to take, even if he deserved it.

Finally, a man Cassie didn't recognize sat on the other side of Richardson's place, a Dr. Holly, according to his placard.

The five of them waited for the chairwoman, Senator Rosen-Lee, to speak again. She was an extreme left-leaning progressive member of the Senate who usually seemed to have a fair amount of anger inside when she appeared on camera. It was apparent now, too. She glared down from her raised position directly at Justin Richardson's empty seat, leaned back and spoke to an aide, who hurried through the door that Landry and Holly had entered through. A few seconds later, he reappeared, spoke to the Chairwoman, and sat down behind her.

She banged the gavel again.

"This hearing will come to order!" Without waiting, she launched into her introduction. "We are here today to hear testimony regarding the possible involvement of psychiatric drugs in mass shootings. We have had a horribly tragic event recently, and my heart goes out to all of the victims' families and loved ones." She looked directly at Cassie and nodded slightly. "However, as terrible as those attacks have been, we cannot go off on witch hunts. Now, I will introduce our witnesses and we will hear their statements." She looked down at a paper in front of her.

"Dr. Benjamin Holly is a licensed psychiatrist and an advisor to the Psychopharmacology Office of the Food and Drug Administration. Next, Mr. Michael Landry is Chief Executive Officer of Alexira Labs, maker of a prescription drug known as Orensafam. Next, and *absent*, was to be Mr. Justin Richardson, President and CEO of Provachem Pharmaceuticals. Beside Mr. Richardson's empty seat is Mrs. Renata Reyes, Deputy Commissioner of the U.S. Food and Drug Administration. And beside Mrs. Reyes is Mrs. Cassandra Stevens, a newspaper reporter and the mother of a son killed in the Travis High School Shooting. Mrs. Stevens, please accept this entire committee's and my own sincere condolences for your loss."

Cassie nodded as the senator smiled at her.

"All of you, please stand, raise your right hand, and say 'I do,' after I read this oath. 'Do each of you swear to tell the truth, the whole truth and only the truth, in this proceeding?' "

Each of the people on the panel said, "I do."

"Good. Please be seated. Now, after each of you gives your statement, the members of the committee will each have fifteen minutes to ask questions. Dr. Holly, we will hear your statement now, if you have it."

Benjamin Holly thanked her and properly addressed the committee, his voice and calm manner sounding confident as he made a clear statement of the FDA's position on the approval process of all drugs. He referred several times to what he called the unjust vilification of the agency and its practices, glancing to his left at Cassie at various points.

Next came the CEO of Alexira Labs, Michael Landry, a dapper, bearded early-fiftyish man who used his statement to make a broad appeal to the public to see his products as a weapon against "diseases like mental illness." Cassie sat and watched the committee members, holding her rising irritation and telling herself her turn was coming. Her fear was giving way to angry resolve.

The chairwoman made a curt comment about Richardson's absence, only saying she had not been informed about it.

The statement of Renata Reyes was short. It said, in effect, that her agency took no official position on the matter of prescription drugs being involved in shootings. The most telling statement she made was, "The presence of pharmaceutical products in a killer's blood does not automatically mean that they had any part of the cause for the crime. These people had food in their stomachs, as well, but nobody blames hamburgers for bad behavior."

Despite herself, when the woman made that statement, Cassie let out a breathy "Ha," then grabbed her glass of water and tried to pretend it was a cough. She said a quiet "Excuse me," as the other woman continued and finished her statement.

Then, as her name was announced again, Cassie's stomach began to turn upside down. She took a deep breath, and her throat constricted. Then she heard Zach, behind her, clear his throat loudly and speak her name, and it brought her back to the present. She coughed and began reading.

"Good morning, Madam Chairwoman, and distinguished members of the Committee—" She read her statement in as strong a voice as she could. She knew it was long, and she heard impatient sounds from some of the other witnesses. But now, it didn't faze her. At a couple of points, the audience actually applauded lightly, and a man somewhere, gave out with a loud, "Yeah!" at one point, gaining a single gavel rap and sharp look from the chair. Then, it was quickly finished. It had taken just over eight minutes. Too long, but they had allowed it.

As she finished, she heard the FDA woman beside her emit a heavy sigh, and thought she might have seen her shake her head slowly from side to side in a gesture of denial.

"Thank you all for your thoughts. I will yield to the Distinguished Ranking Member, Senator Carlos Rivas. Senator Rivas?"

"Madam Chair, I would like to reserve my time for later, if that is acceptable." He glanced at Cassie with a quick smile.

"So ordered, Senator," she answered, a bored note in her voice. "So, we will then hear from Senator Curtis Hocking. Senator—"

"Thank you Madam Chair," the elderly black senator said, his voice sounding quiet but clear through the sound system, "and thank you to all of our witnesses today. It is clear that we have a problem in this country. A problem of violence, often expressed through gunfire, and often with guns that private citizens should not even be allowed to own, and often, as you know too well, Mrs. Stevens, aimed toward innocent members of society." He shook his head, looked down at his papers, and sighed.

"It happens all too often. But, why do they kill? I do not believe, as you have outlined in your newspaper columns, which most of us have read, by the way, that these depression drugs are really the cause. You've reiterated your position on that in your statement, and we'll consider it. But, let me ask you this—" He paused for several seconds. "It is relatively rare. Just over seventy mass shootings in thirty-some years? Hundreds of millions of these drugs have been taken by people all over the world? Not to downplay those crimes and the heartache they caused, but if you were right, Mrs. Stevens, it seems the drugs would cause many more than that."

"Senator—" Cassie remembered to reach for her microphone to turn on the switch, as she had been instructed to do only when she was going to speak. "Senator, was that a question?"

"Yes, it was. Why aren't there more killings if the drugs are to blame?"

Cassie pulled the microphone closer to her so she could be easily heard without leaning forward. "Well, Senator, we don't know that the mass killings are the only ones where people are driven to commit acts of violence. Most likely, not. There are also suicides, knife attacks, hostage situations, cars driven into crowds, domestic abuse, gang shootings, robberies, and so forth. I firmly believe, based on evidence I've read and warnings printed in the drug labels, required by the FDA because the dangers are clear and present, that the mass killings are just the tip of an iceberg. They are just the worst of many rimes that these drugs probably cause, as well, and not all of them result in death or even physical injury."

"And how would you go about investigating that?"

"I believe that blood tests and autopsies with complete toxicology screening would show the presence of these drugs in many cases of violent crime. It is a simple procedure. These drugs do hang around for a while in the system."

The old senator grunted and looked at Justin Richardson's empty seat. "I was going to ask Mr. Richardson about his drug bein' discovered in the blood of the Travis High School killer, like your newspaper article said on Sunday, but he's not here. I wonder what he'd say if he was? How 'bout you, Mr. Landry? If your depression drug was found in that killer, what would you say about it? Do you think the drugs you sell are makin' killers?"

"Absolutely not, Senator. We spend over a billion dollars per drug, over several years, to develop a safe and effective product for the public. The FDA approves these drugs after years of testing. Sometimes they don't approve the drugs, and we lose. We wouldn't stay in business, sir, if what Mrs. Stevens claims was true."

The old senator looked at Landry and sniffed, smiling, then shook his head and said, "Madam Chair, I yield back the remainder of my time." He leaned back in his padded chair and looked at his watch.

"Thank you Senator Hocking. The chair recognizes the distinguished senator from Georgia, Mrs. Hargis, for fifteen minutes."

Senator Susanna Hargis reached for her microphone and adjusted it. Her smooth southern accent and rich voice came through easily. "Ladies and gentlemen, this is a difficult issue that we will not solve today. We all know that. We're trying to get facts, if possible. Now, Dr. Holly, I need to ask you about a controversy from the past in your own office. This happened years before you joined the FDA, I know, but I am hoping you will have a position on it."

Cassie liked this woman already. She was an attractive brunette, forty-something, with a friendly voice that made her sound unthreatening. Carlos Rivas had told Cassie that she was one of the most incisive people in the U.S. Senate.

Dr. Holly nodded to the Senator, not knowing what was coming.

She continued in her mild, musical voice. "I've looked into some of this, Doctor, and I've found a memo that came out of your own office, from one of your predecessors, a Doctor Paul Leber. It was back in, let me see, um, 1998. I'd like to read this memo to you and ask you, and then Deputy Commissioner Reyes, to comment on it. Is that okay?"

Doctor Holly nodded, smiling. Cassie noticed, though, that the woman beside her seemed to brace herself with a new posture as she waited for the reading to come.

The senator continued. "This Dr. Paul Leber, for the record and benefit of the other members, was head of the FDA's Division of Neuropharmacological Drug Products, and he wrote this memo in 1998. It regards an SSRI drug like you make—" she glanced at Landry, who squirmed slightly, "—so, here's the memo. He uses the generic name of the drug, 'citalopram,' in the memo. But the name doesn't really matter too much. He's referring here to information about the application for approval on this drug." She smiled, put on glasses with pointed retro-style mother-of-pearl rims, and started reading.

" 'One aspect of the labeling deserves special mention. The Clinical Efficacy Trials subsection within the Clinical Pharmacology section not only describes the clinical trials providing evidence of citalopram's antidepressant effects, but makes mention of adequate and well controlled *clinical studies that fail to do so.*'

"That emphasis is mine," the senator said, removing her glasses and looking up. "Are you all getting this? I know it's hard when you're just hearing it. He's saying some of these clinical trials showed that the drug did *not* work. Isn't that amazing? Okay, I'll continue reading now:

" 'I am mindful, based on prior discussions of the issue, that the Office Director is inclined toward the view that the provision of such information is of *no practical value to either the patient or prescriber.*'

"That's interesting, isn't it? The director of Dr. Leber's psychopharmacology office—your office, right, Dr. Holly?—thought the failure of that drug in trials was useless information for patients and doctors! I'll go on. Oh, by the way, this 'citalopram' he talks about is branded as 'Celexa' in the USA. He writes:

" 'I disagree. I believe it *is* useful for the prescriber, patient and third-party payer to know, without having to gain access to official FDA review documents, that citalopram's antidepressant effects were not detected in every controlled clinical trial intended to demonstrate those effects. *I am aware that clinical studies often fail to document the efficacy of effective drugs, but I doubt the public, or even the majority of the medical community, are aware of this fact.* I am persuaded that they not only have a right to know, but *should* know. Moreover, I believe that labeling that selectively describes positive studies and excludes mention of negative ones can be viewed as being potentially "false and misleading." ' "

She removed her glasses and held them for a moment. "That's interesting, isn't it? What do you think of that, Dr. Holly? And, by the way, I added some emphasis there. Dr. Holly?"

"I'm sorry Senator, it's interesting to hear it, but I was unaware of that memo. I know of Dr. Leber, but I would have to investigate the circumstance surrounding that memo before I could comment in any way."

"Mm-hmm. I thought so. To me, it's pretty clear on its face. And

Deputy Commissioner Reyes? Do you wish to comment?"

The woman beside Cassie clicked her microphone on. "No, Senator, I have no comment."

"Yes. Well, that's not a surprise to any of us, is it? You know, it's interesting to me how some people in the most responsible positions are the least responsive to issues that definitely affect them and their responsibilities. If I may say so, even though I know we're supposed to be asking questions, I think it's a real shame that the American public cannot get a straight answer on some of these things, and that lands right on top of officials like yourselves, Dr. Holly and Mrs. Reyes. There is one other thing I'd like to mention that goes right along with this memo and with this issue."

She reached for another set of papers. "The Washington Post, in 2004, printed an article that said this, in part:

" 'The Food and Drug Administration has repeatedly urged antidepressant manufacturers not to disclose to physicians and the public that some clinical trials of the medications in children found the drugs were no better than sugar pills, according to documents and testimony released at a congressional hearing yesterday. Regulators suppressed the negative information on the grounds that it might scare families and physicians away from the drugs, according to testimony by drug company executives. For at least three medications, they said, the FDA blocked the companies' plans to reveal the negative studies in drug labels.'

"So, I guess we've been through this before, haven't we? I doubt that you folks will have any comment, so I won't ask. Do you?" She waited, but nobody spoke. "Yes, well, it's just a cryin' shame that years have passed and this agency we trust with our health, through examination and approval of our food and our drugs, takes a position that protects pharmaceutical companies from a lot of negatives. In fact, *tells them not to include negative facts on drug labels.* If the

American public knew of that practice, I wonder how they would react?" She stared at Dr. Holly, then Landry, then Mrs. Reyes.

When her gaze got to Cassie, her expression softened. "Mrs. Stevens I truly applaud your efforts to get this information out of the shadows and into the light again where we can examine it once more. A member of my own family was prescribed Pefrexa XR, and a couple of months ago, when your articles exposed that type of drug as such a danger, we talked to his doctor and began withdrawing him from it. As you've told the public, stopping it, or any SSRI for that matter, suddenly, can cause worse damage than the mental illness it's supposed to treat. Until your articles came along, I was as dumb about all this as most of the public, so I owe you a personal thanks." She smiled.

Cassie nodded and mouthed "thank you," uplifted by the vote of confidence.

Senator Hargis then looked over at Justin Richardson's empty seat. "Mr. Richardson, wherever you are, for the record, I do hope you get all that's coming to you, sir." She didn't smile as she said it. "Madam Chair, I yield back."

The Chairwoman of the committee snorted, her expression as sour as it had been all along, and she recognized another member. "The Chair will now recognize the distinguished gentleman from Iowa, Senator Otis Black."

At the far end of the platform, a gaunt Lincolnesque man spoke in a strong voice. "Thank you Madam Chair. I don't have much." He reached for and lifted an electronic tablet device. "I have this here Kindle electronic reader. I read parts of books on it when I get a few minutes. I've got this one book, written by a fella named Stephen King, named *Guns*. It's not a very long book, but he has some good things to say in it. He covers a lot of the problems of the gun violence problem and the mass shootings. But, in this whole book, a short little book as I said, he doesn't mention any kind of drugs connected with mass killers. Not only street drugs, but no prescription drugs, either. What do you say to him and people like him, Mrs. Stevens?"

Cassie paused, trying to think of a sensible way to reply, looking for respectful words, but she failed. She clicked her microphone on. "Senator Black," she said in a stronger voice than she realized, "I think it's ridic—er—questionable that you would appeal to a popular writer of horror novels for any meaningful opinion on the issue of guns and spree killers. King is one of my favorite authors, and I've actually read that little book. It's not too bad, but it's terribly biased, uninformed and misguided. I imagine Mr. King, like most of the American public, is just ignorant of the facts and the warnings surrounding the SSRI issue. And, Senator, going to Stephen King for information about why spree killers kill? Or what to do about guns? Well sir, that's just—just *silly!*"

The room went silent except for a few low groans and murmurs. Cassie heard Zach's voice behind her, quiet, saying, "Easy, Cass. Calm down."

She spoke again. "Senator, I am sorry if my tone does not convey the immense respect I have for your position. I truly apologize for using the word 'silly.' But, sir, you must know that there are much better sources of information on this issue available than a prejudiced ninety-nine-cent ebook by Stephen King. Basing your opinion on what should be done about guns and mass shootings on that book is like basing your knowledge of the Jurassic Period on the Flintstones."

A few muffled laughs could be heard in the audience, which had now filled the seats in the room.

Senator Black chuckled. "Well, ma'am, you are a newspaper reporter and he is a creator of stories. As far as qualifications go, I'd probably call it a draw." He smiled at her, then continued. "And, may I ask, ma'am, where is *your* information from?"

"I have read many, many books by respected authorities in the field, written over a forty-year period, on both sides of the question—David Healy, Jerry Avorn, Gary Greenberg, Ben Goldacre, Robert Whitaker, Marcia Angell, Nancy Andreasen, Irving Kirsch, and several others I can't recall. I have toured Mr. Justin Richardson's drug factory with him. I've talked to doctors, to gun enthusiasts, to people who have investigated the connection between antidepressant drugs and rampage killers. I've studied public records, autopsies where they are available, and literally every source of information I could find. I've been all over both sides of the issue, Sir, and I have discovered the fact—the *fact*—Senator, that antidepressant drugs are extremely dangerous to a certain small percentage of those who are under their influence and to the people around them. The FDA's 'Black Box Warnings' on these drugs bear witness to that fact."

"Well, thank you, ma'am, for your candor." He paused and looked through his bifocals at a paper on his desk. "You know, Mr., ah, Landry, Senator Hargis brought up something a minute ago that reminded me of something. You ever hear the term 'washout'?" He narrowed his eyes at Landry.

"I don't know your context, sir. Can you explain more?"

"I think you know. It's a technique that's used leading up to your clinical trials for your drugs."

"Oh, yes sir," Landry said. "What about it?"

"As I understand it, you test people before the trial begins, to see how they react to placebos, isn't that the case? Can you explain what a placebo is, exactly?"

"It's a replica, in appearance only, of a drug that's being tested, but it has no drug properties of any kind. It's inert, sometimes called a 'sugar pill' because capsules used to have just starch and powdered sugar in them. They are simply inert pills made to look like the real drug, given on the same schedule and with the patient treated under the same protocol as those on the real drug. The patients and the trial conductor, in a double-blind trial, don't know who is getting the placebo and who is getting the real drug. Placebos are a control to see how well the real drug works."

"And those 'real drugs' are sometimes the drugs in Senator Hargis's memo, that she read, that somebody in the FDA said sometimes the drugs fail. So the placebos in those trials must've beat the drugs for effectiveness, if I heard it right."

"Well, that doesn't happen much, Senator," Landry said.

"Mm-hmm. So, tell me about this 'washout' having to do with placebos?"

"We pretest the subject population for about two weeks before the clinical trials begin, to see who in the groups are extra-sensitive to placebos, that is, biochemically or psychologically biased, and we let them out of the trial."

"So, you kick out the people who might actually improve on the placebos, because that might make your drug look bad. That's about it, isn't it?"

"Not at all, Senator. There are just people who get better on placebos. They react more strongly than the normal population."

"And you don't want *them* in your test, do you? They'd make your drug look bad, just like I said. I've heard the whole point of these drug trials, the real goal, is 'beat the placebo.' So you get rid of people who make that harder to do." He looked away from the witness table. "Thank you Mr. Landry. Madam Chair, I yield back."

Cassie had enjoyed the exchange between Landry and the old senator, but she was still itching to be asked more questions. She was relieved when the chairwoman said, "The Chair will now recognize the distinguished senator from Arkansas, Senator Rivas."

"Thank you Madam Chairwoman. It is a great pleasure that I have the opportunity to talk to all of you. I have learned a great deal from Mrs. Stevens's testimony, and I disclose for the record that she and I were friends as interns in this city during our college years. Mr. Landry, we understand that you are in business to make a profit. Can you tell me approximately what percentage of your revenue last year was in the profit column, Mr. Landry?"

"Offhand, sir, I don't have that information."

"Mr. Landry, I find it odd that you have no idea. I'm not looking for an exact percentage. How about giving me something that might be within five percent of the actual figure?"

Landry replied, "Senator, that would not be a good idea, because it could be easily misunderstood. I'm sorry, but I will provide the committee with the information within a day."

"You know that in law school they always told us that you should never ask a question for which you do not already know the answer. I do have the figures for Alexira and Provachem here, from your own corporate reports to stockholders last year."

Landry stared at Rivas without responding.

"It seems that, as an industry, the pharmaceutical industry is truly one of the most profitable on our planet. I congratulate you on your success. Your industry, as a whole, has a profit margin that is between twenty and thirty percent of revenues. The top ten pharmaceutical companies in the United States earned $429 billion dollars in 2014, and the average of their profit margins on that amount was twenty-two percent. That is quite large, would you not agree?"

"Yes sir," Landry answered.

"Pfizer, which was in that list, had a profit margin of forty-four percent. An exception among exceptionally profitable companies! It is a shame Mr. Richardson is not here to hear his profit figures, but I will quote them in any case. (In fact, though, I imagine Provachem will be having a change to its management and to its profit picture after the recent merger failure.) I am somewhat sorry to say that your own companies are not as profitable as some of the others. Provachem was in the high end of the twenty-five to thirty percent range. Mr. Landry, your Alexira company had a twenty-one-point-three percent profit." He closed the notebook he had been reading from. "But, those percentages apply to revenues in the billions, so they represent large amounts of money."

"Do you know, Mr. Landry, what the average profit percentage of some of the big oil companies might be? They get a lot of flak about their extreme profits, you know. I'll tell you. It is between four and six percent of their revenues."

"Sir, is there a question coming?"

"Actually, yes, Mr. Landry, there is. But I would like to ask it of Mrs. Stevens, if you don't mind."

Landry said nothing but was visibly angry.

"Mrs. Stevens," Rivas said, smiling, "I would like to know what you would suggest companies like these might do with that profit, or some of it?"

"Senator—" Landry said.

"Oh, no, Mr. Landry, I am sorry. This is not a question for you."

"May I answer, Senator?" Cassie said.

"Please."

"Yes sir. I believe there should be a continued effort to discover how and why their drugs cause *some* people to go completely out of control. The drug companies *can* afford that kind of research! They just don't want to, though, because it would reflect badly on them. But these are not simple pain pills! They're drugs that are designed to change the way the brain works! When they do it in such negative and sometimes violent ways, they—and we—need to know why. The *public* needs to know why! How else can we prevent another mass murder and other crimes?"

Throughout the room, scattered applause told Cassie she had scored some points with that one. The gavel sounded and the applause died out.

"Thank you, Mrs. Stevens. Mr. Landry, would you like to add anything to that?"

"Senator, with all due respect to Mrs. Stevens, that is an almost impossible task to be undertaken simply to save a couple hundred lives—" The moment he said it, the audience buzzed as he tried to cover it up. "What I mean, what I mean is—" The collective audible gasp in the audience covered up the rest of his words. He waited until the noise died down. "Senator, that was not what I meant to say."

"That is obvious, Mr. Landry. Go on."

"I'd like to clarify what I meant. Every year, tens of thousands of people are killed in automobile accidents. I don't see very many senate committees meeting to solve the problem, at the expense of the car companies. One hundred thousand people die every year from *properly* administered drugs. Nearly as many die annually because of doctor-caused and hospital-caused illnesses."

"Yes," Rivas said calmly, "we know this. It seems you would not be a very good witness for the defense, sir! I will yield back my time, Madam Chair."

The chairwoman gaveled and said, "I thank all of the witnesses. We will break for lunch and resume this hearing in two hours." She gaveled, and the room immediately erupted into loud conversation.

THIRTY-FIVE
SEPTEMBER 13, 2016. TUESDAY

"Could you believe that Landry guy?" Zach said after Cassie stood and turned to him.

"Pretty bad!" Cassie said.

"Ha, yeah. Maybe he's been taking some of his own drugs."

Carlos Rivas had rounded the long, raised platform and stepped down onto the floor beside them. He shook both their hands. "Cassie, and Zach, what an excellent beginning!"

"Thank you, Senator," Cassie said. "But do you think we're going far enough? Do you think we're being specific enough?"

"I believe we are. I have been in many of these hearings, and the information that has already come out of this one is more specific and more enlightening than I've seen in some of them. Don't be discouraged, my friends. We are making progress. And we will make even more this afternoon. And you are doing a wonderful job, Cassie!"

Cassie smiled and nodded, but wasn't sure she agreed.

He noticed her expression. "Cassie, the only thing I know for certain about this capitol is that, if it moves at all, it moves very slowly. You will continue, I hope, with your articles and research, and keep us on our toes. Don't worry, we have started a ball rolling here today, and it has a better path than the misguided gun control efforts that came out of past tragedies."

"Well, Carlos, I hope you're right. I did this all for Mark and for all the other innocent victims, you know." She couldn't help her eyes getting moist.

"I know you did, Cassie, and like I said, you have done a wonderful job. For now, I am sorry, but I must go and meet with my staff. You can go to the cafeteria, on the floor under us, where they have an excellent lunch selection. I'll see you during the next session, yes?"

He shook their hands, smiled, and disappeared through the doors behind the raised committee members' platform.

Zach said, "He's a great guy, huh?"

"Mm-hmm," Cassie said, "You know, I've got one huge question and I forgot to ask Carlos."

"Yeah?"

"Yeah! Where the heck is Richardson?"

He looked at her. "Good question. Nobody but Carlos mentioned him, did they?"

"Just the Chairwoman. She didn't say much." She shook her head and made a mental note to ask Carlos why Richardson hadn't shown up.

"I wonder if he'll be held in contempt?"

"Ha! Yeah. He would be if I had the chair! That was good, what Senator Hargis said." She chuckled as they waited for the elevator.

"What was it? I must've missed it."

"She said, for the record, to Richardson, she hopes he gets everything that's coming to him!"

"Ha! I couldn't agree more!"

Justin Richardson had timed his departure from Houston to appear to be normal for the Senate hearing. He'd told them he would appear without counsel, and his lawyers had objected. He'd told them to go to hell and felt good about it. Knowing that nobody in Houston would look for him and the company jet, and also knowing that the committee wouldn't know he was missing until he didn't show up for the morning session, he grabbed his go bag and left. His other bags, several of them, had already been loaded onto the plane. The pilot was curious about why he wanted to go to Atlanta when they could have flown straight to DC, but knew Richardson too well to risk asking questions.

Richardson's only regret was that his beautiful young wife would hate him for this. But, truth be told, he was getting tired of her.

She wouldn't be the first he'd left, and she'd get over it. She had money, and that was all she'd ever wanted. He had left her a quitclaim deed to the house, both of the Mercedes, and the Ferrari. It was saying goodbye to that Italian racing red 458 Spider that was hardest of all. If he had thought farther ahead, he would have shipped it, but there just wasn't time. He would send the divorce papers from Sweden. His resignation from the company and distribution of his shares to the non-executive employees was something that made him feel good about himself. It didn't matter to him that they were suddenly not going to be worth much.

He had cut all his ties. The coastal vacation house in Malmö, Sweden, would be ready when he arrived. He looked forward to seeing Estrid again. She would welcome him, as always, with a wonderful hot meal and warm bed.

He looked at his watch. Half past noon. He finally began to relax as the plane was pushed back from the refueling station. The engines throttled up slightly and the plane taxied under its own power to join the takeoff queue.

His trip had begun seven hours earlier when the Gulfstream had taxied out and pushed itself into the sky, the last time he would ever take off from Texas. His cell phone had rung and he let the call go to voicemail, with a message that he was in a meeting and not available. It wouldn't matter anyway, after all the dust settled.

He was already disconnected in almost every way, and he had only one regret, that he hadn't had a chance to at least talk to that reporter from the Dallas paper, if for no other reason than to give her a smug smile or laugh.

He would sleep during the fifteen-hour flight to Sweden. He had just closed his eyes when the twin engines both slowed. He heard a slight squeal as the brakes were applied and the plane's nose dipped suddenly. Of course, this wasn't unusual. Traffic was always busy on the apron of the large private aircraft terminal at Atlanta and the starting and stopping could be expected.

But it surprised him when the engines wound down even more,

as if they were being shut off. The plane braked to a complete stop.

"What the hell is going on!" Richardson demanded. He looked out the left side. Two large black SUVs had stopped in front of the wing, halting the plane.

The copilot emerged from the cockpit and said, "Sir, the—" something, and the rest of his words were covered by mechanical sounds as he opened the outside door and lowered the stairs.

Richardson remembered his loaded Glock 30 in the briefcase with his cash and gold, but abandoned the thought.

A serious-looking young man in a dark suit entered the cabin, showed the copilot a sheet of paper, and turned down the aisle into the wide seating area. As he headed toward Richardson, another man entered, looked around and ushered the copilot back into the cockpit.

"Supervising Special Agent Brian Simmons, Federal Bureau of Investigation, sir." He held out an identification wallet toward Richardson, who glanced at it. "Justin Richardson? Please stand up, sir."

"What's this? So I missed a damn senate hearing!"

"Justin Richardson," Simmons answered, a puzzled expression on his face, "you are under arrest for suspicion of the crimes of conspiracy to commit murder, conspiracy to commit a felony, obstruction of justice, lying to a Federal officer, extortion, and murder. Here is the arrest warrant." He handed Richardson the same sheet of paper he had shown the copilot.

"What? What the hell!" Richardson said, grabbing the paper and glancing at it, a note of fear in his voice.

"Please turn around, sir," The agent commanded.

Richardson, breathing hard, did as he was told, leaning forward to clear the short ceiling in the jet. He endured a quick pat-down search.

"You have no right—" He stopped talking when his left wrist was grabbed and the click of a cold steel handcuff was applied. His right wrist was pulled back and the other cuff locked around it. His shoulders slumped.

"Justin Richardson, you are being placed under arrest by a Federal agent. You have the right to remain silent. Anything you say or do can and will be used against you in a court of law." He turned Richardson around to face him and the front of the plane, double-checking his jacket pockets in case the pat down had missed something. "You have the right to an attorney. If you wish to have an attorney and cannot afford one, an attorney will be appointed to represent you. Do you understand these rights as I have stated them to you?"

Richardson's eyes narrowed. He nodded.

"Please reply verbally, sir."

"*Yes*, dammit!" Richardson barked. He let the agent guide him toward the other agent and the exit door at the front of the cabin.

"We will help you down the steps." The agent took Richardson's elbow and held it firmly.

With that, Richardson moved slowly forward and avoided the eyes of the other agent. He glanced back at the opulent interior of his company jet, then was guided down the steps and into one of two black SUVs parked at angles in front of the plane's left wing.

He said nothing as the agent put him in the back seat and secured a seatbelt around him. The two agents got into the SUV. Its engine came to life. Without waiting, it wheeled around to leave. The other vehicle, apparently staying behind with the plane, didn't leave.

Richardson realized that his life as he knew it was ending, without fanfare or appreciation for all the things he had accomplished. He bristled, indignant and infuriated.

As the SUV paused before leaving the apron, he raised his head to look out of the heavily tinted side window and finally realized this was his last glimpse of the gleaming robin-egg-blue and cream Provachem Gulfstream jet.

A word popped into his mind. *Unfair!*

THE END

A REQUEST
From The Author

Thank you for reading this book! I trust you enjoyed it and found some interesting facts.

As Dr. David Healy said in his Foreword to *Pillaged*, in essence, the issue of whether antidepressants can cause suicide or homicide is not just a story about adverse effects. It truly is a *central issue* in modern medicine and one Big Pharma would like to avoid. I agree, and I fervently want to get my version of this message out through this book.

WILL YOU TAKE FIVE OR TEN
MINUTES TO ASSIST ME?

Reviews are the lifeblood of publishing. They make *all* the difference. I need honest reviews of the book so that potential buyers will know how good the book may be, what to expect, etc.

Please go to https://www.amazon.com/dp/0972956719/, the sales page for this bok, and click the star rating. On the next page, you can post your honest review of this book.It will help other readers and it will help me.

It will take only a few minutes to provide your thoughts, and it will help! Thank you, sincerely! -- Bill Cory

GRATITUDE

DECEMBER 10, 2015. THURSDAY.

I am grateful for the advice provided by Larry Brooks (storyfix. com), which guided me toward the final draft of my story.

My greatest thanks also goes to Dr. David Healy, who agreed to read a book from a stranger, not knowing what it was about, not knowing he was mentioned in it, and not knowing if it was worth reading at all. He agreed to receive it and look at it, and then, to my utter amazement, offered to help generate interest in it!

This was the fourth full draft of this book. It is as good as I could make it, but it would have been much less than it is if not for the help and honest criticism of two editors.

As a copy editor, Roberta Peters is absolutely excellent. Her sharp eyes saved me from dozens of typos and miscellaneous grammatical errors that I never caught despite many re-readings. I can't say enough thanks for the time and effort she expended to help a Facebook friend, and I hope someday we can meet in person.

And, my content editor, Sherry Cory, my dear and always patient wife, was incisive and insightful with her questions of detail and continuity. She saved me from receiving many emails that would have started with, "I don't think you meant to ...." They say you shouldn't accept criticisms or compliments from people who love you, but Sherry went past that caution and gave me honesty I didn't expect. She could have a new career doing this, if she wanted to.

Thank You from the bottom of my heart to all of you for your invaluable contributions to this novel!

AFTERWORD & NOTES

THIS IS A WORK OF FICTION, but the facts and figures cited have been gleaned from research in over fifty authoritative books in the field of pharmaceuticals and psychiatry, plus information saved in a folder containing a dozen gigabytes of medical journal articles, videos, blogs, illustrations, and web pages of pharmaceutical companies, the FDA, the Congressional Record, and other authoritative sources. Information from news media is also noted there. All of the websites in the text are real websites.

In the following pages are my attributions and sources of information. For the sake of continuity throughout the book, I have not used note numbers and have relied here instead on page numbers and the sentences where the information begins. Page numbers are related to the print version. For electronic-version readers, the links in this section are clickable.

page #   **Starting sentence and attribution or explanation**

25   "The barrel of the Russian Saiga Shotgun smoked." Saiga 12-ga shogun is no longer legally imported, but it can be purchased here and there

91   "One of the latest books, *Pillaged* ..." Dr. David Healy is an internationally respected professor of psychology, psychiatrist, psychopharmacologist, scientist and author of over 20 books. His main website is _www.davidhealy.org_.

91   Maris, R. (2015). *Pillaged: Psychiatric Medications and Suicide Risk.* University of South Carolina Press

91   "The question of whether antidepressants and other psychotropic drugs ..." from *Foreword* by Dr. David Healy, to above book, *Pillaged.*

94   "Obviously, every shooting is done with a gun ... " Reference to Mother Jones website, *http://www.motherjones.com/special-reports/2012/12/ guns-in-america-mass-shootings*; refer to the data on the spreadsheet shown at this page: *http://www.motherjones.com/politics/2012/12/ mass-shootings-mother-jones-full-data*

96   "Yeah. It was *Wesbecker*, and I agree." Joseph Wesbecker's family sued Eli Lilly & Co., but the jury found for the Defendants. Judge in the case thought something wasn't right and sought to change the verdict, but had to sue in the Kentucky Supreme Court for legal permission to change the verdict. He was granted that permission based on case law in Kentucky; the official verdict was therefore changed. See: *http://www. breggin.com/index.php?option=com_content&task=view&id=72* . Also search "Standard Gravure Shooting" on wikipedia.com.

99   "Roseburg, Oregon, the most recent before this ... ." It is commonly assumed of the psychiatric profession that antidepressant drugs are the normal and expected treatment for depression. The killer in Roseburg, Oregon, in late 2015, was reported to be under psychiatric care.

106   "He walked to one of the chairs and sat. 'Just so you know, ... terrorist shooting at Ft. Hood in 2009 ...' " This shooting, by Maj. Nidal Hasan on Ft. Hood, Texas, was called "workplace violence" by the military, though Hasan was a known supporter of Muslim jihad, had emailed with Anwar Awlaki, and was found to be taking antidepressant medications that he, a licensed psychiatrist, prescribed for himself.

108   "Right Now, after the Chattanooga shooting ..." Chattanooga shooter Mohammad Abdulazeez was using drugs. He murdered five US service members, who were not allowed to be armed. *http://www.cnn. com/2015/07/20/us/tennessee-naval-reserve-shooting/*

110   "She clicked the cylinder back into place." Smith & Wesson model 686+ is a .357 mag/.38 spl, 7-shot revolver.

120   "Cassie looked at the sample box in her hand." The text of the FDA-rec-ommended warning for antidepressants being prescribed to children and adolescents is reproduced on the next page. To see the actual "Black Box" and requirements for providing the warning, go to this web page: *http://www.accessdata.fda.gov/drugsatfda_docs/label/2005/20152s035lbl.pdf* .

The text of the "Black Box" at the above link is accompanied by this statement: "This medication guide has been approved by the U.S. Food and Drug Administration for all antidepressants." The text, reproduced below, is required to be in a bold-lined box at the beginning of the medication guide.

"Suicidality in Children and Adolescents

"Antidepressants increased the risk of suicidal thinking and behavior (suicidality) in short-term studies in children and adolescents with Major Depressive Disorder (MDD) and other psychiatric disorders. Anyone considering the use of [Insert established name] or any other antidepressant in a child or adolescent must balance this risk with the clinical need. Patients who are started on therapy should be observed closely for clinical worsening, suicidality, or unusual changes in behavior. Families and caregivers should be advised of the need for close observation and communication with the prescriber. [Insert established name] is not approved for use in pediatric patients. (See Warnings and Precautions: Pediatric Use)

"Pooled analyses of short-term (4 to 16 weeks) placebo-controlled trials of 9 antidepressant drugs (SSRIs and others) in children and adolescents with major depressive disorder (MDD), obsessive compulsive disorder (OCD), or other psychiatric disorders (a total of 24 trials involving over 4,800 patients) have revealed a greater risk of adverse events representing suicidal thinking or behavior (suicidality) during the first few months of treatment in those receiving antidepressants. The average risk of such events in patients receiving antidepressants was 4%, twice the placebo risk of 2%. No suicides occurred in these trials."

129   "Secondly, many of them in the last few years... ." The popularity of First Person Shooter video games is lamentable, and they are implicated in many mass shootings. This is well-covered in the book, *Stop Teaching Our Kids To Kill. (Grossman, D., & DeGaetano, G. (Rev. 2014). Stop Teaching Our Kids to Kill: A Call to Action Against TV, Movie & Video Game Violence. New York, Harmony.)*

129   "Beneficiaries? ... They are the pharmaceutical giants, and they are the most profitable large companies on the planet." BBC report online, "Pharmaceutical Industry Gets High On Fat Profits." Linked at: *http:// www.bbc.com/news/business-28212223*

136   "Hello Chris. If you're available ..." The use of ghost writers by the pharmaceutical industry—writers who are hired by the drug maker to create fake "peer reviewed" articles for medical and psychiatric journals—is a continuing problem. Some journals are beginning to curb the practice. See: *http://davidhealy.org/pharmageddon-is-the-story-of-a-tragedy/*

138   "As the commercial began ..." The American Psychiatric Association's *Diagnostic and Statistical Manual of Mental Disorders*, Fifth Edition, is the "most definitive resource for the diagnosis and classification of mental disorders," according to part of its description on Amazon.com. The book describes over 500 mental disorders. It is used as described, with questions asked by the doctor, which, if answered in specific ways by the patient, forms a diagnosis. Some people swear by it; others vilify it. (*Diagnostic and Statistical Manual of Mental Disorders: DSM-5. [5th ed.]. [2013]. Washington, D.C.: American Psychiatric Association.)*

153   An excellent overall view by Robert Whitaker of the history of psychiatry in the United States. (Whitaker, R. [2010]. *Anatomy of an Epidemic.* New York: Broadway Books.)

155   *Pharmageddon*, by the aforementioned Dr. David Healy, of how Big Pharma came to be so big and powerful, and the dangers brought along with that power. Unsurpassed explanation of how pharmaceuticals use ghostwriters to fool the public and professionals. (Healy, D. [2012]. *Pharmageddon*. Berkeley: University of California Press.)

156   "Elevations or decrements in the functioning of serotonergic systems per se are not likely to be associated with depression." (Whitaker, p74, *Anatomy of an Epidemic*)

156   Citizens Commission on Human Rights International (CCHR). Founded by Thomas Szasz and Erving Goffman and initially connected with the Church of Scientology. A non-profit organization established in 1969 that opposes psychiatry. *www.cchr.org* .

156   "As Robert Whitaker writes... , 'At that moment, Eli Lilly and all of psychiatry had achieved a public relations victory of lasting importance.' " (Whitaker, p294, *Anatomy of an Epidemic*)

157   YouTube.com video of FDA Advisory Committee Hearing, Sept., 1991, in which citizens testified of the suicidal and violent effects of SSRIs. *https://youtu.be/Om2J9g-ssKo*

160   *Dying For A Cure*. Well-written first-person account of polypharmacy's effects. Beddoe, R. (2007). *Dying For a Cure: A Memoir of Antidepressants, Misdiagnosis and Madness*. Milsons Point, N.S.W.: Random House Australia.

160   " 'Yes, really. Her driver had therapeutic levels ...' " See *https://www.washingtonpost.com/wp-srv/inatl/longterm/diana/stories/paris0911.htm* . Henri Paul's blood tests, ordered by the French court, revealed fluoxetine.

161   "Have you run across the 'Learned Intermediary Doctrine' in your reading?" This refers to a principle of law used by pharmaceutical companies, more in Europe than the USA, but it is appealed to here as well. See *www.davidhealy.org/welcome-to-the-humiraverse//#sthash.dpuf*

161   "Yes. Several studies have proved the link to autism, but the news media is so in love with their Big Pharma ad money, they won't touch it." PubMed.gov. *http://www.ncbi.nlm.nih.gov/pubmed/17547888* . CNN.com. *http://www.cnn.com/2014/03/27/health/cdc-autism/* . British Journal of Psychiatry. *http://bjp.rcpsych.org/content/205/2/95* .

169   "Linnie pressed on. 'But the writer of this memo ...' " Dr. Paul Leber was Director of the FDA Clinical Pharmacology Office. Quoted in *The Emperor's New Drugs*, by Irving Kirsch. (Kirsch, I. (2010). *The Emperor's New Drugs: Exploding the Antidepressant Myth*. New York, NY: Basic Books.) Also see: *http://www.accessdata.fda.gov/drugsatfda_docs/nda/98/020822a_admindocs_corres_P1.pdf*. (Page 30 of 40.)

191   Fourth leading cause of death in hospitals. Adverse drug events are now the fourth leading cause of death in hospitals. *http://davidhealy.org/about-data-based-medicine/* also *http://articles.mercola.com/sites/articles/archive/2011/02/04/death-by-medicine-an-update.aspx*

191   "Allow me to quickly describe the high points of the entire drug approval process, from discovery to prescription." This process is not as cut and dried as we often assume. Often drugs are prescribed that have not been adequately tested. One commonly known example is Thalidomide. But there are many others that have been withdrawn from circulation by the FDA and foreign agencies after they've proven to be injurious or fatal. See *https://en.wikipedia.org/wiki/List_of_withdrawn_drugs*.

193   "Drugs do a hundred different things but in a trial everyone is guided to ignore the ninety-nine other things and focus on just one thing–does this drug work for whatever it is the company is interested in." Quote from Dr. David Healy's blog. See at: *http://davidhealy.org/lost-in-medication-the-crusoe-report-3/*

194   "Nobody had ever prevailed to any great extent." Regarding Joseph Wesbecker trial. See previous reference from page 96.

202   "Lately, I've been writing a lot about SSRI drugs—antidepressants that have been sold to the world public as an effective treatment for depression, but that often do not work and create many well-known side effects. Those are listed in the FDA labels for the drugs, available to read for every drug on an FDA website at *www.fda.gov/drugsatfda*." Enter the brand name or generic chemical name of any drug, and you get a database of dates and documents, including links marked "Label," "Label Available," and so forth. Click the links for the complete label, of which most of the public is completely unaware.

261   "Because of the committee meeting?" Lobbyist traffic in the senate office building hallways is heavy, especially with the 1,300-plus such
reps hired by PhRMA (Pharmaceutical Research and Manufacturers of
America). and other concerns. They have the most lobbyists of all, with
over three per Congressional Representative and Senator.

266   "The C D C says these legal brain altering drugs are used by eleven percent of Americans. *Eleven percent!* But over *half* of these people *have
not seen their prescribing doctor in a year!"* See CDC information:
http://www.cdc.gov/nchs/data/databriefs/db76.htm

266   "According to a 2008 study, over 60% of patients take SSRIs for two
years or more. Over 14% take them for ten years or more." *Ibid.*

266   "But in a few individuals, ..." Adverse reactions to drugs. According to
the FDA, "An adverse reaction is an undesirable effect, reasonably associated with the use of the drug, that may occur as part of the pharma-
cological action of the drug or may be unpredictable in its occurrence."
21 CFR 201.57 (g) (*http://www.accessdata.fda.gov/scripts/cdrh/cf-
docs/cfcfr/cfrsearch.cfm?fr=201.57*)

266   "In 2013, the top five SSRI antidepressants accounted for over 148 million prescriptions, in the United States alone." Compiled from IMS
health statistics: *http://psychcentral.com/lib/top-25-psychiatric-medi-
cation-prescriptions-for-2013//*

267   "I propose to you that the 'partnership,'... 'User fees' is the term they
use. If *ever* there was a conflict of interest, this certainly is one!" The
PDUFA, is described here: *http://www.fda.gov/Drugs/DevelopmentAp-
provalProcess/SmallBusinessAssistance/ucm069943.htm#P27_459* .
These "user fees" are presented in a positive light, but when many
drugs are approved that are later recalled for lack of safety and effectiveness, it causes a thinking person to question the propriety of having
the drug companies pay the approval agency's expenses.

267   "The FDA advisory committees are populated by consultants paid by
pharmaceutical companies. It's a perfect setup for corruption. This

should be questioned and investigated." See the YouTube videos, where advisory committee members are identified by their company. This is still typical in the industry. *https://youtu.be/Om2J9g-ssKo*

267   "Prescription records and gun purchase records could be matched." HIPAA would be an obstacle, but something could be done! Open up HIPAA to the extent that mental illness *treatment* can be included in the Form 4473 background check, and cross-check it with receivers of prescriptions for psychiatric drugs. It would most likely help cut the rates of crimes such as those in this book, and probably others perpetrated by previously non-criminal actors.

278   "The senator continued. 'This Dr. Paul Leber, for the record and benefit of the other members, was head of the FDA's Division of Neuropharmacological Drug Products, and he wrote this memo in 1998.' " See *http://www.accessdata.fda.gov/drugsatfda_docs/nda/98/020822a_admindocs_corres_P1.pdf* . See page 30 of this 40-page photocopy (page 11 of Leber's 12-page May 4, 1998 memo regarding citalopram ((Celexa®))). The quotes in the fictitious Senator's question are direct quotes from this page. This is revelatory of the FDA's favoring of the health of pharmaceutical companies over a well-informed public.

280   "She reached for another set of papers. 'The Washington Post, in 2004, printed an article that said this, in part:' " See this article at this link: *http://www.washingtonpost.com/wp-dyn/articles/A9802-2004Sep9.html* .

283   " 'Mm-hmm. So, tell me about this 'washout' having to do with placebos?' " The washout process is used in randomized clinical trials. Hypothetically, its purpose is to rid the study of people who will respond well to placebos, thereby giving the "real" drug more demonstrated effectiveness compared to placebo. This is not an accepted verdict by all researchers. See also: *http://www.ncbi.nlm.nih.gov/pubmed/8570378* .

284   "It seems that, as an industry, the pharmaceutical industry is truly one of the most profitable on the planet Earth." This is a true statement. The figures here are taken from a BBC report online, "Pharmaceutical Industry Gets High On Fat Profits." See: *http://www.bbc.com/news/business-28212223* .

BIBLIOGRAPHY
LISTED BY PUBLICATION YEAR

Andreasen, N. (1984). *The Broken Brain: The Biological Revolution In Psychiatry*. New York: Harper & Row.

Breggin, P. (1991). *Toxic Psychiatry: Why Therapy, Empathy, And Love Must Replace The Drugs, Electroshock, And Biochemical Theories Of The "New Psychiatry"* New York: St. Martin's Press.

Kramer, P. (1993). *Listening to Prozac*. New York, N.Y., U.S.A.: Viking.

Breggin, P., & Breggin, G. (1994). *Talking Back To Prozac: What Doctors Won't Tell You About Today's Most Controversial Drug*. New York: St. Martin's Press.

Healy, D. (1997). *The Antidepressant Era*. Cambridge, London. Harvard University Press.

Valenstein, E. (1998). *Blaming The Brain: The Truth About Drugs And Mental Health*. New York: Free Press.

Breggin, P., & Cohen, D. (1999). *Your Drug May Be Your Problem: How And Why To Stop Taking Psychiatric Drugs*. Reading, Mass.: Perseus Books.

Tracy, A, PhD. *Prozac, Panacea or Pandora?*. Cassia Publications.

Cohen, J. (2001). *Over Dose: The Case Against The Drug Companies : Prescription Drugs, Side Effects, And Your Health*. New York: Jeremy P Tarcher/Putnam.

Breggin, P. (2001). *The Antidepressant Fact Book*. Cambridge: DaCapo Press.

Brown, B., & Merritt, R. (2002). *No Easy Answers: The Truth Behind Death At Columbine*. New York: Lantern Books.

Spitzer, R. (2002). *DSM-IV-TR Casebook: A Learning Companion To The Diagnostic And Statistical Manual Of Mental Disorders*, Fourth edition, text revision. Washington, DC: American Psychiatric Pub.

Whitaker, R. (2002). *Mad In America: Bad Science, Bad Medicine, And The Enduring Mistreatment Of The Mentally Ill*. Cambridge, MA: Perseus Pub.

Maxmen, J., & Ward, N. (2002). *Psychotropic Drugs: Fast Facts* (3rd ed.). New York: Norton.

Strand, R., & Wallace, D. (2003). *Death By Prescription: The Shocking Truth Behind An Overmedicated Nation*. Nashville: Thomas Nelson.

Angell, M. (2004). *The Truth About The Drug Companies: How They Deceive Us And What To Do About It*. New York: Random House.

Avorn, J. (2004). *Powerful Medicines: The Benefits, Risks, And Costs Of Prescription Drugs*. New York: Knopf.

Goozner, M. (2004) *The $800 Million Pill*. Berkeley. University of California Press.

Newman, K. (2004). *Rampage: The Social Roots Of School Shootings*. New York: Basic Books.

Healy, D. (2004). *Let Them Eat Prozac: The Unhealthy Relationship Between The Pharmaceutical Industry And Depression*. New York: New York University Press.

Abramson, J. (2004). *Overdo$ed America: The Broken Promise Of American Medicine*. New York: HarperCollins.

Hawthorne, F. (2005). *Inside The Fda: The Business And Politics Behind The Drugs We Take And The Food We Eat*. Hoboken, N.J.: J. Wiley.

Frankfurt, H. (2005). *On Bullshit*. Princeton, NJ: Princeton University Press.

Jackson, G. (2005). *Rethinking Psychiatric Drugs: A Guide For Informed Consent*. Bloomington, Ind.: AuthorHouse.

Kassirer, J. (2005). *On The Take: How Medicine's Complicity With Big Business Can Endanger Your Health*. New York: Oxford University Press.

Earley, P. (2006). *Crazy: A Father's Search Through America's Mental Health Madness*. New York: G.P. Putnam's Sons.

Evans, I., & Thornton, H. (2006). *Testing Treatments: Better Research For Better Healthcare*. London: British Library.

Gibb, B. (2007). *The Rough Guide To The Brain*. London: Rough Guides.

Beddoe, R. (2007). *Dying For A Cure: A Memoir Of Antidepressants, Misdiagnosis And Madness*. Milsons Point, N.S.W.: Random House Australia.

The PDR Pocket Guide To Prescription Drugs. (8th ed.). (2008). New York: Pocket Books.

Bass, A. (2008). *Side Effects: A Prosecutor, A Whistleblower, And A Bestselling Antidepressant On Trial*. Chapel Hill, N.C.: Algonquin Books of Chapel Hill.

Christensen, L. (2008). *Surviving A School Shooting: A Plan Of Action For Parents, Teachers, And Students.* Boulder, Colo.: Paladin Press.

Torrey, E. (2008). *The Insanity Offense: How America's Failure To Treat The Seriously Mentally Ill Endangers Its Citizens.* New York: W.W. Norton.

Breggin, P. (2009). *Medication Madness: The Role Of Psychiatric Drugs In Cases Of Violence, Suicide, And Crime.* New York: St. Martin's Griffin.

Chalmers, P. (2009). *Inside The Mind Of A Teen Killer.* Nashville, Tenn.: Thomas Nelson.

Cullen, D. (2009). *Columbine.* New York: Twelve, Hachette Group.

Langman, P. (2009). *Why Kids Kill: Inside The Minds Of School Shooters.* New York: Palgrave Macmillan.

Olsen, G. (2009). *Confessions Of An Rx Drug Pusher.* New York: IUniverse Star.

Goldacre, B. (2010). *Bad Science: Quacks, Hacks, And Big Pharma Flacks.* New York: Faber and Faber.

Kirsch, I. (2010). *The Emperor's New Drugs: Exploding The Antidepressant Myth.* New York, NY: Basic Books.

Whitaker, R. [2010]. *Anatomy of an Epidemic.* New York: Broadway Books.

Greenberg, G. (2010). *Manufacturing Depression: The Secret History Of A Modern Disease.* New York: Simon & Schuster.

Hall, M. (2011). *Dear Bully: 70 Authors Tell Their Stories.* New York, NY: HarperTeen.

Healy, D. (2012). *Pharmageddon.* Berkeley: University of California Press.

Sharpe, K. (2012). *Coming Of Age On Zoloft: How Antidepressants Cheered Us Up, Let Us Down, And Changed Who We Are.* New York: HarperPerennial

Diagnostic and Statistical Manual of Mental Disorders: DSM-5. [5th ed.]. [2013]. Washington, D.C.: American Psychiatric Association

Frances, A. (2013). *Saving Normal: An Insider's Revolt Against Out-Of-Control Psychiatric Diagnosis, Dsm-5, Big Pharma, And The Medicalization Of Ordinary Life.* New York: HarperCollins.

Greenberg, G. (2013). *The Book Of Woe: The DSM And The Unmaking Of Psychiatry.* New York: Blue Rider Press.

King, S. (2013). *Guns.* Philtrum Press (Amazon Kindle Single ebook)

Marcum, J. (2013). *Medicines That Kill: The Truth About The Hidden Epidemic.* Carol Stream, IL.: Tyndale House.

Goldacre, B. (2014). *Bad Pharma: How Drug Companies Mislead Doctors And Harm Patients.* New York: Faber and Faber.

Grossman, D., & DeGaetano, G. (Rev. 2014). *Stop Teaching Our Kids to Kill: A Call to Action Against TV, Movie & Video Game Violence.* New York, Harmony

Maris, R. (2015). *Pillaged: Psychiatric Medications and Suicide Risk.* University of South Carolina Press